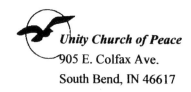

BATU

The Transformation

Emil Toth

PublishAmerica
Baltimore

First printing

ISBN: 1-59129-497-5
PUBLISHED BY PUBLISHAMERICA BOOK PUBLISHERS
www.publishamerica.com
Baltimore

Printed in the United States of America

DEDICATION

*This book is dedicated to everyone who is on the glorious and inspiring
quest to discover truth and love within them.*

ACKNOWLEDGEMENTS

While the original Batu manuscript was a work of inspiration the hard work of editing was not. Since no venture is made alone, I must acknowledge the editing and help of my friend Joyce Hug. An early edit by Rosemary Horvath pointed out inconsistencies. Final edits by Barbara and Joseph Gatto gave the work its final polish. I owe a great deal to the love in my life, Suzanne Gibbons, for her evaluation and suggestions that gave the work greater depth and clarity. I also wish to thank my agent Karen Carr and my publisher for believing in Batu. I remain eternally grateful to all of them.

My heartfelt thanks go to my former wife, Barbara and my children Susan, Sheryl, Cynthia and Jim for their long-standing patience and understanding. Barbara has made me aware that spiritual growth comes in many forms and guises.

The strong influence dreams and visions have in my life has found its way into this novel. Impacting it even further has been the friends I have come to love. We have been challenged by our relationships. We have faltered. We have grown.

Batu's inspirational story dramatizes her heroic mission of self-empowerment and the startling ways she draws attention to injustices. Since none of us are truly separate from the other, each of us contributes in composing every heroine or hero. We all have missions in life. Some of us may have a heroic mission that impacts many people by becoming a persistent voice that makes a community aware of injustices, or of the danger of toxic waste or clear-cutting a forest or of crippling prejudices. Most of us are involved with the difficult missions of dealing with illness, raising children, providing food and shelter and sharing love. All of them are important, none more significant than the other.

As you wind your way through the characters presented in this story, you might be able to identify with one or more of the missions they have. My hope is that you will.

~ ET

CHAPTER
ONE

From across the village center, Tomudo saw Batu walking leisurely toward the group. The chattering children happily gathered before him, waiting for him to begin the story session. The fluid, sensual motion of her walk always stirred him. As he watched her approach, his heart quickened. Tomudo reveled in her presence. His eyes flickered from the children to her a number of times, as she closed the distance. Tomudo saw the early heat had left tiny beads of perspiration above her full upper lip. Their eyes met. She smiled, revealing rather large, white, evenly spaced teeth. Her cheekbones were set high and prominent on her face with her brow sloping back gently to her hairline. Her most striking physical attribute lie in her widely spaced, green-flecked, light brown eyes. In the depths of her eyes, one could detect the quick intelligence that set her apart from nearly everyone in the tribe. They hinted of the intellectual confidence she possessed. The black hair covering her delicate ears hung tightly waved down to the middle of her neck. While of average height, she was broader of hip than most of the other women in the village. Her honey-brown colored body moved leisurely toward the talkative group.

When Batu had reached her eleventh season, her thin frame slowly filled out. Her childishly lovely face had changed into one of startling beauty. While the physical changes were taking place, she became aware of how she affected the men and men-children of the village. Unobtrusively, she observed their reactions to her growing beauty and came to the conclusion that no other woman held their attention as she did. She took great pleasure in the feeling of superiority and control over them and used it to bolster her self-confidence. Because of the success she had in discussions with Tomudo and her father and debates with her father, she also became confident in her intellectual superiority.

For Batu, detecting how men reacted to her became a game of observation. Some men stared blatantly, while others veiled their interest. Gradually, she became adept at detecting the quickened heartbeat pulsing in their necks or the slight perspiration on their upper lips even though the air was pleasantly warm. While in social conversation, she had become aware of their slightest stammering or pause. Now and then, she caught the quick movement of their eyes over her body if they thought she would not notice. Often she found their desire amusing. Most of the time, she felt flattered by all the attention her beauty drew to her, yet on occasion, she became irritated by their obvious stares. As she grew older and honed her logic and debating abilities with her father, she became confident and desired recognition for her intelligence at the tribal level but only received it at the family level.

While women were able to converse with the men socially, they had to refrain from debates or discussions involving tribal legends, traditions or laws. The strict role women were forced to play resulted from the interpretation men had of the historical stories orally handed down from generation to generation. The Kahali men had attributed the social, ethical and moral downfall of the ancient world to the decay of the family. Batu doubted that was true and had grave reservations that men should rule the family and dispense discipline. It chafed her that the Kahali women were subservient to men and could not serve on the council. With all of these restrictions in place there was little room for women to develop their independence or hope to assume an office of authority. As she grew older, the laws, along with tribal tradition, were sources of immense irritation for Batu. In spite of the fact her father helped develop her intelligence and independence within the confines of her home, she could not understand why women chose to simply allow men to rule their lives.

Batu stopped at the rear of the group, lowering herself on her haunches, as she had so often in the past. Currently in her sixteenth season of blue skies, she often attended the teaching sessions for the sheer pleasure of being able to engage Tomudo in discussions during and after the sessions. She was the only woman to dare break tradition and sit in attendance after her twelfth season. Such breeches of tradition irritated most of the villagers. Because Batu continued to come, the villagers covertly condemned Tomudo's leniency and doubted that her father had ever reprimanded her.

Noticing that Tomudo was waiting patiently to begin his first story, some of the children settled in and grew quiet. Tomudo's responsibility included teaching the Kahali's oral history, laws, legends and traditions. Through these stories he instilled knowledge in the children and male adults. While no men were present at this one, they, like Batu, continued coming to the sessions in order to participate in the discussions and debates. A great deal of leniency prevailed if children missed sessions, especially with the women-children.

Tradition dictated that it was not considered essential for the women-children to gain a great deal of knowledge. When they reached their twelfth season the women-children participated in the rite of passage and became women. At that point their formal education concluded. Any further knowledge would usually be acquired in the family setting by way of discussions, if men allowed it.

Tomudo raised his hands for quiet and started telling an amusing anecdote about his first encounter with an otter. He used the story to capture their imagination and as a prelude to the study session. It elicited the laughter he had anticipated. Long ago he had begun prefacing each study session with such stories to catch their attention and set the children at ease. Ever since its inception, the children enjoyed the sessions more and were eager to participate in the discussions.

For this session, Tomudo had selected five stories. The first was by far the most important, and he had told it many times previously. Even now, the Age of Corruption story held a strong fascination for him raising questions of how it occurred and why. The next story, the Stewardship of Nature, explained the importance of living in harmony with nature and each other. The other three supported the first two stories and emphasized the importance of the lessons.

"I have selected this story from the collection that makes up our history. It is called the Age of Corruption. How many of you remember it?"

A flurry of hands punctuated the air.

"Very good! Who remembers the first sentence of the story?"

A woman-child named, Chitonch quickly raised her hand. A shy youngster named Kyler timidly raised his hand.

Selecting Kyler specifically because he felt Chitonch knew the answer he asked, "How does it go Kyler?"

He stood and hesitantly answered, "In a very remote period..."

Although he could not recall the complete sentence, Tomudo praised him. "Very good, Kyler."

Looking at Chitonch he asked, "Can you finish it for Kyler?"

Grinning she rose saying, "In a very remote period of our history our forefathers lived in huge villages called cities."

Pleased, Tomudo returned her grin. "Excellent. Thank you both."

He began his recitation expressing the feelings he had for the story. He had discovered that the more emotional he became during the telling of a story the more lasting effect it had upon the children. "So, in a very remote period of our history our forefathers lived in huge villages called cities. The number of people living in any one of these huge villages was so great that one man could not count them in a single cycle of the Great Sun.

"Most of the villages banded together into huge groups called nations and ruled over very large areas of land. Some of these lands stretched from one sea to the other, others were much smaller. In some of the nations, their skin color was mainly of one hue, while in others, all of the hues were present."

Arunde raised his hand.

Seeing it, Tomudo stopped. "Yes?"

Arunde stood. "Why is it we do not have all of the colors in our tribe?"

"A very good question Arunde. As people with various skin hues found our village, they bonded with those who were already living here. In the passing generations we eventually became a blend of all of the colors. Our varied brown skin color is a blend of the black, brown, red, yellow and white hues."

He looked over the children and asked, "Does anyone remember the connection between the temperature and eye coloring?"

Several hands darted up.

He pointed to a slightly framed woman-child. "Lehe, can you tell us?"

"The cooler the air the lighter the eye color."

He posed another question to Lehe. "If we are all of one skin color and the temperature is hot, why does our eye color vary?"

She responded immediately. "Because we have inherited the coloring from our ancestors, and it has not been affected as much as our skin color."

"Excellent, Lehe." Tomudo posed another question to them. "Can any of you explain another way we can identify our heritage?"

Chitonch raised her hand.

Tomudo waited.

Marot, an older man-child raised his.

Tomudo nodded at Marot.

Marot stood up. "We can also tell by our hair color."

Tomudo praised him. "Very good."

Looking at Chitonch he asked, "Can you add anything to what Marot has said?"

She stood up smiling. "Yes. The amount of curls we have in our hair also indicates our ancestry."

Smiling in return, Tomudo said, "Excellent. Perhaps we will eventually all have dark skin color. Many generations from now our eyes may all be dark and our hair may also turn dark and curly. As you know that is the way our ancestors looked when they left this land to settle the earth."

He looked at Arunde. "Have we answered your question to your satisfaction?"

Nodding his head, Arunde answered, "Yes."

Tomudo smiled saying, "Then we shall continue with the story. They lived in huts called buildings which were large and contained separated areas. The buildings were constructed with openings in the thick walls covered by a clear crystal-like substance that allowed them to see outside of the building without going to the entrance or leaving it. They lived and worked in these buildings. Their knowledge was so advanced that they were able to control the weather inside of the buildings. Many buildings were constructed in the cities. This was done by placing one living or working area on top of the other. Some of them were so high the tops of them could not be seen when it rained.

"During this same era knowledge was of supreme importance. The children went to large buildings where they were taught many great things. Those of superior intelligence continued to learn. Normally, the more intelligence one had the greater the position he or she held in the community.

"Their knowledge was so great they were able to move over land and sea and through the sky in objects they constructed called vehicles. As their intelligence grew, so did their ability to construct things of beauty as well as things of destruction. They had even controlled the power of the jagged light that precedes the thunder when it rains. By using this power, our ancestors were able to light the cities and create very complex goods and weapons. This very complexity nearly destroyed all life on earth, by corrupting both the air and the water.

"The immense number of people living on earth created unimaginable demands on the land. Forests were destroyed to grow vegetables and fruits. The removal of such vast areas of forests altered the weather. The rising water, of the melting polar regions, flooded coastal lands. Droughts caused famine over vast expanses of the earth. New illnesses developed, baffling men of medicine.

"In spite of all their vast knowledge, the number of people who thrived upon the inadequacies of others grew. Traditions were neglected." Tomudo paused for emphasis. "During the Age of Corruption, some of our ancestors honored tradition and law. Their numbers grew nearly as fast as those that abhorred the law and tradition. Men of science constantly warned the Elders of the impending disaster to nature, but they were not taken seriously. Only a few nations heeded the warnings. Their efforts to curtail the corruption came too late. They could not restrain the defiling of Mother Earth, and she began purging herself. It also angered the Great Sun and temperatures rose around the world. Long seasons of draught and famine menaced vast regions of the Earth. Pestilence ravaged the Earth. Both the poor and wealthy nations suffered tragically."

Tomudo paused and smiled at Batu. He continued on with the story hoping his voice would not betray his desire for her. "Wars erupted. Unscrupulous nations unleashed horrendous man-made explosions contributing to the destruction and death. Natural catastrophes began occurring in places where they had never happened. Volcanoes erupted over Mother Earth spewing enormous amounts of ash into the air blocking out the Great Sun for many cycles of blue skies.

"Nearly all who lived in the cities lost their lives in the prolonged struggles and conflicts. Even their great, layered buildings did not survive the onslaught. Those that survived crumbled with age and gradually became unrecognizable.

"With the corruption to Mother Earth, multitudes of people died. Those that survived were afflicted by the Great Sun. Illness ran rampant over the lands. The masses of people could not escape the gods' searing wrath. The man-made explosions caused mutation in men and animals. Most of the mutated people and animals died. The descendants of the mutated animals were crazed, ferocious and were a constant threat. Even docile domesticated animals turned upon their owners. Other forms of life did not escape the raging gods. Many people tried to hide from the gods to elude the havoc. Some were successful, but their numbers were few.

"The people who mutated were terrible to look upon. Many of the disfigured mutants died quickly. The few mutants that did survive had tremendous strength. They bore children and terrorized the normal survivors."

A young man-child named Bola waved his hand in the air. Tomudo acknowledged him with a nod of his head.

"Are there any mutants left on earth?"

"A very good question, Bola. We think we have chased all of them out of our area. I am not certain if any are around now. They could well exist."

"Did any of our people get hurt?" asked Bola.

"Yes, and we hurt some of them. Our warriors had to kill them to drive them off."

Looking at Bola, Tomudo raised his eyebrows questioningly. The child shook his head, seeming to have answered his own question.

"Some people managed to live because they had a supply of pure water and food. Pure water was one of the most decisive elements in surviving. The survivors lived in constant peril.

"With the passing generations, our ancestors slowly came together on this land. The land and water were slowly restored. Our ancestors had a very diverse religious background. The religion and philosophy we have, evolved from their thoughts and experiences. Men became protectors and the heads of the family. Women were entrusted to rearing children and supporting the decisions of their men. Our Kahali ancestors were taught to respect the earth. As seasons came and went traditions and myths were established. These were passed on orally to provide continuity and purpose to our lives. Because of this new philosophy and religion the Great Sun provided us with abundant game, food and water.

"It is here on this land that the Kahali tribe settled. On this fertile land, we have learned to honor the goddess, Mother Earth. We, the Kahali, have survived the age of corruption because we live in harmony with each other, nature and our religion.

"This story and all of the rest are remembered and revered in the minds of the Teller of the Stories from the first to the one speaking to you now."

The story captivated the children, as it had so many times in the past. It had become the most repeated story in the historical collection and bore telling several times each season. Tomudo's eyes scanned the children to see if there were any questions. They came to rest on Batu. A challenging glint claimed her eyes, as she stood up. Recognizing her wish to speak he nodded his head.

"May I ask a question?"

"Of course."

"During the era of history the story speaks of, did our ancestors look unfavorably upon someone possessing a great deal of intelligence?"

The children were straining their necks to look at her. They were all aware that Batu's presence broke with tradition. They remained quiet, anxiously waiting Tomudo's reply.

Tomudo surprised the children by calmly replying, "I have thought about that very same thing myself. It seems that intelligence may well have been revered."

A trace of a smile flickered across her face. Buoyed by his honest and calm answer she asked, "Could it be that women were allowed to acquire as much knowledge as men during that era?"

He stared at her finally understanding where her questions were leading. Thinking her question over, he reasoned it out and answered, "Yes, even though it is not spoken of directly in the stories, I have found indications that it was allowed."

She breathed deeply and spoke. "Do you think women are capable of critical reasoning?"

He deliberated in answering and looked at the children briefly, wondering if he should continue the discussion. Not wanting to displease Batu, he replied, "Yes, but they have not demonstrated it as well as men."

"I am aware of that. Perhaps repression may be the reason for this difference. What do you think?"

Furrows appeared on Tomudo's brow. "I am not aware of any repression, Batu."

"Possibly because you have never looked for it," she snapped back.

Ignoring her tone of voice, he replied, "I have had no one speak of repression to me until this moment so how can I be aware of it?"

"Then it is right that I make you aware of it. Why is it the men can acquire knowledge by entering into debates at these story sessions and women are not even allowed to attend?"

"You are attending."

"True, and I am breaking tradition by doing so."

"But, you are not breaking any of our laws, so I have allowed you to attend these sessions," he countered.

"I will admit that is true, but why are women not given this same liberty to attend without the stigma associated with breaking tradition?"

"I cannot answer that."

Her eyes narrowed as she asked, "Why not?"

He touched his forehead with the fingers of his right hand as if to draw from his mind the correct reply. "Because I do not have a story to guide me and tell me what to say to you."

"Are you afraid to speak on your own? Must you always consult the stories before you answer a question?"

"I am not afraid to speak, but a wise man always seeks counsel when it is available."

"Since only you know every story handed down from generation to generation, is there one that speaks of why women are forbidden to acquire knowledge?"

"Women are not forbidden to acquire knowledge. If they were you and the rest of the women-children would not be here."

"That is true, but we are greatly discouraged at entering into any discussions where we could increase our knowledge. Why is that? Why are we being repressed?" Batu asked pointedly.

"There are a few stories that hint of the reasons, but none that are specific," he responded.

"And could those stories have been used to create fear among our ancestors?" she asked tersely.

"I could not answer that with any authority, Batu."

Batu's forehead crinkled with intensity. "I ask you again is there a story or law that specifically forbids a female to acquire knowledge once attaining womanhood?"

He answered immediately. "No."

"Are you sure of this, or are you afraid to answer me truthfully?"

"I am not afraid to answer you. If you must have an answer from me, as opposed to what is stated in our stories, it will be a conjecture. I think women may have used their knowledge just as unwisely as did men and contributed greatly to the dishonesty and downfall during the age of corruption. I am certain that is why our men fear it will be repeated."

"Do you realize with that statement you have admitted that women were of the same mentality as men?"

He looked at her silently and admired her logic.

Batu threw her hands on her hips and raised her voice in emphasis. "In my opinion, if the women would have been in power, there never would have been an Age of Corruption. We women have been under the domination of our Kahali men for countless generations instead of being equals. It is unjust. If we were to be given the opportunity, we could easily demonstrate that we are as intelligent as men. And it is my opinion that if we women would have been in power during the Age of Corruption it could have been prevented. We never would have been so foolish as to jeopardize the health and welfare of our children."

Batu's defiance caught Tomudo by surprise. No one had ever been so challenging with him. In his role as apprentice, and now as the Teller of the Stories, he displayed emotion only when the stories demanded it. At the council meetings, debates between two opposing men did become heated, but he and the other council members were seldom challenged. Being confronted by Batu, he was slow in recovering his composure. Gradually, he felt his tension dissolving and his mind eased back into its reasoning mode. He admitted to himself silently that there could be a slight chance that what she said held some truth. If it were so, then why had the ancestors neglected to tell of it? There appeared to be more questions than answers surrounding the subject.

His eyes fell away as he searched for an answer. As he did he became cognizant of the children again. They were so still he had forgotten they were present. He realized they were waiting for his reply as eagerly as Batu. His answer was crucial. If he blundered, the impression would be lasting on the children. He chose his words carefully.

"We are both guessing at what happened in the past. Concerning women's abilities, I can only tell you what our history tells us. There is little that speaks of these things. Anything else I would say would not be upheld by the stories."

A broad smile appeared on her face. She knew she had won the debate. She realized he had capitulated in such a way that the stories were upheld for the children. She also saw that he was open to her opinions and willing to discuss and debate them. He did not seem to have any fears of being chastised by the council or men of the tribe for having entered into a debate with her. She nodded her head slightly, in approval of her silent conclusions. She hoped that the opportunity would present itself to engage him in another debate. Having accomplished what she intended to, she decided to defer her other questions for another occasion. If he were not speaking as the Teller of the Stories, the discussion may have taken a different direction. She recognized that he would be a challenge to her in any further debates. He would be a welcome change from always discussing such things with her father. The last time her father came close to winning a discussion with her was more than two seasons ago.

Her infectious smile surprised him. He returned it with one nearly as engaging. A vast difference existed in the two smiles. His came about by way of admiration of her intellectual and conversational abilities. Her smile was brought on by her victory over the man spoken of as the most intelligent in the village.

As his thoughts of admiration faded, he wondered when it was he had become emotionally involved with Batu. He knew it happened before he had come to admire her intelligence. He had been witness to the formation of the stunning beauty she now possessed. He had never seen a woman so gifted by the gods on a physical and mental level. As she matured, her inquisitiveness and logic constantly amazed him. In his memory, she had missed only one session. Many times, she approached him after the sessions for clarification or requested to hear further stories. He obliged every request she made with tenderness and patience.

He knew of the stories surrounding her and her father. Everyone in the village did. Her exuberance, curiosity and eagerness to engage her father in intellectual discussions had often been the focal point of village conversations. It had become a source of divisional undercurrent in the tribe. He chose to ignore that aspect of her personality. He chose instead to center his attention on her beauty and intelligence. No one in the tribe had her intensity to acquire knowledge. Hopefully, as she matured, her open defiance would fade and slowly be crowded out by her eagerness to learn and bear children.

CHAPTER
TWO

Szatu laid aside the squash she had just washed and concentrated on shelling the nuts collected a few cycles ago. Hearing Batu enter, she glanced up about to ask for her help, when she noticed the grin on her face.

"Why are you grinning so?"

"I have just come from the story session and had a debate with Tomudo."

"Debate? What do you mean debate?"

"I have debated with him."

Szatu threw up her hands. "You know you are forbidden to enter into a debate with men. You have shamed us again. Why have you done such a foolish thing?"

"I could no longer just sit there and not ask him why women were not as intelligent as men!"

"But you are not supposed to do it. What would happen if all of the women would do such things? Their work would not be done. Their men would be shamed and there would be disharmony amongst family members."

"Mother, I have done these things with Father and we have not had disharmony in our family."

"That is because your father is not like other men. He loves you and takes great pride in your intelligence. That is why he allows you such liberties."

"Tomudo is just like Father," Batu countered.

Szatu turned reflective asking herself if Tomudo could have come from the same mold as her man, Aahi; and would he allow her to engage him in other debates under council pressure?

"It matters little what I think about this. It is your father's thoughts and feelings that are important. We will continue this talk when he arrives." Brushing the problem aside until her man came home, Szatu said, "Come, help me clean these nuts."

While Batu's hands were busy with the nuts, her thoughts kept going over the talk she had had with Tomudo. She smiled now and then as she ran it over in her mind. She could find nothing she would change.

Szatu glanced at her child and wondered where she ever got the courage to do such bold things. Batu had shown signs of having a very clever mind while very young but also prone to be contrary and extremely independent. She never could comprehend where Batu's stubbornness and argumentative nature had come from. It seemed she always had to have her way. Almost from the moment she could talk, Batu had easily manipulated them into doing what she wanted. Szatu often anticipated Aahi's displeasure with Batu. When Aahi had become angered, she always interceded for Batu by soothing his feelings. Yet, from past experience she knew he rarely remained angry for more than a moment. Aahi's love and tolerance for Batu always took precedence over anything she did, thus making it virtually unnecessary for her to intercede. She took another look at Batu and grinned in spite of herself. Batu's independent nature obviously came from Aahi. He continually allowed Batu to break with tradition, thus fueling her defiance of tradition. Secretly, he relished it, possibly harboring some anger for a tradition that denied his child from ever receiving formal recognition for her talents. While the responsibility to punish Batu lie upon his shoulders, she knew he would never consider it. Love always kept him from holding so foreign a thought.

The gods had bestowed upon Batu beauty and intelligence, of that Szatu was certain, but she also knew how fickle the gods could be and how quickly they could withdraw their favor.

Confident that the next rising of the Great Sun would provide a catch, Aahi returned empty handed from checking his snares in a nearby grove of trees. He looked forward to seeing his family and eating a good meal. He walked past the fire where the leg of the curl horned antelope sizzled. Its tantalizing aroma filled the air. He entered the hut and upon meeting his woman's eyes bent slightly at the waist, showing his respect and kissed her on the cheek. She returned the salute and kiss.

Aahi stretched. "It is good to be home." Seeing the strange look on Szatu's face, he asked, "What is wrong?"

"Batu has openly debated with Tomudo."

A furrow appeared on Aahi's brow as he looked at Batu and spoke. "How did that come about?"

"I wanted to know about the women of the past."

"We have discussed that. Why did you have to ask him?"

"Because you do not know all of the stories that would shed more light upon what women did."

"How did Tomudo react to your questions?"

"He answered them as you would have, Father. I found no deceit in his replies."

"And you never will my child, for he is a man of honor and integrity."

Aahi's eyebrows shot up. "Did he seem angry with you at any point?"

"No. In fact we left smiling at one another."

He scrutinized her and could not tell from her demeanor whether or not she won the debate. He knew that when he entered into one with her it always turned into a battle of wits.

Unable to contain his curiosity any longer, he asked, "And how did the debate go?"

Smiling for the first time since he had arrived, she said proudly, "If I were to judge it, I would say he was impressed that a woman could think so clearly."

"And did you win the discussion?" he queried.

"Why do you ask, Father?"

"Because I want to know how you fared against the most intelligent man in the tribe."

"Yes, I clearly won!"

His eyes could not hide his approval. She had developed far beyond his expectations. He had long suspected that his creation had no equal in the tribe. The many seasons that he had cultivated her conversational and debating skills finally came to fruition and culmination. He felt prouder of her than he had at any other moment in his life. If a shortcoming existed in her upbringing, it lay in his failure to alleviate her stubbornness and overactive pride. He also realized those very shortcomings had contributed to her excellence in other areas.

The reality of her actions and her breech of tradition settled in. He could not openly praise her for breaking with tradition, but he could hardly punish her for something in which he took such great pride.

The slightest bit of concern remained on his face as he spoke. "You knew fully that you were breaking with tradition again, Batu?"

"Yes I did."

"There will be a great deal of talk about this matter at the baths and at the council. I know some of the people may not talk to us for a while, but that has happened before. We have even lost a few friends because of your independence, but no laws were broken, and as long as no evil comes from this, we will survive, and I will always stand beside you."

Having voiced his concerns, Aahi now smiled expansively. "It is a shame we do not have any wine, for I feel like celebrating."

He gathered Batu in his arms and held her proudly. "Ah, if only you were a man, you would receive accolades, from Tomudo himself, in the form of an apprenticeship."

As they ate their meal, Aahi continued to be jovial. Several times, Aahi made Batu repeat portions of the debate with Tomudo and savored every word.

After the meal, Aahi relaxed outside the hut, replaying the episode in his mind. A short while later, Batu and Szatu exited the hut and made their way to the running water to bathe. His eyes followed Batu, as she and her mother walked across the village center. He shook his head. It had been amazing to watch her grow intellectually. Unfortunately, her intelligence had a darkness surrounding it. It came coupled with a stubbornness, which rendered her inflexible. When she felt she was correct, she would never relent to anyone.

He sighed. When she accepted a man in union, he would be facing a huge undertaking in trying to control her. It could be the cause of great difficulties between them. Care would be needed to choose the right man for Batu. While the responsibility rested with him, he also wanted to please Batu.

His eyes followed the women he loved, until they made the turn to the running water. Now, he thought, would be as good a moment as any to review the men he considered worthy to be in union with his child. Narrowing the choice to three had been an easy task. The rumors of Kiirt's abuse of his deceased woman eliminated him. Banaar was far too young and immature, and Stoven far too old. The final selection would be more difficult. The last time he had gone over the men he felt Tomo to be the best choice. It mattered little that he had only lived seventeen seasons, for he had already shown courage and skill on the warrior treks and hunts. He had seen him track, and it would not be long before he would be superior to his father. Whenever he saw him throw the spear it nearly always hit the prey, and his ability to make and place snares placed him among the best in the tribe. He would always be a good provider. Another important factor was that he came from a fine family.

His other choice, Zenon, had already seen twenty-one seasons and eagerly sought Batu. Although not a very good a hunter, he would provide stability to the union, which Tomo had not yet shown. In addition he had a very able mind, and would possibly provide some stimulation for Batu's intellectual appetite.

Lastly, there was Tomudo. If he were younger, there would be no man to compare with him. Already thirty-two seasons old, he had outlived his previous woman in union. He would bring prestige to the union. Being a member of the tribal council, he commanded respect. That respect would also be given to Batu upon their union. Tomudo unquestionably was the most intelligent man in the tribe. One hindrance he had was his age, another the possibility of his being sterile. His previous union left him childless. If the union did not provide a creation, and Tomudo died, Batu would be in jeopardy of being banished from the village. He could not take the chance of placing his beloved Batu in such a dangerous predicament. Aahi knew that a man rarely chose a woman as a mate if the woman had already been in union. The enticement of having Tomudo as a member of his family was great, but the risks far outweighed the benefits.

Even after the analysis of the three men, Tomo still appeared to be the wisest choice. He prayed his decision would be the correct one, for he could not bear to see Batu unhappy. Goodness, she had given him such joy so many times; it would be difficult to live if she were unhappy. He looked at the waning light and knew Szatu and Batu would soon be returning from their baths, and he would be heading for the water himself.

Szatu allowed Batu to move slightly ahead of her, so she could watch her out of the corner of her eye. She wondered if Batu would ever stop surprising her. The child had grown up too quickly. The moments from her birth till now seemed to have taken place in the span of a few short breaths. Although impossible, she wished to keep her near her forever. Soon, Aahi would make his final selection for Batu's mate. There certainly were enough suitors. Her intelligence and contrariness did not scare them away. They all overlooked such things in favor of her beauty. Even her penchant for breaking with tradition did not scare the men away. Szatu knew that first and foremost they desired her. It was obvious they all felt she would be subservient to them. She was not that sure of it. For Batu's sake, she hoped that her man would learn to live with her rebellious and independent nature, if not, her life would be miserable.

Both child and mother's step was lively. Small patches of tall grass clung to the soft, warm earth here and there on the wide path, occasionally brushing against their legs as they passed by. The path ended at the water's edge, where past churning floodwaters formed a large cove out of the pliant earth. A large accumulation of reeds growing on the bank received the burden of the current and curtailed any further erosion. The cover of reeds provided the necessary material for a covey of weaverbirds busy weaving and mending their nests in the nearby trees. Their chirping threatened to drown out the women and women-children talking in the water. The birds were a constant source of delight to the young bathers. They often paused to watch the birds in flight, swooping and darting in and about the reeds.

Cimini saw Batu and Szatu and waded to where they were about to enter the water.

Batu and Cimini smiled at each other.

"Szatu, how are you?" Cimini asked cordially.

"I am fine, Cimini. And you?"

"Well, thank you."

Szatu glanced at Batu and Cimini. "I am sure you two want to talk. I see my friends waving to me."

"Goodbye, Cimini."

"Goodbye."

As Batu and Cimini walked out into deeper water, Cimini nudged her. "Is there something you want to tell me?" she said with a wide grin.

"So, you have heard."

"Of course. Was Tomudo mad?"

Furrows appeared between Batu's eyebrows as she reviewed the event. "No."

"Do you suppose he did not get angry because he wants you to be his woman?" Cimini asked eagerly.

"I suspect so. It is apparent he is not as tied to tradition as the other men." Smiling broadly, Batu continued, "That is a quality I admire in him."

"Tomudo may not be the most handsome man in the village, but he is one of the gentlest. He is extremely kind with children," Cimini pointed out.

"Are you desirous of him, Cimini?"

"I would be a fool not to want him. Unfortunately he has not spoken to my father. I have watched his growing interest in you. He has had no eyes for anyone else."

A broad smile settled on Batu's face. "It is true. He has noticed me."

"Humph, just a little," Cimini, said in an exaggerated manner.

Turning serious, Cimini questioned Batu, "What did your father say about the debate?"

"He showed concern that I broke with tradition, then turned genuinely proud of what I did."

"And I am proud of you too, Batu. I wish I had been there to see it," Cimini said wistfully.

"Come with me next time," urged Batu.

"My father would never let me, Batu."

"Perhaps the cycle will come when all women will be allowed to attend."

Grinning, Cimini said, "When it does, you will be the cause of it."

Tilting her head, Batu smiled smugly, pleased with the thought.

Nearby Oliva caught sight of Batu talking to Cimini; she dove under the water and swam toward them. Surfacing, she wiped the water from her expansive face, clearing her eyes in the process. Cimini and Batu exchanged greetings with Oliva.

Unable to control herself any longer, Oliva giggled and looked at the women and children who were looking in their direction. The children at the story session had been quick to tell everyone what had transpired.

Oliva leaned toward Batu confidentially. "I heard what you did at the story session," said Oliva who was having trouble holding back another giggle and finally let it loose.

Always impatient with Oliva, Batu exploded. "Idiot, why are you giggling?" she asked indignantly. "I did nothing that was funny."

Despite hurt feelings, Oliva sheepishly said, "I meant no offense, Batu. It just seemed so funny for a woman to enter into a debate with the Teller of the Stories."

"It would seem funny only to one who could not understand anything," snapped Batu.

Ignoring the obvious verbal injury, Oliva asked, "How were you ever able to do that with Tomudo?"

"I just began asking questions."

"But you have done that many times," Oliva stated.

"This time I challenged him," Batu said smugly.

Oliva leaned closer to Batu and asked, "Did he get upset?"

"Tomudo is not a man who gets upset," replied Batu.

"Was the debate a great challenge?" Oliva asked.

"It was quite easy. Actually, it was not as much of a challenge as I imagined it would be. He is more intelligent than my father only because he knows all of the stories of our village."

Oliva frowned. "Why did you do it?"

"I had two very specific reasons. First, I wanted to match my wit against his to see where I stood against our most intelligent male."

"And how did you do against him?"

Caustically she replied, "If you would have asked the children you would know I was superior to him."

The hurt in Oliva's eyes was lost to Batu. Somewhat cautiously she continued questioning Batu. "What did you talk about?"

"I wanted to discover the roles women had in the past," she said impatiently.

"But we are not supposed to talk about such things," Oliva pointed out.

"Do you think I do not know that?" Batu stated angrily.

"But you always get in trouble because of what you say," Oliva countered.

"Trouble means I am doing something. I am not just a lump of flesh."

Shaking her head, Oliva offered, "Father would not allow me to do such things. He would punish me terribly."

"How do you know?" Batu countered. "You never do anything you are not supposed to do."

"I know, Batu. I know."

"Well, I do not want to be like all the rest of the women."

Puzzled, Oliva asked, "Why not? Why do you want to be different?"

"It is unreasonable to imagine that everything should remain the same. Excitement comes from being different. At least I give everyone something new to talk about," Batu said smugly.

Batu nodded toward the bathing women. "Listen to how excitedly they are talking and whispering about me," she said, smiling in satisfaction, as she sprayed her eyes on the bathers. "I have given them much to talk about in the past and I will do so in the future."

Oliva turned and looked at the other women who were obviously talking about Batu's behavior. She smiled weakly and admitted to herself that Batu's words were true. Many were the times she envied Batu's keen mind and knack for creating excitement. And now, she had yet another reason to envy her, her beauty. For the third season her father had not received any offers for her to be in union, while Batu's father had received more than she could count on one hand. More and more her less than comely face had come to rule her life. Again, she would have to wait until next season to see if any man wanted to be in union with her. Life held no charm for Oliva. Disgusted, she wondered why she was not exciting and fair of face like Batu. Oliva sighed and thought the gods were cruel to have bestowed a dull mind and an equally dull face on her.

Watching Batu washing herself, Oliva could not imagine entering into a debate with her father much less a learned man like Tomudo. She wondered what it would be like to have everyone's attention focused upon something she did or said, or on the way she looked. She surmised it would be exhilarating and provide a sense of pride. Unfortunately, she could not think of anything she could do to put herself in such a position at the moment, yet in the past few seasons Batu had been the center of attention many times. She wondered why the gods favored Batu with such qualities and failed to bestow them on her. She could not fault Batu for what the gods did. Unfortunately, when they made her, perhaps the gods had been ill, she rationalized. When they made Batu, it appeared they felt well.

Oliva knew she would put up with Batu's occasional vanity and meanness. At least Batu confided in her. Batu held nothing back in the telling of the strange things she did and the discussions she had with her father. Thankfully, the gods left her with the pleasure of Batu's company. Many were the moments she envied Batu, but she also valued her friendship and consequently contended with her cutting remarks. But she was not alone in recognizing Batu's faults. In the past she had overheard conversations among many women who felt Batu to be too vain and disrespectful of tradition.

Oliva shrugged her ample shoulders in resignation to fate. Unwilling to cloud her mind any longer, abandoning all her thoughts of envy and remorse, she ducked under the water, grabbed Batu's legs and gave them a tug, sending her sprawling into the water. Batu ejected from the water sputtering and ducked Oliva with Cimini's help.

Szatu waded further into the cool swirling water. It soothed her warm skin. She always enjoyed the leisurely baths and the easy chatter and laughter of the women and children. As she approached her old friends Margit and Shevel, they were smiling. The smiles could not hide the eagerness beneath. They were waiting to discover why Batu had openly debated with Tomudo.

Margit spoke as Szatu drew next to them. "So, once again your Batu has caused us all to talk about her and wonder why she broke with tradition. Glory to the Great Sun, one moment it is this, then it is something else. Who knows what she will do next?" Margit smiled and made a movement with her shoulders. "We have been in suspense long enough. Tell us why she argued with Tomudo."

It pleased Szatu to be able to share her intimate knowledge of what transpired. She related the conversation in detail.

Shevel listened to Szatu relate the story, while glancing now and then at Batu, Cimini and her creation, Oliva. Szatu finished talking and Shevel asked, "When he was told of the discussion, what did Aahi say?"

Szatu, who had also been looking at Batu, turned her attention back to the women. "I was not sure how he would react, but he..." She paused because of Shevel's presence and altered what she was about to say. If she told everything it would put Aahi in an awkward position with the men, and Shevel took pleasure in other peoples problems and awkwardness. She continued, "He stood stern with her. I am certain he will deal with her properly. Disciplining Batu is his responsibility." Szatu glanced back at Batu and could not help but feel proud of her courageous, if not foolish, action.

Margit looked lovingly at Batu. How many times had she wished she had created a child like Batu? she mused. Unfortunately, the gods had not blessed her, and her man Janos, with a creation of their own. She often wondered if she and her man were being punished for something they had done. Was that why their union had not been fruitful? Whatever the reason, she had long since stopped talking to the gods about the lack of a creation in her life. The gods were simply not aware of her existence or interested in her desires. But with Batu near her, she could at least take pleasure in her exploits. She considered herself fortunate to be a close friend of Szatu, for the friendship allowed her to be near Batu. While Batu was an infant, she held her lovingly and imagined her to be her own. As a toddler and youngster, she filled Margit's life with merriment. Later, she watched Batu grow in beauty and then in intelligence and then into the most adventurous woman-child in the tribe. With friendly and loving pride, she admitted to herself that no woman in the tribe could match Batu in beauty. More than once, she had looked at Batu's hips and thought how easy it would be for Batu to have children. Batu would fill Szatu's home with a joyful noise from her creations. Unconsciously, she shook her head. If it were not for Batu, her life would be as barren as her body.

Shevel followed Margit's eyes to Batu. Now as so often before, she masked her true feelings toward Batu. How could someone as good as Szatu create someone so vain, aggressive and disrespectful of tradition? Batu did have an appealing face and body, and seemed somewhat intelligent, but she had an appalling personality. She paled next to her own Oliva. Oliva's heart was pure. Oliva never caused her any sorrow or reason to raise her voice in anger. She always behaved like a woman. She never broke with tradition. Batu's actions and speech were uncontrollable, impudent and conceited, and she could never understand why Aahi did not beat her. What angered Shevel the most was how the men in the village watched Batu. It disgusted her to see the way men looked at her. They acted as if no other woman existed. She had even caught her own man, Mato admiring her. How could they look at a woman who did not hold with tradition? With a sudden rise of anger she thought justice would be served if Batu would not be able to bring forth a creation. It would be horrible if the village had to contend with another like her.

Turning her attention to Szatu, Shevel said smugly, "It is too bad Batu is not more like you. Perhaps she would be more obedient and could be accepted by the other women in the tribe."

Wistfully Szatu replied, "Batu is Batu. She has always been fiercely independent and unique. I have never tried to bury those qualities. I love her as she is, Shevel."

Scrutinizing Shevel, Szatu felt certain if the gods had given Batu to Shevel she would have been broken in spirit and never would have accomplished the things she had in life. Batu was fortunate to have a father so willing to endure her craving for independence and zest for discussion. Few men in the tribe would be secure enough to have withstood Batu's constant probing and debates. She challenged both of them in their philosophy on subjects they rarely had given a second thought to, let alone discussed between them as man and woman. They were inclined to accept things, as they were, Batu could not. There were moments when she felt Aahi would have been justified in being harsh with Batu or even punish her, but he never reached his limit with her. Aahi endured everything for Batu.

Szatu knew many of the women held Batu in poor regard, yet there were a few women who openly admired her. They even took pride in her escapades. Realizing those women took pleasure, in some vicarious way, in Batu's independence and intelligence; she easily put up with Shevel's innuendoes.

Feigning interest in her bathing, Szatu proceeded to change the subject, not wishing to cause ill feelings with her friend.

CHAPTER
THREE

The Great Sun rested at the three-quarter mark. Tomudo sat on a small, weather worn log bench situated near the entrance to his hut. It bordered the village center and sat at the foot of the path, which ran parallel to the running water. The wide path, one of four directed at the cardinal points of Mother Earth, served as a thoroughfare for the villagers. His eyes appeared to be closed. He had used this innocent deception often. He watched Batu intently through slightly opened eyelids. She tended the fire near her hut across the village center. At the rim of the center and to his left, a small group of men were trying to stare inconspicuously at her while discussing her in soft monotones. He had feigned sleep many times and gained knowledge in this very same manner.

By now the whole village knew of the incident between him and Batu. The fact that it happened did not surprise him; it astonished him that it did not happen sooner.

He had intently watched Batu mature and delighted in it. He did not have that privilege with his deceased woman, Jocas. He had never paid that much attention to Jocas until the moment he saw her overwhelmed with emotion. Prior to that she was just another one of the children at the sessions he taught and later, one of the women of the village.

As he watched Batu, he marveled at the feelings he had for her. He began to notice the precocious Batu at the age of eleven, when she began showing signs of physically maturing. Even as a little child she seemed to have a grace and agility that the other women-children did not possess. Even now, these qualities were easily overlooked, because of her facial beauty. As she sat on her haunches by the fire, he stared at her abundant breasts moving sensuously. He felt himself stirred even at this distance. He hoped he had impressed her father, Aahi, with how much he wished to be in union with Batu. There were many men seeking to be in union with Batu, yet he felt confident he had the most to offer her.

At the story sessions, he had been impressed with her conspicuous intelligence and maturity. He knew it to be a direct result of her parents.

While talking with her father, Aahi related several stories from her early life, which indicated not only her cleverness, but also her philosophical development. While some men would be fearful of such qualities, to Tomudo, those qualities enhanced her character.

A sudden movement by Batu caught his eye, and he focused his attention on her once again. She rose from her haunches and stretched. Her arms moved lazily over her head as she arched her back causing her breasts to jut skyward. The act was a natural one for Batu, but he and the men observing it viewed it as sensuous and naively provocative. She seemed totally unaware or uncaring of the men looking at her. They, on the other hand, were keenly aware of her and whispered and smiled. Unexpectedly, she turned and went into her hut to the dismay of all. Staring at the entrance to her hut, Tomudo wondered how he was going to control himself when she would do these things if they were joined in union. Hopefully, when she became his woman, the men would be more cautious and respectful. He grinned wryly. He had to admit that he was willing to contend with such guileless acts, which provoked occasional discourtesies from the men, as long as she was his. What concerned him more were her acts of independence he had witnessed.

Tomudo leaned back and closed his eyes. His thoughts of Batu faded and began to center around his past. It seemed only a few moments ago that he had first heard Tonilla, the previous Teller of the Stories, reciting the stories he loved so well. He had listened in fascination to the story of the Tribal Flood, riveted to a spot at the feet of Tonilla. From that moment, his every thought and desire focused on being selected as the next Teller of the Stories. He made it a point to spend every free moment he had in the company and service of Tonilla.

Young Tomudo's efforts did not go unnoticed. He impressed Tonilla by his sheer persistence. While still in his tenth season, Tonilla selected him to be his apprentice. With the selection, Tomudo's dream became a reality. He studied with a fervor that both surprised and pleased Tonilla. It took Tomudo five seasons to remember the tribe's stories, a feat that matched Tonilla's own abilities.

Tomudo reached the age of twelve and completed his Rite of Passage to become a man. At that point, he began attending the council meetings, although he could not contribute his opinions. That privilege would be accorded him upon Tonilla's death. After the meetings, Tonilla took great care to explain why he aligned himself on one side or the other in the discussions and problems of the villagers. Tonilla constantly encouraged

Tomudo to ask questions until he felt assured that he fully understood why he had voted for or against a particular decision. In this fashion, Tonilla instilled in Tomudo the wisdom he now displayed in the meetings.

Tomudo, like all of the men, learned to hunt and build his own snares. When he became the Teller of the Stories, he, like the other members of the council, did not have to provide for his own food. Even though he sat on the council, he did not want to lose his skills and occasionally went on hunts and set his own snares.

In his seventeenth season he became bonded in union with his woman, Jocas. Small of stature and with ordinary facial features, she had not been selected for union in her first available season, her sixteenth. He considered himself fortunate that she had not been selected. He first became drawn to her at the Ceremony of Unions. She stood near him observing the ceremony. For some unexplainable reason, he had been drawn to watch her throughout the ceremony. While the vows were being exchanged, her eyes filled with tears. Unobtrusively, he looked to see if any of the other women, who were not in union, were reacting in the same manner, and found none so effected. Through that single observation, he concluded that she had a deep sensitivity. At that moment, he knew he wanted to be in union with her.

He proclaimed his intention to her parents immediately after the ceremony. Having been accepted by her father, he presented himself at the hut of her parents the customary six times, as prescribed by tribal law. At three of the meetings, he spoke to Jocas alone to verify that his impressions and desire were correct. Talking to her only solidified his feelings for her.

The union proved to be one where both of them grew in their love for each other. She brought to the union tenderness and gave her heart to him completely, holding nothing in reserve. Their inability to produce a creation stood as the only area in their lives that lacked fulfillment. Before she could give birth, she contracted a fever. The efforts of the Talker Healer to save her were in vain. Unable to withstand the fever's ravages she died. Her death devastated Tomudo.

In his pain, he sought solace from Taja, the Talker Healer. Taja's sincerity and compassion had become a source of comfort in his loneliness. Taja worked patiently to turn Tomudo's feelings around by guiding his thoughts to the joy Jocas had brought to his existence.

His twenty-sixth season of life proved to be horribly bleak. While struggling to overcome the loss of his woman, two more tragedies befell him. The first, the death of his father, left him without any immediate family.

The second, Tonilla's death, stunned him nearly as deeply as the loss of his father. He found solace with Taja and refuge in his work on the council and teaching the children.

The council served as the sole governing body of the tribe. It enacted the laws, settled disputes and organized the ceremonies and festivals. Each of the five council members represented a unique aspect of tribal life. The Elder was chosen from the older men of the tribe who were noted for their wisdom and represented traditional and conservative viewpoints. The Talker Healer on the other hand, symbolized the dynamic, mystical powers of the Great Sun and Mother Earth. The lineage of Talker Healers carried with it the vestiges of esoteric knowledge. The thread of spirituality wove around the fabric of all the past Talker Healers. He communicated with spirits and the deceased people who were dwellers in the Land of No Shadows. He and the High Priest were the healers in the tribe. The High Priest attended to the woes befallen the tribal members because of religious breaches and contentions with the gods, while Taja attended to their other ills. The Warrior Hunter member of the council brought with it the qualities of courage, cunning and strength, as well as the ability to hunt and snare. The Teller of the Stories preserved all of the stories that guided the village. He taught the children by recitation of the stories. Rounding out the council was the most liked man in the tribe, the Friend of All. He aptly determined the pervading mood of the villagers.

Tomudo held the council in high regard and knew the great trust his predecessor had put in it and in the position he had held. His assessment of the council, made while an apprentice, still held true. In his opinion, of the four other council members, only Taja demonstrated any consistent wisdom. The Talker Healer said little, but his words were always filled with understanding. Tonilla had left Tomudo with the impression that Taja's predecessor possessed the same wisdom and integrity displayed by Taja.

Taja's wisdom became apparent to Tomudo after only several council sessions. Whenever issues became clouded, Taja would patiently outline the errors in the council's thinking and indicate an alternate way of looking at the situation. The solution then seemed self-evident, and they acted upon it with clarity. After a number of such incidences, Tomudo began to evaluate his own position prior to actually making his mental decision. He tried to think in terms of how Taja would evaluate the problem and then proceeded along those lines. Outside of the council setting Tomudo found Taja stimulating, fascinating and loving.

With the current composition of the council, it became apparent he and Taja's personal philosophies set them apart from Mihili, the Elder, Motum, the Warrior Hunter, and Neda, the Friend of All. The three were influenced by Romir, the High Priest, and entrenched in the quagmire of a religion, encumbered with dogma and surrounded by fear and superstition. Even with these restrictions and impediments, Tomudo genuinely felt the council contributed significantly to the welfare of the Kahali people.

Making decisions that affected the tribe eventually affected Tomudo as well. A deep sense of attachment to the tribe evolved from his work. He welcomed the change and the opportunities. It gave his life purpose and direction. And now, his life seemed destined to move in yet another direction. Concerned and anxious, he felt an urgency to know if Batu would become his woman. In previous discussions with Taja, he had never sought his help exactly the way he would now. He knew Taja had the ability to see how events could unfold. With Taja's help, he would seek to insure that Batu would be his woman. Perhaps Taja would influence the future so that his union with Batu would become a certainty. His concern had prompted him to schedule a meeting with Taja. He hoped to have Taja intercede with the spirits and dwellers in the Land of No Shadows. He wanted their blessings and help.

Tomudo moved from his bench, went inside his hut and busied himself preparing his meal. While his hands were occupied with the mundane chore, he thought about Taja. Taja's abilities as a healer held a fascination for Tomudo. He knew that Taja probed into the relationships of those that came to him imploring them to establish harmony in their lives. In Taja's viewpoint, rectifying relationships seemed to be a prerequisite to good health. While he treated the sores, fevers, cuts and fractures with herbs and poultices, he continually sought to mend their hearts and minds. Taja believed an illness to be the physical sign of a disruption in harmony. While Tomudo could not see the connection, he could not argue with the results he produced.

After finishing his meager meal, Tomudo deliberated on the gift he would present to Taja for his assistance. He knew he did not have to offer anything in return for his help, but he felt a need to thank him in a special way. Making his choice, he picked up the exquisitely carved work of art. The full-length figure of a tribal warrior fit easily into both of his hands. His father had carved it for him in commemoration of passing his warrior tests. It remained as one of the few physical reminders he had of his father, and he cherished it. He would give it to Taja, for his passion exceeded his sentimentality and need for remembrance.

Emerging from his hut, he walked hopefully toward Taja's. Shortly, he would know the powers this mysterious man had over the dwellers in the Land of No Shadows. It baffled him how one man could attain such powers. He scanned the sky as he walked. Several dark, billowing clouds adorned the sky. He hoped they did not shelter a bad omen. He needed all signs to be correct for his desire to become a reality. He knew an element of danger existed in what he hoped to accomplish. A few, seeking Taja's help, were unable to cope with what went on in his hut. They never spoke to Taja again. He had a sense that he would be completely at the Talker Healer's mercy while in his hut. Were not Taja of such high moral character, he would not have been willing to take the risk, but he trusted Taja more than anyone.

Stopping at Taja's hut, he announced himself, "Taja, it is Tomudo. May I come in?"

Taja's appeared at the entrance smiling and said, "Of course, please come in."

"I wish to thank you for allowing me to come. Please accept this token of my appreciation," he said handing him the carving.

Accepting the work of art, he examined it appreciatively, "It is a true work of love. I hope my admiration of it can attain yours."

After admiring it, he set the carving next to an ivory carving of an elephant on one of many shelves in the hut. Taja moved into a seated position on a mat stuffed with soft, white blossoms from a fluff bush. Tomudo took his place opposite him on the other mat. The Talker Healer said nothing giving Tomudo the opportunity to survey the interior of the hut. The first objects to catch his eye were the many clumps of drying flowers, which hung from the ceiling. He noticed that each clump hung carefully spaced so they did not touch one another. To his left, hanging in small separate clumps to dry, were various herbal plants, leaves from several trees and the roots from a number of plants. Some of the clumps he recognized to be coltsfoot, goldenseal, peppermint, wormwood, persimmon and agrimon, but generally they were foreign to him.

Hanging on the same wall were pouches of various sizes containing seeds, powder, herbs and crushed minerals all used in his collection of healing. On yet another shelf, a large stone bowl sat next to an assortment of smaller wooden and stone bowls some with covers others with none. Peeking out from one of the stone bowls was a long stone instrument he surmised Taja used to crush the herbs and minerals. The blend of odors provided a strange mixture of pungent, acrid and sweet smells. Immediately behind the Talker

Healer, a shelf held a small assortment of skulls. One he recognized as human another looked like a serpent's skull. The rest he did not recognize. His eyes wandered to another shelf containing a large variety of beautifully polished stones, which he knew Taja used in his healing. He recognized a few of them and knew of their energy from his own experience but was unsure exactly how Taja used their energy in his healing.

Gradually, his eyes rested on Taja. Taja smiled in a way, which led him to believe that Taja knew what his thoughts were at that moment. This left him slightly disconcerted even though he had sensed Taja's ability to read his thoughts in the past.

"My friend, why have you given me the statue?" asked Taja.

"The moment of decision for Aahi will soon be here. As you know, there are many men who seek to make Batu their own in union. I wish to be assured that Aahi will select me. I have come to ask you to intercede for me," explained Tomudo.

The Talker Healer looked into Tomudo's eyes for a period of several breaths before speaking, "I have come to know you well my friend. When you spoke to Aahi I am certain you spoke eloquently in your behalf. I sense you can accomplish what you want to do. Your heart is pure in this matter. In the past you have shown many signs of understanding Batu and her needs. As for your request, I can do nothing except show you the way to the inner landscape or to the Land of No Shadows. Where you will go, and what happens, I do not know. Perhaps the answer you seek will be given to you in one of those places. Perhaps there is no answer that can be given."

"Why is that?" Tomudo asked.

Taja gazed into Tomudo's eyes briefly before answering. "That is for you to find out. Knowing I can do nothing to intercede, do you wish to proceed?"

"Of course. But you spoke of an inner landscape. What is it?"

"Many times the answers we seek are deep within ourselves. They await our venture inward and are part of what I call our inner landscape. It is here that we create our dreams and many of our visions. It is possible you may enter into this realm as opposed to the Land of No Shadows."

He ended his explanation abruptly, then rose from his mat and stepped to one of the shelves. Selecting a particular pouch, he removed it and returned to his mat. Opening the pouch he took a few mushrooms from it. Beginning with the east, he honored each of the four directions with a silent prayer, as he pointed to each with his raised hand holding the mushrooms. He began to chew them slowly. He closed his eyes and slowed his breath until barely noticeable to Tomudo. Watching Taja, he became aware of a change in himself. The simple rhythmic movement of Taja's chewing had somehow calmed him as well.

Without opening his eyes, the Talker Healer reached into the pouch and stretched out his hand to Tomudo. "Chew them slowly, as you pray to the Creator for purity of heart and for protection."

Tomudo placed them in his mouth. His mouth instantly began to tingle. He followed Taja's instruction. He closed his eyes and formed a simple prayer in his mind. Gradually, as he chewed, a burning sensation replaced the tingling. He became lethargic. His arms felt heavy, as did his legs, and his head felt like it wanted to rest on his chest. A rushing sound caught his attention. It sounded like the wind and increased in volume. Unexpectedly, it stopped.

Tomudo became aware of being in a place surrounded by a heavy haze, reminiscent of clouds that, on rare occasions, hovered near the ground, during the rainy season. Surveying the area to his immediate left, he saw an unfamiliar looking bird perched on a small tree. Except for its bright green colored head, the bird exhibited a soft green plumage. It peered at him with its head cocked at a strange angle. He wondered whether or not to approach it but quickly discarded the idea. From the mist, a huge, ebony warrior advanced toward him. The way the warrior walked told of his connectedness to Mother Earth. The muscles in his body rippled as he approached. Every movement spoke of his power and confidence. Painted over much of his body were white markings resembling the jagged-light that flashes during violent rains. The other markings on his body indicated he had attained the stature of a great warrior. The warrior stopped a few paces from him. He towered over Tomudo. At this close distance, he saw tiny bluish-white jagged lights emanating from every portion of his body. It gave him an imposing, ominous appearance. He sensed the tremendous energy available in the warrior.

The warrior broke the silence. "Why have you come seeking me?"

As he spoke, Tomudo saw tiny jagged-lights spring from his body arcing to his own. His flesh felt singed from the contact with the jagged-lights, and his body shook from the energy racing through it. He feared for his life. Unable to flee, he looked on spellbound. Somehow the energy captured him. When the warrior ceased talking, the jagged lights receded leaving him intimidated and alarmed by the warrior's power. Only after the painful sensation had subsided to a bearable level did he realize the giant warrior's mouth never moved. How could he communicate with me and not open it? he wondered.

Gathering his courage he spoke, "I have come to ask for your assistance. I want the woman, Batu, to be in union with me."

The ebony warrior answered him with a question of his own, "Are you not man enough to achieve this through your own efforts?"

The warrior's mouth did not move, and again the jagged lights leapt from his body to Tomudo's causing him to shake from their energy. The arcing receded, as the communication stopped. His heart hammered in his chest. He had never heard it spoken of or seen a spirit who had such tremendous power at his disposal.

Tomudo answered carefully, not wanting to incur the anger of someone so powerful, "I am but one of many seeking to have Batu become their woman. I seek help from the dwellers of the Land of No Shadows for assurance that she will be bonded to me. I wish to create a child with her and share my humble knowledge with her."

The warrior moved closer to him. The tiny jagged lights stretched toward him as he drew nearer. Some of the tentacles of lights arced across the distance between them. The nearer the warrior came to him the more the lights arced and burned him. He clenched his teeth to keep from screaming and losing face. The warrior pointed at him and moved toward him. Unable to move, Tomudo watched as the warrior's index finger came closer. The warrior touched Tomudo on the chest with his finger. The contact sent Tomudo hurtling through the air.

Lying on the ground shocked and confused, he rubbed his arms and legs to alleviate the burning sensation. Looking up, he found the warrior had vanished. Cautiously, his eyes searched the surroundings for the ebony giant. He found nothing, nothing but the haze. He trembled slightly and hoped the giant would not return. Assured that he was gone, he began to assess what had happened. What sort of magical powers did the warrior have to be able to throw him through space at the touch of his finger? He had never encountered such feats, nor had he ever heard of anyone else tell of it. A quick scan of his body showed he had no lasting visible injuries. Unexplainably, he realized he felt fresh and energized from the experience. Had the warrior somehow given him some of his power? He even sensed his thinking to be clearer than previously. For what reason did the warrior give him this power and clarity of thought? He wondered if, upon his return, from the Land of No Shadows, he would be able to utilize them.

While lost in his evaluation, the hairs on his body started to stand on end. It was the first indication that something was terribly wrong. The feeling he had when the warrior appeared could not compare to the fear building up inside of him. Quickly, he surveyed the haze. A hideous, tortured scream rang out from the depths of the haze. He looked into the haze for movement. He saw nothing. The screams continued and grew louder. The roar intensified until it became deafening. Tomudo fell to his knees in fear, covering his ears.

He scanned the mist feverishly to detect the threat. A creature exploded from the haze. It stood upright but looked like nothing he had ever seen before, or wished to see again. Uneasily, he examined the grotesque being. Its eyes were colored a dull ugly red. They had no visible pupils. The turned up nose revealed huge openings with long protruding strands of greenish-gray hair. The same hair covered its torso and limbs. Its misshapen head appeared hollowed out at the top. Its narrow ears began at the top of the head, near the hollow, and extended down to its neck. The beast had no lips, leaving its mouth fixed in a perpetual snarl revealing large, dull, yellow, canine teeth. A huge depression lay in the middle of its chest, large enough for a hand to be placed in it. Sores covered much of its body and oozed a sickly looking gray, pasty liquid. The joints of the beast were abnormally large and swollen, yet in proportion to the joints; its limbs were very thin. As it lumbered toward him, its ungainly arms dangled nearly to the ground and swayed across its body. In place of nails, it had claws that were longer than the appendages from which they grew. The color of its skin was of a hue he had never seen and served to accentuate its horrible features. To further intensify its ghastly presence, a foul odor emanated from the beast and permeated the air, making it difficult for Tomudo to breathe.

The creature screeched at him, sending vibrations of terror racing through Tomudo's body, "Why have you disturbed me?"

Tomudo, shaking uncontrollably, summoned his courage and spoke, "I have come seeking help from the dwellers of the Land of No Shadows."

A horrible laugh escaped its mouth. "So you imagine I am from the Land of No Shadows? And you believe I will help you? You are a miserable being. You tremble at my sight and you ask for my help. You are a pathetic excuse for a man. You lack courage and show your weaknesses and you expect me to help you?"

Cringing, Tomudo answered, "Yes."

The beast laughed insanely. "I would just as soon kill you as help you, but I will help you if you can defeat me in battle here and now."

Not waiting for Tomudo's reply the beast plodded toward him. Tomudo's terror mounted. Fear caused uncontrollable, spasmodic jerking in his arms.

The nearer the beast came, the stronger its foul, personal odor became until Tomudo could not breathe from its stench. Fear overwhelmed him. He wanted to flee, yet he could not move away from the oncoming menace. The creature's odor overpowered Tomudo. Falling to his knees, his body purged itself orally and anally. The appalling smells mixed and magnified those of the creature's. He would have willingly killed himself, if he could have found the energy and means to do so. Petrified, he fell on his side, the helpless prey of the grotesque beast. Powerless to move, he watched the beast come nearer and nearer. Finally upon him, it tore at the flesh of his thigh with its claws and fangs. Screaming from the intense pain, he could do nothing to defend himself, so paralyzed was he by his fear, weakness and misery. Unbelievably, he retained consciousness. Throughout it all he could not take his eyes from the bloody face of the creature and his own gory body. Still screaming feebly, he saw the beast turn his blood-splattered head and reach for his arm. Holding it in both of his ghastly hands, the beast placed a foot on his body for leverage then wrenched the arm from his body. The excruciating pain racked through him. He felt the warm red, life-giving liquid spurting upon his face, causing his vision to blur no matter how quickly he blinked his eyes. With his remaining strength, he wailed in unspeakable pain. Then, he gasped for air, as his own vomit threatened to choke the life from him. The beast's powerful jaws crushed his neck and the torturous pain reached an agonizing crescendo. He heard his own gurgling scream fade, as he lost consciousness and sank into the enveloping darkness.

Tomudo awakened with a start. His eyes darted about the surrounding haze in search of the monstrous creature. He could not see the beast anywhere. He became conscious of his body. Scanning it, he saw his body remained undamaged and intact. Dumbfounded, he wondered at the lack of even the smallest scratch from the horrible encounter. He sat upright and tried to fathom how such pain could be inflicted and yet no injury sustained.

His thoughts were interrupted by another figure moving out of the haze. An old woman, of rare beauty and exquisite grace, moved toward him. Her eyes held a deep and wise look. Tightly curled hair cropped short, surrounded her round face. Her deep, rich, brown skin was covered, in part, by a soft white material, which did not appear to be of any animal skin he had ever seen. It hung dramatically around her torso, revealing long, well-muscled legs for a woman of her age. The woman exuded a vitality that he sensed not only visually but also on a visceral level. Serenity radiated from her, engulfing his complete being. Content to simply remain uncommunicative, he enjoyed the feelings and sensations associated with being in her presence.

Stretching out her hand, she beckoned to him. Rising, he slowly covered the short distance separating them, marveling at her beauty all the while. Never had he seen a woman of any age so enchanting, so lovely. Stopping a scant arm length from her, he peered deeply into her eyes. A haunting feeling came over him. She had a familiarity about her, yet he could not identify it. He wondered if he had seen her in his dreams. His memory for faces was nearly as good as his recall of stories, so he would not have forgotten someone so stunning. The longer he remained in her presence the stronger the feeling became.

As she placed her hand over his heart, the feelings of peace, love and serenity intensified. He reveled in the sensations. Joy penetrated his heart. He soared with the wave of emotions he sensed, never dreaming such feelings were possible. They grew so intense he lost all sense of self and gave way to the bliss that engulfed him. His head began to slowly spin. Unable to support himself, he fell to the ground unconscious.

Tomudo awakened sitting cross-legged on the mat in front of the Talker Healer. His head had dipped forward. The slight tingle and strange taste of mushrooms still lingered in his mouth.

Looking intently at Taja, he asked, "Was I in the Land of No Shadows or the inner landscape you spoke of?"

"Were there no clues to where you were?"

"I cannot remember. I was too involved with what was going on."

"Bring the visions up in your mind."

After a moment he replied, "Yes, I remember the beast in the vision saying he did not come from the Land of No Shadows, so I was in my inner landscape. What does it all mean, Taja?"

"Why do you ask this of me? You ventured inward, not I," he said with the same intensity in his eyes as Tomudo's.

Looking extremely puzzled, Tomudo replied, "I thought you would be there with me."

"When venturing inward you normally venture alone."

"What does the vision mean?" asked Tomudo.

Closing his eyes the Talker Healer took a few breaths before he answered, "If I told you what the visions mean that would not be fair to you. Their impact would be lost to you. Their significance is intended for you, and it is you who must do the interpreting. You have the ability to understand the experience. Trust yourself. It is your task to determine what your moment in your inner landscape means. There is tremendous knowledge to gain in what you have seen, heard and felt. Use it wisely, thanking the Creator for the gift given to you."

"But what if I cannot understand its meaning?" he persisted.

"You must trust yourself. In reflection you will discover the truth of your experience," Taja answered reassuringly.

Unexpectedly, the Talker Healer closed his eyes, this time in silent prayer. After a few breaths he stood up signifying the close of the meeting. Tomudo rose, thanked him, and left. Walking with his eyes glued to the ground, he noticed his shadow had lengthened on the ground. Glancing at the Great Sun, he calculated he had been with Taja for a quarter of the cycle. The fact surprised him.

Reaching the confines of his hut, he drew the cover over the entrance and sat down. Heeding Taja's words, he concentrated on reviewing what had transpired during his venture in his inner landscape. What had happened was totally unexpected. He had never heard Taja speak of the inner landscape. He assumed the Talker Healer would go to the Land of No Shadows, acquire the information or help he sought, and come back. Instead, he himself went on a journey to an inner landscape that proved to be strange, puzzling and frightening, yet somehow reassuring. Now he had to determine what everything meant. From what little Taja said, he would have to decipher what the three beings in his vision meant. Beginning with the warrior, he mentally listed his attributes. It seemed obvious from his height and muscle definition that he had extraordinary physical strength. The paintings on his body indicated that he had attained a stature given only to the bravest of warriors. He also had a magical power contained in the jagged lights, which he may have derived in some manner from the jagged light of the rains. He wondered if this warrior could use his jagged light to split trees? He remembered the story that told of the woman who had been killed by the flash of the jagged light and how grossly burned she was. But the warrior sent the jagged lights to Tomudo without destroying him. No warrior in the tribe had ever spoken of seeing jagged lights coming from anyone. How did it fit in with what he sought to know? He shook his head in frustration. Despite his efforts to uncover the mystery of the warrior, he could not clearly define his relationship to him or Batu.

Although he did not wish to, his thoughts were drawn to the beastly being. Remembered fear quivered through his body. Like the warrior, he had never heard of anyone ever speaking of seeing a beast of this nature. No one in the tribe ever dreamed of, or told stories of, such a being on a personal or tribal level. Why did it appear to him and why did it attack him? Why did it eat his flesh? Why did the combat need to be so revolting? He still shivered at the thought of how it felt to be torn apart and consumed while conscious. Why did the creature smell so terrible? Why was it so totally ugly and repulsive? Even now in rethinking the events his stomach turned sour and felt as if he were going to vomit. Recalling the experience with the vile creature, his flesh crawled. What message did the creature try to convey to him? It was very evident the beast could destroy him at any moment and with ease.

Feeling certain the woman held the meaning of the visions, he turned his attention to her. Just thinking of her, he felt better. In spite of her obvious age, he felt that any man would want to spend his life with her. It would be easy to love a woman as beautiful and graceful as she. He sensed she had the qualities he had always desired in a woman. Creating a child with a woman so lovely would be the fulfillment of his dream. He recalled how wonderful he felt being in her company and sensing the goodness in her. If Batu would evolve to become like her, their life together would be an idyllic existence. Unfortunately, she was not part of this earth, but what she bestowed upon him he would remember forever. It seemed incomprehensible how easily all of it had been conveyed to him without a word being spoken. He sat in expectation. Nothing came to him.

Shaking his head impatiently at himself, he decided if he were to unravel what it all meant he must organize his thoughts. Very well, he told himself, he would go over everything systematically. First, he had met a warrior with immense power and obvious courage. Next, he encountered a vile beast capable of destroying him. Lastly, he met a woman of beauty and goodness, having a depth of love unsurpassed by any woman he had ever known. He struggled to understand how they were related to him and Batu and his hoped for union with her. Of course the woman could represent the inner Batu, as yet not revealed. He shook his head negatively, in response to his thought. It seemed unlikely that the woman represented Batu, for in her current development, she would be unable to love as deeply as the woman. Yet with patience, guidance and his love, he hoped she could attain a semblance of the woman's qualities. Their beauty seemed to be the only thing similar between them. Batu exhibited aggressive tendencies and intelligence. The woman displayed neither of these. Up to this point Batu was still filled with a great deal of pride and vanity. The woman showed no signs of either. No, she definitely did not symbolize Batu. If not, then what or whom did she represent? The only other person his request concerned was himself, but clearly he was not a woman.

In his steady scrutiny of the events and symbols, he knew that the qualities of the woman were the important issues and not the physical aspects she represented. Why should a woman's qualities concern him? Were the woman's qualities Batu's? Were these what he sought in Batu? Were these what he saw in her? If the qualities of the woman were important, how were the warrior and the beast's qualities important to him? And how was he to integrate them?

As he returned his thoughts to the warrior, his eyes narrowed. He searched back through his life to see where any sort of connection could be made to the warrior. Finally, he recalled an incident while hunting. Motum was part of the group and had led them to a herd of gazelle. The hunting party had felled two of the herd. The scent of blood had brought forth a lone, young male growler that tracked them for some moments before Motum spotted him. He had instructed the group to yell wildly, wave their hands and run toward the growler. The noise scared the beast off. Motum's knowledge of animals and his courage had impressed Tomudo. But how did that relate to him? While he admired Motum, he himself had never had the opportunity to duplicate his courage before he became involved in learning the tribe's stories. He continued the search through his youth and could not find anything remotely close to discovering what the warrior meant to him.

Moving his attention to the beast, he immediately became uncomfortable. Trying to pinpoint the reason for being uncomfortable, he wondered if it was out of fear of being killed or out of fear of being hurt or humiliated, in his relationship to Batu. He knew of other men who loved her but none seemed violent enough to attack him in secret. He felt confident; he was past being humiliated by Batu. She may seem aggressive to most women and men but he looked upon her with admiration, as did her father. Both of them viewed her as a woman many generations ahead of her moment in history. She held a keen mind, which matched his very well. If she did attempt to humiliate him he envisioned himself strong enough to bear it and to even prevent her from such behavior. The fear of being killed was a puzzle to him. He could not imagine any situation that would present itself to him of such a disastrous outcome. Scratching his head, as if to reiterate his inability to fathom that fear, he focused on the woman in the visions. Her image took shape easily in his mind. There seemed little in her face that brought Batu to mind. Even her eyes were an unusual color. The love he felt coming from the woman was something Batu had yet to exhibit to him. He had never felt love from Batu, admiration yes, love no. The only things she and Batu had in common were grace of movement. Nothing else seemed to apply to Batu, but it was conceivable that Batu could develop into the woman.

Letting go of the woman's image he tried to get an overall impression of the event in Taja's hut. Were all of the images significant to him? His feeling was that they were. Were they all related to his relationship with Batu? Again, he felt they were, but how were they related? He seemed no nearer to unlocking their secret then, as when he first experienced the visions. He had to approach the visions in another way. Batu did not seem to be the primary person in the visions. That left only him. What could they be trying to make him aware of about himself? If someone asked him to describe himself he would define his physical attributes and then continue by listing qualities he possessed. No sooner than the thought appeared, he felt something in his stomach that told him he was correct. Qualities! That was the key. He had to look at the qualities of the warrior. Perhaps therein lay the secret to each vision.

Suddenly the pieces fell together easily. Each being he encountered had specific qualities and he must assume each quality to be present in him. An assurance of certainty swept through him. Now, the only thing left to do was to put them into the correct order to determine what the experience meant. The warrior's body markings spoke of his courage and connectedness to Mother Earth. The jagged lights emitted from the warrior represented power and energy. Power could be used for good and evil alike. He had seen the High Priest misuse his power in the past. He had been hunting often enough to see why the tribe chose Motum to represent the warriors. Motum exuded courage, and his keen senses were a tremendous asset on the plains. A true warrior always used these assets for good. He saw that at certain times in his own life he had used these same assets in ways to benefit himself, and at other times to benefit the people he knew. There were many examples of power used for good and evil within the stories of history. The evil resided within him, as an ever-present aspect. He accepted that, but he knew he had it, for the most part, under control. Yes, yes, he admitted to himself, he knew about the evil force, and he knew he had to control it in the same manner as he controlled goodness and love within himself. It seemed self-evident to him now.

Sighing, he measured his thoughts carefully. If he is to be bonded to Batu he must be grounded in the same way the warrior is with Mother Earth. He must also be in control of himself and of the powers within himself. The power he possessed must be used for the good of everyone, not only for himself. He had learned that as an apprentice and at the council meetings. Could it be that the union with Batu would produce situations where his self-control would be tested in unforeseen ways?

Having felt he understood the warrior's message, he turned his attention to the beast. He shivered anew at the thought of the creature devouring him. Could that be it? Could it be that in some way he could devour himself? If that is true, then, he must control the beast within him and not allow it to surface. But how and why would he devour himself? he wondered. What was it Taja once said? It was something to the effect that if we are unable to control ourselves, we destroy ourselves. Destroying and devouring is one and the same thing. He felt he had interpreted it correctly.

He focused on the beast's head and chest depressions. They seemed to indicate the absence of the organs in those areas. The beast had neither a mind nor a heart. Without them he himself would be a beast. His heart and mind gave him stability. When properly used, they contributed to a person's wisdom. Without wisdom he could destroy himself and those he cared for and loved. His thoughts ran over some of the talk concerning Batu's actions. He had to accept the stories for he had not seen them in person. With so many rumors, he knew there had to be some truth to them. He had been present on two occasions when he heard Batu berate her friend Oliva. It demonstrated that she had not used her heart during those moments. He could not help but wonder if the beast was in some way intertwined with Batu. How could the beast represent Batu, who is so beautiful? No, he corrected himself; the beast was symbolic of how mindful he must be in his relation to Batu. He had to be wise. How else could he make her his mate and keep her? He had to earn her love after they bonded or the union would be devoured and end in disaster. So the beast symbolized his words and actions that can destroy a relationship.

Content with his interpretation of the beast, he concentrated on the woman. The most important qualities of women are to nurture and enrich lives. It stood to reason that those qualities would have to be used if he is to win and keep Batu's love. He would need to nurture the love Batu kept hidden so well under her egotistical mask. They were also aspects of himself that gave comfort and sustenance to many people he encountered. The woman represented attributes of the mother, creator, forgiver, and lover.

It became increasingly evident which qualities were essential to make their union prosper. For it to be a success, he must be in complete control of himself and not allow any evil tendencies to surface and devour their relationship. For this to happen, he must attain and use his heart and mind wisely. His mind must be clear and able to understand what may stand in the way of their productive union. He must have the courage and wisdom of a great warrior and the heart of a tender, loving mother. Mothers give of themselves fully, unselfishly and completely, in order for her children to flourish. That same mother is also a mate and as such, must provide her man with enough attention and love for the relationship to remain vibrant, fulfilling, and cherished.

Tomudo smiled content with the logic of his thoughts and confident he had interpreted the visions correctly. He felt he could accomplish what he wished to do. Bowing his head, he gave thanks to the gods for the ability to decipher the information and for a safe return from his venture into his inner landscape. Continuing his prayer of thanks, he touched upon Taja's help and the assistance of the gods who most likely were the creators of the vision. Satisfied that Aahi would choose him, he relaxed. His first venture into the realm of his inner landscape had been terrifying, engrossing, and enlightening. Above all, it established a new insight into his inner-self. Having had the experience, he felt certain the answers to questions and the solutions to problems dwelt there for himself and everyone willing to seek them.

CHAPTER
FOUR

The Great Sun rose steadily above the horizon, splashing its brilliance on the land. The pale companion, Sun With No Heat, also hovered in the bright blue sky. Together they heralded the celebration of the Rite of Preparation. The ritual prepared the men and women who had reached their sixteenth season of life for union. Previously, upon entering into their twelfth season of life, they participated in the Rite of Passage. This ritual allowed them to be recognized as men and women of the tribe.

The Rite of Preparation, like the Rite of Passage, was taboo for the opposite sex and thus the women's Rite of Preparation was held separately from the men's. Their ceremony was short but extremely decisive. The men's ritual was long and arduous, lasting four cycles. Two of the cycles were spent on the plains and two in the jungle demonstrating their courage as warriors and hunters, as well as their survival skills.

Romir, who would be conducting the women's rite, carefully slipped the chain of bones over his head, fondling it for a moment. The habit of fondling it came about long ago, when he had become the apprentice to the High Priest, Tekumsha. The feel of it always gave him pleasure. More than anything else, it symbolized his stature as the High Priest.

It seemed but a moment ago that the incident had happened that steered him to his current position. He and three other male children were on the plains playing a game of warriors. He and Tulu were paired against Jeham and Muwah. They were using sticks to represent spears in their play. He had just deflected a blow from Jeham and countered with his own aimed at Jeham's shoulder. Jeham deflected the blow, only to have it careen off and hit him on the head.

Jeham screamed, "You did that on purpose!"

Romir defended his action. "No. You deflected my blow and it landed on your head."

"You lie," charged Jeham

"Why would I lie?"

"Because I was beating you."

"You were not," angrily retorted Romir.

The unexpected blow from Jeham's stick caught Romir flush on the cheek. Lights exploded in his head. The blow laid the skin open. Blood oozed from the cut. He staggered backward. Still reeling, another blow landed on top of his head splitting the skin. The third blow missed his head and fell on his shoulder numbing it. The next hit the side of his knee and he crumpled to the ground.

Jeham jabbed Romir with his stick. "The next time you do something like that I will hurt you worse. If you tell anyone I did this I will beat you again."

Jeham glanced at the others and motioned for them to leave.

Slowly, Romir righted himself to a sitting position. The effort was too much. He retched. The earth spun. He lay down and waited for the feeling to pass. When the spinning stopped, he dragged himself away from his retching. Little by little anger crowded out the feeling of pain in his body. Jeham would pay for what he did. He had to figure out a way to get even. It would not be easy to beat him physically, for he was two seasons older and stronger. Unable to think of a way to retaliate, he sought help from the gods. Recalling how the High Priest encouraged the tribe to pray to the gods, he went about formulating his prayer. He asked the gods to punish Jeham for his wrongful act of violence. He repeated the prayer incessantly until the sky darkened and his stomach growled. He limped back to the village where he would have to explain to his father what happened. He repeated his petition well into the darkness and through the next several cycles.

That same season found Jeham, Tulu and Muwah playing in a nearby grove of trees. Jeham, making his way through the branches of one of them, missed the markings of the dead limb. He moved too far out on it. The branch snapped with a loud crack and sent him plunging to the ground awkwardly. His head struck a protruding rock. A pool of blood quickly spread out underneath his head. The parched ground absorbed it as his life spirit fled his body.

Romir was as shocked as the rest of the tribe to hear of Jeham's death. As the shock wore off, he remembered his incessant prayers to the gods. He was overcome with emotion. The gods had answered his prayer! Trembling, a great fear gripped him. He had caused Jeham's death. He grew certain of it. He had prayed for it to happen and it happened. The gods had heard his pleas. What the High Priest had been saying had to be true. Indeed the gods were the source of unknown powers. He sat shaking with his knowledge. This one act proved to Romir that some people angered the gods and some pleased them, some were rewarded, some were punished. Such power could not be ignored. He vowed to be among those that pleased the gods.

The incident propelled him to sit at the feet of the High Priest, Tekumsha. The High Priest was a compelling storyteller, far superior to the Teller of the Stories. Some of the stories told of the gods that disposed of those who fell out of grace. He admired the way the greatest of all the gods, Tor, dispensed punishment to those who disbelieved. The stories always indicated the troublesome person never escaped the wrath of Tor. Here was true power.

Romir's dream was fulfilled with his selection as apprentice to the High Priest. His heart swelled with pride knowing he would be one of the Tor's emissaries who would guide the Kahali people.

Early in his apprenticeship, he found the gods did not always deal with troublesome members of the tribe. At such times, Tekumsha would take it upon himself to become Tor's administrator of punishment. It became necessary because some offenders escaped the wrath of Tor, for some inexplicable reason. The responsibility weighed greatly upon the heart of Tekumsha during these moments. He could not comprehend how the people could stray from their religion or from his instruction. He would search his mind and heart at those moments of stress and eventually perform deeds that he considered the will of the gods. They ranged from creating illnesses to the actual death of one man. The measures were rarely employed, due mostly to the religious nature of the people of the tribe. Romir knew of four incidents that forced Tekumsha to resort to such punishment. In most cases of irreverence, Tekumsha would request offenders to appear in the sacred hut, where they would be warned of their offense. Offenders were cautioned that their irreverence displeased the gods and the evil ones would beset them in their dreams and in the Land of No Shadows if they persisted. The warnings usually sufficed to correct any misconduct.

Romir recalled it did not work with Acati. His offenses to the gods and Tekumsha were so disrespectful they warranted his death. Acati's acts of irreverence began when his woman died unexpectedly in her sleep. He became critical of the gods for having taken his mate.

Upon hearing of it Tekumsha and Romir visited Acati. The customary greetings were exchanged.

"This is not a social visit, Acati. We came as High Priest and apprentice. It is common knowledge you are openly talking against our gods. This cannot go on."

Acati stood his ground saying, "I would never have spoken thus if the gods had not taken my woman. They are the ones at fault."

"No, you are wrong," Tekumsha insisted. "We all must die. The gods are not at fault. You are wrong for speaking irreverently. It must cease."

Angered, Acati retorted, "It is easy for you to say such things. Your woman has not died. My woman was only twenty-four. She has left me with two children and no grandmothers to care for them. Did your gods think of that when they took her?"

"Others have also lost their mates. They do not blame the gods."

"I am not like the others. I place the blame where it should be, on the gods."

Romir sat silently half-expecting Tekumsha to strike Acati.

Tekumsha pointed his finger menacingly at Acati. "You cannot go on speaking irreverently. It will anger the gods. It has already angered me."

"Do you think I care what happens to me? When my woman died, I already lost my life. Neither you nor the gods scare me."

Tekumsha's eyes narrowed. "Mark my words well, Acati, you are in danger!"

Acati yelled at him, "You cannot threaten me. Get out."

"You will regret this, Acati."

"Get out!"

Before the meeting, Tekumsha wanted to be lenient because of Acati's loss. Now Tekumsha was forced into action after Acati's blatant disrespect. Knowing further reasoning with Acati would be futile, Tekumsha prepared a vomiting poison, in anticipation of their second meeting. He requested a meeting with Acati. When Acati agreed to the meeting, Tekumsha showed Romir how to prepare the poison and apply it to the inside of the drinking bowl. At the meeting, Acati stubbornly refused to atone. Realizing that further talk would be of little use, Tekumsha changed the subject and got Acati to relax by talking of the most recent antelope hunt. After Acati relaxed, he brought out wine to show they were still friends. When he left, Acati had no hint that he had been poisoned.

Three cycles later, Acati became ill. In an effort to expel the poison, his body vomited so often and so harshly blood appeared in his vomit. It devastated his intestines, producing uncontrollable bowel movements and dehydration.

A few cycles after Acati had been stricken, Tekumsha and Romir visited his hut. Tekumsha impressed upon him the illness happened because he angered the gods. Acati would hear none of it. After he regained his strength, he remained a troublesome menace to the religious welfare of the tribe. Tekumsha decided Acati would have to be silenced.

At the next dawn, Tekumsha and Romir left for the jungle to gather the fever-inducing plants. They moved through the foliage cautiously, mindful of the serpents and other lurking predators. At times, they had to use their long blades to chop their way through the dense foliage. The Great Sun neared the quarter mark as the dense jungle undergrowth began to give way to the towering trees and sparser vegetation below. Here they were able to walk without using their long blades. They walked a short distance when Tekumsha located the area where the fever plants grew under the forest canopy. Carefully, he pointed out the plant and its distinctive features to Romir. Romir etched the area in his mind. Then, taking great pains not to get any of the oozing fluid on his skin, he helped cut the leaves from several of the plants. At the sacred hut, the High Priest showed him how to crush the leaves in a bowl and collect the liquid, leaving behind the pulpy residue. The very slow-acting poison ideally suited their purpose. No one would be able to associate their meeting Acati with his death and thus no one would know they were exacting the punishment for the gods.

As with the other poison, Tekumsha showed Romir how to line the inside of the drinking bowl with the poison. Romir summoned Acati to the sacred hut.

"Romir and I have asked you here to formally warn you that you have angered the gods. You must stop your irreverent talk, now!"

"We have had this discussion before. I am not afraid of the gods or you."

"But you saw how the gods made you sick before. Any wise man would cease such talk, in favor of his health."

"I have recovered. I will die when I want to. The gods have no power over me."

"You are wrong, Acati. The gods have tremendous powers to heal and to injure."

"Then why did they take my woman? She never hurt anyone. She never spoke wrongly of the gods."

"I cannot answer for the gods. What the gods do is a mystery. Only they know why they do what they do."

"They are stupid, Tekumsha. They show no wisdom. If they were wise they would not cause pain and suffering."

Romir's eyes widened at the offensive remark. Tekumsha clenched his teeth to keep from screaming at him. He kept quiet until he composed himself.

"And you show no wisdom with such irreverence. I implore you to cease such talk."

"I will not stop. Only death will cease my talking against the gods."

Wondering if the gods themselves had spoken through Acati, Tekumsha peered at him saying, "I can see talking about this is not getting us anywhere. Let us forget it for now and speak of happier moments."

Acati felt proud that he did not back down to Tekumsha. Although the situation was strained, he did engage them in social conversation. When Tekumsha offered him the berry wine, it pleased him.

Tekumsha played his part shrewdly. He never let Acati suspect mortal danger lay in the wine bowl. Acati left, content that the High Priest, Tekumsha and his apprentice, Romir had not frightened him.

Acati died four cycles later. At the burial, the High Priest denounced Acati and warned the villagers not to incur the wrath of the gods. He emphasized the importance of following the precepts of their religion. The harmony of the religious life of the tribe had to be protected. Preservation of their religion was of the utmost importance. Without their religion the wrath of the gods would destroy them all. They had nearly destroyed all of the people who lived during the era of corruption. One uncompromising fool could jeopardize them all.

Romir learned the importance of maintaining respect for the position as High Priest and keeping the people attuned to their religion from Tekumsha. It became his obsession. He had employed the use of the vomiting poison twice in the five seasons of his reign as High Priest. Unlike Tekumsha, he had no remorse, only a sense of power. Any opposition to their religion was taken as a personal affront. Whenever it occurred, he longed to see the disrespectful and foolish person suffer. With each offender he had followed his mentor's methods, but he was less lenient than his predecessor. He desired retribution for the humiliation he suffered. He felt frustrated at being unable to talk the members into changing their attitudes. He felt denied the opportunity to conquer them with what he considered his superior reasoning skills.

When he resorted to poisoning them, Romir was amazed at how quickly the dissident person would call upon him to be their emissary and plead to the gods for forgiveness and healing. As the transgressors lay ill, Romir would point out to them that their transgressions had caused their illness and the Talker Healer could not heal them. He would assure them that if they repented they would be forgiven. He told them if they repented, he would pray for their quick recovery.

He ran his hand over his chain. The act brought his thoughts back to the present. The women's ritual had become his favorite. It always thrilled him to be present at their Rite of Preparation. Being the only man to know what transpired at the ritual flooded him with excitement. It was taboo for any man, except the High Priest, to know what went on during the ritual. Presiding over the function presented him with a tremendous sense of power.

Attending the Rite of Preparation for the first time, as an apprentice, his feelings were quite different. The culmination of the ritual involved the women impaling themselves. The act horrified him. He cringed when they screamed. How were they able to do it to themselves? he wondered. With each successive ritual his aversion lessened and his fascination increased. As he entered into manhood and bonded with women, he became excited even at the sight of the women coming into the clearing. As they lowered themselves onto the stake, he could hardly contain his excitement or conceal his arousal. While they impaled themselves, he often visualized each one lowering herself on him. The ceremony excited him so much he found it necessary to seek out a woman to physically bond with immediately after each ritual. After attending the Rite of Passage for some seasons, he detected the same sense of power and arousal in Tekumsha. Breathing deeply, Romir smiled looking forward to the ritual just a few moments away.

Seated on the bench outside her hut, Batu waited for her mother to come out. This season, Batu and fourteen other women were preparing themselves for union. Her mother had described the proceedings, even going as far as to caution her not to eat anything at the dawn meal, fearing she might eject it during the ritual. She had followed her mother's advice and refrained from eating. An apprehensive feeling settled on Batu. She wondered how she would react to the ritual. Would she feel afraid or cry out in pain? Would she become embarrassed or look awkward to the others, as she performed the ritual? She knew she could withstand some pain but was unsure of herself in spite of her mother's reassurance.

Szatu emerged from the hut interrupting Batu's thoughts. A slight touch upon her arm by her mother signified the moment had arrived for their departure. They walked slowly to the ceremonial ground. It sat located in a large grove of trees bordering the running water. Passing through the village center, they saw a small group of men with their fathers. They were waiting for others who were part of the male ritual. Soon they would make their way to the plains, where the male ritual would commence. Walking with her mother, Batu's mind filled with anxious thoughts concerning the ritual.

They left the village behind them. Neither spoke as they approached the woods. Finding the faint path leading into the dimly lit, shadowy interior, they followed it for a brief period. The dappled light flickered on them through occasional breaks in the trees. They came to a clearing. Located in the center of it were fifteen starkly ominous poles standing roughly one hand short of groin height yet each varying slightly in height. At the base they measured about four fingers in diameter. Four fingers from the top, they tapered sharply to one finger in diameter. The slender point was three fingers in height.

Batu's eyes riveted upon the stakes. They were ominously grotesque. Suddenly, the whole process of the Rite of Preparation seemed primitive, totally unnecessary and brutal. The stakes loomed starkly in the light of the clearing. She looked at her mother to see her reaction. She could read nothing in her eyes.

A twig snapped. It drew her attention to the path. The High Priest appeared with three mothers and their children. Her gaze lingered briefly on the tribe's religious leader. He is an ugly man, she thought. How could any woman stand to be near him? He was the only man who she could not stand looking at her. Whenever she saw Romir in the village center, she went into her hut in order to avoid his gaze.

A huge man, the High Priest had a large barrel chest and a stomach that reflected his ravenous appetite. His calves were unusually spindly and out of proportion to the bulk they carried. His forearms were thin while his upper arms were inordinately fleshy like his thighs. His large, round face made his deep-set eyes seem beadier than they already were. The eyes lacked signs of compassion or intellect but did display his cunning and shrewdness. In unguarded moments they exhibited a fierce and unrelenting look. The sickly yellow tint to his eyes added to his ominous appearance. The sacred necklace, composed of numerous small bones from various animals, including that of the tawny growler, adorned his neck. His armband and loincloth were fashioned from the skin of the growler. The mutant growler had replaced its descendant the lion, now nearly extinct, as the most feared predator on the plains. The sheer strength and ferocity of the growler had long fascinated him. Because of it he had fashioned every piece of clothing he owned from its skin.

The nostrils of Romir's small nose were not flared and caused him difficulty breathing the tropical air. Clenched in his stubby, fat-fingered hand was a staff. Atop it sat the skull of a monkey. Its eyeless head glared portentously into space. Romir reached the clearing and immediately noticed the troublesome Batu had already arrived. He swiftly took in her beauty. His gaze came to rest on her breasts. This woman would not escape union, he told himself. He knew of many that were seeking her for their own, and he understood why they wanted her. But her past actions indicated she would be trouble for any man. In his eyes, she had many faults. Despite them, he, like most of the men, was not immune to her stunning beauty. He had been present on a few occasions when men had stopped talking to watch her. Like them he lusted for her. In spite of his desire to bond with her, he would do nothing until she performed the ritual of preparation. Only an idiot would risk bonding with her before then. The strong taboo would put him in jeopardy of losing his testicles, his manhood and quite likely his life. He admitted to himself he wanted to feel those breasts against his chest, and to have her beneath him, bonding with her, until he had his fill. If indeed he would get a chance it would not come until after the ceremony. Perhaps her father would choose to keep her in his hut. If that were the case, he would devise some way to test how willing she would be to bond with him.

The other celebrants and their mothers trickled into the clearing. The apprehensive reaction of the celebrants to the stakes did not escape his scrutiny. Who would scream the loudest? he wondered. Would there be any that would resist crying or making a sound? It happened rarely, but it did happen. His eyes rested longer on Batu than on the others. He could feel the blood pumping faster in his body just thinking of her lowering herself on the stake.

While his mind had wondered, the celebrants and their mothers had drifted into the ritual sight. Carefully looking over the group of celebrants, he saw they were all present. The group had quieted their whispering and stood ready. Clearing his throat, he raised his voice and said, "The celebrants will now position themselves in back of the ritual shafts and face me. The mothers will stand behind them."

After they positioned themselves he continued, "We have assembled thus to participate in the Rite of Preparation. With this ritual you will prepare yourselves for union with your men. We have gathered in this manner for unnumbered consecutive seasons. This traditional ritual signifies your coming of age both physically and religiously. After this ritual you will be able to be united with a man and participate in bonding and in the creation process. The severing of your tissue and opening of your passage is the final preparation needed to conceive. Upon completing the act, you may enter into union in the eyes of our religion and the gods."

He paused to clear his throat of an accumulation of phlegm. Turning his head, he expelled it and wiped his mouth with his hand.

Batu cringed at the sight and wondered if the others were as repulsed by the act as she.

He began to sing. The lyrics told of a woman whose beauty caused a god to seek her for his own in union.

Upon finishing the song, he looked at each woman before he spoke, "The moment is at hand for each of you to prepare yourselves for the man you will bond with once you are in union. We will begin with Boco, while the mothers sing the inspiring song, Sacrifice of the Virgin."

Batu inwardly thanked her mother for arriving early and choosing the last stake, knowing the order from her own experience.

Boco hesitantly positioned herself above the pole. The women sang of the virgin who sacrificed herself to one of the gods to gain his favors and love. Boco holding the tip of the shaft with one hand opened her flesh to allow the point to enter her body. Then, slowly, she lowered herself on the point. Her face contorted with fear. Feeling the sharp pain, as she impaled herself, she cried out and jerked herself free from the shaft. Sobbing, she turned and lurched to her mother who held and comforted her, while tears ran from her own eyes.

Romir signaled for the next woman to perform the impaling ritual. The woman cried out but did not weep. The mothers sang the brief song, Sacrifice of the Virgin, for each celebrant, as they performed the ritual. The next three celebrants all cried out. Tears streamed from their eyes. Romir motioned for Luwan to begin. She lowered herself onto the shaft, and held her breath. At the moment of breaking her passage tissue, she let her breath escape in a rush. She neither cried nor sought comfort from her mother. Romir openly admired her courage by nodding his approval. A woman who could endure the impaling without a sound would be desirable in union. Such a woman would obey her man and know how to bear children well.

His excitement rose with each performance of the rite. He wondered if any of the women were able to see how aroused he had become. In the past, he had partaken of the pleasures from several of the women who had impaled themselves. Each one became a new prospect for his form of impaling.

The last celebrant was Batu. He found it difficult to conceal his lust for her, as his eyes lingered on her breasts. He signaled for the women to begin singing, and then waved his arm in her direction ceremoniously. As she stepped up to the pole, her gaze caught its sinister presence. For a moment she glanced toward the High Priest and then turned unexpectedly to face her mother. The act caught the mothers by surprise. They halted their singing. Szatu's heart began beating wildly. She had seen that defiant look on her creation's face before and openly cringed.

Batu turned back to face the High Priest and proclaimed, "I have grave doubts that this ritual can prepare me for union with a man. If I cut myself on the arm it will not do anything for me except cause me to have pain and to lose my blood. I am fighting to understand how this ritual is any different. I have witnessed these women become prepared for union in your eyes and in the eyes of our religion. You will not witness another. Impaling myself will not prepare me in my eyes. I choose not to participate in this barbaric ritual.

"I declare before you and all of the women here, that I am now prepared to be with a man in union. Whether you believe I am or not, does not make any difference to me. I know I am a woman, and bonding with my man will break my passage. Some grotesque stake whittled by you will not break it. This ritual is disgusting and demeaning enough. To have you stand there and witness it adds to the shame and degradation."

Batu turned and looked at her mother standing with mouth agape. Szatu was as shocked as the others witnessing the rebellion. Throwing her shoulders back, Batu walked briskly to the path leading back to the village.

The words were like a knife in Romir's stomach. She had spewed out her irreverence defiantly, catching him by surprise. He listened to her dumbfounded. His arousal instantly disappeared. When she stopped talking, it took him a moment to retaliate. He screamed after her, "Batu, you will be punished for your impudence and disbelief. When you die, you will be thrown into the area of demons in the Land of No Shadows. Mark my words well! You have brought shame on yourself and your parents, as well as the tribe. The gods will not stand for this!"

Rooted to the spot by his bewilderment, he could do nothing more than watch as her mother ran to catch up with her. Silently, he cursed her and swore to deal with her ruthlessly. To the women before him, Romir growled loudly, "Such acts of impudence and disrespect for tradition are what brought catastrophes upon our ancestors, during the Age of Corruption."

Pointing his finger at the women he warned them, "Even the vehicles of destruction that flew in the air during that age were no match for the forces unleashed by the gods. I can only hope that the wrath of the gods will not spill over onto the rest of us because of Batu."

The High Priest watched Szatu leave the group. "Take care that you teach your children to respect tradition or you will be chasing after your child who has violated tradition."

He cursed Batu silently, knowing that the one who needed to hear his words the most had fled his presence. He could see the women were shocked and upset with Batu. What they felt could not compare to his anger. Hastily, he concluded the rites, wanting instead to run after Batu and beat her unconscious.

Batu had ruined the ritual. He chose not to linger and talk with the women as he normally did. He left the ceremonial grounds as soon as he ended his speech of congratulation. In rage, he kicked the ground on the path, sending dirt flying. Still growling aloud, he sounded like an angered beast. A woman had never insulted him. How could a woman show such disrespect for him, his position and tradition? His anger mounted with each step that brought him closer to the sacred hut. No woman had ever committed such an irreverent act. None! Such intolerable behavior could not go unpunished.

The fading admonitions Romir yelled at her meant nothing to Batu. Her mind rested clear of any taint. She felt no remorse for what she had done, only relief. Hearing someone coming after her, she turned to see her mother running toward her. She waited for Szatu to catch up. Drawing up next to Batu, Szatu said nothing. Deep in their own thoughts, they walked in silence. They broke free of the trees. The Great Sun's brilliant light felt warm and exhilarating on Batu. Walking in the light, a flood of reassurance washed over her. She knew she had done the right thing. Looking at her mother, Batu smiled, hoping to ease her mother's thoughts and misgivings. It did not change the forlorn look on Szatu's face.

Szatu had waited until she was reasonably calm before she spoke. Frowning she said, "Oh, Batu, what have you done? Do you realize you have broken our tradition and angered the High Priest? How could you do it?"

"Mother, I did not know I was going to do what I did. I saw the ritual as barbaric and disgusting, and I could not submit myself to it. I may have gone along with it for your sake had not the horrible High Priest been there. With him looking on, I was repelled as much by him as the ritual. I could not degrade myself with him present. It revolted me to see the women impale themselves with him leering at them. He knows nothing of who I am and of my desires. But he stood there and had the audacity to speak to me and them of union."

She stopped talking for a moment and then went on. "Aside from all that, it was worth doing what I did just to see the look on his face." Incredibly, she laughed as she recalled his reactions.

In spite of the gravity of the situation, Szatu had to agree with her assessment of the High Priest. She had thought him loathsome, but she had always been afraid to mention it to any of the other women. She also felt uncomfortable around him no matter what the occasion. She kept these thoughts from her child.

"You will again be the topic of harsh conversation and may lose some friends," she warned Batu.

"Mother, if I worried about such things, I would be afraid of doing anything. My only true friend is Cimini. She alone has understood my desires. The rest cannot be considered friends. I shall be able to contend with the talk, as I have in the past. I only hope you understand how I feel about all of this."

Preoccupied with her own thoughts, Szatu did not answer her immediately. She knew what Batu did would deepen the division in the tribe. From past experience, she was aware that the tribe held no soft emotions about Batu. They did not simply like her or dislike her. She elicited much deeper feelings. Some of the women admired and loved her. The majority was not enchanted with her and despised her aggressiveness. The men were totally different. In her they saw a rebel and a threat to tradition. They hated her for that, yet they grudgingly acknowledged her to be the most beautiful and desirable woman in the tribe.

Szatu rubbed her forehead. She wondered when Batu would stop causing such turmoil. Aloud she said, "It is hard to understand you, Batu. You are so rebellious and independent it frightens me. What will you do when you no longer have your father and I near you to accept you and your actions? Your man will not be so lenient as your father."

"I have already thought of it, Mother," she said without elaborating. Reassuringly, she placed her arm around Szatu's waist. Several strides later she playfully bumped her hip to her mother's and smiled warmly. For Szatu it was not comforting to know Batu had given it some thought, nevertheless it did surprise her. She took a few strides while thinking, then, giving into Batu's playfulness. Spontaneously, she returned the bump to Batu's hip. Both of them giggled in release of the tension.

They continued walking slowly to their hut. Szatu wondered what Aahi was going to say when they told him of the incident. She would have to think of a way to tell him without breaking the taboo against speaking of the act that consummated the rite.

Aahi saw his women coming. Immediately, he knew something had happened. Not only did he read it in their faces; he saw it in their slow walk. Szatu had the look of a worried mother. He stood up as they neared.

Directing his eyes to his woman, he asked, "What is wrong? What happened?"

Batu grabbed her mother's arm to prevent her from answering. "I have not fulfilled my Rite of Preparation. I refused to impale myself."

Puzzled and shocked he asked, "Impale yourself? Why would you do such a thing?"

"It is part of the ritual to prepare myself for union," she replied.

Szatu could not be stilled now. The panic was evident in her voice as she spoke. "Batu, you have broken the taboo! You are not to speak of such things to a man!"

Aahi responded to the disclosure with a wave of his hand silencing his woman. Instinctively, he lowered his voice in the event anyone was in the neighboring huts. His own voice sounded strained. "The damage has been done. The taboo has been broken, so speak to me of this impaling."

Szatu detected the agitation in her man's voice and apprehensively listened while Batu told in detail of the ritual and how each woman had to impale herself on the stake. She could not believe her ears. The cautioning of the taboo was nothing to Batu; she told her father everything.

Aahi was startled to hear the details of the mysterious Rite of Preparation. His brow tightened. Szatu was correct; a man should not hear such things. Batu had broken with tradition, and she had broken the vow of silence. To break the vow was a tremendous taboo, and he unwittingly had been a participant in it. The shame was his as well. It may be they all had to fear the wrath of the gods for what had transpired.

Seeing how disturbed he was, Batu regretted her actions for his sake. Perhaps she had gone too far this time, even for him.

"Father, I am sorry if I shamed you," she said in honesty.

Gauging her emotions through her eyes, he saw her sincerity. He was proud of her for apologizing. He drew her to him, stroking her hair, but the worried look did not leave his face.

"You are fortunate that the family patriarch is the one to deal with those who break with tradition. If it were the council or the High Priest you had to contend with, you would be severely punished for this breach of conduct.

What you have done troubles me, but I forgive you. My concern is for all of us. Breaking tradition in such a manner is either a sign of great foolishness or of great courage and honesty. I know you to be no fool. I have always stood beside you in the past and I will now. What troubles me is that you broke the taboo. You must not speak of telling me about what transpired at the ritual. I do not want others to know you have broken the taboo. If anyone finds out you have told me things that are against the law, I will be cast out of the village. This will affect your mother as well. You must swear you will not speak of this to anyone. Do you understand?"

"Yes, Father."

"Breaking with a religious tradition is in itself a tremendous blow to our family. You will lose face as well as we. Unfortunately, there may be problems with the High Priest. The future will be treacherous. It will be necessary for you to be ever vigilant where he is concerned. He will not easily forget what you have done and may seek retribution through the gods."

He released her, suddenly weary, he rubbed his eyes as she confessed, "I did not break the taboo in defiance. You need not fear that I will speak of it, Father. It was not my intention to involve you."

"Batu, whenever you do something it always involves us. You must come to understand that before you do great harm to us." Sighing heavily he drew her and Szatu into his arms. "You have always been impulsive, Batu. It has led you into problems in the past, and we have survived. We have lost friends in the past, and it is possible we will lose some again because of what you have done. What is important is that we always stand united now and in the future."

Managing a worrisome smile to the women in his arms he tried to reassure them saying, "No man has two more beautiful and courageous women by his side anywhere on Mother Earth."

CHAPTER
FIVE

Romir's anger drove him to the Teller of the Stories' hut. Tomudo heard the High Priest's angry voice calling out to him. "Tomudo, it is Romir. I must talk with you."

"Of course Romir." With a wave of his hand, he beckoned the large man in. "Please sit down."

Without accepting the offer he began his harangue, pacing irritably in the small confines of the hut. "I have just come from conducting the Rite of Preparation for the women, and I was shocked and angered by Batu's words and actions. I have never been held in disrespect by any woman and neither have the High Priests before me."

"What has happened?"

"Everything has happened! Batu has not completed her Rite of Preparation and has grievously insulted me in front of the other women. It is unfortunate that only her father can punish her for breaking with our religious tradition. If she were mine I would beat her until she could not walk.

"I must warn you that if you take this woman as yours, she will cause you nothing but misery. To be involved with such a woman will lead you to disaster. Mark my words well, Tomudo, Batu is trouble. Women like her have always brought disaster upon men. Women like her corrupt men."

Waving his hand in opposition, Tomudo said, "You are talking out of anger, Romir. I have always found Batu to be highly principled."

"Your view is colored by your desire for her, Tomudo. Do not seek to enter into union with her. She will show you nothing but disrespect. She will bring shame upon you and your position, as a council member."

"I am truly dismayed by your attitude toward punishment, Romir."

"How did you expect me to feel about it? She humiliated me at the ritual."

"You are correct. I should not expect everyone to feel the same way as I do about breaking with tradition, especially you who reveres it so highly," answered Tomudo.

"If she has done wrong, it is Aahi's place to release me from my promise," Tomudo informed him.

"It would not surprise me if he did not do so," countered the High Priest. "If he had not allowed Batu such liberties in the past, she would never have done this and all of the other things to aggravate our people."

Irritated, Tomudo said, "I am not as sure as you that she really intended to aggravate anyone."

Tomudo moved toward the huge man and said, "I will wait for Aahi, and I promise you, I will discuss this matter with him."

"This has gone past discussion. You must take action. Do not be beguiled by her face and form. Her beauty must not suck you in. Do not make her your woman."

"I am well aware of Batu's impulsiveness, Romir."

"This is not impulsiveness. She is irreverent, disrespectful and vicious. I warn you, Tomudo, she is evil."

Tired of his ranting, Tomudo placed his hand on the High Priest's shoulder and guided him to the exit. Though he felt impatient with Romir, he recovered his poise and said diplomatically, "I thank you for worrying about me, Romir. It is appreciated, and I will take what you have said and weigh it in my decision."

In parting Romir said, "Mark my words well. If you take her as your woman, she will bring you disgrace." He lumbered away, the anger evident in his huge body.

Tomudo watched Romir disappear down the path. While he mulled over Romir's outburst, he caught sight of Aahi making his way toward him.

Visibly showing the pressure he was under, Aahi exchanged greetings and came directly to the point. "My friend, have you heard of the incident?"

"Yes. The High Priest just left. He told me Batu has broken with our religious tradition."

"It does not surprise me that the High Priest would run to tell you what happened. He is probably at Mihili's hut now."

"I am not pleased with what he said, Aahi."

"Are you concerned about her breaking with tradition?" asked Batu's father.

"No, what worries me is Romir's anger. He spoke of how he would beat Batu, if she were his responsibility."

"Such words do not set well with me either. Thankfully, it is not his responsibility to discipline her, Tomudo."

Tomudo shook his head in agreement. "I am sure you did not come here to talk about the High Priest. What brings you here, my friend?"

"It is with great reluctance I say this. Since Batu has not fulfilled her Rite of Preparation and broken with our religious tradition, I release you from your decree of wanting to make Batu your woman."

A long pause ensued before Tomudo spoke. "I have not answered hastily because I wanted to choose the correct words. It is true that she has demonstrated little regard for convention and tradition. In fact she seems to have caused more turmoil and talk than the rest of the people of our tribe combined since she has been old enough to talk. All that matters little to me. I love her too much to let Romir's anger, or the villagers' wagging tongues, keep her from being mine."

Aahi's eyes were unflinching as he answered, "Your words are true. She has been troublesome, and I have been extremely lenient with Batu. It would have been easy to squash her spirit." He hesitated, and then made up his mind to share an intimate fact with the man waiting so patiently for him to speak. "When young, I witnessed my mother's spirit beaten down by my father. It broke her heart and mine. I vowed never to do it to my woman or my creation. This is why I have been so lenient with Batu. If you still want her as your woman, it is in your hands. You are free to say you do not want her."

Without hesitating Tomudo answered, "I have not changed my mind Aahi. I am greatly impressed that you and Szatu have allowed Batu to grow up being true to herself. Rarely do parents allow a child to develop their personality as freely as you have done. You have encouraged her independence and that will create opportunities for my own growth. I pray my love proves to be as unconditional as yours. I truly hope I am wise enough to give her what she needs to continue to grow."

Aahi looked into Tomudo's eyes and saw the younger man's honesty. He parted wishing Tomudo were younger. If he were, it would be easy to decide upon him to be Batu's man. He walked away slowly, hoping the meetings with her other suitors, Tomo and Zenon would go as smoothly as it did with Tomudo.

Tomudo sat and reflected on Batu's contrary behavior. Assessing the number of times she was the center of some controversy, he had to admit that it seemed to be escalating. But throughout all of her adventures and misadventures, her rebellious nature and penchant for causing disturbances did not appear to harm her relationship with her parents. He hoped it would be the same with him.

He wondered if she would continue her displays of independence after being bonded to him. If she did, his life with her could well be chaotic. As she grew older and gave birth to their creations, hopefully, she would begin to be more complacent and accepting of things. He smiled inwardly, the solution could be to keep her filled with new life and then she would be too busy to be concerned with independence. Having children of his own was an extremely important part of his life. Batu would provide him with strong and intelligent children. With the passing of his woman Jocas, he swore if he ever bonded again, he would create a child as quickly as possible. Already past the mid-point of his life, he longed to hold a creation of his own to his heart. Visualizing Batu's broad hips, he felt them to be well suited to bear a child. His passion flared up, as he held her image in his mind. He longed to have her in his hut, in order to demonstrate his love for her.

Romir's talk with Tomudo did not go as he had expected. Tomudo seemed cold to his warnings. Preoccupied with his thoughts, he made his way back to his hut. His parched mouth hung open. Inside the hut he removed the cover of his drinking bowl and drank deeply from it. Anger and confusion raced drunkenly within him. How could the gods let an act so vile go unpunished? Why had the gods left Batu alive? What was the reasoning behind it? The questions raced through his mind, but there seemed to be no reasonable answers.

He had to talk with Aahi. This insanity of Batu's must not be allowed to continue. He headed toward Aahi's hut. His walk slowed. He struggled with how to impress Aahi that he must punish Batu severely. Still deep in thought, he found himself in front of Aahi's hut.

"Aahi. It is Romir. May I enter?"

Szatu went to the entrance and looked at Romir. He easily detected the uncertainty on her face.

"My man is not here. He has gone to see Tomudo."

"As he should after what has happened," snapped Romir.

Romir saw the reaction on her face, but, to her credit, she replied in a level tone. "If you wish to wait for him, you may do so out here." Turning abruptly, she retreated inside her hut, leaving him looking at the entrance.

His anger flared up again. He slammed his bulk down on the bench cursing Szatu under his breath for her rudeness. A moment later, Szatu exited with Batu in tow. He glared openly at Batu. Without talking to him, they walked in the direction of the running water. Romir watched them, his stomach churning.

Returning from his amicable meeting with Tomudo, Aahi was disheartened to see the High Priest waiting for him. Romir stood up as he approached.

"What took you so long? I have been waiting to speak to you about Batu's irreverent behavior."

"Please, let us discuss this inside away from the eyes of the village."

Romir took notice of the inordinate amount of people gathered in the village center. The word of what had happened had spread quickly. Seeing them, he would have preferred to berate Aahi in front of them, but he opted to follow Aahi inside. Aahi motioned the High Priest to a bench and sat down himself.

"Have your woman and Batu told you of what happened?"

"They have."

"This is the most grievous in a long list of things your creation has done. It must stop now! In the past I have not shown my anger toward Batu for it did not involve our religion. Now it involves me. I demand that you punish her severely for her irreverence and disrespect, not only for our religious law but for me."

"I am sorry for what she has done, Romir. Believe me, I will take steps to insure that she does not do it again."

"That is what you should do, but you must also punish her."

"I will handle that as well."

"Like you have done in the past?" The High Priest shook his head violently. "No, that is not good enough. She has shown contempt for me, and it must not go unpunished. You have not taken the switch to her once in her life. I have never seen a mark on her body. If she were mine, she would have been beaten long ago when she first erred. You cannot put it off any longer. Now is when you should beat her."

Upset, Aahi's eyes became slits. "Batu is my child, my responsibility and this is my family. I am the sole dispenser of punishment in my home. Each man is given that responsibility by our law. It is I who will deem how to correct Batu, not you. We already have some who are too eager to correct their creations by the switch."

Hatred flared in Romir's eyes. "You will be sorry you have taken this stance. The gods are not forgiving, especially where it concerns their religion. If you do not punish her the gods will. Batu had better beware, and you as well."

Romir catapulted from the bench and stormed out of the hut. Seething, he stomped back toward the sacred hut. Satisfaction eluded him. Talking gained nothing. He had to take action. He felt certain he wanted retribution more than the gods did. They had not done anything as yet. It could very well be they were waiting for him to do something. He would have to take it upon himself to devise the punishment and administer it himself. The gods would not have to wait until she became a dweller to enact their retribution. The gods' earthly emissary would eagerly do it here. This would be the first time any High Priest would dispense justice to a woman. Woman or not, vengeance would be his, and he would make certain it would be slow and telling. In destroying her, he would destroy her father.

Touching the weathered skin of the growler, hanging at the entrance, he entered the sacred hut. Nearly twice the size of the other dwellings in the village, it served as the focal point of the High Priest's secret religious celebrations. The interior consisted of small benches set against three of the walls. On the other wall were grouped the remains of a growler, the mutated offspring from the lion family. The tail, paw, a section of the entrails and head were hung on the left side of the sacred wall. On the right side, a ceremonial headdress, designed to ward off evil dwellers from the Land of No Shadows, hung as a mute reminder of the forces of good and evil resident there. Next to it hung another headdress. This one aligned the spirits of the animals of prey with the High Priest's energies. A huge wood carving of the radiant Great Sun hung from the most prominent position on the wall. All the past High Priests honored the power of the Great Sun. He would need it by his side now against Batu. Hand rubbed with aromatic oil, it stood almost half as tall as he did. An exquisite work of art, it depicted the deity with many beamed arms reaching out from its oval, stern-faced center.

He removed the chain of bones from around his neck and returned it to the sacred wall. Sitting down he tried to calm himself. The moment cried out for him to think clearly. This would take a great deal of thought. He could not rush the punishment. If he did, it would draw attention to him. She would undoubtedly be in union with a man shortly. It might be of benefit, if he prayed to the gods and asked for guidance in his dreams. Yes, it would be proper to ask why such contemptuous behavior was allowed to go unpunished. After carefully thinking it through, he concluded that the wisdom of the gods would deal with the wrong she had committed. He had to put his trust in the gods. Eventually, she would be brought to her knees before him and she would ask for his forgiveness. The only thing remaining for him to do was to make his plea to the gods insuring that it become a reality.

A deliverance bowl, fashioned from the wood of an indigenous nut-bearing tree, sat on the lone shelf. The figures of a lion, growler and an elephant were intricately carved on the outside of the bowl. The inside of the bowl contained a large rayed depiction of the Great Sun. It measured two hands in diameter and four fingers deep, with the overlapping lip one finger wide. The ceremonial deliverance bowl had been used in all of the previous High Priest's initiations. The beauty and delicacy of the finely polished bowl stood out as the only other artistic article in the hut. Grabbing the large water bowl, he poured water into it. Empowering the water, he repeated his sacred vows anew to sanctify himself, while he slowly let the water trickle from the bowl onto his head. It ran through his hair down his forehead, neck and massive torso.

Romir did not bother to wipe the water from his body. His eyes roamed over the objects on the sacred wall. Moving in front of the wall he set his knees on the earth before it. Bending at the waist, he placed his head on the ground. After clearing his mind, he began his petition to the gods for protection from all forms of evil influences and to deliver Batu to him.

Whenever someone opposed him, he always sought help. He found that help in the sacred hut, from the gods and the power items. He let his eyes roam over the power items. Making his choice, he stepped to the wall gathering the items from it. This time was no different from all of the others. He consistently chose the growler's remains whenever he sought assistance, or needed some form of fortification. Drawing the power from them to himself, he assured himself that he would have power over everyone.

The paw symbolized swiftness and agility. With it he would deal a savage blow to his enemies. The head, with its huge jaw, represented the ability to crush everyone who opposed his views and beliefs. The entrails empowered him to consume the opposing person's energy and power, leaving him defenseless. The tail enabled him to ward off any unknown parasitic individuals. These objects of power allowed him to both protect himself and be endowed with the qualities of the growler. With them he assured himself of the conquest of anyone stupid enough to oppose him.

He went to the wall took the entrails of the growler off and hung it around his shoulders. Next he took the paw and the tail from the sacred wall and sat on the ground facing the sacred wall. Holding the paw in his right hand and the tail in the other, he began to chant the name of Tor, the greatest of all gods, over and over until he felt completely calmed. During all of this he gazed at the huge wooden depiction of the Great Sun.

Taking a deep breath he began his plea in a voice shaking with emotion.

"Oh, unseen gods of light and of the dark,
giver of life, destroyer of all, I seek to divine
the reason why you have not struck
down the irreverent, Batu. Such impudence
must not go unpunished. Indicate to me that
you wish me to be your avenger. Let my dreams
show me the way to accomplish this feat.
Guide me to see what action I must take.
Let retribution be yours through my hands.
Clear my mind to accept your guidance.
I willingly shall be your instrument
in the execution of your punishment."

He sat still, feeling the power of the growler flowing through his body. With the prayer completed and the energy coursing inside of him, he felt a sense of invincibility. Vengeance would come. Now he must be patient and wait for a sign from the gods. Rising, he returned the power articles to their places on the wall. As he left the sacred hut, a sense of well being flowed through him.

Despite his fervent prayer, several Great Suns rose and set without receiving a sign to guide him. Without guidance from the gods, he began to think of ways to entrap Batu and deal with her. None seemed appropriate. None seemed to ensure that he would not be implicated with her death. If he invited her to his hut to discuss her improprieties, she surely would refuse to come. Having a woman break with tradition presented new difficulties for Romir. He desperately sought revenge, but he was afraid his involvement would be detected. He could not afford that. He had to be patient and wait for the correct moment to exact his punishment.

A few cycles later his dream of illumination occurred. In it he saw Batu standing before him. The Great Sun rose from his left and moved slowly through the sky. It reached its zenith and lazily began its descent. As it sank, it drew his attention to Batu who stood to his right. As he looked at her, she began to sway from side to side. Her eyes were rolling in their sockets, and she seemed to lose all rigidity in her body. Losing her balance, she fell forward on her hands and knees and looked up at him submissively. He closed the distance between them. Grabbing her head, he pulled her up crushing her to his chest.

He awoke breathing heavily, finding he had ejaculated. Smiling openly, he knew it to be the sign he had been waiting for from the gods. The dream was a good omen. It exhibited his dominance over Batu. Elated, he smiled to himself. The clarity of the dream astonished him. He saw she would be brought to her knees in submission before him. The Great Sun held a prominent position in the dream, and it prompted him to believe it was divinely created. The surprising conclusion also seemed to promise physical bonding with Batu. Though unexpected, it seemed appropriate. It would be an added atonement for her transgressions. He would not be gracious in his bonding with her. He meant to dominate her and satisfy himself with no thought to her needs. The gods had spoken to him by way of his dream. His faith in the gods had been restored once again. Retribution would come, and he did not have to jeopardize his position to act. He would safely view the wrath as it unfolded.

Looking at his soiled loincloth, he removed it and put on his other one. Bending down, he retrieved the soiled loincloth and walked from the hut to the running water to wash away the remains of his dream.

CHAPTER
SIX

Sleep did not come easily for Batu. There were too many things to think about. She knew her father's decision to be imminent concerning who her mate would be. She knew he had narrowed his choice down to three men. Zenon did not impress her. He was just too ordinary. She easily ruled him out. She sensed that her father favored Tomo. Of the three men he was the most handsome and oozed sexuality. His strong sexual appeal interested her. Closing her eyes, she brought up his face and figure and imagined them in an intimate embrace. She lingered with the image for a few moments and then withdrew her focus.

Tomudo was interesting and extremely intelligent. The only drawback with Tomudo was his age. Tomudo, at thirty-two, would likely die before her. But, certainly she would have a child by then and she would not have to fear being banished. "That law is as insane as the Rite of Preparation," she said to herself. She could not understand why the tribe upheld such a barbaric law. The law stated that a woman must be exiled from the tribe, if her man died and she had not given birth. Unable to survive by themselves on the plains, or in the jungle, these banished women surely suffered horrible deaths. To her, women were as essential to the welfare of the tribe as men were. If the tribe deemed a man worthy, because he could provide food, then why not let women who lost their men learn how to acquire their own food? That would eliminate the burden. The women would have worth. The law seemed to insure men's existence. And why not? Men created the laws. She saw it as horribly unjust. Hopefully, some event or moment in the future would alter the law to make it more just. For now she would have to accept it despite its stupidity.

Tomo's skill as a trapper and hunter were well known. Her father often spoke of him after coming back from a hunt. Reflecting upon Tomudo's position in the tribe, she knew they would never lack food. Men who served on the council were supplied with food from the tribe's community cache. Each man contributed to the cache. It was mandatory that every tenth kill or catch of meat be given to the community store. The council members monitored the distribution of the food to the women who had been in union, but lost their men and had a creation from that union. This held true even if that child no longer lived with the mother in her hut. Women who were never in union and still living with their families were also allowed to remain in the village, by virtue of the fact the father was still a provider. Men were never forced to leave the tribe, for they had contributed to the food cache during their productive seasons of life.

The only thing left now was to sleep and let her feelings guide her decision. She had no idea who her father had chosen but it mattered little. In the past, she had used her logic, cunning and charm to win her father over to her way of thinking. She had done it many times and was thoroughly confident that she could do it again. When it was necessary to persuade him, she generally could do it easily. A few logical points, a smile at the right moment, a burst of laughter and he would capitulate to her desire. Rarely did she have to use complicated arguments to sway him over to her point of view.

Her mother confided to her that the other women-children rarely tried to win their fathers over to their way of thinking. That meant her relationship with her father was very unique. She had discovered that fact herself a few seasons ago by simply listening to the mothers discuss their families. During those moments, she also gathered that apart from her mother, most of the women held to the more traditional view about family relationships. Tradition, and the stories learned as youths, impacted them to such a degree that they considered themselves inferior to the men in the tribe both physically and mentally. She abhorred such nonsense. Evidently some shared her views, for more than once a few of the women made it known they were delighted to see that she had the courage and intelligence to present her thoughts to her father. Yet, she also knew that the majority of women were opposed to her aggressive nature and the way she conducted herself with her father. They favored the traditional ways. They knew men grew angry and resentful when women challenged their authority or demonstrated their intelligence. They considered avoidance of conflicts with their men essential to preserving a peaceful family atmosphere. Here is where she felt her father more secure in his manhood than the other fathers. He always welcomed her intellectual discussions and her demonstrations of independence. On some occasions her mother had defended her position in defiance of her father. In this respect her father had no peers in the tribe. In essence he was as radical as she was.

Not surprisingly, there were a few women in the tribe who worried about Batu's upcoming union. They were fearful that the man she would be bonded to would not allow her to express herself as freely as her father. These women considered Aahi an unusual man. If her man's love lacked the strength of her father's, or if he was insecure in his manhood, he would not permit her to speak openly. Through their conversations and experiences with Batu, these few came to realize she possessed great intelligence. Being in union with the wrong man could crush her dreams.

Batu stretched lazily and looked forward to the rising of the Great Sun. She closed her eyes and fell asleep with the ease of one untroubled by anything, and with the confidence of one who feels they can correct anything, if it does go wrong.

The first thing to appear in Batu's mind upon arising was the face of the man she wanted as her mate. She had eaten and now sat on the bench outside her hut, arms encircling her legs, listening to a nearby songbird. For Batu it sang of freedom. She sat waiting for the correct moment to approach her father and proclaim her choice of mate. Every encounter with her father gave her the confidence she needed to broach still another area of routine, or of tradition or of tribal life. There were so many injustices that had touched her life. Some were appalling, while others were simply irritatingly restrictive. It would be wonderful if in the future she would be in a position to change things. She wondered if this was why her father consciously allowed her such freedom in their talks. After some further thoughts she shook her head knowing it unlikely that the other men in the village would take any woman seriously. Grudgingly, she had to admit there appeared scant chance of a woman having any impact now or in the future concerning tradition or the laws.

Hearing her parents laughing, she got off the bench and went inside. With her father in a jovial mood, she seized the opportunity and approached him.

"Father, I need to speak to you."

"About what?"

"Have you come to your decision concerning to whom I am to be bonded?" she asked tentatively.

"Yes, Batu. After much consideration, I have chosen Tomo."

Batu nodded her head in recognition and said, "I have given the matter of who my mate is to be a great deal of thought. Bonding with a man as handsome as Tomo has a tremendous appeal.

"Bonding is going to be a fact of life in union, and I am uncertain if Tomudo can fulfill my desires. But the mental aspect of life is of much greater importance to me. Here, in the mental realm Tomudo far surpasses Tomo. I crave knowledge more than sexual pleasures. Tomo would be unable to offer me the intellectual stimulus I seek so desperately. Tomudo is the repository for all the historical tales, the myths and legends of the gods, and the laws and rituals. I know there are many stories Tomudo does not share with the children at the study sessions. I want to learn all of them. I feel I crave this more than anything else. He also commands respect because of his position on the council. If I were to become his woman that respect would be accorded to me. That also has a certain appeal to me. While thinking about Tomudo, I saw my life continuing to be interesting, and intellectually challenging. Because of these things, I have chosen Tomudo."

Szatu's mouth dropped open in surprise. She did not expect this to happen. She wondered silently, had Batu gone too far this time? She remained quiet. Aahi's role is to handle Batu and to make important decisions. She knew that. Neither she nor Batu were allowed to oppose him in important decisions. Attentively, she waited for Aahi to deal with her.

Aahi's first impulse was to say she should not be meddling in his decisions and not to question him. He chose to remain quiet and gather his composure. There was no need to hurt her with his reply.

"The decision is mine to make, Batu. I have made it after very careful consideration."

Batu raised her hands in defense. "I know you have taken great pains to make your decision, Father. I am concerned that you have not asked me how I feel about a decision that will affect me for the rest of my life. It would seem wise to hear what I have to say," she argued.

Aahi absorbed her words. Indeed, he had not sat in council with her. Knowing it to be his decision alone, he chose not to consult her.

"I am listening."

Seeing she had already made an impression upon him, she weighed her words carefully. "I would not be truly happy with Tomo for he lacks the intelligence I seek in a man. He would be unable to teach me what I desire to know. I would soon grow bored and unhappy even though he is so handsome."

"That would not happen because you would soon have a child. You would be too busy to become bored," her father replied, planning the future for her.

"I do not wish to have a child until later in my life. I wish to learn what I can now. Later, I will be too busy raising a family. Who knows what I may or may not be able to do in the future? Now I have the desire to learn and Tomudo can share his personal philosophy with me and teach me all of the stories he knows. Tomo cannot offer me that. Tomo would be good in his role as a provider, but I would have to be the teacher with him. It is an unacceptable role for me. I doubt Tomo would be willing to learn anything from a woman. He appears to have the same stringent ideas of all the other men. They define the roles to sharply for men and women. I do not want that kind of a man. You have spoiled all of that for me, Father. Lastly, he would surely not allow me the independence of thought or speech you have. I think it would be different with Tomudo. In the past, Tomudo has shown he is willing to allow me to discuss things. I am sure he will do so in the future."

The clarity of her thought processes and the reasons she presented impressed Aahi. The fact that Tomudo would be the most secure in his manhood and would not squash her desire to continue her pursuit of knowledge was a formidable argument. In fact, Tomudo alone would possibly share what he knew with her. Tomo, on the other hand, would need to feel in control of Batu. It would not take long before he would see he had no control over Batu and feel threatened by her superior intelligence. He may even resort to physical force to establish his authority over her. Looking at it from that viewpoint, Aahi felt compelled to agree with his creation.

Looking intently at her, he wondered which of the gods blessed her with such reasoning powers. Many were the times he had wished she were a man so she could be on the council. With her intellect and creativity she would have been easily chosen for the position of the Elder or Teller of the Stories. None of his ancestors had ever been on the council. It would have been a great honor. As a man, she would have revolutionized the thinking of the tribe. As a woman, she would be able to do nothing and would forever be an irritant to the village. If Tomudo was willing to share his knowledge, she could learn everything he knew. With his wisdom and intelligence, he might also be able to influence her.

Wanting to test her, he asked, "What if Tomudo is no different than Tomo? What if he does not speak to you as an equal, like your mother and I have all your life? What if Tomudo is filled with tradition and is unwilling to share his knowledge with you? What will you do if these things are true?"

"Father, if he is my bonded man, he will give me everything. I see in him some of the qualities you have in yourself. He has allowed me to attend the story sessions and most recently allowed me to openly debate with him. I am placing my life on this judgment," she answered.

Aahi, earnestly concerned for her, said, "You are confident of this, but what will you do if he is not so open-minded as you think? I saw you grow in knowledge and independence through the seasons of your physical growth.

He will have you thrust upon him without the benefit of the slow changes that I have seen take place in you. He may never bend to your desires."

Batu reached over and placed her hand over his. "Father, I will gladly risk it with Tomudo, for with Tomo I see even greater risks. Being in union with Tomudo offers me more opportunities. I beg you to reconsider. Trust me. I would not be happy with Tomo. With Tomudo I have a chance to be who I want to be, and do what I want to do."

Searching her face, he knew it would be impossible for him to alter her thinking at this late juncture. If he forced her to obey him, he risked angering her, or worse, losing her love and placing her in a union of unhappiness. He knew he would capitulate to her desires. It had been so all of their lives. He could never hurt her or deny her anything no matter what she said or did.

Remembering how many times he had felt her to be teaching him, he openly smiled. He could not remember exactly when it happened, but she seemed to surpass him in intelligence seasons ago. How was it possible for one woman to be so intelligent and independent? he wondered. If only she could express her love as well as she could present her arguments; she would be the consummate woman. He recalled the Talker Healer telling him that she would be a woman of destiny after he had looked at the lines in her palms. She was so small then, hardly seven seasons old. Perhaps bonding with Tomudo would fulfill destiny. He hoped it would, but felt only the gods knew the future.

Aahi looked at his woman, Szatu. He saw the concern in her eyes, wondering if he would relent to Batu's request. He smiled at her to reassure her that he would not hurt their creation. His gaze moved to Batu. He grinned fondly at her. His life with her had been filled with excitement and joy. How would he exist without her in his hut? He shook his head not wanting to think of it. The coming seasons would be filled with many wonderful moments for Tomudo and few for himself. He hoped Tomudo would face those opportunities with the wisdom he had displayed at the council meetings. If Tomudo restricts Batu in any way, it could destroy her spirit and zest for life.

With the knowledge gained from their talk, he grudgingly agreed with Batu. Tomudo did fit all of the qualities Batu wanted in a man. He alone could come remotely close to living in harmony with her.

Reaching his decision, he stood up, stepped over to Batu, and drew her up to him. He embraced her saying, "Once again you have convinced me. I have thought of these things, but not from your viewpoint. My fear in choosing Tomudo lie in the brevity of the seasons he has here on Mother Earth. But since you are willing to risk it, I have reconsidered my decision. I will choose Tomudo to be in union with you."

Squeezing him tightly she said, "Thank you, Father."

Releasing him, she turned and saw her mother's open arms welcoming her. She rushed to be embraced.

Mixed tears of happiness and sadness formed in Szatu's eyes. "Your father has shown his wisdom and deep love for you. Be happy, Batu, and give us many strong and beautiful creations to play with."

Batu looked directly into her mother's eyes. "Many seasons may pass before I usher a new life onto Mother Earth. There is too much I want to do first."

CHAPTER
SEVEN

Shadows stretched across the village center. Aahi walked upon them to Tomudo's hut.

"Tomudo, it is Aahi. May I enter?"

"Aahi, welcome. It is good to see you."

"I am the bearer of good news, Tomudo. I have come to inform you that I have selected you as Batu's man in union," he said happily.

Overjoyed, Tomudo replied, "You honor me, Aahi. I have longed to hear those words from you!"

"You will be a welcome addition to our family. We all respect and admire you. I want you to know that Batu has always admired you for allowing her to be present at the story sessions. I also want you to know that she has always lived in an atmosphere of independence. I am certain all of the men who wanted her would not be able to live easily with her. Other men were reluctant to offer themselves because they were afraid of her revolutionary nature. It has always been thus with Batu. Even as an infant her actions were independent. For me, the process of adjustment came about over the period of cycles and seasons in the face of her actions and thoughts. I have extended many privileges to her and shared all I know with her because I not only love her and admire her but also feel strongly there is something unique within her nature. I am reluctant to restrict her in any manner.

"I will tell you openly, I am very proud of Batu. I love her deeply and do not want to see her hurt. I trust you to be a wise man, Tomudo. I hope she can fill your heart, as she has mine."

Tomudo, at first taken back by Aahi's words, now spoke. "Aahi, I am honored to have you speak so openly. I will not destroy your trust in me. I have watched her grow into womanhood. I love Batu. I want my life to end with her in my arms and my children surrounding me. Anything she wants to know, she but has to ask."

Aahi nodded in admiration of his words. The very words seemed to forge a deeper friendship with Tomudo.

"Your words are well spoken. I have decided it would be appropriate to have you as our guest for the last meal of this cycle. Of course this would not be considered as one of your six final meetings with Batu before your union. No one has to know."

"You surprise me happily. Thank you, Aahi. I will be there."

Being invited to Aahi's hut for a meal broke with tradition and it surprised Tomudo. Perhaps it was Aahi all along who was the revolutionary and passed those tendencies to Batu. He could not recall any man being invited to a meal with the woman he was to be bonded with. It placed him in the middle of a precedent, but at this point, he did not want to concern himself with what anyone would say. His main concern rested in making Batu his woman.

After a few exchanges of pleasantries they bid each other farewell, Tomudo assuring Aahi that he would be there at the proper moment. Aahi left feeling more convinced than ever that he had made the correct decision.

The meal was lavish by tribal standards. As he ate, Tomudo could scarcely take his eyes off Batu. Szatu delighted and charmed Tomudo. Tomudo had never really had the opportunity to speak to Szatu much. Her simple honesty and tremendous love for Batu touched him. Aahi obviously adored his creation. One only had to look at him when he spoke about her, or when he looked at her, to be able to see the depth of his love. His own deep love helped Tomudo overlook Batu's brakes with tradition. He understood how Aahi could not punish Batu.

The pace of the conversation never slowed. Batu surprised him by revealing her sense of humor. He found it difficult to always focus his attention on her parents as they spoke. Everyone had questions to ask of him and he of them. He left impressed by them and hoped he had done the same. Tomudo felt certain that Batu's nature would follow her parents'. Eventually, she would become as gracious as they and would be a fitting mother of his creations.

The first full Sun With No Heat after the rains had arrived. It heralded the Ceremony of Unions. The tribe began congregating near the Great Sun Circle shortly after their first meal eager to celebrate. Each celebrant entering the center was greeted with mirthful cheering. The High Priest arrived and the tribe gathered around the ceremonial couples. Batu stood proudly among them, keenly aware of the eyes of the men upon her. A row of flowers set in her hair encircled her face. She beamed happily. Next to her, Tomudo and the other couples waited to be joined in union.

Romir raised his voice. "We gather here, as the Great Sun looks upon us, to join these men and women and make them one, through their union. The gifts you men are about to give to the mothers will not repay them for the many seasons they have kept their children safe and loved. The gifts are symbols to remind them of what they have lost, and to remind you of the great value the mothers place upon them. You may now present your gifts to the mothers."

The men presented their gifts to the mothers. Tomudo presented Szatu with an intricately carved wooden statue of a wapiti, saying, "Please accept this humble token. It is a sign of my appreciation. Thank you for accepting me into your family."

After the presentation of the gifts they remained standing in front of the mothers.

"Those men who would be in union must now honor the mothers of your chosen women."

Tomudo placed his hands upon Szatu shoulders. "Thank you for raising and caring for Batu. I accept the responsibility for taking care of her until I die."

The High Priest continued, "Those men who would be in union must now honor the fathers of your chosen women."

Tomudo stepped over to Aahi and placed his hands on Aahi's shoulders as a sign of his respect and friendship.

The High Priest declared, "Those of you who would be in union must now proclaim your love to your chosen women."

Tomudo stepped back into the circle in front of Batu.

Looking into Batu's eyes, Tomudo said lovingly, "I pledge my love and life to you, Batu." Placing his hands on her shoulders, he said, "I vow to care for you until I die."

Romir called out, "You women who would be bonded to these men now present yourselves to your men and vow your love for them."

Batu, as a symbol of her trust, faith and subservience to Tomudo placed her hands in Tomudo's.

"I vow to be your woman, Tomudo, until I die."

Having completed their vows, Tomudo held both of Batu's hands and raised them above their heads symbolizing their union. Batu and Tomudo embraced as the villagers applauded and cheered all of the celebrants.

When the tumult died down the High Priest shouted triumphantly, "You are now bonded. May the Great Sun shower his abundance upon you."

During the festivities Romir approached all of the participants to wish them well, except Batu. The slighting had not gone unnoticed and would be whispered about at the baths for many cycles. Romir's affront bothered Tomudo, but he felt too happy to approach him and make an issue over his overt omission.

Tomudo struggled through the pleasantries. It seemed an eternity before the shadows stretched across the center. The festivities had quieted down. Several small groups lingered in the remaining light. This had been the first time he ever felt his position on the council served him negatively. He felt obligated to remain at the festivities longer than the other bonded couples, because of his position.

Bidding farewell to Mihili, the last council member to leave, other than he, he made his way over to Batu. She was engaged in a conversation with her mother, father and another woman.

When the opportunity presented itself he said, "Batu, we should be departing. Aahi and Szatu, I know the wapiti carving is an insignificant gift next to Batu's worth. Please accept my humble thanks for all you have done in raising her."

Tomudo placed his hands on the shoulders of his second father. Aahi returned the show of respect and friendship. He did the same with Szatu. She surprised him by also embracing him.

She smiled warmly. "Go in peace. Love my Batu well," she said emphasizing her acceptance of him.

In parting Aahi said, "The gods have blessed you and put you together for eternity by this sacred union. May they guide you in your journey through life. Till we meet again, Tomudo."

Aahi had mixed feelings. He felt sad about losing Batu and also happy for Batu, as she entered her new life with Tomudo.

Batu hugged her father then her mother. Withdrawing from her mother's embrace, she blinked her eyes rapidly to clear away the tears. Szatu, knowing her own eyes were filled with tears, marveled at Batu's tears. Batu's emotional display caught her off guard. This was the deepest sign of emotion she had ever seen displayed by her creation. Perhaps, in the future, Batu would realize the great realm of emotions that had been held in check by her intellect. In the past she and Aahi were unable to penetrate that barrier. It would seem that having a man and leaving their home might have already begun to change her. Throughout her life, Batu had always been on the receiving side of love. She rarely demonstrated her love for either Aahi or her. For some reason she had never really learned how to return it or perhaps never felt inclined to display it. It may have been their fault, due in part to how they reared her. Perhaps in the future Batu would exhibit to Tomudo what she and Aahi were unable to elicit from her.

Turning to her man, Batu smiled self-consciously and brushed away her tears. "I am ready, Tomudo."

Joining hands, they walked the short distance to Tomudo's hut. Inside he drew Batu to him. Her eyes did not hold the passion his displayed. In her eyes he saw the slightest sign of apprehension. It surprised him and he cautioned himself to move slowly. Gently, he ran his trembling hands over her back, while they embraced. Its softness yielded to the pressure he applied. He moved his hands down her back and found her loincloth. Undoing the knot holding it up, it fell silently to her feet. Cupping her buttocks he squeezed them gently and felt her tremble in response. His hands moved slowly around her hips. Both of them were breathing deeply. He crushed her in his arms, feeling her body pressing on his. His hands explored further and he savored the sensations. He opened his eyes and gently pried her away from him to look at her again. He cupped her breasts in his hands. Feeling their fullness heightened his desire. He pressed against her, as he guided her to their sleeping mat.

Passion glazed Batu's eyes. His fingertips deftly moved over the newly found sensitive areas. She shook with anticipation. Having explored the lush soft contours of her body with his hands, he now covered them with his lips. Starting at the inside of her calf, he slowly moved up one leg then the other. Moving his hands to her stomach, she quivered in response. He let his lips caress it and moved to her breasts. He tenderly showered them with kisses. Finding her nipples, he instinctively drew on them delighting in the pleasure.

Sensation after sensation rippled through Batu. They were more than she had expected. Her body reacted involuntarily. It moved on its own, delighting in each new feeling. The pleasure of his lips drawing upon her nipples thrilled her and she moaned uncontrollably. He stopped and she longed for him to continue.

The strength she felt in his body surprised her. Her body felt so different from his. She ran her hand over his body finding him thrilling and quivering to her touch, as she did to his.

Tomudo teased her nipples with his fingertips. They were taut to his playful caresses. He moved to her ears and slid his lips and tongue over the tiny folds, causing her to shudder with delight. He gently kissed her cheeks, forehead and eyes. Pressing his lips upon hers, he marveled at their soft fullness.

With increasing excitement, he found his hands again seeking the soft swells and undulations of the body he had desired to touch for so long. He felt her hands exploring his body with equal pleasure and excitement. Locking into the embrace of love he slowly made his entrance into her virginal body. He felt her passage membrane resist his entrance. Applying pressure he felt it break and felt her reflexive action of the pain. He moved cautiously not wanting to hurt her any more and impair her passion. Eventually, his gentleness was rewarded with her slow and rhythmic response. His passion soared, yet, he controlled himself, wanting to be gentle and cultivate her needs and desires. He did not want her to be submissive or afraid but a willing and loving partner in their exploration of physical love. He wanted to create an atmosphere of mutual desire and inquisitiveness. By allowing her to experiment and discover the joys of bonding at her own pace now, it would hopefully insure her desire and pleasure in the future. The intimacy of bonding served as a natural expression and extension of his love for her. He wanted Batu to come to that same realization.

Batu felt the pain caused by his penetration. It made her wince. Almost immediately, she recalled her own words at the Rite of Preparation. An image of the ritual stakes flashed before her mind and quickly blurred as Tomudo covered her face and neck with kisses. This is the way the gods intended her tissue to be broken. The pain receded. Unconsciously, her body moved in union with Tomudo's movements. The fears and inhibitions she had at the start were lost in the throes of her desire to fulfill her rising passion. The escalation caused her body to perspire freely. His quickening passion matched hers. Both their bodies tasted the splendor of love and finally quivered in climatic release.

The experience left Batu breathless. Nestled in his arms, she savored residual sensations. Questions floated lazily around in her head. She had never imagined the sensations flowing through her body would be this strong. Why had she responded so passionately? Could it be because she loved him? Was it the sheer physical delight? Whatever the truth, she marveled at her body's ability to act of its own volition so easily. Bonding drew something from her body that she could not fathom at the moment. She wondered if loving Tomudo would be uncontrolled as well. Her thoughts were interrupted as he began to kiss her eyes. She quieted her mind in favor of her emotions and the physical sensations sweeping through her.

Later, she lay spent in his arms, amazed at the sheer physical pleasure she had experienced. How could she have moaned involuntarily so often? She had never done that except when surprised by some pain. This time it came about from pleasure. Having him within her gave her an exhilarating feeling. The awareness of her body completely fascinated and overwhelmed her. How could it be that she sensed being one with Tomudo even as they consumed their passion? How strange and wonderful. Breathing deeply, she smiled and clung tightly to him. The unique scent of his body mingling with her own pleased her.

When her mother spoke of the act of bonding, she did not dwell on the emotional and sensual aspects of the experience. She spoke of the practical and functional applications. Did she do so because she wished her to discover the glories of it herself? Whatever the reason, it pleasantly astonished her. She also did not expect Tomudo would be so amorous. Were all of the men so apt in the art of bonding? Thinking about it, she grew certain that he was more considerate and skillful than most men. She thought of the times she had bathed and had heard the stories about men who simply satisfied themselves. Some of them had little or no thought about their women. Tomudo seemed to think of her needs.

In spite of how satisfied she felt, she glanced up at the shelf on which her birth beads sat. The beads sat as a silent reminder of her promise not to bear a child until she herself was ready. Composed of a single piece of twine, the birth beads contained twenty-eight seeds, eight of which were different in nature from the others. The habit of moving a seed from the left side of the twine to the right, as she awakened with the new dawn, began with the first flow of blood from her body. Her mother took great pains in instructing her as to its use and value. She silently thanked the ancestors for their care and knowledge in determining the cycle of conception. Fortunately, the gods granted her a predictable cycle. Despite the immense pleasure bonding gave her, she knew she must be careful when they bonded. Brushing the thought from her mind, she laid her head on his chest and watched the rise and fall of his stomach in the waning light.

Tomudo marveled at Batu's tremendous sexual appetite. Prior to their bonding, he could not be certain if her body, so sensuously perfect in form, could be matched by the emotions of the woman within it. He feared that anyone so intellectual would not be able to respond emotionally. His skepticism proved to be unfounded. Prior conversations with her pointed out her devotion to reasoning and not emotion. He felt it important to continue to slowly develop her emotional side. Elated, he reassured himself the future would only serve to strengthen their compatibility.

He felt her embrace tightening. Instinctively he squeezed her in return. He smiled happily. The response and enjoyment of their physical bonding far exceeded his expectations.

As the cycles passed, they continued their explorations in the realm of passion. Tomudo's amorous demands were met eagerly with Batu's own passion. On the ninth dawn after their union, Batu, upon awakening moved the first dark colored seed on her birth-beads to the right. She knew she would need to refrain from bonding, or risk conceiving.

With the darkened sky the moment came for her to establish her independence. As they lie on their mat, Tomudo became amorous in anticipation of bonding.

"Tomudo, we must not bond. I can conceive now," she informed him.

"But that is what I wish. I want you to conceive."

In opposition, she said, "You wish it, but I do not."

His eyes reflected his confusion. He was about to criticize her but caught himself. Calmly he spoke to her. "Batu I seek to bond with you, so we may create new life within you. I am eager to have our creations about me before I am an old man. Jocas did not give me a creation, and it has been one of my regrets. I do not want to be without one in my life."

"I understand how you feel, Tomudo, but I am not ready to have my body distorted with a child inside of me. I am young and we have the future to provide you with all the creations you wish. But not yet, not yet," she replied impassioned with her own feelings.

"Batu, you do not know how deeply I feel about this. I will comply with your wishes now, but it will not be thus for long."

Unwillingly, he turned his back to her knowing if he spoke further his words would be harsher and promote an argument between them. He must be rational and keep their relationship warm to win her love. The next several cycles would be dreadful for him. He hoped he would be able to restrain himself and not force her to bond with him.

Batu's words were only part of the truth. She knew that if she were to have a child she would not be able to pursue her desire for knowledge and anything else that may come to her mind. She wanted to learn all of the stories he knew. There would be no hope to gain them if she bore a child. Her energy would be diverted to child rearing and she would be trapped like all the other women. She saw no reason to bring forth a creation now. It could be done when she began to lose her figure and the wrinkles began to appear in her face. By then she would have gained the knowledge she felt she needed. With all of her other desires fulfilled, the moment would be right. No, she was not ready. Conceiving a child would come when she wanted and not before.

CHAPTER
EIGHT

A vibrant crimson glow hovered on the horizon. The early light from the Great Sun caressed the underside of the rare clouds, holding forth the promise of a glorious dawn. The changing colors pigmented the clouds in an ever-brighter kaleidoscopic fashion, proclaiming the arrival of the provider of life. The vermilion orb revealed itself to an earth already teeming with activity. Animals and birds anxiously sought to acquire and consume their first meal. All were ready and inquisitive to see what territorial boundaries needed to be reestablished or could be expanded.

The traditional period of celebration of Batu and Tomudo's union reached its conclusion. Their dawn meal had been consumed. Tomudo's apprentice, Coloma, would soon arrive to continue his instructions. Tomudo had selected Coloma to be his successor, as the Teller of the Stories, based upon his observations of the young men and men-children during the story sessions. The evaluation consisted of a few simple tests of recollection. Coloma fared excellently. Pleased and proud to be selected, Coloma knew it honored not only him, but also his whole family.

While waiting for the arrival of Coloma, Batu touched Tomudo's arm, "I know Coloma will be here shortly. I wish to sit with you and listen to the stories."

Tomudo had anticipated her request and smiled knowingly, "I have no objections. In truth, I am pleased you are interested."

Batu smiled broadly, finding her assessment of Tomudo to be correct. She felt certain no other man, except for her father, was secure enough in his manhood to allow her such liberties.

This would be her first non-social encounter with young Coloma. On occasions she had seen him, as he went to Tomudo's hut for instruction. Her other contacts with him had been at the story sessions. From those sessions she had gleaned that he did not have as inquisitive a mind as her own, but he did seem intelligent and remembered things very well. She wondered if Coloma's ability to recall matched her's and how he would react to her presence at the instructions. Would he think her to be beautiful? More than likely, he would be respectful and only gaze guardedly upon her. She was used to such behavior from men.

After this instruction, she would be able to easily determine how he felt about her. Being in union with Tomudo helped her to further understand why she affected men as she did.

Coloma arrived and greeted them from outside the hut. Tomudo welcomed him, as did Batu. Coloma greeted both of them formally, respectful of their positions in the tribe. It had been awhile since he had seen her this close. Her beauty astounded him. Like so many of the others in the tribe, he was infatuated with her. He had always thought her the most desirable woman he had ever seen. Now, being so close to her, he found it difficult to keep his eyes off her face.

Taking his usual position on a small mat across from Tomudo, Coloma awaited his teacher's instructions. He had been coming to the hut for over two full seasons and knew the routine well. There were four basic groups of stories he had to learn. The first group of stories he had already learned covered the tribal laws. Currently, he was committing to memory the tribal history, next would come the traditions and rituals, then the legends of the gods. Last to be committed to memory would be the names of the past council members.

He felt it a great honor to be the one selected for such a powerful position in the tribe. The respect accorded anyone on the council was something he had become aware of after he began his instructions. He had secretly thanked the gods many times since being selected as Tomudo's apprentice. The change in his parents' attitude toward him became immediately noticeable. There were five other members in his family and he had not received much attention from any of them. Upon his selection it all changed. They became attentive to him as well as boastful and proud of him.

Folding his hands in his lap, Tomudo asked Coloma, "What story in our history concerns our decision to settle on the land we occupy?"

Coloma was caught in his preoccupation of trying to observe Batu seated behind Tomudo. In her presence he had become unraveled. The question took him by surprise. He had learned the story during the recent rains.

"I recall the story, but I have forgotten the name," Coloma answered honestly.

Batu smiled, sensing her presence confused Coloma.

Coloma's inability to recall the story did not concern Tomudo. He felt Batu's presence prompted his problem and knew he would overcome it in a few sessions.

"It is called Takahums' Lost Hut. You did well in answering truthfully. It is a trait you must always have when you are the tribal storyteller. To maintain the tribe's trust you must be above reproach. Now proceed with the story as you recall it."

Batu admired how skillfully Tomudo made Coloma feel that he did the right thing being honest and truthful. She reminded herself to be honest in all her conversations with her man, lest he lose respect for her.

Coloma began reciting the story. At times his recitation differed with the story. Tomudo corrected him. No word could be altered. In this manner, the legends, traditions, rituals, history, and laws were kept scrupulously intact from one Teller of the Stories to the next. Batu focused her attention on the stories Tomudo taught Coloma and committed each to her memory.

The Great Sun neared its zenith as Tomudo ended the session. In parting he said, "You have done well. Keep the corrections in mind when you retell the stories to yourself after your meal. We will see you again at the next new Great Sun. Keep well, my friend."

Coloma rose from the mat.

"Thank you, Tomudo." Then looking at Batu said, "Goodbye, Batu." His eyes fell momentarily to her breasts as he passed her.

Batu smiled broadly at Coloma. She was aware of the quick glance he had given her. Turning to her man, she wondered how to form her words.

Noticing the look in her eyes, Tomudo asked, "What is it? Speak your thoughts."

"I wish to be present whenever you instruct Coloma so I can learn all of the stories."

Tomudo returned to his mat. "I had anticipated your desire. It pleases me you wish to be present. I see no reason why you cannot be present. There are many stories that Coloma has already learned. If you also want to learn these then I will teach them to you separately."

"You can teach them to me after our dusk meals," she said happily bouncing down next to him. "I know I can remember the stories better than Coloma. All I need is the opportunity."

Upon appraising her statement he replied, "I know how strongly you desire to learn, Batu, but your ability to recall a story is yet to be tested."

Batu replied emotionally, "I can recite all of the stories Coloma learned this cycle. Is that enough proof of my ability?" Without letting him reply she continued, "You have carefully picked him because he has the best mind in the tribe among the males, yet I am better than he."

Tomudo retorted, "Do not talk such foolishness. It often takes three or more sessions to remember just one brief story word for word without error. You cannot remember four stories after listening to them only one cycle. It is impossible. It is a painstakingly slow process, done so as to eliminate any mistakes."

"I will prove to you I have learned the stories Coloma has recited. Will you listen?"

"Of course."

She began with the first story of Takahums' Lost Hut. Her voice lacked the inflections necessary of a good storyteller, but he attributed it to her concentrating on the words and not the theme of the story. He needed to correct her once. It centered on Coloma's lapse of memory. She went through the other stories and again faltered at the points Coloma had problems. In all, Tomudo had interrupted and corrected her six times.

Angry with herself she said, "I am sorry, Tomudo. You were correct. I did not learn them without mistakes."

Astonished, he raised his hand and waved it at her. "You have no need to apologize. You have learned in one sitting four stories better than most people could learn one story. I have taken great pride in knowing I have learned our stories, yet you have humbled me. In this recitation you have shown me your recall is superior to mine."

"Is what you say the truth?"

"I am not in the habit of telling untruths, or saying things to flatter someone."

Smiling elatedly, Batu said, "Then you have paid me a great honor."

She slipped her arms around him and clung to him feeling she could accomplish anything if given the opportunity. As she began to pull away, Tomudo would not release her. He drew her to him tightly. His hands sought the sensitive and sexually charged areas of her body. Gently he laid her down. He knew she fully accepted him as a teacher, provider, protector, and partner in physical bonding, but he needed and wanted her love. He wanted it to become a reality quickly but understood the need for patience. He knew her head ruled her in all phases of her life, but he had already discovered her passion. During moments of passion, her mind set aside such things in favor of her body's desire. Their bonding, while charged with energy, still lacked any words of endearment from her. He hoped the act of bonding would soon become an act of love and surrender from her. He knew the moment would come when she would openly declare her love for him. He needed to be patient. What troubled him was her refusal to bond with him during the cycles she could conceive.

The sessions fell into a pleasant routine for Tomudo, Batu and Coloma. Coloma wondered about Batu's presence at the sessions, but he had too much respect for Tomudo to question him about it. Eventually, he became used to her presence, and his level of concentration came back to normal. Batu also began to take less notice of Coloma. Having accepted his presence and his quick-guarded glances, her attention now centered on the stories. She always sat in the same location on their sleeping mat with her legs crossed and her back up against one of the upright supports of the hut. She remained thus until the end of the instruction. After Coloma left and they had eaten, she would relate the new stories to Tomudo. Her capacity to recall the stories continued to amaze Tomudo.

Tomudo had decided the best way for Batu to learn the stories of the tribe's history that Coloma had previously learned was to have Coloma repeat them in her presence. In that way Coloma would benefit greatly, and in a relatively short period, she would have them committed to memory.

The more comfortable Batu became with her new environment the more impressed Tomudo became with Batu's abilities. She quickly acquired a feeling for the theme of each story. Listening to her recitations, he noticed that she often placed emphasis on words and phrases that defined the story in a way he had not envisioned. When it happened, he seized the opportunity to discuss her feelings and reasoning during these moments of discovery.

Having heard from Batu's father of her reasoning skill, he ventured into discussions with her that forced her to use logic. He found her use of deduction excellent. When he found her reasoning to be illogical he patiently pointed out her flaw. At times she fought to prove her position, but eventually she did come to realize her error. The errors were usually centered on her own prejudices that she had been totally unaware of at the moment. In his estimation, she was already at a level with the men who were considered the best in the village at reasoning. At times she detected flaws in his own logic, and he had to concede to her the point or the discussion. As the cycles passed he thought her interest would wane. It never did.

Half the season of blue skies had passed by and the only shadow, in their otherwise light filled relationship, was Batu's insistence on not having a child. With every refusal, Tomudo felt troubled that Batu denied him the thing he wanted most. His desperation grew despite the great pleasure he derived from their union. Bonding and their intellectual discussions did not fulfill all of his needs. He wanted a child. The void in Tomudo's heart could not be filled by anything or anyone except a child of his own. Batu seemed oblivious of the deep rift it caused in their relationship. The strain kept building in Tomudo.

The face of the Sun With No Heat glowed softly on the darkened earth. It had become full for the fifth time since he began instructing Batu. As he sat in its light he came to his decision. He had to openly declare her intelligence. He decided to speak to the council about Batu. The meetings were held in the meeting hut every tenth rising of the Great Sun. They were to meet again after the zenith meal of this cycle. During these meetings the villagers were able to bring their problems and questions to the council, where they could be arbitrated and answered.

Tomudo arrived at the common meeting hut to find the others already there. They greeted him cordially. It had been six seasons since he first sat down as a member of the council. In that span, he had come to know the abilities of each member quite well. The Elder had been chosen from the men of the tribe who had exhibited wisdom in discussions and debates. The position represented the traditional and conservative views of the tribe. Mihili, the Elder, had been a council member for ten seasons and had demonstrated his reasoning abilities often in discussions prior to having been chosen for the position. The High Priest, Romir, who often became privy to everything that went on in the meetings, influenced many of his decisions. Next to Mihili's right sat Wapur, his apprentice of six seasons.

The Warrior Hunter, Motum, sat next to Wapur. As the Warrior Hunter he represented excellence in hunting and snaring and displayed courage, cunning, and strength in battle. Those qualities caught his predecessor's eye, and he was made an apprentice at the age of fourteen. At the death of his teacher he became the Warrior Hunter. His huge, well-muscled body rested easily as he sat quietly. At twenty, he was the youngest member of the council. If they were ever threatened, the tribe would turn to him for their leadership and survival.

To Mihili's left sat Neda, who held the position of Friend of All. He attained it because of his popularity. His easy manner and an infectious laugh made him liked by everyone. He aptly determined the pervading mood of the villagers from constant interaction with them. His predecessor had selected him as the apprentice Friend of All prior to his death two seasons earlier.

Seated next to Neda was the Talker Healer, Taja. Taja had attained his position the season before Tomudo became the Teller of the Stories. His mysterious abilities allowed him to walk in the Land of No Shadows, the land of the deceased. He and the High Priest, Romir, were the healers of the tribe, although their methods of healing differed greatly. Taja, though only a season younger than Tomudo, clearly stood out as the wisest member of the council. At the meetings he talked little, but when he spoke his insight to problems proved to be unparalleled. If issues were clouded, his questions cleared the air. If an injustice could not be seen, he made it visible. Having never been in union with a woman contributed to his enigma.

Next to Taja sat Coloma. He would succeed Tomudo and become the next Teller of the Stories and the teacher of the tribe.

Mihili opened the meeting, "Let us begin. Who wishes to speak?"

Tomudo swept the ground in front of him with his right hand. "I have come upon an unusual person in our tribe. It is my woman, Batu. I have allowed her to be present during the instruction of Coloma. She has demonstrated great ability in recalling the stories I have taught him. In her initial session she learned four stories. These same four stories have taken Coloma several sessions to learn." He turned his head toward Coloma. "All of you know Coloma's ability, yet she surpasses him. Even I am no match for her memory."

Pausing for effect, Tomudo continued, "It is rare when we can add to the stories of history. The last story to be added concerned Motum's single-handed kill of a growler. I wish to add to our folklore the story of her unusual memory."

Mihili caught the quick glances from Neda and Motum and knew they were looking for him to make his feelings known before they would commit themselves. He sighed. Another problem had reared its ugly head. At age forty-four, they seemed to weigh more heavily upon him. It seemed that he had sat on the council all of his life. There were many times he wished he had not accepted the position. As for Batu he knew of her aggressive behavior and breeches with tradition. If he ignored or refused to take a positive approach with this request, he would alienate his long-standing friend. Impulsively, he decided to have her brought to the meeting. If she were not as good as Tomudo suggested she would fail in her demonstration. This seemed to be an easy way to extricate all of them from a sensitive situation.

He placed his hand on the ground signifying his wish to comment. "I know you to be a man of integrity, Tomudo, so I take what you say to be true.

Before we vote on this I wish to hear the stories she has in her head. Can you bring her here now?"

Pleased to hear Mihili's willingness to consider his proposal he quickly replied, "If the council so desires, I shall get her."

Looking at the other members Mihili could see no dissent in any of their eyes. "It is good. Let us cast our decision to bring Batu here."

Mihili voiced his affirmation. Each member in his turn voted in the affirmative. Coloma and Wapur, being apprentices, could not vote.

Mihili's eyes settled on the proud Tomudo. "Go. Bring her to us."

Tomudo rose and walked out of the hut, moving swiftly to tell Batu the news. He had refrained from telling her of his decision to approach the council, but he now felt certain she would be happy.

Entering their hut, he found her busy repairing a woven reed basket.

"Batu, I have told the council about your gift of recollection. I also told them that I wish to create a story about you and make it part of our history."

Surprised she stared at him in disbelief. If it became a reality, the story about her would be passed down from one generation to the next for as long as their tribe existed. The impact of what he said made her heart race. Exuberantly, she threw her arms around him.

"Why have you not told me of this before?"

"I did not want to tell you for fear they would reject my idea. The council wants to have you recite some of the stories to them. Will you come?"

She squealed in delight at the prospect!

He grabbed her arm and they walked rapidly to the common hut. As they walked, she questioned him. "Why have you done this?"

"I have thought about our first debate, while we were not yet in union. Perhaps you were correct. We Kahali do not fully appreciate our women. It may well be our ancestors also did not appreciate them. Maybe a story will help to alleviate our prejudices."

"But I am surprised the council would even consent to hear me."

"It surprised me as well. Fortunately Mihili did not seem to want to argue the issue."

At the entrance Tomudo announced their presence and they were told to enter.

After the greetings, Mihili directed his comments to Batu. "Tomudo has spoken of your gift of recall. Before acting upon his proposal, we would like to hear some of the stories you have set in your mind. Please recite the first four stories you heard."

Deliberately she looked at each member of the council and began with the first story she had heard. At first her delivery was hesitant. As she gained confidence she began to lose herself in the telling of the story, eventually becoming animated and at ease.

She told all of the stories and waited expectantly. Mihili addressed Tomudo, "It would be appropriate if you told a story she and Coloma have not heard and for both to retell it."

Surprised by the request, Tomudo thought about it and saw the wisdom in it. "I have not told any of the stories of our legends to Coloma or to Batu, and I know you have knowledge of many of them. I will select one from them that you know."

Selecting one of average length he began to recite it slowly and evenly.

Thankful that her initial moment of nervousness faded Batu easily recalled the story and retold it with one error, smiling as she completed her recitation.

Mihili nodded his head in approval. "Coloma, please recite the story."

Coloma faltered in his recitation several times and forgot one sentence completely.

At the conclusion of the recitations, Mihili, hoping to throw her off, requested the telling of three additional shorter stories of tribal law that he knew. In each case Tomudo first told the story and Batu recited it next and Coloma last. She was nearly flawless, erring only twice in the telling of all of the stories. Coloma on the other hand made several errors and struggled badly with the middle story forgetting three complete lines.

Amazed, Mihili looked at Batu with admiration. He scanned the council members and said, "We have been witness to Batu's memory. She has done well. It is for us to decide what to do."

Turning his attention back to Batu he said, "We wish to thank you, Batu. We will let you know of our decision."

She thanked the council for her audience and left. Mihili looked at the others with obvious consternation in his eyes. "It is obvious she has a true gift. Does anyone wish to speak further on this matter?"

Taja swept the ground. "It is very evident Batu is gifted. I propose we have Tomudo create a story of her gift."

Mihili asked the others, "Are there any other words before we vote?"

He paused for a reply. When none came he continued, "Let us now say affirm or decline to Tomudo's request."

Grudgingly Mihili took the positive initiative. "I say affirm."

Motum answered, "Affirm," as did all of the others.

Looking at a proud Tomudo, Mihili said, "We now advise you to create an appropriate story of Batu and recite it to us at our next meeting."

Pleased with himself and proud of Batu, Tomudo found it difficult to concentrate on the business conducted during the rest of the meeting. At its conclusion, he walked briskly back to his hut, eager to see what Batu's reaction would be to his unexpected action. As he passed through the entrance of their hut, she threw herself on him hugging and kissing him wildly.

With a wide grin he asked, "Are you pleased?"

"Oh Great Sun, of course I am. What did they say after I left?"

"I have been requested to present the Batu story to them for affirmation at our next meeting," he said squeezing her to him.

"Will you tell it to me first?"

"Yes, that way you will learn another story, one that will not put you to sleep," he said teasing her.

"When have you found me asleep, except when we are bonding?"

He smiled at her humor. "Perhaps this is a good moment to put you to sleep."

Batu smiled and drew him tighter to her. He slowly began to run his hands over her body. Looking into her eyes, the smile faded. In its place, he detected her rising desire. He moved slightly away from her and let his eyes rest on her beautifully sensuous breasts. He leaned to kiss her delicate neck, slowly moving his lips to the swell of her breast. He placed his hand on her breast and felt the nipple harden in anticipation. He undid her loincloth. Her breath quickened. His lips slid down her breast and encircled her taut nipple; his tongue caressed it until she moaned in pleasure.

She placed her hand over his mouth, "No more talk," leading him to their sleeping mat.

Batu's passion elated Tomudo. Their relationship would be perfect, if only she were as willing to bond on those cycles she could conceive. But those times she refused him were a drain on his patience. It took everything he had within him to control himself. Uncertainty filled him. How long could he endure her putting him off? When she refused him he felt dreadful, rejected and at times angry.

He swept his dark thoughts aside unwilling to cloud the moment. Tomudo's love spilled forth to their bonding. Being within her and holding her gave way to a rising sense of oneness with her. It had since they first bonded. He held her tighter, wishing to have his body melt and fuse with hers. He whirled in the vortex of his love and passion.

Batu's happiness and desire to show her thankfulness resulted in her rising passion. Her thoughts were swept away by the consuming desire. She responded to Tomudo with eagerness. Letting her body have its own freedom of expression, she flowed with it through the valleys and mountains of her experiences. When at last she lay quietly in his arms, it came from luxurious exhaustion.

CHAPTER
NINE

The council approved Batu's story. The dedication date was set and was upon them. The people assembled in the village center. Mihili, the Elder, raised his hands for quiet. "It is rare when we are able to witness the creation of a new story. This story will be preserved with the others for as long as the Kahali tribe exists. Among the Kahali is a member of outstanding ability and we have gathered here to honor her. The council has heard Batu recite many stories, giving us proof of her great memory. We have thus asked Tomudo to create a story of Batu's ability to remember stories. Tomudo will now recite it."

Tomudo took Batu's arm. They stepped away from the crowd and walked the short distance to the center of the gathering, where Mihili stood. With Batu by his side, he began his recitation of the new story.

"In the Kahali village, when Mihili, the Elder, Wapur, his apprentice, Motum, the Warrior Hunter, Taja, the Talker Healer, Neda the Friend of All, Tomudo the Teller of the Stories, and Coloma his apprentice served on the tribal council, a woman named Batu displayed great skill in recollection. She is the creation of Aahi and Szatu. Her man in union is Tomudo, the Teller of the Stories. He is the creation of Tamko and Boroki. During the course of teaching Coloma..."

Beaming with pride, Batu listened attentively. When Tomudo finished his narration, the crowd applauded. Most were courteous, some were enthusiastic, and some applauded grudgingly. A few shouted their approval. Villagers pressed to be near Batu and Tomudo. She basked in the attention unmindful of the jealousies and resentments present. Many praised Tomudo for his composition choosing to linger with him longer than with Batu. She did not notice.

Some, disgruntled with her past actions, gathered in small groups, and refrained from congratulating Batu. The most noticeable of them was the High Priest. The hatred he bore for her found vent in his open criticism of her contempt of religious tradition. He did not remain in the center long. The humiliation he suffered because of her, at the Rite of Preparation, still burned in his belly. He chose to leave and secluded himself in the Sacred Hut, praying for her deliverance to him.

As the well wishers filtered away from them and congregated in small groups, Tomudo and Batu seated themselves in the soft, warm sand of the village center with Aahi and Szatu.

"We are pleased with your story," Aahi said beaming. "It has brought us great pride to have Batu so honored with a story created by her own man."

"There are far too few stories about women and now our Batu has one devoted to her," added Szatu smiling broadly. "You have been chosen by the gods for this honor, Batu."

Szatu felt certain Batu was the most beautiful woman in the tribe, but was never entirely certain of her reasoning, intellect, and memory abilities. The doubt no longer remained. She stood above the others. Aahi and she could justifiably be proud of her.

Batu laid her hand on Tomudo's. Her thoughts raced as quickly as her heartbeat. What would she attain next? How exciting would it be? It thrilled her to be surrounded by the whole tribe and given such adulation. The recognition had been more than she had ever hoped would happen. Friends joined their little group for brief periods and left. Gradually, the village center emptied. With the Great Sun sinking, Batu's moment of honor came to a close.

Tomudo and Batu ate with her parents, visiting with them until their faces became indistinguishable in the quickening darkness. Batu could not bear to see the cycle end. Her moment of glory would not be the same when another cycle began with the rising of the Great Sun. She bubbled with excitement as they strolled the short distance to their hut.

Inside their hut Tomudo held her close to him. "You have filled me with pride." Moving slightly away from her, he took her face in his hands. "Only the birth of our child could make me prouder. Come, let us bond now and create life within you. Forget about your beads and your ideas of not wanting to conceive. I want to fill your body with my seed and create a child."

Pulling away she said, "Tomudo, we have spoken of this before. It is the wrong moment. You know I wish to wait. I do not want to be bloated and be too busy or too tired to learn."

Tomudo spoke with passion. "Forget your idea of learning for the moment. Bearing a child is more important. How can your heart not ache to hold our creation and know the joy it can bring?"

"Please do not ruin this moment for me," she pleaded.

He ignored her plea. "Other men would not be thwarted by your words. They would simply take you and plant their seed within you." His eyes reflected the puzzlement in his heart. "How can you continue to deny me a child?"

She turned her head.

"Have I given you any reason to be cruel to me? Have I not taught you all you desired to learn?"

Batu's mouth contorted in her effort to remain silent.

He took her by the shoulders and forced her to look at him. "Do I speak the truth?"

She glared at him choking on her rage. How could he spoil her moment?

He stood silent waiting for her reply. She remained still. The darkness kept him from seeing her reaction adequately, but he felt the anger surge from her, buffeting him like blasts of wind from a raging storm.

In spite of the anger he sensed, he continued, a deep urgency forming his words. "This must end! Things have to change. I vow that I will no longer bond with you until you are ready to create life within you. My love for you has not diminished, but this is the only way I see to make you come to your senses."

Looking at his outline, the words burned into her heart. He was turning on her. How could he do that? Words of protest rang in her mind, but could not pass her lips.

Exasperated, he waved his hands saying, "I have said enough. It has pained me to say what I have."

He waited for her words. None came, leaving her unspoken anger to envelop them. When she did not reply, he lay down on their mat and turned his head away from her, unwilling to chance that she would see his tears in the darkness.

Batu had listened to his words without making a reply. Her throat constricted and did not allow her to utter a sound. Anger roared through her. The blood pounded in her head threatening to deafen even her own thoughts. How could he ruin the happiest moment of her life? The whole tribe had just honored her and now her man tore her happiness from her.

He spoke of love, but if he truly loved her why did he attack her on this glorious occasion? She at least was honest and did not tell him falsely that she loved him. She did not speak untruths. She cared for him and longed for his touch, but she knew that did not constitute love. When she became aware that she loved him, she would tell him. It seemed inconceivable that he truly loved her as deeply as he said he did, for he would not have hurt her as he did.

His vow was idiotic. He would be the one seeking to bond with her. She was positive of it. He desired her body too much to stay away from her. She would show him how foolish he was for making the vow. If this is to be a test of wills she will be the victor. In the past, she had always triumphed over her parents and friends. His passion would make him capitulate. He was too weak in his resolve. She felt certain of it.

Neither of them slept well that darkness and for many following. True to his word, Tomudo did not seek to bond with her after their confrontation. He longed to hold her and bond with her, but she showed no signs of wanting to discover the truth in his words. He wondered if he had been too hasty with his vow. At least before, he could give the love she needed to be stable and warm in their relationship. Now, she had turned cold, unreachable and worse, untouchable. He struggled with different approaches to heal the wounds and resolve the horrible situation in which they were enmeshed, but it mattered little what he said. Her ears and heart were not open to him.

Batu remained angry. Whenever she evaluated what had happened, she felt wronged. She reasoned he would soon realize his mistake and beg for her forgiveness. She had never deceived him. She had made her intentions and desires known to him at the outset. He had hurt her terribly. Anger clouded her reasoning. Whatever significance his words contained lay lost within her. The possibility of her viewpoint being wrong never entered her mind.

Many cycles had passed before Batu's buried passion began to betray her. While bathing with her mother, Szatu moved away from Batu to a small group of women. Left alone she became preoccupied in her thoughts. Her mind drifted to the pleasures of bonding with Tomudo. As she washed her breast her hand lingered upon it. Oblivious to everything and everyone around her, Batu lost herself in the echoes and images of remembrance. Only when her mother stood next to her did she break away from her intimate thoughts.

"Batu, is something wrong?" her mother asked trying to be as polite as possible after seeing her unmoving for so long and with the far off look in her eyes.

Distressed she blurted out, "No."

She ducked under the water to compose herself. Surfacing, she continued to bathe, engaging in an animated conversation with her mother to shield her embarrassment.

During their dusk meal, Batu and Tomudo spoke little. Tomudo regretted his vow from the moment he uttered it. He ached for Batu, yet no matter what he said the barrier between them existed. She seemed to be hurt beyond any expectation of reconciliation. As the cycles wore on he saw her personality visibly change. She no longer talked to him about anything except the stories, and rejected all overtures of his embraces.

In the darkness, Batu lay next to Tomudo. His heavy breathing told her he was asleep. Out of habit she placed an arm over him, then, realizing what she had done quickly removed it. She cautioned herself for growing weaker in her resolve.

With the onset of the change of seasons the rains grew heavy and confined them to their hut. Much of each cycle they bore in miserable silence. Tomudo often sought to eliminate the tension with humor and social anecdotes. At times Batu seemed on the verge of relinquishing the bitterness in her heart. Occasionally, she smiled and entered into pleasant conversation, which made their problem seem non-existent. Even during those moments, Tomudo's attempts to touch and hold her were rejected. As Batu slowly receded into her shell, Tomudo cursed himself for his vow.

The turmoil caused outward manifestations in Tomudo as well. At times he caught himself muttering or pacing the confines of the cramped hut like a caged animal. Whenever he discovered these actions, it surprised and dismayed him that he could not control them.

The season of rain ran painfully long. During the long, dreary, rainy cycles, only Tomudo's love for Batu kept his hopes for understanding and reconciliation alive within him.

The promise of new life came with the arrival of the first cycle of blue sky. With it the villagers gathered in the middle of the village center around the three Great Poles. Romir and the council members formed a human circle around the Great Poles. Two paces behind them the villagers gathered in rows to form outer circles.

The High Priest raised his hands to the Great Sun hushing the crowd. "Oh Great Sun, giver of life, we are gathered here to thank you for the rains that blessed our land. Regeneration is assured. We give you praise and thanks for the bounty you provide. Allow us to fulfill the promise of the blue skies and create new life and maintain the old life. Protect us from corruption and all forms of harm."

Lowering his hands, he walked over the rocks comprising the pole circle to view the shadow of the tallest pole being cast on the rain pole. He observed the shadow had covered the pole completely. He raised his hands to the Great Sun and cried out for all to hear, "The Great Sun has seen fit to provide us with the correct amount of the life-giving rains. The land and we shall prosper once again. We thank the Great Sun for its providence."

As he lowered his hands, the tribe cheered and the drums began their staccato rhythm. They punctuated the cheering. Almost immediately, some of the children began to dance to the infectious beating of the drums. In a few moments, all of them were dancing gaily. The rhythm flowed freely and spontaneously in their lithe bodies.

The drums stopped. The young dancers paused to catch their breath, waiting for the beating to begin again. The drum bearing the deepest sound soon resonated across the village to the surrounding countryside. Romir hailed to the crowd for the Dance of the Poles to begin. The adults formed a large double circle around the Great Poles and began the dance. Other drums flowed into the cadence of the first forming the melody to a driving, pulsating beat.

The celebrants' bodies glistened with perspiration. They repeated the dance over and over again until the drums ceased. The children joined the adults. The drums sounded again giving the youngsters the opportunity to perfect their skills dancing alongside the adults. The children were enthusiastic, if not as practiced as their elders. The elders smiled and laughed as often as did the youngsters at the mistakes they made. The dance continued for a long period. It enabled the youngsters to hone their skills by repeating the routines.

When the drumming ceased, the dancers raised their arms and voices in a chorus of spontaneous shouting. As the shouting subsided, the dancers raced for the running water to cool their heated bodies and quench their thirst.

Trickling back to the center, they congregated into small groups. They talked of the forthcoming first hunt, the rains, and the anticipated beauty of the flowering plain and of their families. When everyone had returned from the running water, one of the men took up his reed flute and began to play Honor To Our Deceased Hunters. Three other men next to him raised their flutes and joined him at the chorus. The villagers gathered around them and raised their voices in harmony with the flutes, singing as they walked to be near them. Several songs were sung before the music stopped. Toko, the most talented of the drummers, began to beat out the rhythm of Thanks To Mother Earth, upon his drum. The other drummers and flutists picked up on the rhythm, while the men performed the ritualistic dance. At the proper moment, the men-children joined the dancers and offered their bodies in thanks to the goddess through their dancing.

After the ritualistic dances Batu and Tomudo joined Aahi and Szatu. The women quickly entered into a discussion about the repairs that would be necessary to mend the huts. Tomudo steered Aahi away from the women and chose a spot where they could talk without being heard.

"Aahi, I am in need of your wisdom. Batu and I are having difficulty."

"Szatu and I have sensed as much. Since neither of you said anything, we felt it best to refrain from interfering. What is the problem?"

"It is complicated. I want to have a creation and she is unwilling to grant it to me now. To further compound everything, I have vowed to not bond with her until she consents to have a child."

Aahi's eyes widened. "I see. If I may be blunt, you have created a dilemma." He shook his head forlornly. "Knowing how stubborn Batu is, I am not sure how you can resolve so grave a problem."

"I have cursed myself for making the vow, but I could not go on living as we did. I desire to have a family. It is horrible how this has become the divisive point in our union. It should have brought us closer together."

"What is done is done. You must now wait it out until something changes," advised Aahi.

"I am not certain I can. My patience is being tested to the limit. This has gone on too long. It is affecting our relationship."

Aahi saw the pain in his eyes. "A man's desire should always be honored. That is our tradition. But Batu has broken with tradition often. I know her willpower. She will not bend. She often kept applying pressure in our discussions until I conceded. On many of those occasions, I capitulated not only because of my love for her, but because I simply could not think of a way to win the battle of words. In the last few seasons, it was a rare event when her mother or I won an argument with her.

"I can see you love her deeply and will not beat her into submission. For that I am thankful. A few in our tribe would not be so inclined. I feel to hurt one you love is wrong, but I could never get Batu to fully understand that she could hurt someone with her words and ideas. In that, I have failed. She has always had a tremendous amount of pride. It became evident in our debates. She was relentless in her desire to excel. Somehow I could never get her to understand that her pride could hurt others. Perhaps my deep love for her caused me to fail.

"In you, Tomudo, I see a strength that I did not have to resist her will. I pray that the gods give you the continued strength and patience to endure. Szatu and I have seen her sweet loving side, but only rarely. Unfortunately, her mind has always ruled her. If you can reach her heart, I am certain you will be richly rewarded. But to do it you must have patience, great patience."

Grasping Aahi's shoulder, Tomudo voiced his appreciation. "You have given me wise counsel. Indeed, it is also what I have felt about Batu. I, like you, have a love for her that has no boundaries, yet my patience is being tried greatly."

Nodding his head in understanding, Aahi said, "Such is life. We are tried in many ways, my friend."

They walked back to their women, Tomudo hopeful that the new season of blue skies would also bring about a change in his relationship with Batu.

Tomudo entered the village center after having checked his snares and spotted Batu sitting on the bench in front of their hut. She watched him approach. Batu smiled at him as she saw his catch. The catch was small, but it made him happy to provide food from his own efforts. The young antelope would be a pleasant change from the diet of scaly swimmers.

After dressing the carcass, he hung it up on a nearby pole to drain the blood from it. Having drained the blood, he marked it with his brand then walked to the smoke hut and hung the carcass up. He made his way back to the hut, entered it, and smiled warmly at Batu.

"Come, the sky is crystal clear and the air is filled with a freshness that beckons us to taste of it. Let us go to our place overlooking the plain and enjoy the beauty of this cycle."

She smiled in response. It would be pleasant to walk through the fresh grass and lounge in the shade of their tree. They walked down the path past the huts on either side, coming to the huge softly undulating grassy flatland of the plains. The ground flowers were not yet blooming, but the grasses provided a distinct, sweet smell. Approaching their favorite place nestled on the rim of a small stand of trees, a soft breeze caressed them. They sat near each other, their arms almost touching. Tomudo singled out her scent among the many he detected. Batu's scent was so distinctive he felt certain he could find her in the dark among many women.

He broke the silence as he looked at her profile. "The antelope will be a welcome change. I saw the tracks of others so we may have another to eat soon."

"You have done well, Tomudo, I also welcome the change," she said, without looking at him.

His gaze slowly covered her neck and fell to her breasts. He longed to hold her close. He wondered if she would be agreeable to bond here as they had so often before. Reaching for her chin, he moved it so she would have to look at him.

"Batu, being apart like this is maddening. We must set our differences aside. I love you more than life itself. Here, now, under the light of the Great Sun, let us bond and seek to create life within you. Every cycle we are without a creation robs me of the joy of being with it.

"It pains me to have our relationship so strained. We should be lovers and creating children. Let us forget everything we have said in anger and give our bodies to each other in love."

His words stirred her. She yearned to be held and touched intimately, and to yield to him as he asked, but she did not give in.

Her voice rang with emotion. "The gods have blessed me with a mind that is quick and able. If I begin to raise children, I will not be able to use it, as I do now. I have a need to know things and if a child is present, I will not be able to as I wish."

"That is not so. You will be able to teach our children. I will continue to teach you as well."

"No, there will not be enough moments to do it. I am afraid I will also change. Things never remain the same. You see our union and needs with your eyes and I with mine. Perhaps I will be ready to be with creation in the next season or the one after that, but I do not wish to bear a child now."

Disheartened, he questioned whether the misery they experienced was worth what he wanted. He knew they should not remain away from each other, but his vow, now, seemingly rashly made, did exactly that. Perhaps, where it concerned his woman, losing face should not matter to him. Perhaps he should give in. If he did, she may become aware that she loved him.

Tired of struggling with his thoughts, he stretched out on the warm ground and let the beauty of the moment slowly ebb over him. Taking a few deep breaths, he eased into assessing the surrounding environment. Batu's presence gradually became only one part of the panorama of sensations he experienced. In his relaxed state, she commanded the same attention, as did the sounds from a bevy of birds, and the snorting of zebras in the distance. The gentle breeze brought an unidentifiable, elegant fragrance to his nostrils. It partially masked the pungent odor of the earth's decaying material in the woods behind him. The myriad of smells floating in the wind stimulated his attempt to identify each individual odor. He identified as many as he could, then propped his head against the tree and surveyed the lush, green plains. In a beautifully resplendent and mystical dance of nature, the fresh grasses were bending and swaying to an insistent breeze. With their movement, the inherent color they held became lightened, reflecting the cascading rays of the Great Sun. His gaze shifted to a cluster of flowering bushes They showed evidence of the glorious color the buds contained. The bushes were on the verge of bursting open and displaying their crimson petals. The pollen within them would be an invitation to the tiny, quick humming winged birds. He closed his eyes and called upon his memory to host the delicate sweet fragrance of the flowers. He breathed deeply, as if to gather the remembrance of their fragile, fleeting scent in one inhalation. Capturing the scent, he smiled, pleased with his ability to bring it all back. It would not be long before the ground flowers would be sending their own buds out to burst forth enriching Mother Earth's breath. He opened his eyes and slowly scanned the crystalline, blue sky. On the horizon a cluster of puffy, white clouds hung suspended, seemingly fashioned from his imagination. He blinked his eyes and refocused them, wondering why the clouds held such a hypnotic influence upon him. He remembered Taja speaking of being on mountains of such height the tips were hidden from view by the clouds. He had difficulty conceiving anything so huge could exist. Since his union, the dream of making a trek to the land of mountains seemed inconceivable. He had other ventures to absorb his energy and occupy his mind.

A sudden movement at a nearby stand of trees to his right caught his eye. A pair of elands had emerged and grazed leisurely upon the grass. The female, swollen with her creation, appeared ready to give birth. They kept a wary eye upon the humans cognizant of danger even in the serenity of the moment. He focused on the pregnant mother and thought of the natural and rhythmic bonding and birthing processes. It is only in we humans where the complications occur, he reflected. He hoped to see his Batu filled with their creation soon. Perhaps seeing the pregnant eland foretold of things to come.

CHAPTER
TEN

With Tomudo having gone to the council meeting, Batu took the opportunity to walk out to her and Tomudo's special place on the plains. There, she reclined against the familiar tree. She recalled that Tomudo had been coming to this spot long before their union. When he first brought her here, they had bonded, rested and drank in the beauty of the plains. Then, as now, it sparkled with a myriad of color from the ground flowers. A feeling of peace filled her. The breeze, although warm, refreshed her, allowing her the pleasure of its relaxing caress. How good it felt to be away from Tomudo and to have a reprieve from the incessant talk of creating a child.

She looked up to watch the leaves gently waving and lazily closed her eyes. Within moments, her breathing became heavy, and she fell into a slumber. In her sleep, she saw a vision of someone covered with mud approaching. The person stopped short of her. An unknown aged woman also appeared, carrying a large wooden bowl. The bowl carrier stopped near the mud-covered being and poured the liquid contents of the bowl over its body. It appeared to be water. The water flowed unceasingly from the bowl cleansing the mud from the being. A bird caught Batu's attention. It flew around them in a circle. She had never seen plumage like it. A bright pink plumage covered its head, and a rich green plumage its body. Even after it stopped singing, the trill of its delicate and rich song lingered in her ears. Focusing on the two figures, she saw the water had completely cleansed the mud from the being. Mysteriously, the being had no breasts or genitals. The circling bird caught her attention. It flooded the stillness with a haunting, mournful song. Unexpectedly, it swooped toward her. She ducked to avoid it.

Startled awake, she thought the images real. The dream had a vividness she had never experienced. How very odd she thought to see someone who showed no signs of being a man or a woman. A shiver went through her body as she pictured the being covered with mud. It left her with a sinking sensation in the pit of her stomach. Reflecting on the dream, apprehension grew quickly inside of her.

Breathing deeply, she pushed the dream out of her thoughts. She caught sight of a flock of white cranes on their way to the running water, where the huge shallows had formed previous to her lifetime. In the shallows, the cranes were able to feed on the abundant scaly swimmers that gathered for their own feeding.

The ability to fly always struck an envious chord in her. There existed a freedom in flight that could not be compared with any other means of movement. Creativity never ceased to amaze her. There seemed to be no end to the differences she saw on Mother Earth. The jungle in particular had such variety and mystery yet she had never ventured into it. Her father had always told her it was not a place for a woman. The dangers were too great. Knowing he would not take her to the jungle, she never bothered to ask him to take her to the Sumati and Hamor villages. She wondered if Tomudo would take her into the depths of the lush jungle vegetation and then to the Sumati and Hamor villages. She wanted to experience such things before giving birth. Having a child would drastically curtail her from seeing them. Suddenly, she realized that this would be a way to strike a compromise with Tomudo. If he took her to these places she would consent to bearing their child.

Happy with her thoughts of having found a solution to their problem, she walked rapidly back to the village. Tomudo was not in their hut so she busied herself with preparing their meal.

Tomudo arrived and she exclaimed excitedly, "I have been thinking about a way for us to reconcile our differences."

His eyebrows shot up. "I am pleased you have," he said enthusiastically.

"I have never told you about some of the other reasons why I did not want to bear our child just yet. I am willing to learn the stories while I am bearing our child if you take me to see the great forest and to the Sumati and Hamor villages. You could even teach me the stories while we were on the trek and the necessities of survival."

The elation in Tomudo's eyes faded. "Batu, you ask the impossible."

"No. No, I do not."

"Yes you do. Even the most accessible of your requests is fraught with danger. The jungle is teaming with serpents, leopards and boars. I have not been in the jungle for many seasons. If I was experienced I would take you, but I am ill experienced. I would be an inadequate guide and could not protect you properly. Our warriors keep the area around our village free from predators, but anything past a day's journey must be considered dangerous. We would need to ask others to take us and none of the men would be willing to take a woman. No man would be willing to break with tradition to do it."

"You could learn what you needed and then take me," she offered.

"It would take many trips to become acquainted with all of the dangers. If I could find someone to teach me it would consume much of the season of blue skies."

"And what of the trips to the villages?"

Rubbing his forehead in exasperation, he answered, "Going to Sumati would take at least nineteen cycles. Hamor is more than twice that distance. Both trips would be dangerous. One of the stories of our history tells of seven Kahali men who ventured to find other humans. Only four returned. The others were lost to predators. They were gone a full season of blue skies and returned just before the rains. What you ask of me is next to impossible. I do not have the skills to cope with what exists on the plains or to take you on the running waters so great a distance. I am a teacher not a warrior. I am sorry."

"So am I."

"If it were possible, if it were safe, I would take you."

"Yes, I am sure you would," Batu whispered dejectedly.

Several cycles later, Batu awoke drenched in sweat to find she had the same dream about the mud-covered being. The same dreaded apprehension she felt with the first occurrence of the dream gripped her again. Knowing little about dreams, she felt at a loss to explain it or to grasp its significance. The mud-covered being elicited a queasy feeling at the start of the dream, but as the dream came to a close she felt better. Try as she might to keep the dream from her thoughts it kept haunting her. Unable to shake the eerie feeling, she vowed to talk to Tomudo about it.

After eating their dusk meal, she laid her hand on Tomudo's. "I need to speak to you of a dream I have had. I had the dream two times and have strange, apprehensive feelings about it. I even sense a form of fear about one of the figures. I do not know what the symbols represent, and I cannot determine what the dream is trying to tell me."

Inwardly, Tomudo smiled, pleased that she had come to him with a problem. If he handled it properly, this might be the opportunity to repair the recent setback and the damages incurred over a season ago with his vow.

He chose his words cautiously. "If I can help you, it will make me happy. But I have heard, if a dream is to be interpreted correctly, the one who dreams it must think it out. There is one man who has helped others with dream interpretation, the Talker Healer. He is the only man I would trust to interpret your dream. He is the one who might be able to help you, Batu."

Pensively she peered at him, "I am uncertain... No, I do not think I want to do that. What if I told you the dream? Perhaps you may have had one like it and could help me."

Unwilling to stifle her plea for assistance he said, "I will try."

Tomudo listened intently, absorbed by the dream. Had she not been so distressed, he would have delighted in the way she gave emphasis to the places holding dread or threat to her. He listened in amazement, as she orally constructed the imagery in her dream. The natural flow of her story absorbed his attention.

When she finished he told her honestly, "The only symbol I am familiar with is the bird. Normally, it is a positive symbol and usually foreshadows a major event. Other than that I cannot help you very much. Outside of the bird, I have never had any of those symbols in my dreams. On the surface, I can see nothing that might be threatening and cause your unrest."

Sharing with her these few facts, he concluded by saying, "The only thing I can say with certainty is some important event will happen to you. I am sorry I could not be of more help, Batu."

"Oh, but you have helped me tremendously. Before this I knew nothing."

Impulsively, she moved to embrace him, but caught herself and instead gave him an embarrassed smile. She turned and went outside and sat down on the bench. Well, she thought, at least I know the bird represents an important event to come. Could it be that the gods are going to reward me again in some manner, as they did with my own story? she asked herself. Perhaps the tribe will give me recognition for being the most intelligent or the most beautiful woman in the village. This could be her reward from the gods for the anguish Tomudo had been putting her through.

Smiling smugly, she directed her face to receive the last rays of the Great Sun and silently thank him for making her happy once again.

The dream recurred frequently. So frequently that Tomudo talked to Taja about it and spoke of trying to get Batu to see the Talker Healer. Batu refused to see Taja about the dream. She accepted each occurrence as an affirmation of the wonderful event to come. The uneasy feeling it caused receded. In its place grew a sense of anticipation. With it a new level of energy flowed through her. There were times she felt invincible, believing to be somehow chosen for a great event. At other times she felt she could soar through the sky, as she had always wanted to do as a woman-child.

The cycles wore on. Batu vacillated between her expectations and the lack of any tangible evidence of the glorious event. Without any favorable signs of such an honor, she became sullen and short tempered with everyone. Whenever Tomudo would broach the subject of her apparent change in personality, she would become angry and leave the hut. On one such occasion, Batu sat beneath the spreading branches of their favorite tree on the plains. She felt positive that the event she longed for was near. Weary and frustrated, she closed her eyes and fell asleep.

Upon awakening, Batu looked at the Great Sun and saw it had moved almost a quarter of the way through the blue sky. She felt warm and extremely thirsty. Rising to return to the village and quench her thirst, she became dizzy and had trouble focusing her eyes. Something was wrong... Some illness had crept into her body while she slept... With unsteady strides, she began to weave her way slowly back to the village. Stumbling now and then, she managed to cover half the distance to the village before her energy left her. She fell to the ground. Her mouth was parched, and she needed water. Gathering strength from her reserve, she edged back to her feet and plodded slowly toward the village, each step more difficult than the last. The earth and sky spun wildly. She collapsed, the air expelled from her lungs with a rush.

Tomudo's concern grew to alarm. Batu did not appear for their dusk meal. He had already contacted Aahi and Szatu. They did not know of her whereabouts. Remembering she frequently went to their tree on the plains, he trotted quickly out to it. Drawing near the clump of trees, he saw a crumpled form on the ground. Racing to it, he recognized it to be Batu. Perspiration covered her body. She was feverish. He maneuvered her onto his shoulder and made his way back to the village.

Nearing the village, he called out to one of the villagers. "Kalmann, run and fetch the Talker Healer. Tell him Batu has a fever, and I am taking her to my hut."

Inside the hut, Tomudo laid Batu on their sleeping mat. From the shelf, he grabbed the bowl containing their water and her bathing bag and began applying the water to cool her. He started with her head and worked his way down to her stomach. The Talker Healer entered the hut unannounced.

"She is feverish," he exclaimed. "I have been wetting her to keep her body cool."

"You have done well," Taja reassured him. "Please light your torch."

With the added light, Taja quickly examined her body. Finding no fresh wounds, he knew an animal or serpent did not inflict her fever. From a pouch hanging at his side he extracted a small bag and handed it to Tomudo.

"Put a pinch of this sage in her drinking water. Make her drink whenever she is awake. You can even put some in the water you bathe her with to reduce the fever."

"How much of the medicine should I put in the drinking water?" asked Tomudo.

"As much as you can easily hold between your pointing finger and your thumb. The sage should be put in a drinking bowl half filled with water. Let the potion stand awhile before administering it."

"And how much in the bath water?" asked Tomudo.

"About four times as much as in the drinking water," instructed Taja.

With concern evident in his voice Tomudo asked, "Can I do anything more to help her?"

"No. Until we know what is causing the fever, continue what you are doing," answered Taja.

Relieved to have the medicine and Taja present, he took a deep breath. Meanwhile, Taja went to the shelf and removed their drinking bowl, assessed the volume of water in it and removed a large pinch of the sage. Dropping it into the water, he swirled it around and set it down. The particles settled to the bottom.

"She may awaken at any moment. I have prepared the first bowl of the fever medicine for you. When the fever breaks, or if she becomes worse, come for me," he said placing his hand on Tomudo's shoulder.

Patting Taja's hand on his shoulder, he looked up at him, "Many thanks, Taja."

Placing the bag of medicine on the shelf, Taja left silently passing Aahi and Szatu and a few other members of the tribe that had gathered outside. Some were holding their water bowls, which they had filled for Tomudo to use.

Szatu and Aahi entered, "We have brought water for you to use. Others have also done the same knowing you will not want to leave Batu's side."

Szatu knelt beside Batu and placed her hand on her brow. Concern showed on her face as she turned to Tomudo. "I will return later to refill the bowls. You will be occupied and may not have the moments to do so yourself."

Tomudo embraced Szatu patted her back, hoping that it would somehow reassure her that Batu would recover. Releasing her, he placed his hands on

Aahi shoulders.

"We shall be praying for her recovery," Aahi said knowing the danger.

"Thank you, my friends. And please thank the others for me," he said to them in parting.

Tomudo turned his attention to preparing the coolant. He dropped four pinches of the sage in the large water bowl and swirled it around. He began to bathe Batu's body with the sage water, each touch filled with the love he had been unable to show her for so long. Later, Batu awakened delirious. Tomudo managed to get some water mixed with the medicine into her. He held her until she lapsed into sleep, and then continued applying water to her body as darkness overtook the light.

Tomudo awoke with a start to find he had fallen on his side while sitting next to Batu. He wondered how long he had been asleep. The last thing he remembered was sitting on his haunches by Batu's side. Fortunately, he had not fallen over onto her. He stepped to the entrance and stretched. A quick glance outside told him it would soon be dawn. Dipping the bathing bag into the solution, he applied the liquid to her fevered skin. He noticed a slight swelling on her right thigh, approximately half the area of his palm. Thinking it to be a reaction to the fever, he liberally applied water to that area. As the light became stronger he saw swellings of various sizes covering her entire body. A groan escaped his lips as panic seized him.

Szatu appeared at the entrance, as Tomudo rose in anticipation of rushing to the Talker Healer. The look on Tomudo's face sent Szatu's eyes to Batu. "What happened?" she exclaimed.

Tomudo told her of finding the inflamed and swollen areas on her body as he woke up, but could not explain what they were.

"The Talker Healer said to awaken him if she became worse," he said.

"You stay. I will go," she said, disappearing into the emerging light of dawn.

Tomudo remembered Taja had said that illnesses were often caused by troubled relationships. Did pitting his will against hers contribute to her illness? If one of them had given in this would not have happened. He shook his head. He never dreamed a woman could have such strength of will.

A few moments later, Taja entered with Szatu. He eased down to the ground next to Tomudo. Seeing the swelling, he asked, "When did this happen?"

Without looking at him, Tomudo answered, "In the last half of the darkness. What is it?"

112

He answered in a voice so quiet that Tomudo and Szatu strained to hear him. "I have seen this only once. A man developed these same swellings. Within the next two cycles these swollen areas will begin to form crusts that look like silvery-white scales."

Anxiously Tomudo asked, "How soon will these scales go away?"

Without removing his eyes from Batu, Taja answered, "The illness remained with the man until he became a dweller in the Land of No Shadows. He had it upon his arm and under his loincloth. I have never seen it so wide spread. I will prepare some comfrey salve for you to apply to the swollen areas. When she is strong enough, she can do it herself. The salve will give her some relief, but it will not cure the illness." Looking at both of them, he continued, "If the illness stays with her, a sign will appear on the nails of her fingers. They will be marked with small pits. These pits will remain as long as the illness remains."

Rising from Batu's side, he moved to the entrance, stopped to look over his shoulder and said, "Keep applying the water until the fever is gone, and give her the fever medicine each time she awakens. I will be back soon."

The Talker Healer returned, carrying a small bowl with the precious paste. Taja knelt between Tomudo and Szatu and dipped his finger into the mixture. "You can apply the salve on the inflamed areas even before any crusting appears. I did not do this with the man who had the scales. I waited until the scales appeared to begin the application. With Batu you may begin before they appear. It may lessen the intensity of the illness. Apply a little of the paste on each area that is swollen, and on the scales as they appear."

He proceeded to smooth a minute amount of the paste onto a small area of her forearm, "There is no need to put more than a slight film on the swellings or scales should they appear."

Taja rose to leave. Rising with him, Tomudo placed his hands on the shoulder of the Talker Healer. His eyes spoke the words his lips did not form. Taja rested his hands on his shoulders in return, understanding Tomudo's inability to speak.

Szatu, now standing, waited until the men were through with their farewell before she said thankfully, "May the gods be with you, Taja."

After sharing some words of encouragement with Tomudo, Szatu also left.

Tomudo fell to his knees next to Batu and began applying the salve slowly and methodically. He touched her hair lovingly. Their union was more disquieting and tumultuous than he ever suspected it would be, but despite all of the pain and frustrations, he never thought it unfortunate to be in union with her. They had shared wonderful moments before he made that fateful vow and felt certain they would again. Within himself he sensed her indwelling goodness. To Tomudo, it was as distinguishable as his ability to smell her scent. Like a butterfly she somehow had to break free of her encumbering cocoon. The vanity she had developed for so long served as her encasement, trapping and burying her love, and crippling her personality. If she did not break free from her vanity the beauty within her would never be seen. For Batu the moment had not yet come.

During the darkness, Batu awoke mumbling incoherently. Tomudo quickly cradled her in his arms and succeeded in getting her to swallow some of the medicine. She fell asleep before he could lay her back down on their mat.

Three cycles later Batu awoke. The dawn light had already given color to the objects in the hut. Seeing Tomudo still asleep, she reached for the drinking bowl to quench her thirst. Crying out at the sight of her arm, the bowl slipped from her hand and made a thud on the ground. Tomudo swung his body deftly to a sitting position.

"Tomudo, what has happened to me? What is this on my arms and body?" Panic filled her voice. Her eyes reflected the uncertainty of her thoughts.

"You fell ill with the fever and we have applied a salve to ease the inflammation. You have slept for almost four full cycles."

She examined her body in horror. The initial stages of the scaling spared no part of her body. Fearful, she asked, "What is wrong with me? Why is my body swollen? Why is it so blotchy? Why does it itch so?"

"It is some type of rash. Taja will tell you more, when he sees you again."

Looking again at her arm, she saw something foreign under the salve. After wiping the salve off, she tried to brush away the small, white, crusty-looking scales underneath. They would not brush off. The process only further irritated her skin.

"What is this on my arm? It burns and itches. Have I touched some ivy?"

Unable to avoid the problem any longer he told her what Taja said it might be. Her eyes now held a wild desperate look, "What do you mean scales? Is this to be over my whole body? How soon will I be rid of them?" her voice rose in panic, while she fired the questions at him.

"The scales or crusts may appear anywhere on your body. I am not certain how much of your body will be covered, or how long they may stay. Taja gave me some of the salve to put on the scales and swellings. We can put it on the new swellings, now, if you wish."

"Of course I wish it. I do not want this to spread over my body. How often can we apply it?"

"I did not ask," he answered quietly, berating himself for not doing so. "He said to apply it when you were uncomfortable. I am unsure if more applications will hasten the healing."

"I want this ailment to leave me quickly, so we must apply it often. Apply it to the scales on my back, and I will do the rest of my body."

Looking at the amount he had in the small bowl, he saw he would have to apply it sparingly. After he showed her how to apply it, he applied the salve to her back.

The salve, when first applied to her body left it strange in appearance. It reminded her of how the men looked after having painted their bodies in preparation for the first hunt of the season. Unlike their painted bodies, which held a great deal of symmetry, the application of the salve followed the irregular pattern of the swellings and lacked symmetry. Her eyes kept roaming her body. She could not keep from examining herself, yet when she did, she felt revulsion, distress and anger. Finally in frustration, she burst into tears. She struggled to regain her composure, only to lose it with another rush of tears. Tomudo could not pacify her. What could he say, when he himself could not comprehend why the gods would do such a cruel thing? He sensed she could bear any other illness without such emotion, but this affected her beauty. Although courageous and head strong, this illness brought her to her knees. She was no match for it. Unable to find the right words to give her comfort, he watched her suffer.

Darkness had begun to creep into the village. The Talker Healer announced himself at their hut. He examined Batu visually and waited for the questions he knew were sure to come.

Batu's eyes grew dark. "How did I get this?"

"I am uncertain."

"When will this illness leave me?"

"Again, I am uncertain," confessed Taja. "I will begin to prepare more of the balm immediately. Apply the salve to the areas of discomfort as often as you feel it necessary, but do not waste it."

His answer did not satisfy her. "Will it be with me three cycles of the Great Sun, ten or twenty? Let me know how long I must endure this," she asked desperately.

"I do not know, Batu. I will bring more of the balm, when the Great Sun is high in the sky again. I am sorry I cannot give you a definite answer."

"Will this swelling and crusting be reduced by the medicine?"

"It may. We will have to wait and see. Do you have any other questions?"

"What good is it to ask them? You have said nothing of value," she snapped at him.

"I am sorry," he said evenly, "I cannot give you any words of encouragement. If you have no other questions, I am going to leave. I bid you both farewell."

Tomudo glared at Batu. He was about to ask her to apologize, but thought the better of it. Directing his attention to Taja, he said apologetically, "I am sorry. Thank you, Taja."

Batu kept staring at the empty entrance. Darkness crept into their hut. She remained sullen and withdrawn. Tomudo felt she needed to be held, but he hesitated in doing so because of the sensitive condition of her body. The other thing that prevented him was the present condition of her mind. He would have to be content with being able to express his love by simply being there for her.

Hoping his presence, words and deeds would be sufficient to console her, he asked, "Is there anything I can do for you?"

"Yes, bring my beauty back to me."

She covered her face and wept.

CHAPTER
ELEVEN

Aahi left to talk with the High Priest. Szatu began weeping shortly afterward. Crying had overtaken her life since Batu's disease. Szatu had brought Batu onto Mother Earth and never expected her child to suffer so terribly. Batu had always been blessed in the past. Now, she seemed cursed. What was the reason? Batu remained the crowning glory of her life, an ongoing reminder of the goodness of the gods. Sadly, life and the gods turned sour and unfair. In some unfathomable way, Batu had fallen from grace. Szatu seemed certain it had to be a reflection on Batu. There could be no other way to interpret such a tragedy. Her life of joy and pride left her totally unprepared for the pain and sorrow engulfing her family. She had no recourse but to trust in the gods. She had nothing else to hold onto. Soon, they would come to their senses and Batu would recover. Until then, she would pray for Batu and hope she would once again return to the good graces of the gods.

Aahi found the High Priest in the Sacred Hut and called his name.

Romir appeared at the entrance. "What do you want?"

Aahi's eyes were slits as he directed his question to the High Priest. "Are you behind my child's illness?"

"What are you talking about?"

"You know perfectly well. Batu humiliated you. You threatened Batu and me. How did you do it?"

"Aahi, you are not making sense. You had better leave before I get angered."

"You could have easily placed some strange ivy where Batu always went on the plains. You were sufficiently angry to do it. Did you put the juice from the leaves and stems around and on the tree?"

"What are you babbling about? I did no such thing."

"Did you seek the help of the gods in punishing Batu? How could you ask the gods to inflict such punishment upon her? How can the gods allow such shame and pain to happen to one of their favorite creations?"

"Favorite? You believe that Batu is a favorite of the gods? Your concept of the gods is incorrect. How can they like a woman who has no respect for religious tradition? Answer me that, Aahi. I see why Batu has gone so far astray. I see why she has no respect for tradition. You have instilled in her these wild notions. You are confused and have passed that confusion onto her."

Aahi was unable to say anything.

"Ah! You have seen that I am right. My advice to you is to go back to your hut and pray that the gods do not inflict the same illness upon you or your woman, Aahi."

"I do not care if you are the High Priest, Romir. If I ever find out that you have prayed to the gods to injure any of us or that you have done something to cause us harm you will be hurt yourself."

The High Priest stepped closer and put his face next to Aahi's. Anger twisted his face. "Do not threaten me. The gods are always on the side of tradition and the High Priest. Their wrath will take care of people like you and Batu. It always has and always will."

Aahi glared back at Romir. "It will be well if you remember my words." Before Romir could answer he spun around and walked away.

Romir took a deep breath. A slow smile of satisfaction crept onto his face. He had shown the little man who was the greater man of logic. He had shown Aahi that the gods were indeed on his side and that his whole family had strayed from the truth and they were vulnerable to the gods' wrath. He had nothing to worry about, for he stood as the emissary of the gods. He nodded his head in appreciation of how splendidly they punished Batu. In punishing her the whole family suffered. Justice was served. Justice was good. His prayers were answered. In his satisfaction, his smile took the look of a sneer.

Aahi did not feel like he thought he would after seeing Romir. Little if anything went right. He had to admit it had been one of the few times the High Priest made sense. Their religion did stand behind what he said. He felt confused and morose. The frustration he felt before talking to Romir still clung to him. He accomplished nothing except to threaten the man and anger him more. He hung his head, as he walked out to the plains to gather himself.

Batu's thoughts raced wildly. She could not retain anything long enough to examine it rationally. Angrily, she flailed at her swollen thighs. She looked at herself and shook her head crying wildly. She screamed at the gods. "Why have I been afflicted so horribly?"

Tears, she could not control, spilled from her cheeks onto her salve-covered thighs. Her beauty had been a constant throughout her life. Except to utilize it to her advantage, she had not given it much thought. Now, with it gone, she became keenly aware of how much it really meant to her. The latter part of her life, she had placed her mind above her beauty and never worried about it. Her beauty evolved naturally, while her intelligence had been acquired with effort. She worked hard to excel mentally and took great pride in her success. At the moment it mattered little.

Certain that everyone in the tribe knew how horrible she looked, she curled up into the fetus position. How could she ever show herself again? The shame of looking so grotesque surely came from some sort of curse by the beastly High Priest. It had to be a curse. It could not be an act of the gods. The gods had always shown their esteem for her. If she were to be honored again, as her dream foretold, the gods would not allow such humiliation and shame to continue. As soon as the gods noticed her affliction, they would restore her body to its original radiance and health. Patience, she needed patience. The gods would not desert her. This disease would soon vanish and her beauty would be restored.

The Great Sun's gleaming light flooded the earth, shedding its light on hopeful men and women seeking answers to their problems. Batu awoke feeling refreshed. It was the first such awakening for her in many cycles.

Stretching her arms, she noticed the salve covering the crusty swellings on her arms. In those few moments of waking she had forgotten the harsh reality of her body and its grotesque appearance. Instantly, she became aware of the irritation covering her body. Beneath the salve, she could see the crusting and scaling had increased alarmingly. The jewel-like body she once possessed had become hideous. She wept softly. Gradually, her whole body shook uncontrollably, racked by deep, mournful sobs.

Awakening to her sobs, Tomudo, impulsively placed his arms around her to comfort her, only to have them violently struck away, leaving him stunned. Tears formed in his eyes. Before him sat one of the proudest, most beautiful and intelligent woman the tribe had ever produced. Now in a matter of a few cycles her life had been shattered. The loss of her beauty did not compromise his love for her. It saddened him and added confusion and stress to an already troubled union. There appeared to be nothing he could do but continue to pray to the gods for her recovery and to help her in whatever way possible. The Great Sun had surrendered its vigil to the Sun With No Heat. The darkness brought no change in Batu's condition. He watched her as she slept, wishing he were a god and had the power to make her well.

Despite the constant application of the salve, the next several cycles saw an increase in the severity of Batu's condition. Her face, so far free from the swelling, exhibited large blotches that turned into patches of crusts. With their advent Batu's mental state spiraled downward. The visits by her mother and father could not deter her slow descent into the domain of sullen desperation. They, like Tomudo, were helpless and frustrated, unable to ease her confusion and anguish.

Batu vacillated between rage and fear. When her anger consumed her, she attacked her body, scratching it raw. Tomudo's pleas and reprimands, on discovering the open wounds, went unheeded. Returning from his baths, Tomudo often found her wildly moaning and crying, while rubbing and scratching her body. In these agitated states, Batu chose to ignore her wounds. Tomudo had to clean the oozing blood and salve from her body and cover it anew with a goldenseal salve Taja had prepared. Even with his careful attendance, four of the areas she had scratched raw became infected. The one, located on her cheek, concerned him the most because of its proximity to her eye. Another sat on her breast, while the other two were on her left leg. The infections caused Batu to run a fever. Tomudo awakened on the fifth cycle of Batu's fever and found her delirious. He rushed to Taja.

After examining the unconscious Batu, Taja said nothing. Placing a hand above her heart, he sat cross-legged with his eyes closed. Tomudo somberly watched his friend. The silence left his mind to wonder what the gentle man perceived. He sat quietly waiting for Taja to open his eyes. After many moments, he opened his eyes and spoke. "Batu must know the meaning of her recurring dream. If she does not come to understand it, she can die. If she is willing, I will help her in searching for its meaning."

The words sounded ominous to Tomudo. Desperately he asked, "But how is the dream affecting her?"

"Everything causes an effect upon us. The situation reflected in this dream will destroy her or let her grow. It is up to her," he said mysteriously, revealing nothing more. "Is any of the fever medicine left?"

"Yes," replied Tomudo.

"Use it as before. I will bring you more of the goldenseal salve to use on the open wounds. You must keep them as clean as possible."

Tomudo nodded his head.

Placing his hand on Tomudo's shoulder compassionately, he looked into his pained eyes and turned without formally bidding him goodbye. Taja walked out of the hut into the early light.

Shocked and confused, Taja's words rang in his ears over and over again. He sat down next to his woman, swearing he would get her to see Taja. Bending down, he kissed her eyes and lips, and then caressed her hair. As never before, he prayed fervently to the gods for her recovery.

The long vigil allowed him to review what Taja had told him. How did he acquire his knowledge by simply placing his hand over Batu's heart? He had not told him the contents of the dream. That was for Batu to do. His statement that she could die if she did not know its meaning terrified him. Taja would not speak of if he did not believe it could happen. Closing his eyes he vowed to get her to see Taja.

During her illness, Tomudo realized he had touched upon an unidentifiable quality in her. All his attempts at identifying the elusive quality ended in failure. The quality could only be described as a feeling of expansiveness. He could not describe it any better. He resigned himself to simply be aware of what he could not name. He continually came in contact with this essence during his vigil. The very fact that he felt something intrigued him.

Four cycles later Batu's fever broke. Although thinner, she quickly recovered her strength, but the white scales still covered her body.

Tomudo had finished applying the salve to her back and said, "Batu, while you were ill, Taja spoke of the cause of your illness."

Happy that the Talker Healer had detected something, she quickly questioned him. "What did he say?"

"He spoke of your recurring dream being the cause of your illness," he answered cautiously.

"How can that be? What can a dream have to do with what is covering my body?" she asked.

"He was very emphatic about it being the cause. It would do you no harm to see him. I love you too much to see you suffer any more. Please see him," he said imploringly.

Silently, she pondered whether or not talking to Taja of her dream would help her. Resigning to the fact that nothing had helped her up to this point, she quickly broke her silent deliberation, "Very well, I shall speak to him."

Breaking into a huge smile Tomudo said, "I will arrange to have him meet you here. I will leave the hut so you can be alone with him."

His elation struck a harmonic chord in her that she had never felt before. It reverberated through her body. At a loss to explain it, she watched him leave to make the arrangement for her meeting with Taja. For the first time in many cycles, she had something which to look forward.

Taja arrived. His serene demeanor was in sharp contrast to the anxious looks of Tomudo and Batu. He greeted Batu, but received none in return. As he sat down, Tomudo excused himself, leaving them alone.

The Talker Healer took a deep breath then spoke, "If you ever hope to recover from your illness, you need to understand your dream. Are you willing to know its meaning, even though it may be traumatic?" he asked looking deeply into her eyes.

Irritated she answered, "Yes. What could be worse than what I am suffering now?"

He responded with a soft "What indeed!" Pausing momentarily, he took a deep breath and continued, "I am uncertain how you will learn of its meaning. You may discover it now, during this meeting, or the answer may come to you in a different dream, or something else may happen. Whatever happens, if any of the dream figures appear, or others appear, you must question them to find out what their significance is to you. Do you understand?"

"Yes."

"Are you ready to begin?"

"Yes."

He went on with his instructions, "I want you to look into my eyes. Do not speak. Just look into my eyes. Focus your complete attention there."

Gazing into his eyes, she noticed that they were predominately blue and they also contained flecks of green, yellow and brown in them. Continuing to look into his eyes, she perceived a quality in them she had never seen. They actually had a calming effect on her. As she relaxed, she wondered why she had never noticed how peaceful they looked. They seemed to exude the serenity she sensed about him. It surprised her that she saw these things so quickly in a man she hardly knew. His eyes seemed to be constantly changing their expression, as if he sensed her thoughts. He smiled at that moment in much the same way her father did when she rushed to tell him about something she had discovered.

Many moments passed. She kept staring into his eyes becoming aware of a growing sensation within her. It seemed as if little pieces were falling off her body. With each piece she felt more and more exposed. She felt uncomfortable yet knew that it was necessary. As the feeling accelerated, she felt large weights being lifted from her, freeing her from some unknown burden. It continued for some moments, releasing things she could not name. A sense of freedom grew inside of her. She had never experienced freedom exactly like this before, even when she did what she wanted to do in the face of opposition. All of the weights she seemed to be carrying were set aside, leaving her open, exposed and vulnerable, yet unafraid. The extraordinary feeling both surprised her and pleased her. She saw Taja's hand moving slowly toward her. It came to rest above her heart. It felt unusually warm. A feeling of something passing between them came over her. An inner energy and strength flooded her. She suddenly became unconcerned with what others thought about her present condition. That astounded her!

As the eyes of the Talker Healer slowly disappeared, an urging and desire to discover the truth within her swept over her, leaving her enveloped in a cloudy mist. Out of the mist a mud-covered being emerged. It walked slowly toward her. Recognizing it as the being in her dream, she immediately became alert. Stopping a few steps away from her, it stood in silence. Recalling the Talker Healer's instructions she asked, "Why are you here?"

The figure spoke without moving its mouth. "You see before you the self you have chosen to present to others. The soil that covers me is the defense you have put upon yourself. It is also symbolic of the illness that you are now expressing through your body. In this way you have kept others from learning about your true self."

The being stopped its communication. A movement to Batu's left caught her eye. The old woman from her dream appeared. She seemed older than any woman she had ever seen before. Carrying a wooden water bowl atop her head, she began to walk effortlessly toward her. She stopped near the mud-covered being and looked directly at Batu.

Fascinated by her weathered and wrinkled appearance she almost forgot to ask for her help. "Aged one, what significance are you to me?"

"I am the part of you that is eternal and wise. With wisdom you pour out the waters and wash away the elements that hide the being that exists under your defenses. When these barriers have disappeared you will be able to love more fully."

Pouring the water on the mud covered being, she spoke again. "The water is symbolic of your spiritual nature; it is forever present and never ceases to flow within you. Its source is your eternal self, represented by the round shape of the bowl and the androgynous nature of the being. Know that what you have seen is eternal and ever becoming."

The being was now completely cleansed of the mud. Looking at the cleansed being, she felt unsure what the old woman meant by androgynous.

Sensing her question the being spoke, "My lack of organ is purposeful. It signifies that your true self is neither man nor woman. As an eternal being you do not restrict yourself in this way, but in the physical existence it is useful for your development to be represented as one then the other."

The androgynous being and the old woman faded into the mist. The enchanting song of a nearby bird captured her attention. Searching a flowering tree, which had materialized to her right, she finally found it perched on the topmost branch. It had a brightly plumed emerald-green body and effervescent pink head. The song kept changing from a light lilting melody to one hauntingly sad. The bird flew from its perch and came toward her, halting in flight directly in front of her. Fascinated by its ability to suspend itself in mid-air without moving its wings, she watched it spellbound.

Moving past her fascination she asked, "Winged one, what am I to learn from you?"

The bird began to sing in a manner she had never heard before. The song turned to words in her head, "My haunting song is the sorrow in your life. All beings sing it, yet all beings can sing of fulfillment and love as well. My lilting song conveys love in all of its fullness. I sing so you can know that you are the one who creates both the sorrow and the bliss in your life. You are the one who chooses to sing a song of elation or one of despair."

The bird stopped singing and with it the communication ceased. She wondered whether or not the colors had any meaning to her. Before she could vocalize her question, the bird began to sing. The words again formed in her head.

"The green feathers I bear represent your potential for growth and healing, available to you based upon the songs you choose to sing. The crowning glory of pink on my head is symbolic of the love that must be present in you, if you are to truly grow. It is bestowed upon my head to show that the thoughts, which are initiated in the head, must be imbued with love to be of value. The pink color is at the zenith of my body to signify that love is the most important virtue comprising your being."

The song and the words ceased, casting stillness upon the scene. Slowly, the tree and bird faded from view. She waited many moments to make certain no other figures would materialize from the mist. When none appeared, she moved her fingers to help bring her back to her body. She opened her eyes and looked directly into the Talker Healer's eyes. A feeling came over her telling her that he knew what she had experienced. Incapable of comprehending how he knew, or how she knew of it, she sat in silence. Suddenly, she had no qualms about him knowing what transpired in her vision.

Unexpectedly, before those loving eyes she lost the last of her defenses. Tears fell from her eyes, gradually at first and then streamed uncontrollably. When she finally stopped, she felt cleansed, purged of an unknown burden.

Without looking, she knew Taja's eyes were upon her; she knew it with the same conviction that she felt his love. Finally, she looked into his eyes. Again they held her spellbound. They penetrated her very being, uncovering things, forcing her to look upon them, yet they were without condemnation, radiating understanding and love. As she gazed into his eyes, she knew she had cut herself off from her true self just as the wise woman had said. She realized the love she had for herself before this moment had been marred by vanity and arrogance. Her pride and arrogance left little room for understanding and compassion. Refusing to bond with Tomudo had been selfish and shortsighted. If she had loved him, she would have consented to bear his child. She had been foolish to live so ignorantly, so unaware of the value of love and of its giving nature.

She could not bring herself to pull her gaze from his eyes. The longer she looked into them the more peaceful she felt. Those soft pools conveyed the presence of love. She flowed with the gentle and exhilarating feelings. Again she wept. This time she accepted her faults without personal condemnation. Her tears ceased. She leaned over to embrace the body that housed those eyes and sighed.

"Thank you, Taja. Thank you."

He returned her embrace and said softly, "Batu, you are blessed by the love of many people. Thank the Creator for every opportunity you have to return that love."

"I shall. I shall."

Gently Taja said, "You have said nothing of it, so I must tell you; in order for your inner beauty to come forth your outer beauty had to be lost."

Her eyes narrowed with the information. She said nothing in defense.

Rising he said, "My mission here is complete. I must go, but please know that my love is with you."

She rose and stood near him. Reaching out, she touched his arm. Smiling, he turned and left without another word.

His sudden departure left her surprised. She watched him leave, marveling at the powerful emotions roaring through her. They were washing free the inner recesses of her being. The experience left her mind searching for answers that eluded her. About to move away from the entrance, she saw Tomudo coming from the direction of her parents' hut. Nearing the hut he stopped short. A wild smile broke over his face, lighting it up like a child who has received an unexpected gift. Rushing to her, he swept her up in his arms spinning around until they fell on the ground, leaving them both laughing at his impulsive display.

Nestled in Tomudo's arms she smiled at him, "What has possessed you?"

"What?" he said incredulously. "Have you not looked at yourself?"

She looked at herself to confirm his words. The blotchy swellings had disappeared. She swept at some crusts and they came away with her touch. Unwilling to believe it, she wiped at a few more areas and found the crusts came free there as well. The only remnants of her disease were the scabs from where she clawed in frustration at her irritated skin. Smiling and crying happily at the same moment, she clung to him, holding him to her for the first time in over a season.

Releasing him, she dipped her wash bag in the water and ran it over her arms, legs, stomach and breasts, washing the remaining scales away. She ran her fingers over her skin. She did not trust her eyes and needed the reassurance of touching her body. Nothing remained of the swelling and crusts. She smiled again and happily wrapped her arms around her man. Holding him and relaxing in his arms, she became aware of the same emotion she felt from the Talker Healer. The warm, wonderful feeling of love enveloped her.

Before saying what she felt in her heart, she withdrew a bit from him, so she could look into his eyes. "Tomudo, I love you deeply and with every part of my being. I have been so foolish to deny that I loved you. I cannot deny it any longer. It is as tangible as the air I breathed."

His eyes filled with joy. "I have longed to hear those words. Living with you and not hearing those words tore at my heart. I endured it knowing you would eventually realize you loved me." He drew her to him kissing her cheek gently.

Moving her head back, she looked into his eyes, trying desperately to show with her eyes those thoughts she had never expressed. In a voice choked with emotion she said, "Tomudo I am sorry for the pain I have caused you."

"The pain is gone now," he said and drew her closer to him.

She rested her head on his shoulder. Suddenly, she saw how her vanity prevented them from being happy. She wondered if she had used intellect and vanity in a similar manner in her dealings with others? How strange, the very thing she took such great pride in, kept her from seeing the goodness in others and prevented her from being compassionate. With this realization came a renewal in her weeping. Prior to her illness she had always thought people to be weak or overly emotional when she saw them cry, now she saw it as a necessary part of their composition and emotional life.

Wiping the tears from her eyes, she looked at Tomudo, gathering courage from the love she saw in his eyes.

"I have been at fault in our union. I have never thanked you for your love and understanding, nor for the care you gave me while I was ill. You never once said how ugly I looked. You have had reason to be cold and mean to me, yet you always loved me, you were always tender. It has always been you by my side helping me. You taught me what you knew and I returned it with vanity and selfishness. For all those things I am truly sorry. I have been foolish. I wasted so many moments in opposing you and your wish to create a new life within me. If you still wish to create a child, I am now ready to bear you one. I love you, Tomudo. I never knew what love was until now. I never knew what it felt like, or how it could make me feel when I gave it to someone, to you. Hold me. Love me," she whispered passionately.

She crushed her lips to his. Her hands were on his back. She sought the places she remembered that had brought shivers to his body in the past. His hands shook with passion, as he caressed her body. Seeking her breast he covered it with his hand, then his lips. Their passion accelerated until they could not endure being separate. Batu shared her body, giving herself out of love, not desire. For the first time since they had been in union, she wanted to please her man because she loved him. The void she felt, but never filled while bonding, now filled with a rush. She not only satisfied her physical needs but now found her bonding to be an extension of her expression of love for Tomudo.

Batu lay awake savoring the relative calm before the dawn, relishing the quiet moments to think about everything that transpired during the last cycle. In the dark she found Tomudo's chest. He did not stir from his sleep. Moving her hand lightly in a large circular motion, halting it above his heart, she felt its steady rhythmic beat.

"How smoothly your heart beats for me," she whispered. She smiled at her words. With her hand resting above his heart, she shivered abruptly, feeling a cold, non-existent hand upon her own heart. The smile quickly left her face, replaced by a confused frown. In spite of her efforts, she could find no plausible reason why she felt so strange.

Batu and Tomudo settled down to the pleasant routine they had prior to their disagreement. A change took place in Batu's desire to learn. It became tempered, controlled more by her desire to live her life with him as his woman than as his protégée. Often, she playfully teased him, when he finished reciting a story, making fun of one thing then another. At times she drove him to distraction with her hands running over his body. Now and then, her love and desire for him manifested in her eyes. On seeing it, he would smile knowingly and continue the story to its conclusion, then draw her to him. In each other's arms, everything was forgotten, except their love for each other.

Tomudo's gut feelings about Batu were correct. He found her capacity to love profound. Once her defenses were destroyed, the vanity and conceit that had ruled her life were virtually gone. Although shocked at the course of events that precipitated her dramatic change, he was thankful they happened. Thinking of the events and how they unfolded, he found they awed him. The Talker Healer had skillfully brought her to the threshold of understanding. Were it not for his mastery of the inner life, she likely would have perished. He pondered whether all personal tragedy promoted growth as it had in her? If true, then it may well be that a purpose lie behind everything that happens in life and it matters little how it unfolds. It seemed to imply very forcefully that how we face the challenges and opportunities in life add to or detract from who we are. The same could be said for how we relate to everyone. How we relate to people is indicative of whether we use love as the standard to guide us in our relationships. The scabs on her face, breast and leg marred her beauty, but perhaps they were meant to be a constant reminder to her that beauty, just as life, hangs by the thinnest of threads, and is easily snapped and lost. The crucial factor in her remaining alive was her ability to accept the dream's message and to alter her life by letting love be the guiding force in it. The love he felt from Batu, and how she interacted with him, was what he had dreamed their life together would be like. Since her recovery, their conversations were long and intimate and their lovemaking fulfilling. He sensed that happiness finally resided within each of them. He felt blessed.

Their union now presented Batu with the opportunity to experience the joy of giving love spontaneously, without reservations or demands. Having abandoned her position of not wanting to conceive a child, she now yearned to carry their creation. Forgotten were her anger and misunderstanding with Tomudo, which brought about her recurring dream. The transition had unveiled other wonders. It ignited the desire to give her love and her body as well, to her man, her lover. The intense desire to acquire knowledge still rustled within her, but was now surpassed by her need to know her man. They shared endearing words, glances, caresses, and tenderness that is shared by lovers.

The cycles passed by in a wonderfully lazy fashion. Batu's thoughts often turned to the mysterious man who led her out of her personal darkness. It became evident to her that the dream, her illness, her understanding of the dream, her recovery and her ability to feel love so deeply were key points in her life. Amazingly, Taja had been involved in each of them. She could not help but wonder why her life had become intertwined with his. Perhaps in the future he would become more than just an acquaintance. She thought over that statement and smiled, knowing she wanted it to happen.

During the period of Batu's illness, Tomudo had suspended the sessions with Coloma. The three of them easily settled back into the normal routine. Coloma expressed his concern over Batu's illness and his delight in her recovery.

Upon resuming the sessions a subtle change occurred. Batu's relaxed attitude toward acquiring knowledge and her love for Tomudo precipitated a new comradeship between the three of them. The sessions often held casual bantering between them and rang with laughter.

With her newfound happiness, she was unaware of Coloma's appreciative glances until a meeting where Tomudo excused himself. He explained he needed to relieve himself. He told Coloma to repeat the story to Batu and she would correct him, if he made a mistake. While Tomudo was gone, Coloma's glances increased. The number of mistakes he made caused Batu to become cognizant of his watchful eyes. Alone with Coloma, she fell prey to his appreciative glances. This was the first time she had become aware of anyone's gaze since her illness, and it surprised her how good it felt to be noticed again. The feeling had a different twist. It lacked pride. It simply felt delightful to be appreciated.

"Are my scars a distraction to you?" she asked teasingly.

Embarrassed at being caught, he remained quiet for a moment. Smiling boldly he answered, "No. Even with your scars you are the most beautiful woman in the tribe."

The words were a balm to her. She smiled appreciatively at him. The last time any man, except for her father and Tomudo, had ever lavished such praise on her she did not have any scars marring her beauty.

"Thank you. I did not expect any man, other than Tomudo, would ever say that to me."

"I am sorry for being so bold."

"No need to apologize."

Tomudo, entering the hut asked, "What is Coloma apologizing about?"
Coloma's face reddened.

Batu, hoping to relieve Coloma from the burden of telling Tomudo what he had done spoke before he could reply. "Coloma graciously told me he thought I am still beautiful, despite my scars."

Tomudo looked at Coloma sternly. "Is this true?"

Distressed, Coloma answered, "Yes. I hope I have not offended you."

Breaking into a grin Tomudo replied, "No offense taken Coloma. I have not been blind to the appreciative looks of our men toward Batu in the past. I have long been among them myself."

Coloma breathed easier.

"Just see to it that it does not interfere with our work and our relationship," he mildly chastised him.

"It will not, Tomudo. I promise you that."

"Good. Now perhaps you can learn something of value, if you can keep your mind on the stories and your eyes off Batu," Tomudo said good-naturedly.

CHAPTER
TWELVE

The rainy season enveloped the plains and the village, altering the hunting and snaring routine of the men. Whenever the rains eased, the men ventured onto the soggy and treacherous plains or into the nearby groves in quest of meat, vegetation and fruit. Meals, during the rains, consisted of smoke-dried meats and foods stored during the season of blue skies and of the scaly swimmers acquired from the running water. Younger warrior hunters speared the scaly swimmers while the older ones, whose reflexes were slowed, used nets to capture them.

With the first hint of the oncoming change of season, the village became more active. Everyone grew restless. The men were eager to begin the hunts and collect fresh foods. When the Great Sun made its welcome appearance, the tribe conducted the pole ritual to determine how much rain had fallen.

Tomudo also welcomed the opportunity to practice his skill at snaring. Even though not required of him, he enjoyed keeping his skills honed and supplying his own meat.

The Great Sun rose in the brightening blue sky for the fourth time since the rains ceased. Tomudo breathed in the freshness. He made his way from the village to the plains to set his snares. Making his way from the village, he noticed that the light rain that fell, during the dark, had already begun to burn off the foliage. Finding a suitable place, he proceeded to set a snare amidst the scarce brush. While his hands worked positioning the snare, his thoughts drifted to Batu. His inner knowing about Batu's love had been correct; her love matched her will. What he had sensed to be inside of her went beyond his expectations. Her growing understanding of the meaning and responsibilities of love had rewarded his patience. It had not taken her long to regain the weight she had lost. If anything she looked lovelier than before, despite the scars, for now she had the look of a woman in love. It pleased him immensely that her attitude had changed about having a babe, but remained surprised that she had not as yet conceived.

Having set the snare, he backed up ruffling the grass with a small branch to cover his appearance. Had he not been concentrating on Batu he would

131

have seen the serpent. The multi-colored serpent struck his threatening body sending its venom into Tomudo's ankle. Spinning, he saw the bright-colored serpent. Grabbing his long blade, he slashed out instinctively, severing its head, in one swift motion. Looking at the tiny punctures, he saw they were on the outside of his ankle. There would be no way of drawing the venom out by sucking on the bite. Quickly, he made two incisions in the form of a cross over the punctures and began squeezing the fluid out. Pressing the flesh at a spot around the rupture and moving inward, he hoped to contain and eject most of the venom. He kneaded the spot until satisfied he could drain no more venom out. Picking up the serpent, he stuck it into his game pouch. Taking the serpent would help Taja to identify it and determine what medicine he should use. The knife lay where he had dropped it. He sheathed it and left his two other snares on the ground. He began running back to the village. The pace he set would get him there without having to stop and rest. He hoped he would not faint on the way.

He had covered nearly a quarter of the distance. The venom had not begun to affect him. If it reacted slowly enough, he felt he would be spared. Nearing the halfway point to the village he began to feel nauseous. He concentrated on his running, knowing that if he reached the village Taja might have something to counteract the poison. As he neared the three-quarter point his limbs felt heavy. A strange feeling of disassociation crept into his body. Suddenly, he lost the feeling in his legs. They were unable to hold him. He fell. He struggled to his feet knowing that if he remained on the ground he would never survive. He tried to run, but his legs would not respond. He resorted to walking. Even this physical action became difficult. His vision became blurred and gave way to spells of vertigo. The sky and earth merged as images undulated and swirled about him. He closed his eyes in an effort to stem the violent rush of an unrecognizable hallucinatory landscape. The pounding in his ears became a deafening roar, threatening to drive him mad before he died. He threw his hands over his ears as he collapsed on the unyielding earth.

Tiru, returning from setting his own snares, saw Tomudo running in the distance. He speculated about Tomudo's action and kept an eye on him. When Tomudo fell he rushed to his aid.

Examining Tomudo, Tiru saw the blood trickling from the swollen ankle. Seeing the game pouch, he looked into it and saw the serpent. He wanted to immediately put his mouth on the wound in an effort to draw out the venom, but he feared for his own life. Lifting Tomudo onto his shoulder he set out for the village as fast as his burden allowed.

Batu heard the commotion and ran with the others to the swiftly gathering crowd. As she pulled up to the crowd they parted and she saw Tomudo slung across Tiru's shoulder like a slain animal.

Batu screamed and threw herself on Tomudo's body. Moans escaped her as she sobbed.

Szatu arrived and burst into tears. She rushed to the sobbing Batu and held her.

Szatu pleaded, "What happened?"

Sorrow and fatigue showed on Tiru's face and in his voice. "I was returning from checking my snares and saw Tomudo fall. I rushed to him and saw a serpent had bitten him. I checked for a heartbeat, but I could not find one. I hoped Taja could find one and save him so I rushed him here."

Batu kept stroking Tomudo's body and whimpering.

"Please, let us take him to Batu's hut," instructed Szatu.

Tiru shifted Tomudo and was about to carry him in his arms when Motum collected him in his own to relieve the exhausted Tiru.

The crowd accompanied them as Szatu supported Batu to her hut.

Motum laid Tomudo's body on the sleeping mat.

From the entrance Tiru apologized. "I am sorry I could not do more, Batu."

Whimpering, she could do nothing but nod her head in reply.

Motum and Tiru retreated leaving Batu with Szatu.

Dropping to her knees, Batu cradled the body of the man she loved. He had been her lover, her mentor, her hope, and her trust in the future. It all disappeared in a moment. The tears falling from her face were caught by the face of the man she had grown to love and depend on so deeply for understanding. Now he was gone. Only his body remained and that too would be gone soon. Grief clutched at her heart so painfully she doubled over onto his stilled form.

Dimly she heard a voice, "Batu. It is Taja. May I enter?"

Almost inaudibly she said, "Yes."

He entered, nodded to Szatu, and dropped to his knees next to Batu. "I have come to see if Tomudo has left his body. May I?"

Unable to speak she released her hold and laid his body down. Taja bent his head to Tomudo's chest. Placing his ear upon it, he listened for a breath. He then checked for a pulse at the inside of his upper arm and then at his neck. His fingers could detect no signs of blood coursing through Tomudo's veins. He lifted his eyelid and carefully watched for a reaction to the light.

When none came he closed it.

He sat down next to Tomudo's body, closed his eyes and remained motionless for a long period. Finally, he turned to Batu mournfully saying, "I am sorry, Batu, he has gone to the Land of No Shadows."

Only her sobs acknowledged his statement. They punctuated the silence and racked her body.

Unable to restore the body to life, the Talker Healer embraced her bent body. Emotions blurred the rest of the cycle for Batu. Vaguely she remembered Taja leaving. Her parents sat by her side as a steady flow of people came to pay their respects. The shock she sustained prevented her from any sustained conversation with those who came.

When the last of them left she collapsed beside the body of the man she loved. She draped her arms around him in death as she had in life.

Early the next cycle, as the Great Sun cleared the horizon, the council members gathered at Mihili's hut. They talked about Tomudo, heaping praise on the memory of their departed friend. When the Great Sun reached the quarter point in the sky, they reluctantly got up and made their way to Batu's hut. Neda carried the burial stretcher that he had constructed. Tradition dictated that the council members carry the body of one of its deceased members to the edge of the running water.

Arriving at Batu's hut, the council members found Aahi and Szatu outside. A huge gathering of villagers waited nearby. Mihili announced himself and Batu came out of the hut for the first time since Tomudo's death. The men of the council went inside and placed his body on the stretcher, and hoisted it on their shoulders.

Outside, Baruh raised her beautiful voice in song. It lamented the departure of one loved by all. Because of the quality of her voice she initiated many of the songs the villagers sang at tribal functions. The rest of the people in the procession picked up the song at the chorus filling the air with their voices. Exiting the hut, Batu and the bearers of Tomudo's body began their slow journey to the water's edge. Szatu and Aahi followed closely behind with the villagers behind them. The songs of mourning and praise continued until they reached the edge of the running water.

Reaching the burial site, the council set the stretcher with Tomudo's body on the ground at the feet of the High Priest. The High Priest climbed atop a large rock jutting out of the ground and raised his hands to the Great Sun. The soft murmur of the huge crowd quieted. His voice boomed over the hushed throng. "It is with sadness that we gather at this sacred spot to send one of our tribe to the Land of No Shadows. We pray that his journey is safe. We pray that he will defeat the evil ones he may encounter, and not be their victim. We pray that in his afterlife travels he not be torn apart or devoured by the wild ones or be trapped in the eternal fires.

"Tomudo's death starkly reminds us that we all must perish and face these perils. Keep in mind that you do not know when you will be taken away by the gods.

"Tomudo served his people well. Honors were heaped upon him in this life and he will surely attain them as a dweller. I pray that the gods recognize this honorable man in his journeys. May he become a benefactor for us and intercede for the Kahali people with all of the gods and goddesses."

Clearing his throat, he raised his voice in song. The lyrics foretold of conflicts and dangers encountered at the moment of death and in the life lived as a dweller in the Land of No Shadows. Finishing, he motioned to Baruh. She sang another song telling of the hopes and aspirations of those that have succumbed to death. Again, the villagers joined her at the chorus.

As the song ended the High Priest got down from the rock, picked up his skull-tipped staff and moved to Tomudo's body. He tapped the body on the feet, the hands and the head, saying as he did, "May your feet carry you away from evil, your hands fend off any who may cause you harm and your mind be used wisely to gain favor with the gods."

Nodding to the council members, he stepped aside to give them room to send the body to its final resting place.

Internally Romir gloated. That vile, contemptible Batu got what she deserved! The gods struck their righteous blows once again. Although slow the gods were sure in their action. He felt a twinge of shame that he doubted the gods.

The High Priest looked at the huge gathering of people. It would be this way when the moment came of her banishment. There would be many eager to see her expulsion. No one would take more pleasure in her despair than he.

He smiled at the mental image he had of seeing her walking away from the village to a certain death. Catching himself, he quickly altered his face to a grimace, lest the villagers should misunderstand. How fortunate, he thought, that he had not taken any action to punish her and place himself in jeopardy.

The council members picked up the stretcher and waded into the water. The men began to sing a mournful song telling of the loss of a brave and respected member of the tribe. The women sang the chorus throughout the song in counter melody to the men. At the conclusion of the song they released the stretcher. The current caught the stretcher and swept Tomudo's body to its final resting place down stream.

Batu's eyes fixed upon the body of her beloved. Slowly, it drifted into the center of the flowing water. Despite knowing better she expected him to sit up and slide off the raft and swim to the shore. In midstream the swifter current took it out of sight. People filed past Batu and expressed their condolences. She was only vaguely aware of the many sympathetic friends and relatives who spoke to her. Most of them came praising Tomudo and the tribe's loss of a great man. Only a few spoke of her suffering and loss.

The procession of faces ended. Only her parents remained with her at the water's edge. After reassuring them she would be all right, she asked them to leave her alone. Reluctantly they complied with her wish and made their way back to the village.

She watched them walk away, recalling Tomudo saying he envisioned Mother Earth forever giving birth and forever taking life. Each death had to happen to give way to a new life and new hope. She had great reservations with that philosophy.

Batu sat down at the water's edge, looking downstream wondering which predator would be feasting on the body she held so often to her breast. The thought of some creature feeding on his body repulsed her. Falling to her knees, her stomach expelled its food-less contents. Wiping her mouth she screamed, the piercing sound scattered a small covey of birds in a nearby bush.

The High Priest heard the scream as well. He had made his way upstream waiting for the right moment to return and chastise Batu. He had been watching her behind the safety of a growth of bushes. Standing up, he walked to Batu. Hearing the soft footsteps on the ground, she looked up. The devastation on her face told the story of her pain. Pleased at seeing her pain, Romir smiled.

"What do you want, Romir?"

"I have come to tell you the gods are indeed happy," he said sarcastically.

"Then your gods are just like you. They have no heart," she shot back at him.

"You know nothing of the gods, Batu. You have never shown them respect, and now, they are having their revenge. I find that very fitting. To make things more perfect, you are now vulnerable to banishment, because you have not born a child. The Kahali law will not protect you. The only thing that disappoints me is that you are not still cursed by the ugly scales and swelling. I am sorry to see that only your scars remain to make you ugly. You deserve to look even more grotesque than you do. Perhaps the gods will again inflict you in the future."

"You are disgusting. Once again you have proved how rotten you are. At my greatest moment of suffering, you choose to remind me that I am vulnerable. You have driven your hatred deep into my heart. I do not have to stand here and listen to your twisted mind," Batu said quietly. She had no strength to do verbal combat with him. Emotionally drained all she could do was retreat from him. She turned and walked slowly away.

The High Priest called after her smugly, "Whether you realize it or not Batu, you are in quicksand. All I have to do now is wait until the rains come and you will disappear under it."

As she made her way to her hut, Mother Nature's mantle of darkness had already begun to obscure the colors so boldly displayed in the light. The High Priest's words gnawed at her senses and rang in her ears, as she walked. Tears clouded her vision. She had no way to combat him, especially in this sorrowful moment. It took all of her effort to keep from falling to the ground and sobbing. The emptiness in her heart and the searing loneliness magnified the unbearable pain weighing upon her.

It seemed an eternity before she got to her hut and lay down. With great effort, she concentrated on Tomudo. Since discovering the meaning of her dream, his mere nearness had been exciting and comforting. Silently, she thanked him for sharing so much of himself with her and for conveying his love in so many endearing ways. A quiet look, a simple touch and the tone in his voice all sent her the message – he loved her. Even when they were locked in their disagreement, Tomudo had comforted her. During the period when they were disagreeing, she had been stupid for brushing away his arms. How totally unwise she had been to set her vain feelings ahead of his desire for fulfillment as a father. During their period of abstinence, he sought to embrace and comfort her, but she would have none of it. How utterly foolish she had been. Slowly, her arms reflexively encircled her own body, as if the act of doing so could heighten the memory of his embrace and make up for her mistakes.

However brief their moments together were, she felt certain she had loved him even when she did not profess it. When did she first begin to love him? she wondered. Did it happen during the visits he had made to her parents hut, or did it occur while she sat listening to him at the story sessions as a youth?

Looking back upon those moments, she recalled how deeply he had impressed her. She respected him not only for his position and intelligence, but also because of his demeanor and attitude toward her. Now all she had were memories of her moments with him. Closing her eyes, she hoped for sleep and dreams of Tomudo.

Batu sat underneath Tomudo's favorite tree. For the last two cycles, Batu, in addition to thinking of her desperate position, could not get the High Priest's words out of her mind. She could not understand how he could be so horrible and say what he did after the loss of her man. He had not one bit of compassion in his heart. Before that incident, she thought that he might have some redeeming qualities that she may have not known about. Surely a High Priest had some goodness in him. Now she had to question even that assumption. If he did have a spark of compassion, how could he attack her in her moment of sorrow? No one with any compassion would attack someone who just lost his or her mate. There was no other conclusion that she could come to except that he was indescribably evil and had no redeeming qualities. The fact that he could say what he did brought forth a rising anger in the pit of her stomach. Somehow she had to expose him. The village had to know of his dark side. How could she accomplish it? Could gossip bring him down? She answered her own question by admitting it seemed most unlikely. She needed to speak to someone who was wise in the way of relations that had some authority. With Tomudo dead the only person she trusted was the Talker Healer. He had the wisdom, courage and stature in the tribe to deal with Romir. She rose, committing her body to move toward Taja's hut. Certainly, he would help her, after she told him her story.

Having not found Taja in his hut, Batu began questioning people in the village center to his whereabouts. One of the women told her he was still meditating near the running water. Deciding that her problem was more important than his meditation, she headed for the running water. Arriving at his place of prayer, she sat down opposite him. She waited a moment, when he did not open his eyes she spoke his name. As his eyes opened, she noted the far off look in them.

"Batu, what brings you here?"

"I have been angered by the High Priest."

Taja had felt the anger when she spoke his name. He did not reply but lifted his eyebrows in question.

"It happened at Tomudo's burial. Everyone left me to my sorrow at the running water. Some moments later Romir appeared and proceeded to inform me that the gods have taken their revenge on me and that I would soon be banished. How loathsome! At my weakest moment he came to gloat." The anger she bore in her stomach now etched her face. "How could anyone be so inhumane?"

"Anger drives people to do horrible things," Taja answered.

"He has to be exposed for the contemptible person that he is. I cannot let him do this to anyone else."

Taja's brow furrowed as he spoke, "Is it others you are worried about or your own injury?"

"What do you mean?"

"I am asking you to examine yourself. You must know why you are doing things. If you do not, then how are you able to know yourself? You cannot go on deceiving yourself."

Batu's eyes grew wary as she weighed his words. After a long introspective silence she replied, "You are right. I am eliciting your help to prevent the High Priest from doing it to me again because I am angry, and I am suffering. Can you help me?"

"In all honesty, I am not certain what I can do. It is true he spoke to you at an inappropriate moment, but as the High Priest he can warn you about actions and speech that run contrary to the Kahali religious philosophy. All I can do is to speak to him about his terrible insensitivity. I will gladly do that."

With a look of anguish, Batu asked, "Is that all you can do? You cannot silence him?"

The Talker Healer's face spoke his reply.

Batu's eyes flared as she asked, "How can someone so horrible be the High Priest?"

"Having attained any position in life does not guarantee that a person is ethical and honorable. Unfortunately, the High Priest is controlled by his hidden demons like so many of us," Taja answered.

"If I understand you correctly, one of his obvious demons is his anger," Batu interjected.

The Talker Healer nodded affirmatively, then said, "And you have that same demon in relationship to Romir."

Her eyes narrowed as she searched his face and let her body speak to her in order to see if he was trying to hurt her. Nothing she saw or felt led her to believe other than he was attempting to help her. She let the statement sink in. Examining how she felt about the High Priest, she conceded Taja's statement was true and gave a slight nod of agreement. The anger showing on Batu's face a moment ago now showed frustration and sadness. "Why must life be so hard to bear?" She slowly shook her head. "Why must pain be a part of our lives?"

Taja reached over and took her hand. "Our very existence on Mother Earth petitions sadness. One has to simply look at what takes place on the plains. There are predators everywhere. On the plains the animals that are weak, young and old lose their lives every cycle. The pain of death and injury is part of their lives. We must contend with it the same as they, but in addition we also injure each other in our relationships by our words and actions. Our lives are much more complicated because of our intelligence."

Batu interrupted him. "With our intelligence you would think we would not injure each other."

Taja cocked his head and answered, "Intelligence does not always provide what we need to make the correct choice of words or action. Intelligence must be yoked with love to give us wisdom. Many times wisdom is brought about through pain of death and in the suffering brought about in a relationship and the emotions experienced from it."

A quizzical look formed on Taja face. "After listening to my words, do you still want me to speak to Romir for you?"

Suddenly dejected, she said, "No. It seems I have my own demons to conquer." She rose abruptly, ending their talk.

They embraced briefly and Taja said, "Please come whenever you need to talk or face your demons."

She looked into his eyes but said nothing.

Back in her hut, she collapsed on her mat, in sheer exhaustion. The meeting was not satisfying to her. The expectations she had were not realized and left her fatigued. It had drained her spirit. She closed her eyes thinking how hostile her environment had become since the death of her man. With her arms clutched around her body, she fell into a fitful sleep.

Batu found the cycles following Tomudo's death tortuously filled with tears and loneliness. On the fifth cycle after his death she awoke and stretched her arm out to touch Tomudo. Startled at not feeling him there, she bolted to a seated position, only to remember his passing. The fear of an uncertain future gripped her. It trampled the prospects of any happiness from her life. Her thoughts raced in a dreadful, descending spiral of an ever-darkening nature. She threw herself on the mat sobbing. Clenching her teeth, she muffled a scream of distress.

Eventually, Batu's thoughts revolved around her defenseless position. Without a man, she was utterly vulnerable to the law of expulsion. She knew the law well. Clear and decisive, it stated a woman in union who lost her man to death and did not have a child would be expelled at the first rain.

The last woman to be banished from the village had been Nehti. It had happened six seasons ago, yet it emerged instantly in her mind. She had only spoken to Nehti on those rare occasions when they bathed near each other. Laughter seemed to be her forte in life. With Nehti around it seemed as if everyone laughed more. In spite of being so well liked, no one helped her. Her only fault lay in the fact she did not have a babe before her man died. For that, she was cast out of the village, as if she had no worth whatsoever. She recalled how Nehti screamed at the council, while the tears streamed down her face. Her usually happy face set distorted by fear and hatred. She remembered searching the faces of the council. Tomudo's face showed the sorrow he felt for Nehti. The face of the Talker Healer appeared on the verge of crying. Tomudo's face showed distress. The faces of the other council members and the High Priest did not bear such deep emotion.

The law seemed totally archaic. Casting a woman out of the tribe because of food shortage was insane. Surely, they could have divided the food so that the woman could live. During her life, she could remember only one season when the draught had nearly dried up the running water. During that period, the small herds of animals and predators competed with the village for the water in the deeper pools. The warriors had to constantly patrol the area to keep a safe perimeter around the village, but an animal in her memory had killed no one, and no one starved to death. The council should reserve such severe action to violent crimes. The stupidity of the law was conspicuous. It seemed incomprehensible that a reasoning council would allow such a law to remain in force. Game was abundant. The fruit, roots, nuts and leafy plants were always plentiful. The running water contained an ample supply of scaled swimmers. No one ever went hungry.

Ultimately, it mattered little what she thought. Without a man doom sat in her lap. She would have to leave the village and the two people she loved. Leaving her mother and father would be another form of death. She would never see them or be able to talk to them or to be able to feel their love. Each of them would be alive but in all reality each would be dead to her upon being expelled.

Her thoughts drifted to what she would experience upon being cast out.

In what revolting manner would she die? She hoped death would not be in the jaws of some growler. Shuddering from the very thought, she instinctively rubbed her arms hoping the end would not come so gruesomely. Perhaps the best way would be to be bitten by a serpent like Tomudo. It would be fast. It had been for Tomudo. The suffering would be brief. Closing her eyes, a vision of his body flashed in her mind as the current caught the raft sending him floating quickly downstream. Surely the running water would be the quickest way to end her life. If she walked out as far as she could, expelled the air from her lungs, then submerged herself in the running water, her body would be swept downstream and through some quirk of fate might end up next to his body. That seemed the most sensible way to die. The struggle would be brief. There would be very little pain and she would be taking her own life, not subjecting herself to the gory ordeal of death by some beast. It was settled. If she could not find a solution to keep from being banished, she would end her life in that manner. She would wait until the very last possible moment before her expulsion. In that way she, not the council, would control the moment of her death. Shaking her head, she knew that ultimately her feelings would determine what she actually did.

Her thoughts continued to dwell upon death. Death held many fears for her. The Land of No Shadows always held a great many uncertainties. She hoped Tomudo would be there to meet her. The whole realm of the dead seemed mired in mystery. The High Priest never spoke of how one looks in the Land of No Shadows. The High Priest's warning of the evil ones ran through her mind. Did they torment everyone who became a dweller? She could recall nothing said about whether food was provided, or if it was at all necessary to eat. Everything about the realm seemed so vague. The High Priest never explained things. He only made threats and cast fear into the people causing a great deal of apprehension about the afterlife. Their religion should have prepared them for such a momentous journey. She recalled that the Talker Healer spoke to the dwellers. He seemed the most likely to know what existed in that mysterious land. She would have to speak to him about it.

Waving her hand, she tried to drive the gloomy thoughts from her head. Grudgingly she admitted to herself that she savored living even if it would be without Tomudo. Nehti obviously savored life. If she had not, she would not have screamed at the council. She, like Nehti, feared death, yet if at all possible she hoped her intellect would prevail to extricate her from her situation. She would not let terror paralyze her into just screaming or crying.

She would do something to help herself before that moment.

The insufferable law! The injustice angered her. Not only did she lose her man, she would have to face the humiliation, anguish and terror of being banished by her own people. Law or no law, she would not capitulate to such a decision without fighting it. Ultimately, the best way to fight it would be to gather her resources and determine what she could do to save herself. Throughout her life she had fought to achieve what she desired and had won. That same determination would now have to serve her in saving her life. The High Priest would not stand and gloat at her banishment for there would be none.

CHAPTER
THIRTEEN

Coloma walked across the village center and made his way toward Batu. He spotted her sitting on her bench. He halted in front of her looking uneasy.

Shading her eyes, she peered up at him from the bench. "I have come to tell you how very sorry I am about Tomudo's death."

Her mouth made an attempt at a smile and failed. "I am glad you came. I know you regret his passing."

"That is true, but at the burial I saw how mournful you were and it seemed as if you did not know who all spoke to you."

His insightful assessment surprised her.

His hand touched her shoulder. "If I can help you please let me know."

Surprised at his offer, she said, "Thank you. Other than my father, no man has offered anything to me. I am not sure what I need or what I should do. I'm still numb from the loss."

"If it helps you, I miss him a great deal. He not only was my teacher but my friend."

"Tomudo also spoke of you as a friend, Coloma."

"I cannot tell you how proud he made me when he selected me as his apprentice." Coloma quit speaking and poked at the loose ground in front of him with his foot. "I feel lost without him. I do not think I am ready to be making decisions as a council member."

"You will do fine. For a while you may have to try to imagine what Tomudo would have done in the situations you are faced with. Later, with experience, you will feel comfortable in your role."

"Thank you. Your words are a comfort to me, Batu."

"And your appearance is a comfort to me."

A quiet settled between them. Leaning forward, Coloma placed his hand on Batu's shoulder again in friendship.

Batu patted his hand. "Thank you."

As Coloma disappeared down the avenue to his hut, Batu remembered Tomudo had not been able to teach Coloma the stories concerning the tribe's rituals before he died. A glimmer of hope arose within her. Without them the tribe would suffer intrinsically. The foundation for all tribal activities rested in the oral transmission of the stories from one generation to the next. While the ritual and legends were not the most important stories, they were needed. Their heritage depended upon them. If the integrity of the rituals were not present, the council would be seriously handicapped in their ability to act clearly and concisely. They would be unable to make proper decisions, if they did not know the exact wording of the rituals. Without the exact performance, like the traditional ritual of the first hunt, the hunt itself might end in disaster.

She had to think things through. A mistake could be fatal. If she approached the council correctly, she might obtain immunity from expulsion. Her position had merit. At the very least the council would grant her a reprieve from the law to teach Coloma. It would take this sunny season, the rainy season and the next season of sun for him to learn the stories. The advantage belonged to her. She would wait until just before the rains to make the announcement of her proposal. There was no hurry. The longer she waited the more it benefited her position. Searching her mind, she could see no way they could force her to teach him without making concessions to her. If they did not allow her to remain in the village, she would not instruct him. Short of torture they had no leverage over her.

The instinct to live kept her mind searching for solutions of survival. Slowly, she mulled over the alternative to capture Coloma's heart. He had shown interest in her physically. When he had just left he even placed his hands twice upon her shoulders in a sign of compassion and friendship. If necessary she could enchant or even beguile him. He would become a man in another season and she could be united with him then. He seemed reasonable and intelligent and his youth would contribute to his pliability and her success.

Batu closed her eyes and let the softness of dusk engulf her. The Talker Healer's face took form in her mind. The scene of Nehti's banishment accompanied it. Surprised at the intrusion, she drove it from her mind, only to have it reappear. Her attention focused on Taja's face, as he watched Nehti. Tears streamed from his eyes and cascaded down his cheeks. This was not the way she remembered it to have happened. She had never seen Taja crying. She watched in fascination. Try as she might she could not recollect having ever seen a man crying in her dreams or visions.

The vision slowly faded, not so her interest in Taja. She seemed drawn to him. The mystery that shrouded him fascinated her. Conceivably her interest in him may have come about because he was the only man, other than her father, who looked at her without desire in his eyes. Her mind kept rummaging through her relationship with Tomudo and Taja, one man a memory, the other a mystery. Tired and frustrated she turned over on her side and finally succumbed to sleep.

Several cycles later, while Batu wove a new hemp rope, Neda, of the council appeared at her hut surprising her.

"Batu, I have come to request your presence before the council."

"Why do they want me to come?"

"You will be told when you are before the council," he said unwilling to discuss the reason.

Setting the unfinished rope aside, she accompanied him to the council hut. The usual greetings were offered. She sat down on an empty mat and caught Coloma looking uncomfortably at her.

Mihili spoke. "Batu, we thank you for coming. We want to speak to you of an urgent matter. We have waited for an appropriate moment since the death of Tomudo to speak to you. His unexpected death has left the tribe, and us, in an awkward position. Coloma's instructions were not completed before Tomudo left for the Land of No Shadows. Tomudo informed us only a few cycles before his death that you have accomplished the seemingly impossible task of learning all of the stories. We are asking you to complete the task of teaching Coloma the stories he does not know."

So they knew, she thought looking at each member. "It is true I have learned all of the stories."

Mihili nodded in recognition of her statement. "Good. We would like you to begin teaching Coloma as soon as this meeting is over," he said presumptuously.

"I must tell you that at the pace Coloma learns, it will take this season, the season of rain and the next sunny season to teach him the stories he does not know," she said confidently.

Mihili was taken back by the information.

He turned to Coloma. "Is this true?"

"I am not sure. Only Batu knows how many stories are in the ritual collection," he admitted. His eyes dropped to the ground.

Mihili never anticipated it would take so long. How would the council reconcile the fact she would likely be banished at the conclusion of the season of blue skies with the fact that Coloma would not know all of the stories by then?

As Mihili pondered the problem, Neda moved his hand over the ground. Mihili absently nodded approval for him to speak.

"We must have Coloma learn all of the stories before the rains come. We cannot risk you not teaching him everything before your banishment. He will have to be instructed for longer periods and more often. If necessary he will come to your hut after each meal for instruction."

Neda's show of wisdom surprised Mihili. The suggestion was the most significant and intelligent contribution Neda had ever made.

Wiping the ground in front of him, Mihili praised him. "Neda has spoken with wisdom. If none from the council objects, we will vote upon it."

No one wiped the sand to speak.

The votes were cast, the decision approved. Only Taja dissented.

Mihili looked at Batu. "As you saw we are in accord. Batu, it is our position to have you instruct Coloma as we have prescribed. You are to teach him all of the stories he does not know before the rainy season."

"Have I nothing to say in this matter?" Batu asked.

"What do you mean?" asked Mihili.

"If I instruct Coloma, what will you do for me in return? Will you spare my life?"

Mihili answered, "We cannot do that. It is against the law."

Countering, Batu said, "This is my life we are discussing. I think concessions are in order. I feel we can all benefit. I will agree to teach Coloma, at the pace Tomudo taught him. At that pace perhaps some man would come forward and claim me as his woman."

"That is unacceptable. You heard how we voted," responded Mihili.

"Of course I heard it," she snapped at him. "I am trying to strike a bargain for my life. Now, if I consent to your proposal, what will you do to save my life?"

Neda took the initiative. "For your assistance I am sure we can give you a supply of food, water and some weapons to take with you when you are banished."

Anger flared in Batu. "What? You offer food and weapons when I seek my life? Does not that sound ludicrous? What I want is a reprieve!"

Neda regretted his stupid remark and remained silent.

Motum broke the silence. "We cannot give you an extension, but I will make a long knife and a spear for you," he said earnestly.

"I want a reprieve, Motum."

"I cannot do that."

"Why not?"

"You know why, Batu."

"I want you to tell me, Motum."

He replied softly, "It is against the law."

"You, like Neda, offer me little. A man who is dying of thirst is not interested in a weapon."

Motum looked away from Batu's unrelenting glare.

"The law is clear, Batu. We will not oppose it, nor will we tolerate any opposition to it," answered Mihili.

"So, you want me to instruct Coloma, yet you will not even bend the law, so I would have the slightest chance to survive?"

Mihili said, "We are sorry, Batu."

"Let me take another approach. If I do teach Coloma, would you consider something else in return?"

"It depends on what the consideration is," answered Mihili.

"I want you to alter the law to save me," she said defiantly.

"We cannot do that, Batu," Mihili said exasperated.

With her life at stake she was not willing to relent to him. "You do not speak for the others. I wish to hear from them on this matter."

Perturbed, Mihili saw the determination in her face. He sighed. Placating her he commanded the others, "Let each of us speak our mind on this and vote."

The honor of speaking first went to Mihili, the Elder. "I say we do not need to change or to add another law." Stating his vote first he felt confident the others would stand with him and against her.

Motum stared at the ground. "I say no change."

Neda glanced at the others and then at Batu. "I also say no."

Coloma looked at Batu. His eyes pleaded for her to understand his predicament. He did not want to offend the other men. In spite of his deep affection for Batu he capitulated. "I must regretfully say no as well."

Everyone looked at Taja. He spoke directly to Batu. "No one is above the law. It allows us to live in peace and it guides us through difficult moments. When a law is unjust, it must be amended. The law of banishment is unjust, not only for Batu, but also for all women. We must change the law now." His eyes still clung to Batu's.

Although surprised at Taja's stand, it did not shock Mihili. Taja always seemed to be aligned with the troubled and misguided. The count, although not unanimous, still clearly dictated they were to do nothing.

148

Mihili turned to face Batu and said, "We have voted and we decline to alter the law, Batu."

Glaring at the men who opposed alteration of the law, she lashed out at them. "It is amazing how five men can survive with but one heart. If you, Mihili, were in my position, what would your position be on this vote? Would you think the law to be grossly unjust? It is obvious to me the tribe enacted the law when we had a great lack of food and compassion in our tribe. We have not experienced hunger in my lifetime. What we still lack is compassion. Everything here is in abundance except wisdom.

"Not long ago you honored me in front of our people and now you are going to expel me. The very thing you honored me for is what will preserve the integrity of our stories. Does that not strike you as ironic? Have I changed so much that you would do this despicable thing? Am I a threat to you?

"It would be certain death for me to be banished from the village. I also find it strange that you, Motum, and the other brave warriors have vowed to protect our people to the death, yet you will allow me to wander off and fend for myself against whatever beasts I may encounter. You, Motum, do not know the meaning of the word warrior."

Hanging his head and avoiding her glaring eyes, Motum did not say a word in his defense.

"The laws are made to protect the people. I am one of the tribe. I am no threat to the tribe. You do not need to destroy me, Motum. I am not an enemy. If you lose sight of that fact you lose sight of what it means to be a warrior. What you are doing to me is deplorable. No one with a conscience would do it. Would any of you do it to one of your own creations?"

No one answered.

"You disgust me!" she said continuing her tirade. "Since you have not dealt with me compassionately, I will deal with you in the same manner. I will not instruct Coloma."

Anger and pride vibrated in every sentence she fired at them. Her words scorched the men who opposed her. Mihili and Neda's faces were gorged with blood from the anger her words had created in them. Motum's face reddened from shame. Coloma's face hung dejectedly. He looked away from Batu. She looked at the Talker Healer. Taja sat as he did before, but his eyes reflected admiration.

Furious, she rose and left the meeting without uttering a departing salutation. As she walked angrily back to her hut, she asked herself how she could have thought they would choose to save her. Only Taja had stood beside her. None but he had a backbone to hold their bodies upright. He at least had the courage and compassion to change the law. He alone seemed to be able to sense the injustice of the law.

Just thinking of him, she felt warmth come over her body. His eyes continued to haunt her. She recalled having the same impression the last time they met when she was ill. Being a healer had obviously contributed to his sensitivity. She wondered why he kept to himself. Was he as misunderstood as she? While she and Tomudo were at their favorite tree, she had often seen him walking to the next grove of trees that bordered the running water.

As she let her mind roam freely, she recalled the vision she had of the Talker Healer with the tears flowing down his face. Perhaps he, with his ability to talk to the dwellers in the Land of No Shadows, would be able to answer her questions concerning death. She fixed it in her mind to pry from him everything she could about the afterlife experience. Hopefully, he would consent to speak to her.

In the darkness of that same cycle, Batu awoke from a dream as vivid as the recurring dream she had before her illness. In it Tomudo, Coloma and she were in her hut. Tomudo was instructing Coloma as he had so often while he lived. Abruptly stopping his instruction, he looked at her. Rising, he moved to her side. Taking her by the hands, he helped her up and guided her to his mat. He sat her down and moved to the spot where she usually sat. The dream ended with him looking at her expectantly.

The implication of the dream disturbed Batu. The dream laden with few symbols and free from complication drove the message home. The intention seemed all too clear. Tomudo wanted her to instruct Coloma. What she could not understand was how he could want her to do it after the council rebuked her. They offered her nothing for what she would do for the village and them. Yet in her dream, her man wished her to teach Coloma the stories with no benefit to herself.

Why?

CHAPTER
FOURTEEN

The crushing blow of refusal by the council to consider her counter proposal to teach Coloma, in return for a delay in her banishment, slowly took its toll on Batu. The fear of death seeped deep within her, crowding out hope. The indomitable spirit she had displayed so often waned under the weight of a growing depression. Her decisive nature fell victim to indifference. Nothing seemed to be of any importance. Attempting to rid the ghastly thoughts of her impending death became futile.

Unable to darken the lives of her friends with her feelings, she abandoned them. For a while, Batu continued to seek the comfort and companionship of her parents in an effort to free herself from the murky thoughts that closed in on her. Despite the efforts to keep focused, her mind wandered while engaged in conversation. Death spoke louder and sat nearer than anyone and drew attention away from everyone else. Often, she sat sullen and distant. Unable to help in any other way, Aahi and Szatu would sit next to her holding her hand or placing an arm around her in hopes that their touch comforted her.

The sky had lost its brilliance for Batu; the earth no longer seemed lush. The running water she bathed in seemed more like a muddy tide-pool than a cool, lustrous, shimmering, aspect of Mother Earth. Nothing appeared vivid to her. The earth seemed to be collapsing on her. Every cycle found her staying on her sleeping mat longer and longer. Only in the solace of sleep and imagination could she escape the disastrous thoughts of waking consciousness.

The dismal cycles wore on. Batu stopped taking deep breaths for fear she would smell the approaching rain still many cycles away. Even in sleep she could not escape her fears. Her dreams were cluttered with dark woods, empty, destroyed huts and violent storms. Horrible scenes of hyenas tearing her body apart tormented her closed eyelids.

Darkness crept into Batu's life choking out the light. The sanctity of their tree and the bright open plains Tomudo and she had frequented so often could not release her from the pervasive dark shroud.

Batu lay upon her mat staring into space. The Great Sun neared the quarter mark. She had yet to rise when she heard her father call out, "Batu? Are you in there?"

She rose slowly. "Yes."

Seeing the condition of her eyes, Aahi asked, "Have you not risen?"

"No," she mumbled.

"This must stop my child. You must keep active to keep your mind off of what is to come," he advised.

With an empty look, Batu replied, "I have tried, Father."

Wiping his forehead with the back of his hand, Aahi stared at his creation. He had often lain awake imagining what was going on in her mind. Fear cropped into his mind most often. Anger ran closely behind. He cursed the council for its inflexibility.

Aahi looked sadly at his child. How could the Kahali people honor Batu just last season and allow her to be ejected from their midst this season? Why has no one rallied behind her? He shook his head as much in reaction to Batu's words as his thoughts.

"You cannot do this to yourself, Batu. You are killing yourself even before they cast you out. You have fought all your life. No one ever defeated you. Do not let them defeat you now," Aahi pleaded.

"I am unable to help myself, Father."

Aahi's voice rose. "That is not true! You have always done so. This time should be no different."

"It is. I pleaded and employed my best reasoning upon the council. It accomplished nothing."

"I know that, my child. What I speak of is how you are approaching your death. You are not fighting to stay alive. You have conceded to death."

"What can I do?" she asked helplessly.

Aahi shrugged his shoulder bleakly. "I do not know. Maybe Taja knows." Finding the suggestion encouraging he urged her, "Yes, see Taja."

"What good can he do? He is only one against four on the council."

"I am not talking about the council. Maybe he can help you fight the darkness that is oppressing you."

Although she sat silent, her eyes became alert.

"Did he not help you when you were ill?" Aahi asked her.

"He did," she admitted.

"Promise me you will see him before the Great Sun sets," Aahi insisted.

Shaking her head affirmatively, she closed her tired eyes.

"Good." Pleased his talk with her had accomplished something, Aahi smiled tentatively. Closing the distance between them, he wrapped his arms around her and placed a kiss upon her cheek.

Without fervor she returned it.

Aahi felt her lips on his cheeks and patted her back and released her. "I will tell Mother you send her your love," knowing if she were at all well she would have said it herself.

"Thank you."

Leaning against the entrance, Batu watched her father cross the village center to report what transpired between them to her mother.

Sighing heavily, Batu turned and looked at the small collection of fruits, dried meat and tubers on the shelf. Nothing appealed to her, little had of late. Crossing the hut, she removed the drinking bowl and drank deeply from it. She set it back and walked outside the hut and stared in the direction of the Talker Healer's hut. Sitting on the bench she deliberated whether or not to see Taja. The promise to her father set her into motion. She rose and walked slowly toward Taja's hut.

After greeting each other Taja extended his hands to Batu, and invited her in. She accepted his hands without thinking. He guided her to a mat and sat opposite her.

"How may I help you?" he asked softly.

"Father suggested I come," she explained apologetically.

He moved his head in recognition of her statement.

"Father is worried about me," she offered.

"And are you worried about yourself?"

Pausing to think a moment, she answered, "Yes."

"It is easy to understand why. You are immersed in tragedy," he observed.

"Yes. Yes I am."

Batu sat quietly looking at the man. His compassionate gaze made her feel relaxed. She recalled the last time she had felt it when she had been ill.

"How does that feel?" he asked.

Unable to make sense of his question she asked, "How does what feel?"

"How does it feel to be immersed in such tragic affairs?"

"Horrible!" she blurted.

His eyebrows lifted asking a silent question.

Surprised at her loud reply, she examined the feelings behind the words. "Oh god, it is horrible."

When she stopped, he urged her, "Go on."

"I feel horribly alone," she said quietly.

His eyebrows lifted again.

"There has always been someone near me," she confided. "Now I am alone, totally alone. I lost my man and I am alone. I am frightened. My mother and father are still here, but they are not living with me. I am separated from them. I took a man and I separated from them, and he left me."

Batu's emotions welled up. A sob caught in her throat. Her eyes left Taja's. "He is gone... My man is gone... I loved him, and he is gone."

With a sudden burst of anger, Batu shouted, "He left me vulnerable. Vulnerable!"

Her face twisted with emotion. Tears sprang from her eyes. She turned away from his gentle eyes. When she turned back, her eyes were fatigued with fear.

"I am scared," she said in a small voice.

Taja felt the infectious emotions coming from Batu. Moving closer, he placed his hands over hers.

"I never thought about Tomudo dying," she volunteered. "Even when he spoke of wanting to see his child before he died, I never did. It took the illness to make me realize how he lit up my life. Now, with him gone, the light is vanishing. Each passing cycle diminishes the light. It is as if I am being sucked deep into a cave. I am unable to escape from it. It reaches out and envelops me. I am slipping deeper and deeper into it. I am afraid if I remain in this darkness I will lose myself, and I will not be able to find a way out of this abyss."

Her tears rolled down her face and landed upon her breasts.

"I cannot talk with people. I am unable to think about anything except death and how I will die... My sleep is troubled by ghastly dreams... I hate my waking moments and I am fearful of sleeping."

Shaking her head, she moaned, "Oh Great Sun! This hurts."

As if to verify her troubled state, she exclaimed, "I have stopped eating."

Her eyes pleaded for him to help her, while tears streamed from them. "Am I trying to hasten my death?"

He moved next to her and embraced her. She clung to him sobbing and weeping. Only when the last tear fell did she pull away from him.

"Can you help me?"

His gaze penetrated her. A moment passed before he spoke. "Only if you are brave enough to change."

"What do you mean?"

Shaking his head, he said slowly, "Not now, Batu, not now. You have endured enough for one cycle."

Rising, he extended his hands to help her up. "If you wish to talk again you are welcome to come again." He pressed her hands and released them.

At the entrance she stopped, turned and gazed into his soft, mysterious eyes, then reluctantly left.

Several cycles later, Batu's thoughts drifted back to the stark realization of her drastic situation and that precious few cycles remained for her to learn the mysteries inside Taja. She drew a deep breath and nodded, as if to reinforce he thoughts. Sometimes the strength behind the desire to know things surprised her. Even in the face of death, the desire to acquire knowledge could not be squelched. It had become so ingrained in her makeup that she seemed unable to live more than a few cycles without it bubbling up. Would the Talker Healer be like her father and Tomudo or narrow-minded like other men? Everything indicated that he seemed willing to speak to her on any subject. Would he share his knowledge with a woman? She had thought of Taja several times since she last saw him. Each time she had asked to be guided by some sign as to when to see him again. Having received no omen or sign to guide her, Batu accepted her father's urging and confidently made up her mind to see him.

The air cooled unexpectedly, giving some release from the stifling heat. The refreshing breeze caressed Batu as she walked through the village center. She felt the heat retained by the earth on the soles of her feet. The last time she drew up to his hut she had felt anxious, this time she felt eager.

"Taja, it is Batu, may I enter?"

He called to her from within, "Batu, I have been waiting for you."

Surprised by his reply, she entered and questioned him. "Why do you say such a thing? You did not know I was coming this cycle."

"I say it to awaken you," he said softly.

"But I am not asleep," she answered puzzled by his reply.

In spite of being slightly irritated, she noticed the dreamy quality in his eyes. The way he looked and they way he spoke hinted to her that he might be functioning in a different state of consciousness. She had heard her parents speak of these qualities in reference to him.

The meeting did not begin as she envisioned it would, and she found it disconcerting. She usually commanded how a meeting went, but he had thrown her off balance. Sensing her logical, argumentative approach would not work, she let her speech flow spontaneously.

"Your words are foreign to me, Taja. You must explain them so I may understand."

"If you truly wish to comprehend what I say you will need to know much more than you do. Tomudo taught you the stories but more importantly some of life's great lessons concerning love. I found him to be a teacher of high degree, though few knew him to be. You were privileged and honored to be his woman.

"I am going to tell you something you may not understand or believe. Tomudo's love saved you from yourself."

"What do you mean?" she asked defensively.

"If you had not learned those lessons of love you would have perished and he would have survived."

Her mouth opened involuntarily. Angered and confused by his words, she looked intently at him. How could he speak of such things? What manner of man would speak thus and not tremble out of fear of the gods striking him down? "Are you insane? Only our gods would know of such things."

He made no move to defend himself. He remained mute.

Silently, she questioned his silence. Anyone else would try to defend himself, yet he sat mute. There must be a reason why he would say something so foreign to her. If she was to learn from him, she must accept some of his strangeness and reason it out later. For now, she let the words settle into her mind.

Taja broke his silence. "Why do you seek my knowledge?"

She looked at him incredulously; once again he had somehow sensed why she had come.

Recovering, she replied, "I am not completely sure." After thinking a moment she answered. "Possibly because you always seem to be there when my life is transforming. Now, you have appeared to me in a remembrance-vision I had of the banished woman, Nehti. Inexplicably, I am drawn to you. For what reasons, I am not completely certain. You are correct. I am here because I do seek knowledge from you, but I am not sure of its nature and whether you will share it with me."

He was quiet for a moment and then asked again, "Why do you seek knowledge?"

"Because it is my nature to want to know things."

"Why do you seek knowledge?" he asked again.

Puzzled with his repetition of the question she answered, "To learn."

"Why do you seek knowledge?" he persisted.

A feeling of exasperation surged through her and the truth blurted from her. "Because they cannot take it away from me."

"Who cannot take it away?"

"The council! Men! Anyone!" Her voice rose in bitterness and anger.

Unfazed by her outburst he continued, "I have heard it said of you, and I have seen it for myself, that you are fiercely independent. Do you agree?"

Her shoulders squared. Her eyes glinted. "Yes."

"But you are not independent, Batu. Others can and do control your emotions and circumstances. Your decisions are often based upon others in your life," he said intensely.

"That is not true," she countered angrily, "I answer to no one. I do what I want to."

His eyebrows rose. "Is that true?"

His question seemed to scream for an answer, yet she kept quiet for reasons unknown. She reflected on the question and kept her eyes riveted on his. His eyes softened exuding an unfamiliar nuance that engulfed her. The flush on her face told her he spoke the truth.

"No. The council is controlling my life," she admitted.

He spoke softly. "Ah, Batu, how tenaciously you have clung to and clamored for independence. Unfortunately, you are not aware of the forces that hold you at bay and prevent you from realizing independence fully. You are prone to the same stifling mistakes that others have made. Until you know how you are bound nothing will change."

Defensively, her voice rose. "It was not my fault Tomudo died." No sooner were the words free from her lips than the arguments between her and Tomudo rushed into her thoughts.

Compassionately, he said, "Do not place blame on others or yourself. If you want independence you must free yourself from such thoughts. You must free yourself from blame. Use the past for reference. Let it teach you. If you wish to be truly independent you will be able to achieve it only through peace of mind, great love and detachment from what happens and from people."

"That sounds foolish. How can I love and be detached all in the same moment?"

"It can be done. If you loved Tomudo freely, you would fully realize he is always in your heart and will never cease to exist. True independence expands the boundaries of your existence. When it does not matter if you live or die, you are free. When your only desire is to do the will of the Creator, then you are free."

He continued his explanation. "So, Batu, you see you are not independent or free. You have been trapped into thinking you are free. You still fear death. Anger still churns within your belly because the council is unwilling to change the law of banishment to save you. So, others can hurt you. You thought Tomudo offended you during your period of misunderstanding. I am not blind. I saw you were both troubled." His voice, already soft, trailed off into a whisper. "No, you are not free."

Angry, humiliated, and hurt, she glared at him. Tears ran down her face. Brushing them aside, she wanted to flee. Something told her to remain still and evaluate his words. She agonized over them. The tone of his voice prompted her to go on. The words were harsh, but his voice never rose above a soft conversational level. Did he have the capacity to see her correctly? Did the Creator he kept speaking of bless him with the ability to see into people's hearts? Did he speak the truth? Slowly, she recognized that her vanity was the reason why his words seemed harsh and difficult. With effort she calmed herself and searched his eyes for a clue as to how he felt. As she opened herself, a limitless compassion behind them unfolded for her to experience. It made her realize he had no intention of harming her; he simply wanted to make her aware of things that have been restricting her.

After many moments, she surrendered to him. "Taja, help me. I am tormented and confused by what has happened. Why have I lost Tomudo? Why did I have to get sick and lose my beauty? And why do I now face expulsion from the village? Why has it all happened to me?"

He did not reply.

Seeking relief, she went on, "My moments on Mother Earth are brief and if they are to be peaceful and free from fear, I must learn of your freedom."

She waited for him to speak. He appeared content to regard her serenely in silence.

The quiet gave her a chance to reflect further. Looking past Taja, her thoughts moved to the conversations she had with people who knew Tomudo. They told her of Tomudo's compassion and kindness, qualities she grudgingly admitted she rarely displayed. Throughout her life she had used her intellect and independence while seemingly suppressing those gentler qualities. Pride prevented her from seeing herself clearly in the past. Quite possibly, what allowed her to see that truth was Tomudo's love.

Her eyes made contact with Taja's. "There is much that is beyond me, and I truly want to be free," she whispered passionately.

Soundlessly, and with little effort, he rose from the mat. Stepping over to one of the shelves, he picked up the wood carving of the warrior that Tomudo had presented to him when he sought assistance in his quest to make Batu his woman. His thoughts touched on the long friendship they had shared together.

Batu awaited his reply.

He set the bust back and turned to her.

His voice, soft yet firm, seemed to resonate in her stomach. "What you wish to learn will forever change you, Batu. If you wish to pursue this, you will never be the same as you once were. You were different from others before, and if you wish to learn what I know, it will again cause you to be different in the eyes of our people."

"Being different is nothing new to me."

He nodded and then smiled slightly at her words. "Indeed! It has come about because your parents allowed you liberties no other woman-child has ever been privileged with in our tribe. Their encouragement and openness gave you the chance to develop your own ideals and values. Your inquisitive and courageous nature would have been crushed by most other parents."

He smiled broadly. "I remember when you challenged Halpur at the Test Of Strengths festival six seasons ago. He had just received the applause from the villagers for winning the foot race for the young males. As I recall, you stepped forward and challenged him to race you. While much of the tribe laughed and scorned you, your parents beamed with pride."

Batu looked admiringly at Taja. He may have been the only person to detect how her parents felt. Like all the other festivals, challenges were always being hurled about. She felt she could have beaten Halpur in the race, but her challenge went unheeded, as if it had no value.

He looked at her with pride and love. He would never have dreamed of rejecting her request to acquire knowledge. He knew from his dreams and visions that their lives were to be closely intertwined. His face beamed as he said, "You may come whenever you feel the need."

"Thank you." Wanting to see how he would react to the words she was about to speak, she said them with a hint of animosity, "Your honesty hurt me."

"I am truly sorry."

Batu surveyed his face. The growing shadows made his features difficult to distinguish. Reaching out with her heart, she felt the honesty in his heart. The act would never have been considered prior to her being healed of the scales.

In spite of the darkness, she found it hard to end their conversation. "It is late and I must leave. You have given me much to think about."

Reaching out, he held her hand in both of his. "When you seek the truth about yourself, it can often hurt, but it also strengthens you."

Tilting her head, she thought about his words. Rising she smiled and said, "I look forward to our next meeting. I must tell you; I leave reluctantly, Taja."

"And I am sorry to see you go, Batu."

Opening his arms, she slipped into them without hesitating and held him tightly.

Releasing her he said softly, "Until we meet again I bid you a fond farewell."

"Farewell," she said in return.

CHAPTER
FIFTEEN

The meeting with Taja did benefit Batu. She detected changes within herself. While not free from being despondent and fearful, the feelings had loosened their grip. The unwillingness to eat had disappeared, replaced by a moderate appetite. The dream involving Tomudo, Coloma and her cropped into her thoughts shortly after the meeting with the Talker Healer, pushing out some of the darker ones she had previously entertained. After struggling with the intention of the dream and the attitude of the council for a few cycles, she felt a small ray of hope still remained that the council would show compassion and spare her life, if she taught Coloma. Impulsively, she told Coloma that she would begin his instruction. In spite of her decision, Batu had adverse feelings as she sat across from Coloma for the first lesson. Forcibly, she pushed them aside.

As the cycles passed, the unfavorable attitude she had toward teaching Coloma dissipated, and she began looking forward to the task. A side benefit to the instructions also appeared. Having Coloma in her hut permitted her to recapture the happy moments the two of them had had with Tomudo.

Ten cycles had slipped by since she last saw Taja. In her free moments, her thoughts began centering on the Talker Healer and the emotions running rampant through her. The gnawing need to understand her grief and pain kept alive the need to see Taja.

Finishing her dusk meal, Batu walked to the Talker Healer's hut deep in thought. At the entrance, she called out, "Taja, it is Batu. May I enter?"

Upon hearing her, Taja went to the entrance and returned her greeting, "Of course, Batu. Sit down," he said motioning her to a mat.

She lowered herself gracefully into a cross-legged position.

"Have you come to learn?"

"I believe so."

"Do you have something in particular you want to discuss or can our discussions be led by spontaneity?"

"I do have something on my mind. As you know I am instructing Coloma. It occupies much of my thoughts, moments and energies, yet as soon as I am alone my thoughts center on the loss of Tomudo. I seek to rid myself of the pain," she said in complete frankness. "My sorrow lingers." She shook her head sadly. "My grief is suffocating. How long must I keep suffering?"

The Talker Healer said nothing. His eyes were piercing, yet they expressed warmth and compassion. He remained silent. Moments passed. His eyes never left her. Unexpectedly, tears began to well in her eyes. It surprised her, for they came forth of their own volition. Embarrassed at her inability to control them, her eyes lost contact with his.

When she composed herself, he bluntly asked, "Do you think Tomudo still exists?"

She looked at him quizzically.

He reworded his question, "Do you feel he is alive somewhere?"

"Of course. He is in the Land of No Shadows," she said reluctantly. Her eyes locked on his.

Again he rephrased his question. "Do you believe in your heart that he exists?"

"Yes. I truly believe he lives," she answered.

He looked at her for a long while before he spoke again. "If you truly believe that he lives, then there is nothing I can say to ease your pain. If you feel thus, then he is truly not lost to you. The moment will come when you will be reunited."

"But what of my pain?" She choked up and stopped talking. Unexpectedly, tears again spilled down her cheeks.

"How do I live with it when my heart seeks to be freed from its constriction and loneliness? When do I cease crying and longing for his body to be near me?" Pausing, she took a deep breath as if to gather courage for what she was about to say. "When do I stop screaming silently at him for leaving me?"

The familiar compassion reappeared in Taja's eyes. "Your pain shows how deeply you loved Tomudo."

He touched her hand momentarily. "You will accept his loss in your own way and at the proper moment. Each of us does this in accordance with what is inside of us. Every family has to deal with death. None of us is spared. Tragedy strengthens some and destroys others."

It seemed to Batu that Tomudo's death had brought only destruction. Instead of replying, she focused her attention on him. The experience of gazing into his eyes surpassed that of looking into anyone else's. They had a spacious, mysterious depth to them. As she stared into them, she slowly became aware of a tingling sensation coming from his hand. Some moments later the tingling waned. It gave way to warmth reminiscent of the Great Sun blazing on her hand. The manifestations puzzled her.

He broke into her thoughts. "Your pain will ease. Your loneliness will fade. What will remain will be the memories of his love and kindness."

Still somewhat dubious, she mulled over what she wanted to ask him next.

Both were silent.

Taja waited patiently, and then said, "At times, Batu, when you cannot find what you seek within you, it is best to empty the mind of thoughts and simply let the Creator guide you."

Squinting at him, she found it disturbing to think he might be able to read her thoughts.

In the past, she had tried several techniques to do just what he had suggested and now followed through with one of them. Her effort failed, and she became annoyed at herself.

"Be patient, Batu."

The thought again crossed her mind that he knew her thoughts. Releasing that thought, she slowly let loose of each thought as it arose. Suddenly, the question appeared. She wanted to know how he perceived Tomudo. Her father had already shared what he knew about him, but she had never spoken to Taja about Tomudo. They were close friends and had spent many moments together in friendship and at the council meetings. He would be able to give her insights on a part of his life that she had no knowledge about.

Thinking of Tomudo gave rise to her emotions. Waiting for them to pass, she sat with her eyes cast to the ground. With effort, she fought back the tears and gained control of her emotions.

Tears brimmed in her eyes. "You knew Tomudo better than most. How did you perceive him? What kind of man was he at the council meetings? Was he a good friend?"

Taja closed his eyes and began talking before he opened them. "He was unique among the council. He felt our people's troubles deeply. His ability to use his heart and his mind set him apart from those on the council and from others in our tribe. He had a wonderful way of blending the best qualities within him to achieve an understanding and wisdom few men attain in life. The other council members rarely saw things as I saw them. He often saw things as I did. Because of the way we mutually saw life, we often talked at length about our history, our people, and the goodness within them. Our philosophies were very similar.

"On many occasions the conversations turned to you. Prior to your union, he spoke of how much he admired and respected your intelligence. That, and your beauty, brought him to love you at the tender age of eleven. Although he never proclaimed it, I felt it and saw it. He could have taken a woman in union before you, but he chose to wait till you were of age.

"There were a number of men who made it known to him that he was constantly breaking with tradition by granting you the privilege of attending the story sessions. The pressure they put on him never perturbed him. He maintained his allegiance to you and tactfully told them he would be the judge of whether it harmed the tribe. Even with so delicate a matter as your breaking with tradition, his explanations pacified people to the point where they would end the discussion with much of their anger defused. No matter what the topic, most of his conversations ended in this manner.

"You were allowed to keep on attending the study sessions because he loved you. After you were joined in union he happily taught you the stories of our tribe. He was tremendously proud of you and felt it an honor to be instructing you. There were moments when he spoke to me of the hopes and desires he had for you. He delighted in being your mentor."

He stopped and gazed penetratingly at her. Shaking his head mysteriously, he went on. "Even before your union he spoke of how tangibly he could feel the love you had within you. You had not yet made it known to him, but he felt it. I found it amazing and pleasing that he could be so sensitive of you.

"Many times, he would speak of you and tell me how fortunate he felt to have you as his woman. When you finally expressed your love to him, he cherished it beyond imagination. He had a very loving heart, Batu, very loving. There were moments when we spoke about how different my belief is compared to the High Priest. He even wanted to know about the Creator. Yes, we shared many thoughts, Batu. I feel very fortunate to have had him as a friend."

The words consoled her, soothed her like no other words could ever do. She savored them and breathed deeply, sensing she had reached a new level of understanding in her grief. Peering into Taja's eyes a desire stirred inside her. She wanted to hear more words from this man. She felt compelled to listen to him, to learn from him.

"I have heard you speak of the Creator now and in the past. Who is this Creator?" she asked.

"The village's religion speaks of many gods. What I have been taught by the last Talker Healer, and have come to know, is that there is only one god.

That god is the creator of all that is seen and unseen. The name given this god by the first Talker Healer was Creator. Do you wish to know more about the Creator?"

Her eyes moved upward and to the side of his head in thought. "Is the Creator a man?" she asked suspiciously.

A brief smile flickered on Taja's face. "No. The Creator is neither male nor female, although we tend to apply gender to the Creator in order to relate to it. The best way to describe the Creator would be to say that it has qualities that are loving beyond understanding and concerned with your existence in every way imaginable. It is also the force or energy that supports everything seen and unseen. There have been religions and philosophies that speak of this energy as a feminine or mother quality. It is simply our way of trying to explain the Creator. Our efforts to understand the Creator seems to make us use terms and names to describe what we find difficult to understand. There is nothing wrong with that, it is just the way we function as humans."

Batu stopped him. "But it is easy to see in our village that women are the creators for they are the ones that give birth. Men cannot do that."

"That is true, but if you look deeply at everyone you can see that we all have the same qualities. It is only the degree to which they are visible that makes us look different to each other. Our reality appears to be filled with duality. In truth there is more commonality than duality. Even I will speak in these terms for convenience."

Puzzled Batu asked, "How can that be? Differences exist everywhere and are easily seen. Look at light and dark and love and hate."

Taja replied softly, "It only seems that way. If we look at it from a spiritual view it is completely different."

Batu frowned saying, "But the spiritual realm is not the physical realm."

"It would appear so, but in truth, the spiritual realm gives the physical realm its reality. When we view our physical existence in this light it changes. Let us look at your examples. At what point does light become dark? It is our attempt to measure something that exists as points or degrees on a spectrum. The same is true of love and fear. Can you tell me when love becomes fear or fear love? They are descriptive names for the way we feel but are on the opposite ends of a specific spectrum of measurement. This not only involves duality but it is also subjective. When does my love turn to fear? Does it happen the same moment that yours does? With every opposite we are attempting to apply a measurement to its duality and at the same moment have to deal with subjectivity."

Batu's eyes looked clouded. "In your example you use fear in place of hate. Is not hate a better word to describe the opposite of love?"

"Hate may seem to be the best choice but is not hate based upon our fear of not being loved?"

Again Batu looked away in thought. When her eyes returned to his she spoke. "I think you are right. Fear is the cause of much of what I experience and what I think is detrimental to me. As far as how you went about to describe the poles on a continuum, I am beginning to see what you are saying. So we use the term duality to give us an easy way of dealing with our existence."

"Exactly!" exclaimed Taja.

"But men and women are opposite. How can you reconcile that?"

Taja became intent as he searched for the answer. "Perhaps the answer lies in Clara and Dene. They have tried to be discreet but everyone knows they are in love with each other. Our tribe does not permit them to live together in one hut, but they are bonded to each other. Clara shows all the classic traits of a woman in form, speech and actions, while Dene exhibits many masculine traits. Even Dene's body is much more muscular than normal for a woman. It may be an indication that within each male there are female traits and physical parts that have not fully developed. The same is true of the female."

Batu nodded her head then smiled in recognition of the implications present in Dene. She had wondered about Dene herself but always came up with no explanation. Looking at the man across from her, she knew she had found someone wiser than her father. The stimulation of being in Taja's presence was exhilarating.

The Talker Healer's eyes moved to the entrance. "Darkness is caressing us."

Noticing for the first time that his features were difficult to distinguish, she nodded her head. She looked forward to seeing him again and listening to his unique knowledge. Releasing a wistful sigh, she became aware of a flush of feeling and equated it to the sensation of love. On occasion she had felt it emanating from Tomudo. Coming alert she tried to sense his presence. She glanced about the hut, in an effort to see if anything would offer her a clue to his presence. Finding nothing to substantiate her feelings, her eyes eventually came to rest on Taja.

It came from him! The discovery startled her. She had no doubt that it did. The sensation emanated from him not her deceased lover. She marveled at the strength of the feeling. Puzzled and embarrassed by it, she removed her gaze from him and pried her thoughts away from her feelings. Not knowing what to do with the sensation, she asked in a halting voice, "Taja, may I return to speak with you again?"

Smiling broadly, he replied, "You may come whenever you wish."

Returning his smile with her own, she rose, moved to the entrance and turned. "Thank you."

"Farewell, Batu."

Outside, she questioned the intense feeling of love she had felt. Thinking back, it seemed similar to what she felt when Taja healed her. While disconcerting, because of its unexpectedness, it also felt wonderfully pleasant. The feelings it aroused in her were confusing. Walking slowly back to her hut, his words echoed through her head. He implied she would soon leave her grieving behind and attend to her life. That life was replete with problems. The most urgent of them was finding a way to keep from being expelled from the tribe. She needed to focus her attention on survival, but Taja had captured her imagination.

Inside her hut, she slowly stretched her limbs, closed her eyes, and continued to review the meeting. It helped tremendously to fill out the picture of Tomudo she desired to view. Though not completely at ease with the passing of Tomudo, she felt comforted talking to the Talker Healer. The old desire to acquire knowledge also became more pronounced in his presence. Absentmindedly, she became aware that her mind centered on things other than her grief and her banishment from the village, looming upon the horizon. Yes, she admitted, the meeting had its positive moments and did have a positive effect on her. She looked forward to seeing him again.

Seeking to gather more information about Tomudo, Batu sought out people and asked about their relationship with him. It pleased her to hear people speaking well of him. Some who she spoke to openly showed their animosity toward her and grudgingly shared how they felt about him. Despite these episodes, and the feelings they elicited, she continued seeking to find out what people remembered about him. Through the talks she began to appreciate the admiration the villagers had for Tomudo. Compassionate decisions made while serving on the council, and his fondness of children, had endeared him to everyone. The only point of contention they had centered on her and not with Tomudo.

CHAPTER
SIXTEEN

Instructing Coloma had been keeping Batu away from the Talker Healer. Taja's face kept overlaying Coloma's, as she sat listening to his recitations. She grew restless to see him. Unable to control her desire, she dismissed Coloma and told him not to return until after the first meal of the next cycle.

As soon as Coloma left, she made her way to Taja's hut. Walking toward it, she decided to tell him of the dream that precipitated the instruction of Coloma.

With their greeting aside, they again sat opposite each other. She noticed Taja's eyes held a dreamy quality as he spoke and his voice had an unusual tone to it.

"So, you have come again. Such sincerity means you are on the path."

Curious she asked, "What path?"

"When you seek to know the truth of why you exist, you are on the path."

"Where does this path lead?"

"To self-discovery, to an understanding of who you truly are and where you came from. This wonderfully arduous quest ultimately leads you to the Creator of all, who is never completely knowable or explainable."

She pondered his words in quiet.

"Since you have chosen to set foot on the path we must discuss the value of dreams."

The statement caused her eyebrows to rise. Dumbfounded, she stared at him. Did he read her mind? Was it a coincidence he said the words that would prompt her to talk about the dream? Perhaps the way she looked at him triggered him to say what he did. Whatever the case, she took advantage of his words saying, "Can we discuss the dream that contributed to my decision to teach Coloma?"

He lifted his eyebrows and smiled, but did not say anything. She continued without his verbal approval, "In the dream, Tomudo, Coloma and I were in our hut. Tomudo sat instructing Coloma. He stopped, rose and moved me to the place where he always sat teaching Coloma. He then looked at me expectantly."

"Based solely upon the dream I rescinded my decision not to instruct Coloma, thinking that at some moment in the future the council may look upon me with favor for what I have done and I would be spared from expulsion."

Taja looked at her inquiringly. "And now you wish to know what I see in the dream?"

"Yes, I feel the dream is so simple I should not bother you with it, but I need to know if I saw it correctly," she answered.

"You have seen one level of the dream correctly, however dreams have meanings greater than words because they are constructed with symbols. In your dream the three of you were all symbols. Symbols have many aspects, many meanings. You have seen only the surface meaning of the dream, Batu."

Despite the fact, she asked for his help she became irritated. The tone of her voice challenged him as she asked, "What is it you see in the dream?"

Not disturbed in the least he replied, "What I feel from the dream is that at times you must do things that do not solely benefit you. You must do things in life that benefit others. If you were a mother, you would know what I am talking about. Look at your dream again with this in mind. Look at it as a mother would, who always wishes to please her creations."

Following his instruction, she placed herself in the role of Tomudo's deceased mother and replayed the dream in her mind and questioned who could benefit. Looking at it from Tomudo's mother's standpoint she could find nothing. As she viewed it from Coloma's mother's perspective, the meaning became apparent. Her expression changed. A look of discovery came over it.

"Because of what I am doing, Coloma will not be considered less than the other Tellers of the Stories. He will have the prestige of having preserved all of our stories for future generations. His mother will be able to remain proud of him and not feel shamed."

The Talker Healer smiled. "You now have seen what the dream conveyed to you on yet another level. You must not be content to look at dreams only in one way."

"Yes, I see," Batu replied tentatively.

"Even when you interpret them, other meanings may still be lingering in the symbols. A dream may seem simplistic, yet if you search deeper into it, other meanings may be present that have more significance. You must use many eyes to see what is present in a dream. In this case you used mine, but you can also view it from different perspectives as I have described and thus benefit from those views."

After listening to him, she was silent. Taja waited sensing her sifting the words, evaluating them and coming to a conclusion.

"My dream then was telling me that I should look to do something not for my sake, but for the sake of others?"

"Exactly!" Taja beamed expansively. "The greatest value in teaching Coloma is the unselfishness of the act." He breathed slowly and deeply, speaking in a voice that seemed to grow softer as he spoke.

He leaned over and placed his hands over hers, "You have done well in seeing how you should have acted. The true trial is to accomplish this in the midst of a disturbing situation. That is when your strength of character and wisdom hopefully appears." He smiled reassuringly; his hands still covered her's.

She felt uneasy. His words were hard to accept. She had based her decision to teach Coloma on saving herself. It was difficult to think any other way. Would anyone have done differently? If she ever had designs of changing her feelings, thoughts and actions before her death, she felt certain no one except Taja could help her achieve it.

Her attention drifted to his hands. They felt feverish. With effort she lifted her eyes to his and saw warmth in them equal to his hands. She let herself open to him slowly and could not deny what she saw and felt. It was love. He loved her. It was not enmeshed with bonding. It was pure, without any demands. If a demand existed, it rested in the fact he wanted her to realize the beauty within her. She sensed how freely he gave his love. He accepted her for what she was at that moment, not for what she could become.

Speaking gently, Taja said, "Batu, I know you are seeking to save yourself from banishment, but you must look at your life with different eyes. It is not the length of your life that is important. The height to which you soar is important."

Puzzled she asked, "What is this height of which you speak?"

"Your acts of love for others are the height. How you inspire others and what sacrifices you make for others are the height of life. Your struggle to know your true self is a height. A desire to be one with the Creator is a height, and how truly one loves oneself and others is yet another."

Gazing into his eyes, an assurance came over her that with his guidance she could purposefully set about contending with her possible banishment and concentrate on achieving the freedom he described. With his help she would strive for such heights.

Batu silently vowed to spend more moments with Taja, no matter what the council said, and draw from him whatever knowledge he wished to share. When Coloma came again she would ask him to arrive earlier after the first meal so she would have the last moments of each cycle with Taja.

The Talker Healer interrupted her thoughts. "You have much to think of, Batu. Look at your dream again in your moments of reflection. Rest assured that if you wish to continue, I shall share whatever is appropriate about my thoughts, feelings and experiences. You must understand what I do share with you is already deep within you. It simply awaits your discovery."

"How can they be within me?"

"All knowledge is in everyone. The ability is also there to extract it. The moments, desire, and effort is what we lack, Batu."

"For me, the moments are short. I find it hard to see how all knowledge is present in me," she replied.

"Perhaps as you keep coming here you will begin to uncover some of that knowledge."

"I will come."

His eyes closed momentarily in recognition of her statement. "I will await your return."

She placed her hand on his arm. A rush of warmth flooded her. Love radiated from him. It felt stronger than Tomudo's. She withdrew her hand. Unwilling to leave, she prodded her body to move. Rising, she bid Taja farewell and spontaneously embraced him. He returned the embrace and held her to him until she withdrew.

Back in her hut, Batu's thoughts settled on the dream that motivated her to instruct Coloma, as Taja suggested. Reflecting on the new ideas the Talker Healer had placed in her mind could be difficult. Certainly others in the tribe, like she, did things correctly, but for the wrong reasons. The more she thought about it the more she saw that many people could be oblivious to what they were doing. Why were some people mindful of their decisions and others not? And what of those who are not purposefully on the path of wisdom? Could they still make the right decisions? There seemed to be no end to the complexity and variety in life. To Batu, everyone seemed to be in a different stage of awareness, which, in and of itself, remained a mystery.

She reviewed her relationship with Tomudo. She recalled instances where she had done things out of love for him and in a totally unselfish way. But to sacrifice her moments as Taja spoke of had never crossed her mind. Such unselfishness was foreign to her, yet she now had the choice to discontinue

Coloma's instructions or to continue them. She chose to continue them for the good of the entire village not just for Coloma's mother. That choice sent shivers through her body. Now at last she felt she fully knew what she was doing. She would continue the instructions knowing that the Kahali tribe would benefit from her decision. Nodding her head in approval, she glanced up at the goddess in the sky.

During her wildest rebellion, she had never felt as exhilarated as she did now. A sense of the tribe's heritage filled her. Because of her the village would be able to function as it had for generations. In a flash of realization she knew she had achieved a stature of importance no other man had ever attained. The recognition came to her that she, who had broken with tradition so often, would be the preserver of tradition. She had soared to a height Taja had spoken about. Her eyes closed and she fell peacefully asleep.

Thirsting for his words, Batu had returned to meet with Taja at every possible opportunity. She ate her dusk meals earlier in order to be with him, at times lingering until darkness had settled upon the village. There, in the confines of his hut, an inexplicable bond had arisen between them. Despite trying, she could not explain it satisfactorily to herself.

Some cycles later, Batu sat across from her beloved teacher waiting for him to speak.

Taja's eyes were shining. "You have heard me say that you are on a path of love. Have you ever wondered if there is another person on a similar path?"

Batu's eyes narrowed, as she searched her past. "I know that you are on the path. No, I have not given any thought to whether anyone else would be on such a path. Is there someone who is?"

"Yes there are a few. One of them is Kaathi."

Surprised, Batu replied, "But Kaathi is a mere child. She cannot have seen twelve seasons."

"The true nature of the spirit is present in every life you live," explained Taja. "She has chosen to utilize her spirituality in this life. There are many obstacles she must face in order to accomplish what she has set out to do."

Her interest keyed, Batu asked, "What are the obstacles?"

"I cannot reveal everything to you for much depends on what decisions you, I, she and others make. I can tell you that her life is intrinsically woven into yours and mine."

"How have you come about knowing this?"

"I went to the Realm of Possibilities," Taja announced.

An inquisitive look forged her face as she asked, "Where is that?"

"It is a realm of the creative mind. Choices we make in our lives direct which path we walk. There are moments in deep meditation, when I am able to focus clearly upon one or more paths," he answered.

"How many paths are there?" she inquired.

He answered her with a question of his own. "How many leaves are there in the forest?"

"What does that mean?"

"It means that choices determine the number of paths."

She thought about the enormity of what he said and dismissed it as only a possibility. Choosing to follow her first interest she asked, "Can you go to this Realm of Possibilities for everyone?"

Surprised that she did not want to question him about how choices create paths he replied, "Not everyone and not always."

"Have you looked upon my paths?" she asked.

"I have not done so. I felt where you were going, when you were a child and I read your hand."

"You saw my future in my hand?"

"I saw some of it. Most of it I sensed as I read your lines," he answered.

"Are you going to tell me what you felt?"

"No. What I felt were impressions," Taja explained. "While most of what I saw and felt have become a reality, I have been deceived on occasions. Telling you might jeopardize the future. Let us say that if I saw something drastic in your life and I would tell you about it that might cause you great anguish. Doing so may also alter your future. Whenever I sense dire things, I give advice and encouragement. Hopefully, that will alter the person's personality and provide the personal courage that person needs to overcome the obstacle. Besides, I have found out for myself that it is much more fulfilling to be surprised. Consequently, I live my own life spontaneously."

"Spontaneity aside, it would seem helpful to know my future," she pointed out to Taja.

"Perhaps and perhaps not. What if in the knowing you alter things so drastically that you alter a mission you wanted to accomplish?" he volunteered.

"Hmm. I think I see what you are talking about." Going back to another point, she asked, "Have you spoken to Kaathi about what you have seen?"

"I found no need to do it," answered Taja.

"Why not?"

"I sensed she knew of such things."

"How would she know? Is she able to see into the Realm of Possibilities?" He smiled and would not answer.

"Why have you brought up the Realm of Possibilities if you are unwilling to discuss it?" she demanded.

"I brought it up to let you know that it is a reality. It is a tool that is available the moment you are ready to utilize it."

Not willing to let the subject die, she asked, "What prompted you to venture into the Realm of Possibilities where it concerned Kaathi?"

"Some seasons ago I sensed something in her and went there to help me understand what I felt," he answered vaguely.

Curious, Batu asked, "What did you sense?"

"That is for you to sense yourself, Batu."

"How will I sense it?"

"Quiet yourself when you are with her and be aware of what you feel and what your body is telling you," he instructed. "In the past you occasionally trusted your senses. Lately, you are sensing things when we are together. You are becoming more trustful of what you feel and sense. Be trustful, when you meet Kaathi."

"Will you arrange for me to meet her?"

The Talker Healer smiled saying, "It will happen without me."

Well before the Great Sun appeared, Batu awoke eager to begin the new cycle. After she ate she made her way out to the tree she and Tomudo had sat against so often. She ambled out to it while confusing thoughts and feelings buzzed inside of her. As she neared the spot she looked ahead and saw someone lying in the short grass bordering the tree. Drawing nearer she saw the form of a woman-child.

The child heard Batu and turned toward her.

Batu stopped short. It was Kaathi. The hair on her arms rose. How strange, after having talked about her with Taja to have her appear where she never has been before. Drawing closer, she looked intently at the woman-child for the first time. She saw the child to be small and thin for her eleven seasons, more child than woman. For a child of her age, her soft, oval face was strikingly composed. Auburn hair curled tightly framed her face. As she stopped in front of Kaathi, she noticed the child's amazing azure eyes held an unbelievable depth. Taja had the same quality in his eyes, and she often lost herself in them.

She forced herself to speak. "What are you doing here?"

Smiling brightly, Kaathi answered, "Looking at the face of creation." As she spoke she turned toward the plains and drew silent.

Batu stared at the child's profile thinking how much the remark sounded like it came from Taja. Thinking of him reminded her to still her mind and be open to any sensations or feelings that came to her. Turning slowly, Kaathi looked into Batu's eyes. Batu could not take her eyes from the child's eyes. Something transpired in the look that Batu did not understand. After what seemed an eternity, she burst into tears. The weeping turned into sobs. Her hands flew to her face. The words *Creator, I Love You* kept running through her head, as the tears flowed down her cheeks. Many moments passed before her weeping subsided. Wiping her eyes and cheeks, she saw Kaathi looking at her. They gazed silently at each other, Batu in wonderment and Kaathi in serenity.

Kaathi broke the spell with a simple question. "You come here often, do you not?"

Blinking her eyes to ground herself, she answered, "Not as often as I would like."

"Why not?" asked the child pointedly.

"Because I have been too busy."

"This is where you should talk to the Creator, not in your hut."

A look of incomprehension came to Batu's face.

Shifting to a sitting position, Kaathi rested her back on the tree.

"This tree loves you. I also feel Tomudo's love for you here," the child went on.

Batu fought to whisper, "What?"

"He loves you deeply, Batu."

Thunderous emotions flooded Batu. Tears continued slipping silently from her eyes.

"Tears wash away our pain," Kaathi said wistfully.

Through her tears, she looked at the child, unable to comprehend how she could speak so wisely. At long last Batu responded. "I have found that at times it is the only way to rid myself of pain."

"It is true for me as well," Kaathi replied.

The child's reply surprised Batu.

Growing bolder, Batu said, "I know your family. Your parents are kind and loving people. Surely you arc not telling me that you have suffered in your home."

"I have seen myself in visions crying, and I have felt other people's pain."

Her eyes searched the child's for an inkling of what lay behind them and felt nothing but compassion.

"Would you rather we stopped talking, Batu?"

Sensing she needed to compose herself Batu said, "Yes, I would like to just sit and be quiet."

She settled down next to Kaathi.

They quieted themselves. Completing her affirmations, Batu went into a passive state of expectation. In her head, she heard a trickle of music from afar. By degrees it grew louder. She identified some of the instruments, yet many were left unidentified. The splendor of the music filled her mind like scented petals dancing in the air. The sound played upon her heart reverberating and spreading like delicious wine through every fiber of her being. The wondrous sound reached a crescendo then softly faded.

The unique experience prompted her to remain in the meditative state in hope that it would occur again. When it did not, she slowly brought herself to waking consciousness. Opening her eyes, Batu saw Kaathi smiling sweetly. Had the child influenced her meditation? She longed to ask her yet something held her from speaking.

Kaathi reached over and placed her hand on Batu's arm. "Will you walk me back?"

"Yes, of course."

They walked back in silence. The child displayed wonderment at everything she saw. The woman watched the child.

After Batu had eaten her last meal she could not contain herself any longer and walked eagerly to Taja's hut.

Taja greeted her warmly. "So, how did your meeting go?"

"I should have known you knew I would meet Kaathi. I should not be surprised by such things from you," she answered.

He chose not to comment on what she said. Instead he replied, "So you have spoken to Kaathi."

Aware that he did not comment on what she had just said, she could not help but wonder why. Past experience told her that if he did not answer a question or make a comment he had his reasons.

She replied, "Yes, but I never expected the meeting to occur like it did. Instead of going to her hut, I decided to not see her for another cycle or two.

I chose to go out to Tomudo's and my favorite place overlooking the plains. She was there! I am sure she knew I would be there. She is not a child, Taja."

"My dear Batu, what is she?"

"I am not certain... a wise old woman. She is ageless. It is hard to describe how I felt in her presence. My first contact with you was as a healer. Later I recognized your unique gifts and deep love. With Kaathi it exploded upon me. It overwhelmed me. I burst into tears. Later, as I thought about our meeting, I could find no reason why I did. It was very strange. It seemed as if I had no reason to cry and no feelings were associated with the weeping. The tears did not come from emotion. If you were to ask me now, I could not explain why I wept."

"Was anything going on inside of you at the time you wept?" he asked.

"Yes," she said softly. "I kept saying over and over 'Creator I Love You.' I have never done that either. Later we meditated together and I heard this incredibly beautiful music. I knew I had experienced it because of her.

"I recall that you said I should open myself up to her. I calmed myself and before I could sense anything from her the tears came like a flood. I would have expected such things in your presence, but certainly not from a child."

He rose and moved to her side and embraced her. Returning it she looked quizzically at him.

"She has been waiting for you to mature before she made contact with you, Batu."

The impact of his words startled Batu. "What do you mean mature? I am older than she."

"You are older only in age. In this lifetime she is the wise one. In each life we lead, we take on different roles. We do it in cooperation with the other major role players in our life. In our physical life we seem to be gifted in varying degrees in every facet of our existence. Yet everyone is all wise at the greater self level and thus equal. At this moment in history, Kaathi is here to share her wisdom. Do not think of her as a child. She is a child in form only. Her wisdom surpasses mine in this life. In another life it is likely your wisdom will be greater than ours. Do not let her age or wisdom distract or prejudice you. Let the relationship unfold like an exquisite flower."

Caught by surprise at what Taja had just shared, she mulled over the ramifications of such a belief system and philosophy. She found it difficult to think Oliva was her equal, yet he said it was at the greater self level and not this human level. It still seemed a bit strange to think in another life Oliva could be more intelligent than she. Shifting her mind, she found it perplexing that Taja would not share more of what he knew about Kaathi. It was not like him to keep anything from her. That fact gnawed at her. Why was he so mysterious about the child? For some reason she did not feel completely comfortable with not knowing how their relationship would develop. Knowing he would not discuss the future, she turned her inquiry to her meditation. "Why did I hear that exquisitely beautiful music in meditation?"

"While meditating with her, I have heard something similar. It is her song of life, her song of existence. She shared who she is in music."

Suddenly she became upset at her own annoyance and hoping to cover it she rose. "Perhaps I had better get home and rest."

Rising, Taja embraced her showing no sign that he sensed how she felt. "As you wish."

Batu kept returning to see Taja. His philosophy continually intrigued her. After one such meeting, she was walking slowly to her hut. The meeting with Kaathi had nearly been forgotten and made its way to the dim recesses of her mind. She chose to concentrate on the Talker Healer. His mystical nature always elevated her mood. The words he spoke came from his heart and stirred her own. Pausing outside her hut, she looked upward. A strong sense of inspiration overcame her. An overwhelming panorama of twinkling stars blazed across the darkened sky. She found the Great Sun's mate, the Sun With No Heat, shining brightly. For the moment she lapsed into the teachings of the tribe where many gods populated their religion. This was in sharp contrast to Taja's Creator. She found the face of the goddess on the surface of the Sun With No Heat. A rueful smile found its way to Batu's face. Had the women here on Mother Earth, as had the goddess in the sky, always been relegated to lesser roles of importance? Surely the women gods were ones who created everything. They were the life givers, whereas men and men gods were the life takers. Possibly somewhere in another village their legends told of a different viewpoint and women played an important role in creation. Taja had said experiences were interwoven with the future and the past in ways we could not even imagine. Perhaps she was contributing to bringing about a future where women would be more respected for their contributions. She smiled at her thoughts.

Gazing at the softly glowing orb, she winked at the woman's face on its surface. She sat down on the bench outside her hut, remaining there to look up at the goddess, and enjoy the breathtaking beauty stretching across the sky. She felt contentment in the relative calm of the moment. In scanning the sky she saw a star rush across nearly the full breath of it. An easy smile came across her face. The rushing star was a good omen. She breathed deeply, let her breath out with a rush and returned the smile of the goddess.

CHAPTER
SEVENTEEN

Batu sat leaning against a beam in her hut, waiting for sleep. The talks with Taja had given her a measure of relief from the crippling grief, but she had reservations as to why Tomudo had to die. His death left her completely defenseless. Torn between anger and the longing to have him by her side, she failed to hear the greeting outside her hut. Rising, she stepped out into the dim light and saw Kiirt standing with his hands folded on his chest. He seemed to be holding a pompous pose. Kiirt had been one of the men who formally requested her to be his woman, but her father had eliminated him from contention.

"Batu, I have come to see if you are in need of anything. I want to help you in your moment of grief," he said.

Annoyed at the interruption, and somewhat uncomfortable in his presence, she replied irritably, "I have no need for any help. I want to be left alone."

Taken back by her show of irritation, he stood silent and unsure of where to go with his planned conversation. He had hoped she needed something done. Regaining his composure, he said, "If you need anything you have but to ask me and I will do it."

"If I need help, I will remember your words, Kiirt," she said abruptly. She pivoted as she ended her reply and returned inside.

The soft sounds of his footsteps marked his departure.

"Why is he making an offer of that nature?" she asked aloud. "Does he expect to get something in return?"

Her thoughts went back to when they both attended the story sessions. He had not been very bright. A man with so little intelligence would likely make such an offer to seek the softness of her body and not to console her. The disquieting feeling she had as a child about him returned. Something within him seemed twisted, yet she could not identify it.

In order to survive, she knew she would need a man to ask her to be his woman. Ending up with him would be nearly as bad as ending up in Romir's hut. Shuddering slightly, she brushed the unwanted thoughts of Kiirt from her mind.

With little effort, she focused on when she and Tomudo were locked in feverish embrace of bonding. She never suspected bonding could elicit such pleasures. In spite of the pleasure it brought her, she could not imagine herself involved in such intimacy with another man. She longed for those moments with Tomudo as they talked, laughed, cried, bonded, walked, and sat silently together. Would she ever be able to share herself with any man in those ways? Undoubtedly, she would constantly compare any man to Tomudo and regrettably none would be able to compare to him. Suddenly growing weary, her thoughts subsided. The release she sought came slowly in the thoughtlessness of sleep, and in the comfort of its oblivion.

The Great Sun's light flooded the rich earth, seeking to fill each tiny crevice and crack, allowing nothing to escape its heat. The leaves on the wild bean plants next to the village turned themselves to miss the direct scorching rays of the fiery orb. The rays made their way past the turned leaves, falling upon the ground unrelentingly. Having finished her mid-cycle meal, Batu sat outside waiting for Coloma. With idle curiosity she watched two men in discussion near the Great Sun Circle. Kiirt walked into the village center. She shifted her attention to him making his way purposefully toward her, carrying a small bowl. She frowned. It had been but a scant two cycles since she last saw him.

Stopping in front of her, he extended the bowl to her. "Greetings, Batu. I bring this for you hoping it will give you comfort, when your grief is too great. It is a very fine berry wine. Accept it and find pleasure in it." He placed it in her hands.

Batu frowned. She studied the gift, shifting her gaze from it to him. She had never received a gift from anyone except Tomudo and her parents. With deliberation and hesitation she said, "I accept it and thank you."

He bowed extravagantly. Without speaking, he turned and walked away. With his back to her, he smiled openly. The look upon her face testified to the fact that he had caught her by surprise. He had the advantage in this meeting. This would give her something to think about. Now she would have him on her mind, questioning his generosity and interest. Soon the moment would be right for him to seize the opportunity and make her his.

Batu was surprised. She had expected Kiirt to linger and explain himself further, yet he slowly walked away from her. She watched him until he disappeared. She removed the lid of the bowl and inhaled its aroma. The sweet fragrance lingered in the warm air. Its concentrated smell brought to mind the berries she had collected so often near the banks of the running water. She knew the taste of the wine would reflect the fragrance. Perhaps, in a moment of weariness or crushing loneliness, she would release the contents of the bowl to escape and roam freely in her mouth. She would let it set there and then swallow it, as the maker intended. She would consume it and lose herself in its numbing qualities. Entering her hut, she placed the bowl on the shelf next to her drinking bowl. She turned quickly to check the entrance half-expecting Kiirt to be there with yet another attempt at ingratiating himself to her. The entrance frame remained empty.

A few cycles later, their paths crossed again. Batu sat relaxing outside, as dusk settled on the village, lost in her thoughts about Tomudo. She did not notice Kiirt until he had stopped in front of her. She looked up waiting for him to speak.

Under her insistent gaze he began. "Batu, I know of your situation and I know your father did not choose me as your man in union, but I am here to offer you a solution to your expulsion."

"And how are you to do it?"

"I am here to ask you to be my woman," he said evenly, afraid to show too much eagerness in his voice.

She became acutely aware he had difficulty in keeping his eyes on hers. Now and then his eyes sought out the lushness of her body showing his desire to be greater than his respect for her or his fear of rejection. Now, in the moment of stillness they roamed her body freely. It was very apparent why he wanted her as his woman. His blatant display of lust made her cringe. There were moments when she was aware of the desire in men's eyes but none were ever so daring as what she experienced at this moment. Despite her dislike for him, she knew he offered her a solution to her desperate situation.

Strange feelings of distaste coursed through her as she answered him. "Kiirt, you have caught me thinking of Tomudo and I am unsure of what I am to do. My grief has been too overbearing to allow me moments of thought concerning my survival."

Seizing the opportunity, he responded quickly. "You are filled with grief, but you must also think of how you are going to save yourself."

"I know I must begin to think about it, and I will give your offer serious thought."

"The sooner you make a decision the sooner the threat of expulsion will be removed from your thoughts," he offered her.

"That is true. Alright, I will give you my answer four cycles from now after the last meal," she replied grudgingly.

His voice sounded eager, as he replied. "Very well, I will be here as the Great Sun sets for the fourth time."

Taking a last sweeping look at her, he turned and walked away in long strides, leaving Batu to ponder the offer to save herself. Out of all the men only this one came forth to save her. Were they all afraid of her or what the rest of the village would say? It appeared Kiirt did not fear her independent nature and penchant for breaking with tradition. Perhaps Kiirt played the part of a maverick as much as she did. Or did his desire for her overcome his concern with tradition?

She knew from the talks her father had with Kiirt that he had lost his woman after only six seasons. Traditionally men, even men who were widowed, chose women who had never been in union previously. It would seem that he preferred her to the women who had never been bonded, or it could be that the other fathers had rejected him in the past. Even if she wanted to be in union with a specific man, she could not formally ask him. She would have to resort to cunning to bring it about because women were not allowed to formally ask a man to be in union. In the face of such tradition no man would be brave enough to accept such boldness. Tradition once again dictated what she could and could not do.

The fact remained this one man had come forward for her to consider. In her consideration, she would confer with her father and seek his counsel, for she did not know much about Kiirt.

Coloma would have to wait. She needed to know what sort of man Kiirt was. Getting up from the bench, she walked the short distance to her father's hut, still pondering Kiirt's proposal.

After greeting her parents, she informed them of her caller. "I have just been asked by Kiirt to be his woman. Father, I am in need of your insight. Why did you not consider him as one of the final three for my union?"

"Come, sit down and I will tell you."

Batu sat down on the ground. Her mother and father sat on their sleeping mat across from her.

"I did not consider Kiirt because of the talk both I and your mother had heard. It concerned his improper conduct with Marlem, his widow. We men talk when we bathe just as you women do. We share stories of our hunts and of our families. Many were the times I laughingly told the men of your exploits. Some laughed with me, but many others, like Kiirt, did not.

"Marlem's mother, Bovini, told your mother of what she heard from Marlem. On several occasions, Bovini overheard Kiirt and Marlem arguing, as she was about to visit their hut. More than once, she had heard Marlem cry out while Kiirt ushered threats. Often, she saw Marlem with bruises on her face. Those incidences were not the only ones where she was hurt; it happened many times. I did not see Marlem with these bruises myself, so I must accept Bovini's words to be true."

As Aahi paused, Szatu unexpectedly spoke. Emotion stirred her voice. "We women have quietly spoken of the problems some of us experience with our men. We know which men beat and abuse their women. Thankfully, there are only a few of them. Of course the abused women say nothing, but the huts are close to each other and we hear things.

"Our tradition tells us that the men are to have complete control of the family. But some women choose to speak out and cause their men to become angry. In their anger, a few men resort to violence. They do not know any other way to cope with their mates. These are rare occurrences, except in Marlem's case. I know he often abused her physically. Many times, she chose to bathe away from the rest of the women in hope that we would not see her bruises and see her shame. Knowing of her problems, I intentionally walked near her and saw the bruises. I beg you to be cautious of this man.

"You have not been harmed by your father or Tomudo. If you share your life with this man, you will know what it is like to be in danger of being harmed."

Batu leaned forward, as she posed her question to her mother, "Have you ever spoken to Marlem's mother of this?"

"I would never speak to Bovini unless she spoke to me first. Women do not want to speak of such things, Batu," Szatu cautioned her.

Szatu recognized the look on Batu's face. It appeared every time she felt someone tried to keep her from attaining something. "I need to know where Bovini lives."

Worried, Szatu asked, "Are you going to ask about Marlem's beating?"

"Yes, Mother. I must know if I can control Kiirt should I chose to be his woman."

"Why not just wait to see if another man will ask you to be his woman?" her mother pleaded.

"The Sun With No Heat has nearly gone through two cycles since Tomudo has become a dweller. If no other man has come forward by now, none will. I need to speak to the woman. If I am to make a wise decision, I must have all the information I can gather to make it properly."

"The choice is yours," said Aahi, "As is the way you conduct your life. Our advice is to forget Kiirt, then there would be no need to see Bovini."

"I thank you for your advice, but I must talk to her now more than ever. Now, Mother may I have the directions to her hut?"

Reluctantly, her mother conceded and gave her directions then said, "Please, be gentle and polite to her."

"I will be as tactful as I can."

Batu left her parents' hut and walked deep in thought to her own. In her hut, she quickly lost interest in Kiirt and his request. The light of the new cycle would be soon enough to concentrate on Kiirt, for now she wished to lose herself in the memories of Tomudo. She fell asleep with her cheeks moist from tears she did not think she had left within her.

With her dawn meal eaten, Batu walked leisurely to Bovini's hut. Bovini sat outside her hut. Her eyes were closed and her face was directed to the Great Sun. The last time she saw Bovini had been at the Great Pole ceremony, and it had been from a distance. As she drew near the woman it surprised her how old she looked. Upon hearing Batu's soft footsteps she opened her eyes, shaded them with her hand, and peered at her. Her face broke into a wide, almost toothless grin, "Batu, why do you stop here?"

"You know me?"

"But of course. Everyone does. You have been honored with a story about you, remember? I heard Tomudo recite it to all of us. I know you, and I know of your antics. You were always too busy to pay attention to an old woman like me. In spite of that, I like you. More than once, I have laughed over your exploits."

As soon as Bovini paused, Batu spoke. "As you know Tomudo is dead, and I am without child. I am now vulnerable to being cast out of our village. Kiirt has come forward and offered to make me his woman. Being his woman would allow me to remain in the village and stay alive, but I have heard talk about Kiirt that disturbs me. I need to know how he conducted himself while in union with your Marlem."

The old woman grimaced. "I see your unruly behavior extends to conversation as well, Batu. It is tradition to speak of these things only if the family speaks of it. But then you are seldom ruled by tradition, eh?"

"Bovini, I am sorry to speak of your family's shame."

Waving her arm wildly, Bovini interrupted saying, "Shame? I have not spoken yet and you call it my family's shame. You bear the impudence of youth."

Blushing, Batu said, "I am sorry to presume. It is a fault of mine. But I need to know how it would be to live with this man. This is of greater concern to me than some ancient tradition. I have learned it matters little who begins to talk about a subject first. What matters is whether you are willing to help me from making a grave mistake. This is far more important than tradition. My life and my happiness are at stake. I do not care to be in union with a man whom I fear."

Bovini nodded her head in approval. "I may help you, but what of your own unwillingness? I have heard stories concerning your vanity and unwillingness to help your friends."

"I know, Bovini. I have made many errors in the past, but what matters is whether or not there is a future for me. I need your help, otherwise, I will not have the opportunity to correct my mistakes."

Bovini rose. She moved to Batu and inspected her face. "I see no wrinkles in your face and yet you are already speaking with wisdom." She paused and grinned. "Perhaps you are worth saving. You have displayed courage in the past. It is easy to see why so many people talk about you. You speak your mind. You are not afraid of your elders. What you say is true." Shaking her head she continued, "Helping you is more important then my being angry with you. You have injured my pride, but I will survive it. In my old age I have had precious little to be proud of anyhow. Come sit beside me so I do not have to strain these old legs."

Grabbing Batu's arm, she led her to the bench. After they were seated the old woman spoke, "So you wish to know of my Marlem's life with Kiirt, eh? Well, at first they were as happy as any two in union. Most likely the newness of bonding kept him satisfied. Then in their second season together he began to show signs of his true nature. My Marlem began to have problems satisfying his huge appetite for bonding. The fact she was some seasons older than he may have curbed her sexual appetite, but I deeply suspect she could not stand his aggression and oppression. He berated her when she was unenthusiastic. Eventually, he got so angered he slapped her. He would slap her then apologize and then force her to bond with him. The first time she refused to bond with him after he slapped her he hit her with his fist so hard he knocked her to the ground. At this point, she came to me and spoke of their problem and her shame."

Batu stopped her. "Was she unable to speak to him and determine why he beat her for refusing him? I am certain other men have been refused and they have not beaten their women." She thought of the long period of conflict in her own union with Tomudo.

"She told me she asked him many different questions of why he slapped and hit her. He always gave her various reasons. One of the reasons was that it was her fault she made him so mad. Another reason was he wanted her to bond with him whenever he wished. He felt it to be his right and her obligation." She breathed deeply and continued, "The beatings came about because he felt she did not perform her duty as a woman. I suspect his manhood could have been threatened by her refusals. Later, he beat her if she displeased him about anything. My Marlem did not know how to please him. He was just a shallow, mean, angry man.

"There is something else that bears strongly on how he felt and why he acted so badly. He is a terrible hunter and trapper. We often had to share our food with them. It could have been another source of his anger."

Batu shook her head in dismay at the news.

"In their fourth season of union Marlem became pregnant. But it seems the gods did not want a babe to be born to them. She lost the child. While she carried the babe, things seemed to get better. When she lost it, he became very angry and things got worse for her." She stopped and looked away from Batu and stared at the ground, moving her feet back and forth in the dark, soft, warm sand before looking at Batu again.

Her voice became filled with emotion as she continued. "She began to have long moments of sadness. Her moments were filled with sorrow and terror. She grew thinner and weaker. She could not satisfy him. It mattered little what she did. Everything she did aggravated him.

"He never comforted Marlem after she lost the child. He blamed her constantly. His constant harping only fueled her sadness. She could not bear to live. I feel this is why she died, not because of any sickness."

Batu looked at Bovini's weathered face. It seemed even older now that she shared her sorrow. She reached over and placed her hand on Bovini's. In a voice just audible and filled with emotion, Batu apologized to the old woman. "I am sorry, truly sorry."

Tears fell from Bovini's face onto her breast. Batu waited quietly for Bovini's tears to subside. Wiping the tears roughly from her face Bovini continued, "I know you are a very different and strong-willed woman, but I would fear for you if you were to be in union with Kiirt. I fear you would end up like my Marlem. Why waste another life? Wait, another man will come along. Be patient. You will see. You were the most favored in beauty among our women. Surely some man will remember. Even with your scars you have a strong countenance. Some man will come. Just wait.

"Batu, you have done things other women have not even thought or dreamed of doing. Our hope is in your courage. Do not let your courage turn into foolishness. Do not let this man into your hut and life. He will destroy you. Whether the women in our tribe know it or not, we women cannot afford to lose you. You are the only one among us brave enough to stand up to any man and any injustice, but to live with someone like him is different. His anger and abuse would wear you down. It would surely be your death."

The wrinkles in her face deepened, reflecting the emotions inside her. The old eyes pleaded. She sat wringing her hands waiting for Batu to reply.

Batu wondered if she would ever have occasion to go through such tragedy with one of her creations, if she ever lived to bear one.

"Bovini, you have humbled yourself for my sake. You have shared your family shame for me. I am sorry to have caused you the pain of remembrance." She placed her arms around the frail, stooped body, hoping her embrace would provide the comfort her words could not give.

Briefly, Bovini embraced her in return, and then pulled away. Looking into Batu's eyes for a long moment she said haltingly, "Think long on what I have told you. You mean too much to some of the women of this tribe."

"I will, Bovini. I will."

They hugged each other again. Batu left pondering Kiirt's atrocious behavior. She walked out to the plains seeking out her favorite tree. Stretching her hands out and laying them on the tree, the pent up emotions from her talk with Bovini overcame her. She hung her head and wept. When the tears ceased she sat down with her back against the tree. If Tomudo had lived perhaps she would have eventually seen the stupidity in a tradition that prevented a woman from asking a man to join her in union. Perhaps she could have talked Tomudo into getting the men to rethink their position about it.

Propped up against the tree, she felt him near. She hoped he could, in some fashion, help her with her decision. It seemed unlikely another man would ask her to be his woman. The seamy Kiirt appeared to be the only way to escape death. If she joined him in union, she may simply be exchanging one form of death for another. Clearly, she could not match him physically. It would be on the mental plane that she would have to triumph over him. Yet, a man so shallow in nature and prone to bonding and abuse would not be easy to speak to rationally nor would he be likely to change. Words would have little effect upon such a man.

Bovini had detected the problem correctly. She envisioned most of his troubles had their origin in the inadequacies of his hunting abilities and his need to dominate. In his mind, his lack of skills could very well have caused him great concern and loss of stature in the village. Would anything he learned be able to change his poor self-esteem embedded within him? Not likely. Such a man would release his anger and frustrations on the only person he could control, his woman. She wondered whom he beat now since Marlem had died? Possibly he was more cautious because the woman he now bonded with would not tolerate his brutish actions. Perhaps he has no woman and that is why he sought her out.

It seemed unlikely, she concluded, that she would be able to control a man entrenched in such behavior. Her independence would quickly incite him to anger. A man so ill equipped to handle his own inadequacies would simply beat her for her superiority. It would not be long before she would be in the same position as Marlem.

Wearily, she rubbed her face. Life had turned into a perilous mess. Despite all her thinking, she could not figure out why it all had to happen. There had to be a reason why only this one pathetic, sick-minded man offered her any hope for survival. Was this all she was worth? What good was living ten or twenty seasons or more if they were filled with misery, pain and sorrow? Most certainly, she might perish sooner than that by infuriating him.

She imagined Kiirt beating on her with his fists, and then kicking her as she lay on the ground. It was not a picture she wanted from life. She knew she could not subject herself to such brutalities. After having lived in an atmosphere of tolerance and love, she knew she would rather be dead than live under his dominance. Did living or not living come down to this one decision? No! She would not be beaten and humiliated while she had anything to say about it. She would rather face expulsion and death by some unknown force. If she were ever to be in union again, it would be with a man equal to Tomudo in the depth of his love, his tenderness, his understanding, and in his ability to share his knowledge. It would have to be a man who would have the inner strength to not be intimidated by her strong will and intelligence. Did a man like that exist? Answering her own question she said aloud, "Other than her father and Taja, none."

Lost in thought, she became oblivious to the passing of the Great Sun. The air, heavy with heat, gently whispered through the leaves above her. The rich, green grass spread out before her, rippling and changing hues as it reflected the light. A small herd of gazelles fed and relaxed on the distant grasses. Smiling, she recalled the moments she and Tomudo sat here doing the same thing.

She rose and turned to gaze at the tree she and Tomudo had become so fond of. Affectionately, she placed her hand on it silently thanking it for the comfort it had provided two lovers in the past. Withdrawing her hand, she turned and walked back to her hut.

Dusk slipped away as Batu sat awaiting Kiirt. Agitated, she began to rise from the bench just as she caught sight of someone across the village center. The dim light from the Great Sun, now hidden behind the jungle trees, provided just enough visibility for her to recognize Kiirt, as he strolled toward her. She had waited for this moment and had planned what she would say to him. She did not relish doing it but knew she must. Her eyes searched his face for a sign to indicate his potential dangers. He came looking not at all like a man who had slowly destroyed his woman.

He saw her watching him as he drew near. He had deliberately waited till the last moment to appear. He did not want to show her his eagerness. Now that he saw her face, he became confused by what he saw there.

"Batu, I am here as you have instructed me. What is your answer?"

"No," was her curt reply.

"No, but why not? Has another man offered you union?"

"No."

"Then why no? Alone you are sure to die," he argued. "You have no way of surviving on the plains or in the jungle with the rains beating on you and the beasts of prey hunting you," he persisted.

Looking directly into his eyes she replied, "You insist on an answer, so I will give you one. I am a woman who has been raised in an atmosphere of freedom. I loved a man who allowed me that same freedom in union. You would never seek to fulfill my needs mentally or emotionally. I need a man who I can talk to, a man of intelligence, a man of compassion. What little intelligence you have seems to be lodged between your legs." The muscles in Kiirt's jaw popped out as his hands turned into fists. "You, Kiirt, would use and abuse me. For you the act of bonding would be an act of aggression and dominance with no expression of tenderness or love. With you, my life would be filled with fear, apprehension and oppression. I hate you and your lack of respect for women. It speaks to me of your weaknesses and your warped views. You offer me an extension of my life, but under you I would be dying every moment we were together. You know nothing of being gentle or of loving someone, and I fear you could never learn.

"My answer is no. I would say no to you even at the moment of my expulsion, for you would not save me, you would destroy me."

She looked at him defiantly, prepared for his vocal tirade.

Kiirt could not believe what he heard. Anger roared through him. He exploded! His hands darted out encircling her neck. Hate and rage fortified his strength, as he squeezed her throat. Instantly, Batu's neck and facial veins bulged to alarming proportions. Her face, red and swollen seemed unable to contain her protruding eyes. As her heart pounded wildly in her chest, she clutched at his hands, scratching and clawing to free them from her neck.

Unable to pry his hand lose, and rapidly losing her energy, her consciousness leaked slowly away. With heart hammering, lungs bursting and lights flashing in her eyes, she strained to remain conscious. Everything grew dark as she felt herself whirling. A queer feeling of disassociation replaced her panic. She viewed her now feeble struggle calmly. Her lack of concern and emotional equilibrium puzzled Batu. Unexpectedly, she felt his grip loosen and his hands withdraw from her neck. She fell to the ground and continued being an unemotional witness to the activity surrounding her. She had never experienced such a state of mind before. She observed her body react. It doubled up and gulped air. The sight of Kiirt's right foot engrossed her. The toe next to his large toe was distorted. It bent straight upward considerably shorter than his middle toe. How horribly ugly, she thought. Unhurriedly, she felt her head raise allowing her to view his right hand. The crooked little finger caught her eye immediately. It, like the odd toe, was very short and bent to form a hook and set away from the rest of the fingers. His pointing finger, also short, reached only to the middle of the largest finger. It bent at the second joint toward his thumb. The two fingers combined to give his hand a grotesque, deformed appearance. The deformities somehow matched his warped nature.

Even in the quickly darkening light, and in his rage, Kiirt saw the movement out of the corner of his eye, and turned his head. The movement saved Batu's life. Instinctively, he released her, fearing the passerby would send a cry out to the rest of the tribe. When the cry did not come, he looked closely to see who had entered the village center. The High Priest, Romir walking slowly, looked at them carefully. A brief smile appeared on his face as he watched them. Kiirt squinted, not believing what he had seen. Did he really see the High Priest smile, or was it the dim light playing tricks on his sight? He watched the High Priest until he disappeared. Why had he not come to Batu's aid?

As the High Priest disappeared, Kiirt's thoughts came back to the reality of what to do with Batu. He scowled at her, uncertain how to keep her from talking. He had to use the lack of assistance from the High Priest to his advantage. Grabbing her by the hair, he pulled her head up so she would have to look at him.

He stuck his face next to hers and hissed, "If you speak of this I will deny it. The High Priest has seen us and has not come to your aid. No one will believe you. He will stand by me, if you say anything. If you even whisper of this to anyone, I will be waiting for you and finish what I have started. I will do it when you least expect me."

He bent down and drew her head to within a hand of his face. "If you speak of this, I will not only choke the life from you, but I will cut your body up into pieces and leave it on the plains for the predators to eat. You will not have a body when you become a dweller. No one will know what I have done, and no one will care. Everyone hates you. Do you hear me? Everyone hates you."

Releasing her hair, he growled contemptuously, "For a woman who is supposed to be smart, you are stupid. Now you are sure to be banished. No one will have you as his woman. I hail our tradition for you will most assuredly die. I do not know what I saw in you. Your vanity and pride are as ugly as your scars. I would not put up with either one. I would kill you first. For me you are already dead. You are worthless. You are a crazy woman."

He yanked her hair again, and then released it. Shaking with rage, he spun on his heels. His feet pounded the ground as he stalked away.

"How could a woman be so insane and stupid?" he muttered to himself. Fortunately, it had only been her body that interested him. Aloud he grumbled, "I have other bodies to fill my needs. I always have. I always will."

Unexpectedly, a gust of wind swept a small clump of dried leaves after him, jerking crazily in their flight. Batu's hand came to rest lightly on her neck. She eyed him fearfully, suspicious that in his rage he would return. She heard him muttering angrily as he stormed away. While observing him moving away, her breathing deepened as her trembling body tried desperately to release its tension. Filling her lungs did little to ease her confusion about why she reacted so unnaturally.

Turning, she took the few steps that moved her into the familiar confines of her hut and eased gently onto her mat. She became mindful of her hand, which had been lightly rubbing her neck since her attack. She had an awareness of everything her body did, yet even now it seemed strangely separated from her feelings. Puzzled and confused, she could not reconcile the phenomena. The mind, which had served her so well in the past, now seemed unable to make the necessary associations she needed. Her disjointed thoughts were blown about as easily as the dried leaves she had seen moments ago.

"How could my mind fail me so miserably? I must do something," she whispered. "I cannot go on feeling like this."

In the dim light she focused on a blemish on the upright support of the hut. She concentrated on the discolored area until she felt a semblance of mental stability return.

Lying on the mat, she wondered when the tears would burst forth from her eyes, or when a sob would escape from her lips.

"It is as if the whole thing happened to some other woman, and I am but an observer who can gain nothing by a display of emotion," she whispered to herself. "How can that be? This is not normal," she continued, shaking her head in exclamation, "Yet I seem unable to cry or scream in rage for what he did to me."

She remembered the strange fascination his foot and hand held for her.

"That was why I did not scream out. I could not scream because I was unable to draw my attention away from him. But why did I not run from him afterwards? Ten steps would have put me in the next hut, why did I not run to it for help?" Rationalizing aloud, she answered herself. "Maybe any sudden movement by me would have triggered another violent reaction by him. Perhaps. Perhaps if I had attempted it, I would not be on Mother Earth, but in the Land of No Shadows.

"At least I can tell Father what has happened... Oh gods, what good will it do? He told me not to speak. If I do, he will kill me as I sleep and feed my body parts to the animals of the darkness."

Visions of Kiirt coming into her hut and strangling her as she slept formed in her mind. She visualized him carrying her out to the plains and dismembering her, leaving the pieces of her body to be devoured by some wild creatures. She saw Kiirt leave and almost instantly a pack of hyenas appeared. They sat down leisurely and feasted upon her desecrated, dismembered body. She heard her bones snapping and crunching in their powerful jaws.

Shaking her head she murmured, "No, I will not allow myself to die like that. I have a choice and I will exercise it. I will not speak of what has happened. It is settled."

Wearily she turned on her side, the air rushing from her lungs as she moved. Slowly, she again became conscious of her hand as it rested lightly on her throat. The pain of her attack lay there captured deep within its flesh.

"I seek only to sleep and forget," she mumbled half aloud closing her eyes.

CHAPTER
EIGHTEEN

Kiirt slept fitfully. Dawn broke finding him awaiting the inevitable appearance of the council. The anxiety he harbored kept pace with the slow ascent of the Great Sun, in the crystalline sky. He paced the interior of the hut, the worry apparent in his movements. Occasionally, he stopped and peered out the entrance to see if they were approaching. The Great Sun had reached the quarter mark and still they had not arrived. Perhaps his threats had petrified Batu into silence. If true, he may yet escape with his life and not resort to seeking the High Priest's assistance.

Kiirt's thoughts went back to the attack. His eyes narrowed in recollection of the searing words Batu hurled at him. In his heart, he felt justified for what he had done to her. Her unforgivable show of disrespect had touched off his explosive reaction. The disrespect alone made her at fault for what happened. Any man would have done the same thing in that position, he reasoned. The strange part about it was that he had never even touched her and yet she defamed him. It had taken almost two seasons for his deceased woman to bring him to such anger before he had to correct her. The words Batu used had cut into him as quickly and viciously as any blade could. Angrily, he shook his head. She should never have had said such things to him. She was clearly at fault for not holding to tradition and keeping her mouth shut. A woman should never speak words of that nature to a man.

Sitting down on the bench, he rubbed his face in an effort to ease his rising tension. Arching his back, he kneaded the aching muscles in his shoulder. Letting his head hang down wearily, he rested his elbows on his thighs. When had he last lost his temper? he asked himself. Yes, he remembered easily, it had been a few short cycles ago. His spear missed the mark and he lost the kill of a stray, injured, young wapiti. It would have provided food for him for many cycles. In exasperation, he had run after it until his anger and energy were spent, and he had collapsed in exhaustion.

Since the death of his woman, he had rarely lost his temper with the woman he bonded with. There was no need to; she acquiesced to all of his strange desires. He had never suspected that she had been as perverted and twisted as he.

Hearing voices nearing, he bolted upright and flew to the entrance to face the council with his practiced, innocent look. At the entrance, he found the voices belonged to three men passing by whom he only vaguely knew. He turned and began to pace the hut again.

Why have they not come? he asked himself. What is the meaning of it? The very fact they had not made an appearance could mean she was not going to take any action. It is plausible that the gods commanded her not to speak. Even they may have been angered by her disrespect. Perhaps she knew the High Priest would stand by his side, even if he were not that certain he would. Yes, he thought, she is fearful of an alliance, despite the fact there is none. Slowly, he mulled over the thought of he and the High Priest forming an alliance. Having Romir as an ally had never entered his mind. Buoyed by these thoughts, he moved to the entrance and stepped out into the light. Whatever the reasons were, he was thankful that she did not speak to the council. Even the desperate fear residing in his stomach eased away.

He stretched and breathed deeply. Looking up at the Great Sun, he smiled smugly. Perhaps he had been befriended by one of the gods, maybe even the great god Tor. Yes, one of the gods must be protecting him for some reason. The gods knew the value of a man was much greater than that of a woman. A god would never allow a man to be humbled or destroyed because of a woman like Batu. Drawing some comfort from these thoughts, he took a deep breath and slowly let it escape from his nostrils. Yes, now at last he felt a small semblance of safety.

Mulling over the thought of being protected by a god added even more comfort to his disturbed and distraught condition. He would not be in this position if Batu had been respectful to him. Because of her disrespect, the gods had grown angry with her. The more he thought of it the more he felt there could be no other explanation. One of the gods had looked upon him with favor and would not allow him to be placed in a position that could jeopardize his life.

It felt good. It felt right. He knew he would be safe. He had pleased the gods. This realization fed his line of thinking. If he was indeed protected by the gods nothing could harm him. Perhaps he was invincible. Could such invincibility protect him from an adversary as formidable as the tribe's greatest warrior, Motum? Knowing his lack of skills with weapons, some doubt crept into his thinking. In a test on the warrior's field, it may well be that his arrow or spear would find its mark because of the gods and not because of his own skill with them. It seemed plausible. Yes, that is what would happen in such a test. He slowly grew certain of it. Perhaps that is what the High Priest saw in him that moment he had held Batu's life in his hands. Everyone knew Romir had tremendous powers. Something of such importance would be easily detectable by him.

An exhilarating feeling swept through Kiirt's body. Upon sensing it, he became certain of why he was saved. He smiled widely and strode off to his lover's hut. Such an auspicious moment must be celebrated by bonding with his woman. He would show his supremacy over her and all women as he spent himself on her.

With the passing cycles, Kiirt felt more and more assured the High Priest was pleased by his attack on Batu. Kiirt's feelings of safety and invincibility grew with the cycles. The certainty of his being divinely chosen bolstered his feelings of alliance with the gods. All signs seemed to point in that direction. From Kiirt's point of view, it became obvious the gods were constructing events leading to his becoming the next High Priest. Whether Romir knew it or not, he had already contributed significantly to it becoming a reality.

The forthcoming event of being selected as the High Priest's apprentice constantly pressed into Kiirt's thoughts. He continually envisioned himself as the next High Priest. The sacred necklace of bones hanging from his neck would signify the gods' approval. His confidence grew to overwhelming proportions. Braced by this new confidence he reached a monumental decision to approach the High Priest.

Knowing his mission in life, Kiirt walked proudly and purposefully to Romir's hut. He felt he could accomplish anything with the gods' protection and assistance. He smiled as he recalled how in the past he had cowered, as did others, when the High Priest spoke of the tribulations and destruction the gods inflicted upon their tribe and their forefathers.

Stopping outside Romir's, hut he called out confidently, "Romir, it is Kiirt. I wish to speak with you."

Romir appeared at the entrance. He towered more than a head over Kiirt, giving him the semblance of still being a man-child. His glaring eyes pierced Kiirt. Kiirt stepped backward unconsciously from the gaze. Romir said nothing for a long while and then, surprisingly, he smiled.

"Kiirt, welcome. Come inside."

Romir had wondered how long it would take before Kiirt came to him wanting to know why he had not spoken to the council about the attack.

"Sit down, Kiirt. Do you realize this is the first time you have come to my hut? What brings you here?" he asked pointedly.

Kiirt had gone over in his mind what he wished to discuss many times, yet in the huge man's presence he had difficulty remembering what to ask first and how to phrase it.

Nervously, he wet his lips. "Since that fateful moment you saw me with Batu, I have had many deep conversations with the gods. It has become clear to me why the gods have spared my life."

"You fool!" Romir hissed at Kiirt, "The gods had nothing to do with saving you. I let you live. Me! Do you understand? Me! It was I. You owe *me* your life."

The viciousness in Romir's voice raised the hairs on Kiirt's arms and neck. He swallowed nervously and hesitantly continued with his planed declaration. "In spite of how you feel and what you say, I am certain that the gods have saved me in order to become your apprentice. I am here to declare that I am to be the next High Priest."

Romir's mind reeled. This impudent little worm was telling him what to do. Who did this scum think he was? Did he really think the gods would listen to him? The anger raging inside of him sought release. He exploded into action. His hands were a blur as they streaked for Kiirt's neck. Once in his grasp, he thrust him backward off his feet up against a supporting post of the hut.

Desperately, Kiirt struggled to pry Romir's fingers from his neck. He strained to free himself from Romir's hold. His efforts were futile. The High Priest's eyes bulged in rage. In his terror, Kiirt silently screamed for the gods' help. Romir's image faded as his efforts ceased. He felt himself collapse on the ground. Amazingly, Romir had released him. He panted air into his lungs. Assured he would live, he ran his hand over his throbbing throat. Despite being nearly killed, his first thought was that his plea to the gods had worked. The gods had protected him! Even though he lay in a crumpled heap, at the feet of his would be assailant, his confidence grew. He had no doubt that he would replace Romir.

Romir scrutinized the wretch on the ground. The similarity of situations startled Romir. Batu nearly lost her life to Kiirt and now Kiirt nearly lost his to him. He looked at his hands and then, speculatively, at the disgusting flesh at his feet. This piece of rubbish had almost caused him to take his life and in so doing posed a threat to his own. He would have had to concoct a plausible story to extricate himself from the situation if he had killed him.

Romir kicked him. "You fecal mess!"

Unable to look at him further, Romir turned away and sat down. As he slowly calmed down, Romir admonished himself. Perhaps he made a mistake. There must be a reason why he had allowed this wretch to live. He vowed to uncover it before he let Kiirt leave. Looking at Kiirt, he shook his head in displeasure. How could he use this contemptible man to his advantage? He had not chosen an apprentice because none in the tribe seemed remotely suited for the position. Not one of the men or men-children seemed to show any true propensity for the position. They all seemed to fear him and were thus not inclined to be deeply desirous of the position. The whole tribe seemed filled with weak-willed and weak-minded men. The Kahali needed someone with his own strength and determination to lead them into the future. There were only so many seasons he would walk the earth. Someone had to be selected.

He looked at Kiirt, now seated with his back against the post, looking apprehensively at him. Yes, there must be a reason why he has survived. Perhaps what he said had a smattering of truth. The weasel could possibly have been chosen by the gods to be the next High Priest. At this point, no other man seemed desirous of the position. It did take a special man, one who had no fear, one who would not be skeptical about using the special ways to evoke the gods' justice and one who upheld all of the traditions. Perhaps Kiirt was correct. He glanced appraisingly at him.

There is but one way to find out if he spoke the truth. It would determine if the gods really had chosen him. He would put the little man to the test. Romir went about trying to remember when the last test had been conducted. He calculated it to be six generations since the last test. The goals of the men were different then. Four young men openly sought the position of apprenticeship. Out of that group only one had been willing to perform the test to become the next High Priest. The High Priest should never have revealed what the test was about. The lone man did not have to perform the test. His willingness was enough to win him the apprenticeship. He would not be so accommodating. If Kiirt wanted the apprenticeship so desperately, he would have to go through the ordeal. The test would be the determining factor. It rested in the hands of the gods not his or Kiirt's.

Nudging Kiirt with his foot he said, "I have spared your life, for what you say may have some small smattering of truth in it. We will have to find out how much truth exists in what you have said."

Hearing this Kiirt sat upright. He nodded his head, certain he would achieve what he wanted and desired so earnestly. Not even this huge oppressive man would stop him from his destiny. Yes, that sounded right. His destiny. His fate. His life's work. Kiirt's belief solidified into faith, not only in the gods, but also in his ability to prevail. The last shred of residual doubt disappeared. His faith grew, unshakable and unmovable. His future, marked and unmistakable, stood clearly before him as real as the pain in his neck. He would be the next High Priest. He smiled at the High Priest defiantly.

Surprise registered on Romir's face, as he saw Kiirt smile. The man might be insane, but he did not lack courage. *I nearly killed him and he dares to smile. Perhaps this is the man. We shall see little man. We shall see.* He pointed to Kiirt saying, "If your desire is so great, and your belief is so strong, you will fare well when tested. The test will determine if you are telling the truth about being chosen. If you pass, you will be my apprentice and the next High Priest."

Kiirt grinned openly.

Amazing! Despite my dislike for the scum he shows promise, thought Romir. He lacks fear. Romir had to admit that not even Motum would act fearless in his presence.

"Are you willing to put your desire for the apprenticeship to the test, Kiirt?"

There it is. I have been asked just like the gods showed me. "My faith in the gods will never waver," he said to himself. Aloud he said, "I am ready."

"Good. I will prepare for it and I will make it known to you when and where it will be conducted. Is that clear?"

"Yes."

Extending his hand, he helped him up. It was the very one that almost extinguished Kiirt's life.

Romir appraised Kiirt. The man is only a little bigger than a woman, yet there is something inside of him that defies explanation and reasoning. Whatever dwelled inside of Kiirt, he would shortly know its composition.

Kiirt grasped the hand and bounced up, renewed by the erratic and strange happenings. The very hand that nearly throttled him now offered him assistance. It felt right. It felt good. Everything was progressing, as it should, just as the gods designed it. Walking back to his hut, Kiirt frequently touched his neck gingerly and smiled wildly.

Watching Kiirt walk away, Romir shook his head in disbelief at what had transpired. He had never laid a hand on anyone in anger. He had no need to; there were other, more clever ways of inflicting harm and dispensing justice.

Being well acquainted with his own anger, and the managing of it, the fury bewildered him. The man enraged him, but he could not deny that their lives were intertwined with Batu. Both of them hated her, perhaps Kiirt more so than he, but the judgment of that would have to be decided at some moment in the future. Kiirt's hate could be used to his advantage. He trusted hate. He understood it better than any of the other human emotions. Hatred gave a man purpose. With hate raging in his belly a man could accomplish anything. Hate drove a man more surely than any other passion.

Reclining on his bench Romir went over all of the things needed for the test. He always thought he would find a man worthy of the position, yet never suspected he would resort to the ordeal to select an apprentice. The words and the scene for the test were firmly etched in his mind. For some reason it had captured his imagination when Tekumsha had recited the ways and means for it. Essentially simple, yet extremely effective and decisive, it would unequivocally determine the fitness of Kiirt for the position. He would take great pleasure in its preparation and execution.

For the next several cycles, Romir carefully went over the possible sites for the ritual. The proximity of the final site to a small stand of trees and near exposed rocks at the running water influenced his decision. Upon selection of the site the High Priest informed the council members of the impending test and where it would take place. They in turn let the tribe know not to go near the site during its construction, the test and the deconstruction. He prepared the site in the prescribed manner. It took him longer than he had expected. Having to dig some of the rocks from the shore of the running water lengthened his task. Chopping and carting the wood also took longer than he expected. His body strained under the burden despite the fact he used a sled to transport the materials. The long inactive muscles quivered and ached from the toil. His hands blistered. While toiling in the heat, he cursed Batu endlessly. Completing the task, he quenched his thirst from the water bag and surveyed the site. He hoped the gods were watching his effort and rewarded him for his sense of tradition. The sacred site was completed.

After resting, he trudged back to the village. On the next cycle he informed Kiirt of the ritual site and when to be present. He did not return to his own hut immediately. There were too many things on his mind that needed his immediate attention. He had to go to the sacred hut; there he could prepare himself for the ritual by praying and then mentally go over everything gnawing at him.

Kiirt's mind constantly wandered back to what the test might be. Whatever it involved, he felt destined to succeed. The surety of his faith and trust in the gods reigned high. He looked forward to the test with the anxiousness of a warrior. He liked the sound of it. He indeed was a warrior, a warrior of the gods. Soon he would be an apprentice and would not have to contend with hunting and snaring to exist. In some strange way, he knew none of this would have been possible if it were not for the fact that Romir had wandered into the village center.

Kiirt slept alone without the comfort of a woman. He did not want to waste his energy. The moment cried for him to concentrate upon the test and upon his belief that the gods had chosen him to be the next High Priest. The next cycle stretched out agonizingly. No matter what he did his mind drifted back to the fateful question: What was the test going to be?

He ate his last meal earlier than usual. He wanted to be at the appointed spot at the correct moment. Removing his long blade, he placed it on the shelf. Leaving without it and walking so great a distance without a weapon left him with an uneasy feeling. With one last glance at the knife he turned and left.

A short distance from the village he noticed the faint trail of smoke rising to the sky. It came from the direction of the ritual site. As he drew closer he determined the fire to be exceptionally large. It looked much larger than necessary to keep predators away from them. That fact puzzled him.

The streaking remnants of the Great Sun were fading quickly. He neared the sacred ritual site and saw Romir standing close to the huge fire. The firelight danced on the coveted sacred necklace of bones hanging from the High Priest's chest. Kiirt entered the rim of firelight. Romir raised his hand for him to stop. Kiirt stole a glance at the huge fire only a few steps away, while he waited patiently for the Romir to speak.

Romir had dug the fire pit with meticulous care. The round pit measured four strides across and knee deep. Romir had lined the perimeter with head-sized rocks. On the perimeter, a knee-high protrusion of rocks disturbed the circular pattern. Atop them rested a single flat rock. The sooty rocks gleamed from flames in the quickening darkness. Romir had felled a tightly grained hardwood tree and fashioned the slow-burning logs from it. The logs, at first filled to the brim, were now burned down slightly above ground level.

Kiirt stood several strides from the fire. Even at that distance he felt uncomfortably hot. After his initial quick glance, he had not bothered to look at the fire again. He dared not for fear of missing a sign from the High Priest.

He waited patiently. Sweat poured from every part of his body. He peered at the High Priest and saw the sweat running profusely down his body. When did he intend to speak? Since he did not, he assumed the test involved standing near the fire. From the amount of wood Romir had stockpiled he knew they would be here through the darkness.

The fact that Kiirt remained silent drove Romir to reappraise him. Kiirt had not asked one question, despite the fact they obviously raced through his mind. The characteristic was something he had not anticipated from him. His respect for Kiirt grew.

Prior to Kiirt's arrival, Romir wiped the perspiration out of his eyes, but now he let the sweat run its course down his face lest Kiirt would also wipe his face. He knew that very sweat saved his skin from being roasted. Now and then the sweat wandered into his eyes and he experienced difficulty seeing Kiirt. Still, he did not wipe it away.

Gradually, he saw the heat having a visible effect upon Kiirt. The effects of the heat were mounting within him as well.

Before leaving the village, Kiirt drank deeply from his water bowl. He did not realize that simple act would provide him with an unexpected advantage. The apprenticeship was within his grasp. Never had he been so certain of anything. He felt a surge of exhilaration as he saw Romir's eyes blink quickly to free the rivulets of sweat running into them. He had not as yet had to do it. If this was a test to see if he would fall to the ground before the High Priest, he felt certain he would prevail. The test was not as difficult as he had expected. Kiirt smiled defiantly.

The High Priest did not miss the smile growing on Kiirt's face. The man laughs at me, thought Romir angrily. I am sure of it. The arrogant fool. We shall see who wavers in the end. Such audacity will reap its own surprising reward. I must be patient. It is I who will laugh in the end, little man. He sneered back at Kiirt.

They stood watching each other, their sweat wetting the thirsty ground around their feet. They stood unwaveringly. The fire became an isolated patch of brilliance in an expanding darkness, darkness alive and animated by the ritual. It riveted the two men within the searing boundary of its light. Moments crept by, measured only by the rivulets of perspiration streaming from their bodies.

Unexpectedly, Kiirt staggered forward, catching himself with a thrust of his leg. Kiirt's body was depleting its resource of water at an alarming rate. His mouth hung open. His breathing labored. Perspiration no longer flowed freely from his body. His tongue dried. He longed to drink some sweet-smelling water, to clear his spinning mind, now reeling from the effects of dehydration.

Romir saw the signs and smiled openly. The runt has lasted longer than expected, he admitted. Even I am feeling the effects of this prolonged struggle. I will have to speak while I am still in command of myself.

He wet his lips. "Kiirt, are you ready for your test?"

Kiirt looked at him incredulously. "What?"

"Are you ready for the test?" Romir repeated.

The words pounded in his head. What did he say? He wants me to do that after I had thought the test was for me to stand here longer than he. I am nearly expired, and he now wants me to begin the test. He is a madman! Surely he wants me dead. Squinting, he assessed Romir's face and saw he meant what he said. In spite of his confusion and weariness, he slowly gathered himself and answered firmly, "Yes."

Breathing heavily himself, Romir continued, "This is how you will perform the ritual test for the High Priest apprenticeship. You are to place both hands upon the flat rock jutting from the rim of the ritual fire. You will leave them there until I tell you to remove them. Is that clear to you?"

"What?"

Kiirt's eyes snapped from the High Priest's face and rested on the flat rock. The rock had dozens of fissures of bright white-red emanating from its depths. The rock could clearly brand a water buffalo's flesh three fingers deep in a matter of moments.

"Is that clear?" Romir asked again.

Kiirt focused on the rock. He had to place his hands there? He looked at Romir. The sneer on his face said it all. The man does not even hide his disgust for me. Disgust rose in his own belly. Slowly, it churned and turned into anger. He hissed at Romir. "Yes."

If the gods wanted it to be settled in this manner, then he need not have any fear. The gods had led him this far and he had no reason to think they would not continue to be at his side. Romir would not vanquish him, not now, not ever.

Kiirt did not rush himself. Taking a few deep breaths he silently prayed to the gods for protection. His faith in the gods and his anger for Romir grew to proportions that escaped his own understanding.

Romir saw the change in Kiirt. For some moments he felt a chill run down his back. He felt the anger bursting forth from Kiirt. He had never experienced such anger directed at him, not even from Batu or those he had poisoned.

Unexplainably, Kiirt's mind stilled and his body relaxed. A current of energy surged through his body that he had never experienced before. He turned and moved unflinchingly through the heat and stopped at the pit's edge. He took no notice of his body being singed. Standing still for a few breaths, he spread his feet, bent at the waist and thrust his hands onto the glowing rock.

Expectantly, Romir waited for Kiirt to scream. None came. Startled, he watched in fascination as Kiirt hands remained on the ominously red-hot, glowing rock. The man is not crying out! How is it possible for him to endure it? His hands must be burned through to the bones. If that were so, why did he not smell the burning flesh? He witnessed it but could not believe it. Spellbound for the moment he forgot to call out. Recovering he raised his voice, "Kiirt, remove your hands."

Kiirt did not react.

Romir became concerned. Did he not hear him? He called out again, his shrieking voice shattering the darkness. "Kiirt, remove your hands!"

Kiirt watched his hands dreamily. The sensation of being protected by the gods captivated him. Not only did his hands not feel the searing heat, but also his body felt cool and refreshed. A surge of energy swept through him as strong as his belief in the gods' protection.

Vaguely, as if in the distance, he heard the Romir calling to him. Watching in awe, he removed his hands, then turned and walked away from the fire pit. Outside the ring of the fire's fierce heat he collapsed on the ground.

Romir watched Kiirt walk away from the fire. He made no sound to show he had been burned. It seemed impossible that he could endure such pain without crying out and come away from the pit without making a noise. Somehow, he had miraculously passed the test. The contempt and disgust he held for him moments ago gave way to honest admiration. Somehow, the gods had protected him. He could think of no other explanation. None. The jackal had turned into a growler. He could not choose to ignore such a tremendous omen. Even though Kiirt collapsed, Romir failed to move. While Kiirt lay sprawled on the ground, Romir caught sight of his hands. They appeared to be normal. Kiirt stirred and sat up. His movement prompted Romir. He walked stiffly to Kiirt carrying the water bag. He offered it to the little man and again searched his hands for signs of scorching. None were present! Kiirt drank deeply from the bag and handed it back to Romir. After drinking from it himself, he sat on his haunches and peered at Kiirt. He understood the momentary anger he felt from Kiirt earlier and dismissed it. All of his animosity for Kiirt vanished. He drank from the water bag again and handed it back to Kiirt.

Placing a hand on the younger man's shoulder, he said in honesty, "Kiirt, the gods have seen fit to select you to be the next High Priest. It seems they did have something in mind for you. Now, we both know the reason why I did not cry out upon seeing you strangling Batu. I have been mistaken in my assessment of you. Let us put aside our differences and work for our mutual benefit. Together we will be able to accomplish a great deal. Yes, a great deal. When we get back to the village, I will inform the council that you are my apprentice. You, my friend, have much to learn. This is the most powerful and important position in the tribe. You have every reason to be proud of your selection and proud that you have survived the ordeal."

Kiirt smiled expansively. It had all come true. He would be the next High Priest. His anger toward Romir dissolved with his words. He was the chosen one. With the gods by his side, he could accomplish anything.

The fact the High Priest made no mention of their religion or the welfare of the tribe did not go unnoticed by Kiirt. He now understood that Romir considered himself first and foremost in any of his dealings. Kiirt wondered how important the gods really were to Romir? It seemed conceivable Romir believed himself to be a god or above them.

The suspicion he had for the High Priest could not be detected in his voice, "Yes. It is right for us to work as one for our benefit."

Kiirt's narrowed eyes betrayed his caution, but it escaped Romir.

Romir stood up saying, "Kiirt, please rise."

Kiirt rose and looked confidently at Romir. All fear of him had disappeared. He did not see the huge man as an adversary but an ally. Quite possibly the only one he had in the tribe. Despite this fact, he had to be cautious of what he said and did. Only the future would prove how strong his union with Romir would become.

Romir reached behind him and found the small necklace of bones similar to the one adorning his neck hanging from his loincloth. Ceremoniously, he placed it around Kiirt's neck.

"Welcome to the priesthood, apprentice Kiirt. Wear this necklace proudly for it symbolizes your position as a High Priest and the power accompanying it." Romir placed his hands upon his shoulders in respect.

Smiling, Kiirt returned the gesture.

The alliance was sealed the sacred ritual complete.

Romir drank again from the water bag and handed it to Kiirt. They drank deeply replenishing their lost fluids. They were quiet, each content for the reprieve from the ordeal. After recuperating, Romir retrieved a pile of wood and stoked the fire. He returned to Kiirt's side and they talked of inconsequential things. Soon they would be in the sacred hut where they would engage in serious conversation and concentrate on Kiirt's instruction.

Long after Kiirt fell asleep, Romir stoked the fire for the last time before the Great Sun would appear again. They would remain at the site until the stones cooled and with his new apprentice's help, the deconstruction of the site would begin. In the woodpile he picked up a short branch that could easily serve as a bludgeon with which to kill Batu. He hefted it. Imagining Batu in front of him, he swung it with amazing force and then threw it into the fire. Kiirt would be a more formidable weapon to use to accomplish the same thing without casting shadows upon himself.

CHAPTER
NINETEEN

Batu awoke gasping for air. Her hands flew to her chest, where her heart beat wildly. The dream seemed terrifyingly real. As her breathing calmed, she raised a trembling hand to her head. The emotions connected with the dream overpowered her. She reviewed the dream while her emotions played through her body. In the dream she laid on her back, pinned down by the weight of a huge, odd-shaped rock. It covered her chest and stomach, its weight so oppressive she could not get even the tiniest breath of air into her lungs.

The first impression she had seemed to point to her fear of dying by expulsion. Something nagged at her to dig into the dream further. Going over it again she noticed her hands were not struggling to push the rock off. Oddly they were at her throat. The incongruent action grew in its significance. A shiver ran through her body as the scene of her near strangulation flashed explosively before her. Reflexively, her heels dug into the earth. Memories of the attack kept spewing up. Bit by bit the assault, buried temporarily, surfaced. Kiirt's voice menacingly reverberated in her head.

Batu burst into tears. They were the first she had shed for herself since the attack. She hugged her legs. Long after the tears stopped flowing, she finally released her legs.

Fear and apprehension kept her rooted to the ground as pieces of the attack crept back into her memory. Running the experience over and over in her mind progressively displaced her fear with anger and disgust. Her hands no longer shook from fear. They were clenched. Anger swept through her uncontrollably. In the throes of the emotional upheaval she decided to tell Taja of the attack and made her way to his hut. Once there, she related the dream and the attack that precipitated it. While listening, he realized why he had recently sensed her fear so often and why she bypassed his inquisitiveness of how she felt.

"What do you want to do?" Taja asked.

"I want to go to the council and have him punished," she said icily.

"Are you sure?" he asked.

"Yes."

"Even after so many cycles have passed since your attack?" he asked.

"Yes."

With an affirmative nod of his head he said, "Then I will arrange the meeting. Go to your parents and tell them everything. When the council is assembled and Kiirt is present, I will come for you."

As they embraced, he patted her back reassuringly. Each left the hut deep in thought and purpose.

Taja went to Mihili and briefly explained why he requested a special assembly of the council. They divided the duty to find the members. When all but the High Priest and his apprentice were present, Mihili instructed Neda to get them. Taja left to fetch Batu and her family. The other members milled around filled with curiosity. None dared to ask Mihili why the special meeting was called.

When Taja, Batu, Szatu and Aahi arrived they found that everyone was already seated. Mihili, Wapur, Coloma, Neda and Motum sat on either side of Kiirt and Romir, who sat together. Greetings were murmured grudgingly.

Mihili's eyes showed anxiety as he spoke, "First, I must warn everyone present that whenever a meeting is convened to look into an allegation, that has as its punishment banishment, no one present is allowed to talk about the allegation, now or in the future, to anyone. Is that clear?"

The Elder looked at each person around the circle before proceeding. "It saddens me that we have gathered here to listen to so great an accusation. We do have precedents for such accusations. I have consulted with Coloma, and the law is clear in its wording. If the provocation is severe, and if no intent to kill is present, then the accuser will not be expelled. But if we cannot find any provocation then we must vote in favor of the accuser and the accused shall be expelled immediately from the village."

Mihili looked at Batu and Kiirt, saying, "I will not tolerate any interruptions when someone is speaking. Everyone who wants to speak will have an opportunity. Is that clear?"

After the warning Mihili looked at Batu. "Please tell us what has prompted you to bring this severe charge against Kiirt."

Batu's eyes narrowed and darted to Kiirt as she began to haltingly tell her story. "Kiirt had come to me offering to take me as his woman. I told him I would let him know my answer in four cycles. During those cycles I spoke to my parents about his intentions. They were extremely concerned and cautioned me about him. They told me about what they had heard."

"What had they heard?" asked Mihili.

"They said they heard about Kiirt's abuse to his deceased woman Marlem." She looked disgustedly at Kiirt and then brought her eyes back to Mihili. "In order to learn more about Kiirt I approached Bovini. I asked her about the union between Marlem and Kiirt. Bovini told me that Kiirt had beaten Marlem many times. She warned me not to accept Kiirt's offer."

Agitated, Kiirt repositioned his legs.

"Armed with this information I awaited Kiirt. I confronted him with his brutality. He became enraged and began to strangle me. At the point of near death he released me."

"Why do you think he released you?" asked Mihili.

"Romir had entered the center."

"Why did you not call out to Romir for help?" Mihili pressed her.

"First, I am not sure if I could have called out. My throat did not feel right. Secondly, I did not see him. Kiirt told me the High Priest had seen what happened and did not sound an alarm and would not help me."

Motum swept the ground. Mihili nodded to him. "When did this attack occur?"

"Some thirty cycles ago," she answered.

"Why did you not come forward when it happened?" he asked.

"Kiirt threatened to kill me and dismember me, if I told anyone."

"We would not have allowed that to happen, Batu. If you would have told us and something would have happened Kiirt would have been highly suspect." said Mihili.

"That would mean nothing to me, if I were dead," she fired at him, making Mihili feel foolish.

"Why have you come forward now?" asked Neda.

Batu faced him. "Because the attack has just now surfaced from where I buried it deep inside of me. My fear of being killed was stronger than my need to expose Kiirt."

Neda questioned her again. "If Romir was present, why do you think that he failed to come to your aid?"

Batu looked at Romir as she answered. "Perhaps he would have liked to see me dead."

The High Priest waved his hand in a scoffing manner at her. All the council members, except Taja, reacted and spoke at once. When they calmed down, a brief quiet ensued. Mihili broke the silence. "Is there anything else you want to say, Batu?"

She took a deep breath before she answered. "No."

Mihili turned to Kiirt. "Then we will hear from Kiirt."

Kiirt's raised his voice in protest. "Batu's version is a lie."

Silencing Kiirt, Mihili said, "We will determine who is lying. Just tell us your version of what happened."

"It is true I asked her to be my woman. I saw a chance to save her life. I lost my woman and I felt I needed a woman to fill my life. Batu's beauty, although diminished by her scars, has always tugged at my heart. I thought we could learn to love each other. In all sincerity, it seemed ridiculous to let Batu die. Asking her to be my woman would save her."

Romir could scarcely hide his surprise. Despite having no warning of the meeting's intention Kiirt's remarks were exactly the right touch, conceived with the correct tone and clearly showing his concern for another villager. Excellent!

Kiirt continued, "When I came back to hear if she accepted my proposal, she assaulted me with accusations of abuse toward my deceased woman. She kept harping on me and slurring my character. Then she besmirched my manhood. She said I could not satisfy her sexually because I was too small. Then she said I was a weak warrior and could not hunt and snare. She taunted me saying I did not have the brain of a bird. I exploded. I grabbed her throat to silence her. When I realized what I was doing, I released her immediately."

The hut filled with murmurs.

Mihili raised his voice. "Please."

When it became quiet, Kiirt continued, "In the past, my deceased woman Marlem also harped on me, but she could never match the evil tongued Batu." He glared at Batu.

"Are you finished?" asked Mihili.

"Yes."

Mihili, suddenly weary, breathed deeply. "Since the High Priest, Romir saw what happened we will now hear from him."

Romir eyes scanned everyone and came to rest on Kiirt by his side. He ceremoniously placed his arm around Kiirt.

The overture of alliance surprised everyone.

"Kiirt possesses many qualities unknown to you. Without these qualities, Kiirt could never have completed the sacred and demanding ordeal to become my apprentice. I am convinced the gods have protected him. The fact that he survived the ordeal is an omen that he has been chosen by the gods to be the next High Priest. He will lead and inspire our tribe through our religion, when I am no longer here.

"The matter before you is not a simple one. It has grave consequences. The very fact that in his rage, a rage brought on by the vicious-mouthed Batu, Kiirt came to his senses and released her, speaks highly of Kiirt. I cannot say the same for Batu. She has shown disregard for tradition and disrespect for me. Had Batu not said such vile things, we would not be sitting here now.

"Everything Kiirt has said about the incident is true. I heard her remarks with my own ears. The whole ugly incident happened because of Batu. Kiirt showed remarkable restraint. Had it been me in that same situation, I am not sure if I would have had the coolness of mind to let her go. Kiirt's value for life saved Batu."

Romir removed his arm from Kiirt and sat silently confidant that what he said released Kiirt from any responsibility for what he had done.

Mihili's eyes swept over everyone. "Is there another who would speak?"

Taja's hand swept the ground. "I have come to know Batu well this past season. On her behalf, I know she would never tell a lie. Admittedly, she is unorthodox, and a tradition breaker, but perhaps we are in need of someone like her. One thing is certain, Batu is not a liar. I cannot say the same for Kiirt, for I sense he is not telling the truth. Kiirt has already threatened and harmed Batu, let us not be compromised by his newly acquired position. We must be just in what we do. We must not be intimidated by Kiirt's position or by Romir's support of him. I feel that Romir would say anything in his defense."

Taja's eyes locked on Romir's as he stopped speaking. The biting remarks by the Talker Healer were the first that he had voiced in public. Romir's eyes turned to slits as he glared at Taja. Neither looked away from the other until Mihili spoke. "Does anyone else want to say anything?"

Aahi cleared his throat. "Yes. I want to reiterate what Taja said. Batu has always told the truth, for she has never had to fear Szatu and I. We have always encouraged her to speak freely and honestly all her life. There is no reason to think she has suddenly changed. It should be easy to see who is lying here. Kiirt must be punished."

Looking at each person in the circle, Mihili asked, "Is there anyone else who wishes to speak?" No one's hand went to the ground to speak. In the silence, Mihili tried to remember the last time he had seen Romir place his arm around anyone. After carefully going over it in his mind, he came up empty. It clearly demonstrated how he felt about Kiirt. He believed the High

Priest when he talked about the omen from the gods. The fact that the ordeal came after the attack seemed to indicate Kiirt told the truth. His act may have been highly provoked and he may have recovered his senses quickly. It all seemed very plausible. Stealing a glance at Batu, he could see her doing just what Kiirt had said. Her history of breaking with tradition spoke against her.

Mihili shook his head. "It is horrible to be faced with such a decision. Only the gods really know the whole truth and what rests in each of your hearts. This is terrible, not only for us present, but the whole tribe. If any of these accusations find their way to our people it will divide them. We must remember to not speak of what we talked about at this meeting." He took a deep breath and continued. "I have heard from those that wished to speak, and I am casting my vote in favor of Kiirt because he has an impeccable witness to corroborate his story."

Mihili turned to Taja. "How do you vote, Taja?"

"I say Batu is telling the truth."

"Motum, how do you vote?"

"In favor of Kiirt."

"Coloma, how do you vote?"

Devotion filled his eyes. Knowing how Taja voted he felt relieved that he could vote with his heart. "I believe Batu."

"Neda, you are the decisive vote. What say you?"

"I believe Kiirt."

"Impossible!" screamed Szatu. "Were you not listening?" she cried.

Aahi covered her hand.

Romir clasped Kiirt's shoulder and glared at Batu.

Batu shook her head in disgust and glared defiantly back at him.

Kiirt, wanting to shout out in victory instead, smiled in relief.

"Again, I am reminding all of you that none of this may be talked about to anyone. This meeting is over," announced Mihili.

Dejected and angry, Batu returned with her parents to their hut. Only after she had vented her anger did she relate the complete details of the attack, and her subsequent dream and reaction to it. Their attempts at consoling her failed. Returning to her own hut, she collapsed on her mat drained of energy. The meeting produced little satisfaction for Batu. She knew he would never be approached about the attack again. He was safe. That fact made her safe. That was some consolation.

Resignedly, she rubbed her temples and breathed deeply to ease her tension.

The constant intrusion of thoughts about the attack and the meeting drained her energy. In desperation, she forced herself to think about Taja and his teachings. Gradually, her thoughts centered on his discussion of the Creator. What he shared intrigued her. She knew his evocative remarks about the Creator were but a tiny portion of what he knew. The next time she sat before him she would ask Taja more about the Creator.

Batu had prepared and eaten her meager meal early, wanting to be with Taja for as long as she could. After their usual greetings and embrace she quickly settled down. With no evidence of a meal around, she assumed that he, like she, had eaten early.

Taja's eyes softened as he looked at Batu. "Do you want to talk about the attack or the meeting and how you feel?"

Her eyes turned cold. After deliberating she replied, "No. I have no desire to think about it any more, and I want to put it behind me. I do not have enough moments to waste on him. I want to hear more about what it will be like when I die and meet the Creator."

Disregarding what she said he rested his hand on hers and said softly, "This is the second time you have avoided confronting your emotions. It is imperative that you deal with it and let the Creator's law of cause and effect handle Kiirt. Do you remember the law?"

"Of course." Knowing he wanted her to cover it she went on, "All actions, speech and thoughts will return to affect us be they of a positive or negative nature." Her brow furrowed. "No one escapes the law. So, in order for him to grow, Kiirt will have to face a similar incident like I have faced at his hands."

His eyebrows moved upward in recognition of her answer and then asked. "What if his attitude surrounding that forthcoming incident is inappropriate?" he asked.

"Then he will have to face the situation again until he can forgive and finally love his attacker."

His eyes penetrated hers as he asked, "And what of your attitude? Have you forgiven him?"

Batu's eyes widened. "No."

"Then you have some work to do so you will not be burdened with it in some other life," he said softly.

She gazed at him.

"My dear Batu. It is futile to try to evade such an experience. Inevitably, you must deal with your anger. You cannot hide it. I sense it in you. Such thoughts will only entrap you and deter you from your growth in love. It is better to alter your attitude. Understandably, you may never forget what Kiirt did to you, but you must work toward forgiving him."

"It is easier said than done Taja," she threw at him.

"It is never easy to do. Try understanding Kiirt and what has caused him to become who he is, and what factors contributed to his actions. It will help. You must also recognize that you contributed a great deal to the incident. It is not difficult to see your personalities are in direct opposition to each other. Examine what happened from as many viewpoints as you can. Hopefully, approaching your problem in this manner will make way for some flashes of insight. If insight escapes you, then you will have to dwell upon it until you come to some reasonable understanding and discharge your emotions.

"It is likely that this incident and the energy it created has already stored itself in your body. To locate where that energy is you may need to go into meditation and ask to be shown where it is lodged. If you are unable to locate it in this manner you will have to stretch your body and place it in any number of postures to discover and release the energy again and again until your emotions and the associated energy slowly become discharged. Another way is to allow me to probe your body by massaging it to find where that energy is stored. Once found we can knead it over and over until it is all released. For this to work you must go into the emotions of the event as we maneuver the muscle and tissue. The last method is one that I am not going to reveal to you."

Batu sat considering over his words without expressing herself. The unspoken last method held her attention. She wondered why he had not related it to her. He interrupted her thoughts.

"There are other means available as well."

"What are they?" she asked.

"One method is to find some moment when you and Kiirt were not at each other's throats and concentrate upon that until you feel you hold no ill feelings toward him. When you have reached that point, you must work on forgiving him. Do you want to pursue exploring this further?" he asked.

"No. For now, let me absorb what you have said. I must find my own way with this. Let us talk of more spiritual things."

"But this is spiritual, Batu, and it is the most important thing in your progress at this moment."

Shaking her head dejectedly, she said, "That may be so Taja, but I have had enough of this for now. I am very tired, very tired. I need to sleep."

Both rose and embraced her teacher. Taja stood by the hut's entrance and watched her walk slowly away.

CHAPTER
TWENTY

Early the next cycle Batu appeared at Taja's hut. After greeting and embracing, Taja suggested they walk on the plains. When they were some distance from the village, he sat himself down. Following his lead she crossed her legs as well and sat opposite him.

Taja spoke for the first time since leaving the hut. "Are you at peace with the council's decision?"

Curtly, she answered, "Of course not! They have shown their stupidity and left me frustrated. If the High Priest had come to them and accused Kiirt of trying to kill him they would have not reacted as they did with me. How could they not see that Kiirt and the High Priest were lying?"

She waited for his reaction to her emotional reply. When he made no effort to continue the subject, she sensed that something important occupied his thoughts. Far too agitated to calm down quickly, she confronted him. "What is it?"

Cocking his head, he remained silent.

Taking a deep breath, she tried to envision what he wanted from her. After a moments thought she blurted out, "You want me to forgive them!"

Shaking his head slowly, he informed her, "It would not be meaningful, yet. There is far too much energy stored with this event, and if it is not released, it can harm your body and continue to harm you."

Fully expecting him to say that she should, the reply jolted her.

"But, you cannot escape it. It must be done," he suggested.

Her eyes darted to either side of him, as she explored the meaning of his words. Unable to grasp what he was driving at, she surrendered to him. "What is it you want me to do?"

"Batu, you are a co-creator of all events. The wondrous ones and those that cause so much pain in your life."

"Impossible! Kiirt caused this."

Taja raised his hand from his lap showing his palm to her. "No. Kiirt had his part in the cause, but you were the main cause."

"That is absurd!" she protested loudly.

His eyes widened, "Is it?"

"Yes," she retorted.

"You have challenged me often in our meetings. It is my turn to do the same thing to you. I want you to think over everything surrounding the attack and see if you can discover anything new about it. Are you up to the challenge?"

Having never backed down from a challenge, she silently accepted this one. Batu examined everything leading up to the attack. What came to her mind was Kiirt's abuse of his deceased woman. That showed how brutal he could be, but it was not the cause of the attack. What happened between Kiirt and his woman only demonstrated his abusive trait. Kiirt was the one who approached her with his offer of union. Had he never done so, she would not have been attacked. But, he did approach her and he did react violently. He reacted to her judgmental attitude and disgust of him. In, truth her fiery words were the first injurious act of their encounter. She had attacked his manhood and berated him. He reacted like a cornered animal with nothing left to do but attack. Her outrage of his abuse had been the cause of the attack. It did not excuse it. Nothing could excuse it. At last, she saw what her anger had prevented her from seeing – the truth.

"On examining the attack I see what you say is correct. I caused his anger."

"Good. What remains for you is not only to forgive yourself for enraging Kiirt, but also forgive the council members inability to see the truth, Kiirt's abuses to his woman, and his attack upon you."

Shaking her head sadly, she said, "How am I ever going to do that in this my last season on Mother Earth?"

"All the more important to take action. First, you must rid yourself of anger," he stated encouragingly.

"I am not angry now. I feel cheated, disappointed and foolish that I could place myself in such a situation. I did not come here to find out I am to blame."

With great intensity, Taja stated, "You cannot shunt your anger, Batu. Take this opportunity to get back to it. You need to release it. Allow me to show you one of the ways you can help release the anger. You must get back to that emotional moment when it happened. You have already pointed out to me that you have only this season on earth. Do not waste these moments in anger. Are you willing?"

"I am not sure," she said haltingly.

"Trust me," he said reassuringly.

After a few moments a slight nod of her head told him she would cooperate. "Close your eyes," he instructed, "And recreate the attack in your mind."

She looked at him a long while before she relented. The event unfolded more easily than she expected. She watched as she began berating Kiirt. Knowing what followed caused her breathing to become deeper. Her heartbeat accelerated. She saw his explosion. His hands were upon her throat. Her heart raced. She panicked as she felt his hands constricting her throat. She screamed, "No! No!"

"Stay with it!" he commanded, "Feel it!"

Holding the scene, she saw herself fall to the ground. Slowly, her breathing became less labored. Her facial expression hardened.

Seeing the change, Taja confronted her again. "Use your body to show your anger. You must use your emotions to rid yourself of the energy stored in your body as the event."

The muscles in her arms flexed. She threw her shoulders and arms back then brought her arms forward quickly.

"Good, do it again!" he said in a raised voice.

She repeated the action but quicker.

"Again."

The intensity of the movements grew, as she repeated them over and over. The action became violent. Sweat poured from her. Hate for Kiirt filled her and directed her body. The movements came to an abrupt end.

She screamed wildly.

Tears burst from her eyes.

Her head fell to the ground. She moaned.

"I was so helpless," she whimpered.

Opening her eyes she found Taja's. "He made me feel helpless and weak. He had my life in his hands. You cannot imagine what that felt like. I was powerless. I was at his mercy and he had none. I had no control over myself. He took that control from me. He left me with only terror and fear, and I hate him for that."

Quiet for the moment, tears swiftly filled her eyes clouding her vision of Taja. He scooted next to her and placed his arms around her. "Let them flow," he said softly.

She clung to him tightly. Anger, hatred, frustration and shame found a home in each tear. Bewildered by the intensity of her hatred, she was astounded how easily it came out of her. With her voice filled with emotion, Batu asked, "Why do some of us take our anger out upon others physically?"

Sadness swept over Taja's eyes. "I am still at a loss to answer that, but we are all capable of such acts, if all of the negative circumstances are fulfilled and pressures build. We are comprised of the light of goodness and darkness as well. Some of us control the darkness others do not or cannot. I am sorry I had to put you through that, but I could not allow you to harbor those crippling emotions. You have taken a tremendous step in ridding yourself of them. If you are agreeable we can set aside a portion of each fourth meeting to complete the process."

"You wish me to go through this again?"

"Yes, until no anger remains."

"Let me use another method."

"There are other methods, but I at this moment I think this is best suited for you. You can speed up the process by facing Kiirt and telling him how much he hurt you."

An audible sigh escaped Batu. "No."

He embraced her and patted her. "You have done well this cycle. Perhaps you will truly forgive him before season's end."

Batu had kept her promise to devote every fourth meeting to the eradication of her anger toward Kiirt and the council. The second of their meetings did not have the enormous release as the first. Overall it left Batu spent emotionally and physically. Afterward, she drifted out to her favorite resting place and sat leaning against the familiar tree in contemplation.

The soft sound of feet moving upon the earth caused Batu to open her eyes and seek the source. Expecting the source to be from the Talker Healer, surprise registered on her face, as she saw the woman approaching. The look on Zala's face caused her to become alert. Batu moved smoothly from the sitting position to her feet.

Zala's short, stout body moved over the ground stiffly, as she covered the short distance between them in quick, choppy strides. Her short fingers were balled at her sides. Short, dark, curly hair and thick eyebrows accentuated her dark, brown eyes, darkened further by her anger. Her thin lips, drawn tight into a slit, disposed of the last vestiges of softness the ruddy-skinned, manly face had ever contained. The short, thick neck could not conceal the veins furiously pumping adrenaline filled blood through them.

While Zala was six strides away, Batu greeted her warily. "Zala, what brings you here?"

Zala did not reply. Closing the distance between them, she raised her hands and shouted, "Eeeahhh!" as she violently pushed the wary Batu backwards.

Attempting to catch herself, Batu flung her arms backward. Her left arm smashed into the tree that had supported her a moment ago. Pain shot through her arm, just before her head thudded on the ground setting loose a shower of lights. Shocked by the aggression and pain, Batu lay on the ground recovering. Another scream from Zala sped her into action. She rolled to her side too late to avoid Zala's knee that crashed on her rib cage. Ignoring the new pain, Batu forced herself to a standing position and tottered dizzily only to receive Zala's next rush. Zala's shoulder caught Batu and spun her around. Losing balance, she tumbled to the ground. Ending up some five strides away, Zala turned and readied for another charge.

From the ground, Batu yelled, "Are you insane?"

Ignoring the question, Zala grunted like an animal and raced toward Batu, her eyes wild with anger. Managing only a crouched position before Zala crashed into her, Batu went harshly head over heels. The already damaged arm struck a small rock protruding from the ground creating another jolt of pain. Her jostled head throbbed as she swung around to find Zala, who had skidded away on her side.

Batu's adrenaline now matched Zala's. It smothered the pain as she leapt to her feet. She readied for Zala's next assault. She bent at the waist and knees. Jumping to her feet, Zala raced toward Batu ducking her head in the process. Watching her attacker, Batu deftly stepped aside, and like the men wrestling, heaved at the body racing past her. The shove caused Zala to veer radically off course and crash violently into the tree. Her head struck the tree off-center an instant before her shoulder. The two ghastly noises sounded as one. Zala crumpled to the ground. She lay at the side of the tree without a sound.

For a moment, Batu expected her to get to her feet. When she did not, Batu cautiously dropped to her knees and sought out the vein in Zala's neck, as she had seen Taja do on occasions. The blood raced under her fingertips. Gingerly, she moved her hand over Zala's head. There, on the right hemisphere, she found a quick growing lump and a laceration. Blood covered her fingertips as she removed them. Zala's head would pain her long after her own pain vanished. The bark had left gashes on Zala's shoulder. Blood oozed from them freely. While in Taja's company, she had seen him tend to injuries of various magnitudes. It took no effort for her to decide to let the injuries simply coagulate. Cautiously, Batu probed the shoulder to determine if any bones were broken.

She stared at the unmoving form and wondered what possessed Zala to attack her. Batu's memory had always served her well. Utilizing it now, she could not uncover one instance where she had spoken rudely to her. Nothing seemed to warrant the attack.

The woman, eight seasons her senior, had little social contact with her, when Batu was a child. Even as an adult they had minimal social interaction. Occasionally, they had both been part of a large group of women gathered at the baths to discuss a birth or a religious ceremony.

Glancing toward the village and then to the plains, Batu failed to see anyone. Weighing whether or not to leave Zala alone and find Taja, she decided to remain by her side. Influencing her decision was her need to know why Zala had attacked her.

Some moments passed before Zala moaned softly. Batu moved out of her reach and waited. Moaning again, Zala opened her eyes. She rolled slowly onto her back. A hand reached up to find the source of pain in her head. She spotted Batu. Glaring at her, she found the lump on her head and groaned loudly. Pulling her hand away, she viewed the blood upon it guardedly. In spite of moving her injured shoulder carefully, she winced in pain.

"I do not think it is broken," Batu offered.

Ignoring Batu's evaluation, Zala dejectedly said, "You were the one who was to be beaten senseless."

The declaration furrowed Batu's brow. "But why?"

Shielding her eyes from the Great Sun, Zala said, "Because Kiirt wanted you as his woman."

Shocked, Batu said defensively, "I did not know you were seeing him."

"No one but my parents knew."

The attack began to make sense to Batu. Curious, she asked, "How did you keep your relationship hidden?"

Reluctantly, Zala answered, "We met late in the darkness in his hut. With me he took what I offered in the dark. With you he boldly asked in the light. You cannot imagine how that angered me."

Batu clutched her injured arm. "I have some idea now."

Disregarding what she said, Zala lashed out at her. "He wanted you as his woman, not me! After two seasons of giving myself to him he asked you to be his woman. I have no illusions about the way I look. When I reached the age of bonding no man came to take me from my parents. You on the other hand were beautiful and were always doing something to attract attention.

Even after you lost your looks he still sought you out to be his woman. Do you know how that made me feel?"

Releasing her injured arm, Batu gestured peaceably. "I did not want him. I refused his offer."

"Do you think I do not know that? I paid for your refusal."

Confused, Batu asked, "What do you mean?"

"I mean I had to bear that burden."

"What burden?"

"In the way all women bear such burdens, silently," Zala told her.

Batu persisted. "I still do not understand. What burden?"

"I wanted you hurt, as I have been hurt."

Understanding came to Batu. Without answering she searched Zala's face and found the remnants of an old trauma where he had hit her. Her eyes softened. "He has been hitting you. This is why you wanted to hurt me."

Zala screamed, "Yes!"

Batu flinched at the outburst.

"I wanted you to feel pain, as I have felt it."

Batu looked puzzled. "Me?"

"Yes, you."

In her defense Batu said, "I did not hit you. Kiirt did."

"You were the cause."

"No. No," Batu protested. "Kiirt is the cause of your misery, not me."

"The burden began after your refusal."

"Do not blame me for that. He has it in his history," Batu pointed out.

"Do you speak of the rumors about Marlem?" Zala wanted to know.

"Yes."

"I questioned Kiirt about that. He denies having ever hit his deceased woman."

"He lies, Zala."

"No, you do," Zala retorted.

"How could you believe him after he has hit you?"

Stunned, Zala blinked as if becoming aware of that fact for the first time.

Seizing the opportunity to make an impact, Batu continued, "After he came to me, I asked my parents about him. They spoke of the rumors. Against their wishes I sought out, Bovini, the mother of Marlem. She told me Marlem had spoken to her of Kiirt's abuse."

Defensively, Zala hissed, "You lie."

"What need have I of doing that? Go and talk to Bovini yourself."

Frustration showed on Zala's face as she thought over what Batu had said.

Compassion flooded Batu. In a soft voice, she asked, "How long has he been abusing you?"

A hopeless look appeared on Zala's face for a moment before she answered. "Since you refused him."

Moving closer, Batu reached out and covered Zala's hand with her own. Zala jerked her hand away.

In a hesitating voice, Zala unfurled the truth. "When it first happened, I could not believe it. He told me he was sorry. He said he loved me, but it continued to happen." Zala starred at Batu. Anger stirred again inside of her and her face became drawn. "He should have been beating you, not me."

Unable to contain the secret that shrieked to be told Batu whispered, "He has done worse than that to me."

"You lie! What could be worse?"

"I am unable to say."

"Once again you are casting doubts like a woman that gossips," Zala retorted.

"One thing I can say is leave him," Batu said urgently.

"What?" she asked incredulously.

"Leave him," Batu repeated.

Zala's stare changed perceptibly.

"I cannot do that, Batu."

"Why not?"

"Because he has told me he loves me, and I love him."

"What he is doing to you shows he does not love you," she countered. "He is simply a beast using the word love." Batu's eyes narrowed remembering her own encounter with him.

"He is not. He is just angry. Angry at you."

Batu fired back an option. "Threaten him with going to the council."

Zala's forehead crinkled with thought. She made no reply.

"The council is obligated to protect you from him. If you do not want him to bond with you, they can prevent him from doing so."

Zala scoffed. "I cannot believe that they would do it, especially now that he is the High Priest's apprentice."

"They must. It is the law. It is one of the few that protects women."

Curious, Zala questioned Batu, "I heard that you are teaching Coloma the stories Tomudo did not. How does the law read?"

"If a man is not in union with a woman, she can refuse to bond with him. She can refuse to let him enter her hut or take her to his hut."

"And what does the law say about a man abusing a woman?" Zala asked.

"If they are in union the law is too vague. A man can say his woman is disobeying him. If a man is not in union with a woman and he beats her, he is subject to punishment which fits the abuse."

"What is the punishment?" Zala wanted to know.

"He is lashed from three to twelve times depending on the abuse. Knowing the character of our men and how proud they are, I think the humiliation would be worse than the lashing."

"What if the man tries to kill the woman?"

"If it is an attempt on the woman's life, he will be banished from the tribe if found guilty. It matters not if they are bonded."

Too entrenched in her traditional role of the subservient woman, Zala shook her head. "I cannot go to the council."

"You cannot go on like this," Batu pointed out.

Zala cast her eyes to the ground.

Pleading, Batu said, "If you let him continue to beat you, it is the same as abusing yourself."

Zala's eyes shot back to Batu. "You are insane."

"No, I am not. You are to blame for what is happening to you, if you let it go on."

"I am not, you are!"

Ignoring the accusation, Batu said, "Kiirt is the instrument you are using to beat yourself."

Zala's eyes widened. "That is not so."

Batu went on, "If I had a lover and he struck me once and apologized for it I would forgive him. That abusive incident was his fault. If he struck me again and I did not leave him, or insist he see the Talker Healer, I have no one to blame except myself, and in addition my self-respect will begin to erode."

Zala listened intently to Batu.

"Whether it is physical or mental, abuse is the worst form of control. An abusive person does not know the meaning of love, and the one being abused does not know the deeper meaning of it either. It is even worse with parents, for the child has no one to turn to for it is from the parents the child looks to for love, comfort and security. The child can only believe that he is at fault for his parents' behavior toward him. The most difficult situation is one where the child abuses the parents. You are a grown woman who is capable of stopping this abusive relationship. You can take charge of your life before you lose your self-respect and self-worth. End the relationship."

Zala finally spoke. "It is easy for you to say those words; you have had a man and others are seeking to make you theirs. Kiirt is the only man to pay attention to me. He is the only man who has loved me"

Sadness settled over Batu's face. Shaking her head, she confessed, "True, I have had a man by my side in union. Tomudo was a good man." A small smile broke Batu's sadness. "In a quiet way he was a champion of women. I was indeed fortunate. As for all the rest of these men you think I have seeking to be my mate, they are imaginary. Kiirt is the only one to seek me out as his woman. I am not certain why he wanted me. My guess is he wants my body, for these scars have stolen the beauty from my face and form. The Kahali men want women who are traditional and subservient, not radical." Her eyes looked away from Zala's as she searched for the true reason. She continued, "Perhaps that is what he seeks. He wants to conquer the spirit that has dominated my life. Men are in need of winning at wrestling, at hunting and in contests. That may have been his way of showing the tribe that he could conquer me where no one else has been able. Ultimately, if no man claims me, I face expulsion. So you see my lot is not as easy as it seems."

Wanting to know why Batu chose not to save herself yet not wanting to know Zala asked, "Why did you not accept Kiirt's offer? It is better than death."

"If I accepted his offer, my face would look like yours in a short while. I could never be subservient to him. He would beat upon me because of that. I could never cower to him," Batu said bluntly. "Being abused is not acceptable to me, for with it I would lose my self-respect."

She saw Zala wince and wished she had not been so direct. "I am sorry."

Zala stood up. Anger claimed her face again. Her nostrils flared. Her eyes became slits.

Seeing it, Batu informed Zala, "Your anger is misdirected."

"What do you mean?"

"Your anger should be directed at Kiirt."

"How can I be angry with him? I love him."

Spinning on her heels, Zala left. Batu watched her walk away. Discouraged at not having been able to convince Zala to leave Kiirt, Batu shook her head slowly. The pain, unnoticed while talking with Zala, returned as she scooted over to the tree without standing up. Her eyes remained on Zala until she disappeared. She wondered if Zala would leave Kiirt, when the abuse took on greater proportions. Strange, she reflected, how love keeps a person chained to intolerable situations almost to the point of death, and in some cases death is the only release. She shook her head slowly realizing that she would not live to see if Zala's courage could resurrect itself enough for her to leave him.

CHAPTER
TWENTY ONE

A gentle dusk breeze stirred the tall grass that bordered the sloping path to the running water. Batu's eyes drank in the sight now as they did so many common sights since meeting with Taja. It was a practice he recommended for her to become aware of Mother Earth's splendor.

Many of the women and women-children were already bathing and chatting as she arrived. Since her meetings with Taja, she no longer chose to be the center of conversations or to dominate them. Becoming less controversial since the death of Tomudo and abandoning her old disposition, she preferred to inquire about routine family concerns, or simply listen to the social conversations. When pressed into speaking, she offered little in the way of controversy and much in the way of encouragement.

The changes in her temperament, like everything else Batu did, quickly became the topic of conversation for the women despite Batu's efforts to fade from the forefront. Her new character did manage to change the opinion of a few women but most could not forgive or forget what she did in the past.

The water made small wakes as she made her way through it to join her mother, chatting animatedly with a few friends. After greeting them, she began to methodically bathe herself, while she listened to the light conversation of the group. The verbal exchanges did not draw her into the chatter. Content to smile at the appropriate moments during the easy banter, she removed her loincloth and started washing it. The task done so automatically in the past now became significant. Gazing at the loincloth, it struck her that her blood had not soiled it recently. The Sun With No Heat had already been through two of its cycles since Tomudo's death. In her grief and preoccupation with Coloma and Taja, she had not paid attention to her conception cycle.

She stepped over to her mother and drew her away from the others. In a hushed, excited voice she exclaimed, "Mother, my loincloth has not been soiled since Tomudo has died. I believe I am with creation."

Wide-eyed, Szatu broke out into a huge smile and replied happily, "Oh, Batu, this is good news. If it is true, you will not be banished, and you can

228

remain with us." She embraced Batu excitedly unmindful of those looking on.

"If this is true, then I am carrying the creation Tomudo always wanted. His love for me has left the seed of that love within me. At last, my sorrow can turn to joy, for he will live through our creation."

Szatu, nodding her head, while Batu spoke enthusiastically, now spoke, "We must tell your father. He needs to hear this good news. His sorrow has been overpowering for he knows that in several cycles of the Sun With No Heat you could be expelled."

They finished bathing without returning to the women and left hurriedly with their arms around each other, leaving those that saw them embracing wondering what had happened.

Aahi, seated in front of his hut, saw the two women he loved more than his life walking toward him in happy conversation. He had not seen them so light-hearted in many cycles.

"Your faces and bodies bear a happiness I have not seen lately. It is good to see," he said smiling broadly.

Batu stopped in front of her father beaming.

"What makes you so happy?" he asked.

"I am with creation."

"What? Are you sure?" he said enthusiastically.

"Yes!"

"Thank the Great Sun," he said bounding up from the bench hugging and kissing her joyfully. "When did you discover it?"

"Just now while I bathed. I have been so distraught I have not paid attention to the fact my blood has not flowed since Tomudo's death."

"You must inform the council," he instructed her.

She smiled, thankful to see his eyes as happy as they were when she lived with him. Wanting to make him a part of everything, she asked him, "Which one of the members should I inform, Father?"

"The law dictates you should speak to the Elder, Mihili, but if you want to tell one of the others first in confidence I think it would be acceptable," he said thinking of her relationship with the Talker Healer.

She smiled knowingly at him. "No. I will go with your advice. I will speak with Mihili."

Aahi smiled back at her. The old feeling of pride flooded him once again. After so long an absence, it felt good to have the feeling coursing through his body.

Batu remained with her parents. It had been a long while since they had shared happy moments. They spent the moments between dusk and the ensuing darkness talking about the upcoming birth and of Batu's good fortune. It had been many cycles since they were able to speak of the future without being fearful or cautious. Now, they talked eagerly of a future that not only included Batu, but the creation growing within her. When they were unable to distinguish the color of each other's eyes, Aahi and Szatu walked Batu to her hut and happily embraced their creation farewell.

Lying on her mat, waiting for sleep to overtake her, Batu thought how ironic that at first she did not want a creation and now that creation would save her life. She wondered if the Creator had a hand in trying to teach her to allow things to take their own course in life. Perhaps she needed to know of love before she could truly be ready to bring forth a babe. As she looked at the events that had taken place, she still could not understand why she had to lose Tomudo. She could not argue with anyone who wished to say she had been ill-prepared to care for a babe when she became bonded. Those cycles and moments were filled with self-centered thoughts and little else. Sighing deeply, she thought of how much had transpired since her union with Tomudo.

"Oh, Creator, whatever your reasons for the life within me, I thank you," she whispered to the darkness and to her unseen Creator.

The following cycle, Batu told Mihili of her impending birth. She asked him if the number of sessions with Coloma could be reduced since she no longer faced banishment. Mihili told Batu that she would have to present her plea to the council. At the council meeting Mihili presented his concerns and Batu countered with her plea. In the end it was Taja's mediation skills that brought Mihili and Batu to an amicable compromise.

The council's caution in the face of Tomudo's death had already prompted them into action. A new law pertaining to the selection of apprentices had already been enacted. The law stated that after assuming a position on the council that member would have one season in which to select an apprentice. In the past an apprentice had to be selected within seven seasons. As an extra precaution each member who did not have an apprentice had agreed to select his apprentices prior to the end of the next season of sun.

With the threat of expulsion gone, Batu's mind filled with thoughts of the forthcoming birth. The future revolved around the babe growing within her. With her future now secure, Batu saw less and less of Taja. Replacing the meetings with Taja were story-telling sessions with the children in the village center. Some stories were from the repository of stories she had learned from

Tomudo with slight alterations. Augmenting these stories with those of her own making, she delighted and charmed the children.

Batu met with her parents often while carrying her child. They discussed the problems associated with raising a child alone. Wishing to clearly understand what traits were essential in becoming a good mother, she flooded them with questions.

Her existence became happily filled with expectations. More importantly, it now contained the constant living reminder of her love for Tomudo. Unbelievably, the product of their love nestled inside her, growing with each rising of the Great Sun. She had almost given up hope of surviving, and had not dreamed she would bring life onto the earth. Now, this tiny being she carried would secure her salvation. This wonderful babe that she was giving life to, was also giving life to her. All of her cunning, intelligence and beauty could not accomplish what this tiny babe would do. She hugged her stomach and thanked her creation for her salvation.

Slowly and inevitably, her body changed. Marveling at the changes, she often thought of the problems she had caused in her union with Tomudo. How often had she told him she wanted to remain free of a child? Looking at her body now, she thrilled to see it growing larger, and took pleasure in feeling the movement within it. The loss of Tomudo had been a shattering experience, and she had held little hope of ever attaining happiness again, yet now it grew as assuredly as the child within her grew.

Coloma came for instructions less frequently, allowing Batu to luxuriate in her pregnancy. A contented expectancy filled each cycle. She thrived in the slow and happy passage of the moments. In the later stages of her pregnancy her once agile body became cumbersome. Near the end of the pregnancy, she experienced some discomfort, as her belly, laden with child, grew heavy. She endured the unpleasantness joyfully and radiated a glow that reflected her feeling of being blessed.

The light of the Sun With No Heat still ruled the dark sky as the first contraction awakened Batu. She lay on her mat awaiting the next one. It came. Her doubt passed. Her moment of delivery had arrived. Soon, she would be able to see Tomudo's and her creation and to hold it tenderly to her breast. Envisioning the tiny babe cuddled in her arms, a smile played on her lips.

The contractions grew stronger. Batu walked the short distance to her mother's hut. As Batu entered her hut, Szatu knew immediately why she had come. After helping Batu to a bench, she went to the neighboring hut and asked her friend to fetch the birthing-mother. Upon returning, Szatu began making preparations for the event.

When Witok, the birthing-mother, arrived, she placed her hand on Batu's stomach and smiled reassuringly. There were still plenty of moments between contractions. Nothing needed to be rushed. She gave Batu instructions how to relieve some of the tension from the contractions, and then busied herself with Szatu to see that everything was in readiness.

Later, Witok sat with Batu and noticed Batu looking at her side. Moving her hand to her side, she felt her sacred blade. Smiling at Batu she said, "It is with this sacred blade that I will cut the cord and free your babe from you and give it its independence."

Batu smiled hesitantly and said nothing.

The labor took longer than Witok expected. Batu's hips indicated an easy birth and things should have been easy. She became concerned and probed only to discover that the babe's head was not facing the correct way. Batu would have given birth long ago had the body been turned. Batu was tiring. If the babe did not arrive soon, Batu would be too tired to push when the moment came and complications could occur.

Batu's energy waned along with the light. Witok asked that a torch be lit well before it became dark. Her hand moved from Batu's stomach to her groin checking her progress. From the closeness and strength of the contractions she readily determined the birth to be imminent, but until the babe turned Batu was wasting energy. As she gazed at Batu's belly, she saw the babe turn. The babe should appear soon. When the babe did not come, she became concerned that Batu had been in the squatting position too long. Everything seemed to be right, yet the babe would not appear. Sweating profusely and moaning often, Batu neared exhaustion. In the back of Witok's mind, a growing fear took shape. She instantly recalled the last birth that she had felt the same apprehension.

Her constant examination finally revealed the babe's head to her touch. Witok gave a quick smile to Batu. "I can feel your child's head."

Witok thanked the gods for the appearance of the child's head. She said to Batu, "When next you contract, you must push with all of your strength. Your child is ready to be born."

With the next contraction, Batu pushed with what energy she had left. Witok had her hands waiting to feel the head come free from Batu. "Yes, there, it is coming."

As the head came free, Batu felt some release of the pain and pressure.

"Breath deeply, Batu," commanded Witok as she massaged the muscles of her vagina.

Exhausted, Batu did as instructed.

"Once again! With the next contraction push hard, Batu."

As she felt the contraction beginning Batu pushed with her remaining strength. Witok gently pulled on the babe's head and the shoulders came free.

As the babe emerged, Witok saw the cord wrapped menacingly under the arm and around its neck. A reflexive shiver ran through her body. She fought to control the panic surging wildly in the pit of her stomach. The only other time she had seen the cord wound around a child at birth, the result was disastrous. The arm pressing the cord to the body, as it passed through the birth canal, cut off the blood flow and the babe died. Without wasting a precious moment, she grabbed it by the shoulders and pulled the babe free. It was a man-child. Its body color was unnaturally tinted blue. Freeing her sacred blade, she cut the cord and dropped the sacred blade on the ground. Quickly, she tied the cord. Raising the man-child up feet first, she rubbed its back briskly, in an effort to stimulate it to breathe.

The babe did not breathe.

She slapped its hindquarters a few times.

Nothing happened.

Holding the babe by its feet and ankles she turned its body and began to spin around, hoping to force air into its mouth and down to his lungs. As she began to become dizzy, she stopped. Looking at the babe, she could see no sign of life. She twirled round and round again clinging to the babe and desperately hoping for the air to rush into his lungs. Nearly falling to the ground, she stopped. Righting the babe, she checked for a sign of life. She clutched the man-child to her breast and burst into tears, unaware of Batu's crying and screaming. Batu's screams finally pierced through her shock. Numbed, she bent down and gave the stillborn man-child to its sobbing mother.

"There was nothing I could do. Nothing. It rested in the hands of the gods. I could do nothing to save it. I am sorry, truly sorry, Batu."

Batu sobbed uncontrollably. She had seen the look on the birthing-mother's face. It told of the dreadful thing she saw. Her fears were confirmed when the babe did not cry on having its back rubbed.

The horrible feeling shattered Batu.

Joy turned into terror.

Pain seized her.

Her heart felt crushed in her chest.

Agony!

Death!

Batu screamed.

In her misery she took the babe from Witok and pressed it to her breast.

She moaned over and over again.

She rocked back and forth.

Tears spilled onto her creation and into the pool of blood she sat in.

Szatu watched Batu's physical pain cease, as the babe emerged. The sigh of relief had barely escaped from her when she saw Batu's expression change. A moment ago Batu's eyes reflected the joy and anticipation of seeing her child, now abruptly they showed terror, as she saw the color of the babe. As Witok desperately tried to get the babe to breathe, Szatu watched rooted to the ground. Batu's scream startled Szatu. Shocked into immobility, she watched in horror as Batu took the still child from Witok. Batu enveloped her dead creation. Everything became strained and filled with pain. Everything became magnified. Each action pummeled her senses. The moments were enveloped within a bizarre, maddening slowness. It was unreal! Unacceptable! Yet it would not go away. Every movement, tear, sob and word hung for moments to be examined and felt to its extreme. She could not move or speak, illogically trapped as an observer of the unfolding tragedy. Confused and unable to immediately comfort Batu, she stood a mute witness to the pain and suffering.

Having never cursed the gods, Szatu cursed them now. What cruel play of the gods was this? They seemed bent upon dispensing tragedy to her unsuspecting and hopeful family. They were not evil. Why had the gods snatched happiness from them? The gods were less than human to deal such a crushing blow to Batu. Why not take my life? she screamed at the gods mentally. The moments on earth for her were brief. She would have gladly left the earth in order for Batu's creation to live. She would have willfully stepped into the Land of No Shadows to save Batu from such pain. How much more pain were the gods going to inflict upon her family? If Batu had angered the gods, why was this innocent babe made to suffer? Why had the greatest god of all, Tor, not intervened for Batu? The gods often favored Batu in the past. She could not believe the gods would allow her to suffer so harshly.

Of their on volition, Szatu's hands moved to her head and lay themselves atop her eyes as if to prevent them from seeing further pain. Frustrated and angry the tears finally gushed from Szatu's eyes. Their flowing prodded her body into action. She moved to Batu and held her, murmuring comfortingly to her, as she had so often in the past.

The dreadful shriek catapulted Aahi from the bench. At the entrance, he saw Witok place the blood-smeared babe in Batu's arms. He saw the horror in Batu's eyes. Tears made his vision blurry. His throat constricted with the urge to cry out. The pain in his heart crumpled him to his knees. It seemed an eternity before Szatu went to his beloved Batu. Unable to watch the suffering, he turned. If he remained any longer, he would scream out in agony and lose face as a man. Devastated, he forced his shaking body to right itself. Drained of energy, he dragged himself away from the hut. He stumbled often on the way to the plains. There, in the absence of man, he expressed his grief. Only the gods and the creatures of the night heard his mournful cry.

Witok stared at the ground. Mother Earth had not yet completely absorbed all the blood and amniotic fluid from the birthing process. There, in the midst of it, lay the sacred blade she used to cut the life supporting cord of Batu's dead child. Picking up the sacred blade, Witok's hand trembled. Tiny clusters of soft rich soil clung to the wet blade. With an automatic movement she wiped it clean and sheathed it. Falling to her knees, she wrapped her arms around the two sobbing women. Having participated in the tragedy, she hoped her own sobs would provide some absolution. Moments later, she sensed the women needed to mourn in private. With tears still flowing, she rose. Shaken and silent, she walked outside. The task of helping deliver babes was a joyful one. Tragedies such as this one were rare, not so in the past, from what her mother had said. Perhaps she needed to let her child take over the responsibility of delivery. She had not called her to be present because of Batu's wide hips. The delivery should be an easy one, she had thought. She shook her head, wondering whether her child would have noticed what was happening and ventured up the birth canal to turn the babe around earlier. Perhaps that would have prevented the cord from finding its way under the arm. Wearily, she made her way to her own hut. There, within its dark confines, she prayed to the gods that she would never be witness to such pain again.

By the light of the torch, Batu meticulously cleaned her man-child. As she bathed her creation, she began humming to it. With care and love, she washed each tiny crevice free from the drying blood and amniotic fluids. Having dried the babe, she began kissing it. Starting with its toes and feet, she lovingly made her way up its legs. She lingered at the umbilical cord, looking at it in wonderment, knowing it kept her babe alive while inside of her. Reaching his fingers, she played with them as she kissed them, toying with each one. Having honored them, her lips caressed his cheeks, forehead, eyelids and nose, as her tears fell onto the diminutive, still face. Running her hand through his dark, thick hair she noticed his hairline. It had the same distinguishing point, in the middle of his forehead as Tomudo. Tenderly, she kissed the point. Instinctively, she placed his tiny lips upon her nipple vainly hoping he would suckle. His lips did not respond. Fresh tears streamed down her face, as she rocked back and forth and moaned uncontrollably.

Szatu gazed broken-hearted at her own flesh and blood, as she automatically began cleaning the hut. After finishing, she sat on one of the interior benches watching Batu complete the babe's bath. She knew these bittersweet moments would have to serve Batu forever. There would be no endearing exchanges between mother and babe. Future experiences of endearment would never become a reality. There would be no secret knowing smiles and no confidences shared. There would be nothing sweet to recall. Nothing remained but these moments twisted sadly and cruelly by fate, nothing. Szatu's head moved slowly from side to side. Batu's legacy seemed fated to be embroiled in suffering. Unable to look at the two any longer she cast her eyes at the earth. Even there the wet ground stood as mute and ugly testimony of the tragedy, which had taken place moments ago. Her tears dropped silently to the ground disappearing quickly in the dry soil. Only the wretched pain remained visible.

Batu lay on the mat, her babe nestled in the valley of her breasts. Gently stroking her man-child, she began to recite her favorite children's stories. After the stories she sang to the deaf babe deep into the darkness. Finally, in weariness her voice quieted. The sound of an occasional kiss broke the silence. Szatu was about to extinguish the torch. Batu's hand pleaded for her not to complete the action. She turned and pulled her sleeping mat next to Batu. Thoughts of anger, sorrow and confusion held Szatu in their grasp. Much later, with weary eyes, Szatu saw Aahi enter and laid down on the other side of Batu. His hand lovingly caressed her hair.

The High Priest's words at the burial seemed ludicrous to Batu. The words were all the right ones, but they were spoken without compassion. His eyes spoke the opposite of the words he voiced. At Tomudo's burial, and now at her child's, she detected his hostility toward her and the pleasure he reveled in seeing her suffer. The sight of him leaving offered small comfort in her grief. After Romir left, the others slowly made their way past her. Some spoke words of comfort, some chose to touch her arm before they returned to the village. Only her mother and father remained nearby.

She sat on the bank of the running water and turned her attention to the flowing water that had carried away the body of her deceased babe. Batu could not comprehend why joy and happiness always ended in misery. Her life seemed to be swinging like an ill-synchronized pendulum from happiness to sorrow. Pain, distress and darkness kept creeping into her life like ugly predators ready to devour any moments of happiness she experienced. She would have no pleasant memories of her tiny man-child except those when she had carried him inside of her. There would be no such memories of him growing outside of her, no singing her beloved one to sleep, no thrill of him suckling at her breast, no kissing scratched knees, no cherished first word, no cherished firsts of anything he did or said. How was she to live without holding her treasure? She would never share that part of her, which grew even as the babe grew. Her heart yearned to bestow its love on the tender, frail, dependent and beautiful babe. A gnawing doubt festered inside her. Could she ever function in life with a void so large inside of her?

She closed her eyes hoping to see the vision of her man-child. Faithfully it appeared to comfort and console her.

"If only his eyes had opened," she said to the water. She burst into tears. The loss swept through her body yet another time causing her to moan aloud. Hearing her, Szatu leaned over and placed her arms consolingly around her creation. Unable to think of anything to say, she gently rocked her to and fro. Silent tears streamed down Szatu's face.

When she stopped crying, Batu begged her mother to leave her alone. Szatu would not hear of it. Aahi understanding her need gently pulled Szatu from Batu.

Sitting on the ground looking at the flowing water, Batu gave into her emotions and sobbed. Many moments passed before her tears subsided.

Footsteps on the soil made her turn toward the village in anticipation of seeing her parents. Her heart sunk on seeing the High Priest and Kiirt. They stopped near her. Before she could turn away, Romir let his words cut her, "Once again the gods have chosen to honor me and punish you."

Sighing heavily, Batu said, "You must take great satisfaction in seeing me suffer. Go away. Leave me to my misery."

Romir magnanimously spread his arms saying, "Seeing you suffer is my joy in life." A grotesque smile rested on his face. "I must admit there were moments I wanted you dead, but I see now that I derive more pleasure in you alive and suffering. Every cycle you live you will die a little as you think of first losing Tomudo and now your babe. I take great pleasure in knowing that there are many cycles left before the rains come. Each cycle will create worry in you as you think about what manner of death you will experience. When you are cast out of the Kahali village, those thoughts will have already consumed your spirit. All that will be left is for a predator to consume your ugly body."

Kiirt desired to drive his own words deep into Batu's wounded heart, but he knew better than to do so. If he did, he would be the object of Romir's anger back in the Sacred Hut. This moment belonged to the High Priest, not him.

Too filled with sorrow to face the High Priest and his apprentice, she turned toward the running water and said quietly, "Leave me. If you persist in talking to me I shall scream out and tell everyone how vile you are."

Glaring at the back of Batu's head, Romir said, "You have no one to corroborate what you would say. Everyone knows you are insane with grief, and there are but a handful who would give you allegiance. I am leaving only because I have said what I needed to say. My torture is done. Now, I leave you to torture yourself."

Romir grabbed Kiirt's arm as they walked away. A smug look set upon his face. Out of earshot, the High Priest spoke to his apprentice, "Did you take notice of how I did not leave much hope of a future for her?"

Kiirt nodded.

"You must destroy anyone's hope that dares to confront you as she has. That is the way you should leave whoever has wronged you," Romir pointed out to Kiirt. Utterly pleased with himself, the High Priest slapped his apprentice on the back saying, "Let us commemorate what the gods have done and give them thanks in the Sacred Hut."

The High Priest's words left their impression on Batu. Only when the fresh flood of tears subsided did she stir from the water's edge and return to her hut. Dropping down on the mat in a heap, drained physically and emotionally, she wearily closed her eyes and waited for sleep, while her mind raced with memories.

Batu slipped into a morass of agonizing grief. She lived her life in rote. She found it impossible to experience anything outside of her tight confinement of despair. Life became excruciatingly void of happiness, holding little promise of ever being filled with anything of value. Not only had she lost the creation that Tomudo wanted so desperately, she had again lost hope of surviving. Death waited grimly for her when the rains came. While a part of her wished for her life to be over, to end her misery and pain, another part clung tenaciously to the hope that somehow she would be saved from extinction.

Dusk encircled Batu as she sat on her bench. Leaning forward she rested her elbows on her knees and stared at the earth. Even there on the ground, visions of her death took form to taunt her. The thoughts were incessant. Dejectedly, she turned and retreated into her hut throwing herself onto the mat. Wearily she rubbed her eyes and closed them. The faces of Tomudo and her deceased babe slipped in and out of her mind and finally faded into the darkness of sleep.

Overhead, the fiery orb shone mercilessly on the already parched earth. Its suffocating heat paralleled Batu's suffocating despair. The leaves on a nearby tree hung unmoving, yet Batu sat on the bench outside her hut unmindful of the oppressive heat. The loss of her creation bore more unrelentingly in its constancy and more dominantly on her senses than the heat. The heat could be eased with water. There was no escaping the inner pain. Her rational mind tried to determine why the loss of her child held more pain than the loss of Tomudo. Perhaps the sheer immediacy of it bore more heavily upon her. Perplexed, she could not understand how the death of her babe, whom she had held in her arms for only two cycles, could contain such sorrow and heartache.

Unhurriedly, her thoughts drifted to Taja. He had helped her to some semblance of understanding about the death of her man. Why had he not come to console her in her moment of greatest need? He who professed to love her so deeply remained away. Why had he not come? Confused, she closed her eyes to shut out the physical reality in favor of the internal images so often populating her mind. Almost immediately, the image of the birthing-mother and her stillborn babe came to her mind. The vision of the woman rubbing his back, then slapping his behind and finally of her spinning around holding him by his feet in an effort to get air into his tiny lungs kept appearing. The images now, as before, brought tears to her closed eyes.

Through her tears she felt it. It came, as a tender caress upon her weary body. It steadily grew in strength, causing her to open her eyes. Taja stood before her. Blinking her eyes to free them from tears, she looked again to make certain he was not a phantom. Yes, it was he. She should have known it, as soon as she felt the love comforting her. There should have been no mistaking the feeling. Preoccupation with her internal imagery had prevented her from immediately identifying what she felt and from whom it came. Rising from the bench, she threw her arms around him crying uncontrollably as he held her.

Pulling herself from him, she led him inside and said, "I was afraid you would not come."

"Batu, I will always be here for you. Do not doubt my love for you," he said holding her hands, tears flowing from his eyes.

Looking into his eyes, she wondered how she could have ever doubted he would come.

"I have allowed the others to console you first so you would be ready to move from the dark into the light, from pain to understanding, from injury to recovery."

"Oh, Taja, I never thought such pain could touch me again. It is even worse than when Tomudo died. Is it to persist as it did for him?"

Smoothing her hair with his hand, he could have been mistaken for any father in the tribe as he shared a burden with his creation. His voice held the tenderness she sought from him. "The pain that comes from the loss of a babe is deeper and lingers longer than for anyone else. It speaks of the unseen beauty, the unsaid words, and the experiences that would never be shared and of the unknown love that will never be felt by him.

"This like all injuries will heal. Look within yourself for help. We were not created to continually suffer, rather we were created to experience growth from our suffering and, then, to move beyond the suffering. Trust in yourself, Batu. Look to the peace and wisdom of your inner self. The Creator has not left you defenseless to be ravaged by your experiences. Trust in that fact, that truth."

Her eyes bore into his as if to glean the truth in his words. The onrush of truth did not come.

"I hope I shall see you soon," he said releasing her hands.

Smiling, she replied, "Yes. I will be ready soon."

Impulsively, she threw herself into his arms. There in his arms, she hoped in some way to draw from him the strength she needed to be rid of the torment and anguish so deeply burrowed in her heart. Inexplicably, she felt comforted more in his arms than in her parents' embrace. Unwilling to release him, she kept her eyes closed and slowly became aware of his silent benediction of love, accepting it with hope and thanks.

Still holding him, her voice muffled by his shoulder, she said, "Thank you for coming."

She moved to hold him at arm length. The look in his eyes communicated what his lips did not say. She clung to his arm unwilling to release him. When she did let go, tears flowed from her, as she watched him disappear.

The pain in her heart left her for the moment. Her mind filled with questions. Aloud she asked, "Oh Creator, how does he do it? Is he so much a part of me that he can feel what I feel and think what I think?"

She recalled Tomudo had spoken of a quality that his first woman had to feel and sense how he felt. Jocas however did not have the ability to inspire and console him while Taja did. He seemed to achieve such things easily. He had repeatedly demonstrated that he sensed her thoughts and feelings and utilized them in his teachings. She speculated whether a relationship existed between his ability and how far on the path to the Creator he had traveled.

Since her meetings with Taja, her views and opinions had changed drastically. For as long as she could remember, she had always thought the gods favored her. She had measured that favor by her physical and mental endowments. Now she saw that what truly mattered was how well she loved and cared for others and herself.

Sleep slowly claimed Batu, as dusk settled lazily over the silent village. During the darkness of the cycle Batu had two evocative dreams. In the first, Taja and she were seated as they had been so many times before in his hut. He rose and took her hand leading her outside. He raised his eyes drawing her attention to the Great Sun that moved quickly through the blue sky. The dream ended at that point. The second dream found her sitting on the bench outside her father's hut. Cuddled in her arms was her creation. The child smiled at her as she had envisioned it so often in her moments of solitude before its death. As she caressed the infant, the dream ended.

Batu awoke with the dreams emblazoned in her memory. She rose from her mat, went outside, and sat on the bench. The early dawn air held a refreshing coolness. The sky showed signs that the Great Sun would be rising shortly and blessing the earth with life-giving light. This cycle's light would not touch upon the form of her babe, nor could it give it life even if it were to touch it she thought. Gazing at the brightening sky, she remembered how often Taja stressed to find the meaning of dreams upon awakening. Patiently, she began the task of unraveling their meaning. Beginning with the first dream she interpreted each symbol. If Taja and she were in his hut, it surely meant she was acquiring knowledge. But why would she need to see the

Great Sun moving so quickly? Could it be that it might represent the passing moments in her life? The dream could be telling her that she must apply what she has learned to the moments she had left before her banishment. It seemed paramount she needed to apply what she had learned under Taja's tutelage to her environment and relationship. But she had not yet learned all she needed from him. The application of his principles was far more difficult than she had imagined. Perhaps the dream tried to convey that to her as well.

Stretching sleepily, Batu rubbed her eyes and repositioned herself to undertake the task of evaluating the second dream. In this dream, her stillborn babe looked as she had envisioned him so often, alive, smiling, and happy. But in truth, her creation would never do those things. Why would he be shown so filled with vitality? she wondered. It seemed she would be unable to unravel the meaning. Unexpectedly, it occurred to her what its meaning might be. The two dreams were connected! What Taja spoke of now flooded her with a sense of knowing. He had told her that the spirit dwelling in the body never dies. It bore the imprint of the Creator. That implied her babe's spirit lived, and had likely left the body because it had learned some great lesson or had participated in it for the benefit of someone. That someone most likely was her.

Intellectually, she knew she had to grieve, to cry and feel the pain of loss, yet after that, what was to be gained from the tragedy? Somehow, she had to assess her growth in terms of the tragedy. Could it be that through this personal tragedy she must become more aware of the fragile nature of life? These questions were very different from the ones she would have agonized over had Taja not shared his philosophy with her. Undoubtedly, she would have been completely devastated, if she had not met so often with him.

A calm pervaded Batu. Taja had shown her that nothing happens without a purpose, no matter how insignificant it may seem at the moment. Nothing is lost. The Creator wastes no act or word. The treasure of Taja's teachings had made her less fearful and more aware of everything she did. Purpose had returned into her life.

Remembering Taja's instructions, she closed her eyes and slowly stilled her thoughts. Patiently, she waited to see if she could receive a sign that would indicate that she was thinking correctly. In a quiet place, remote and deep within her, she sensed her babe's spirit communicating the message to her, "I am with you."

Batu's eyes jerked open in surprise. Had she really sensed the words from her babe or was it her imagination trying to comfort her? Relaxing, she closed her eyes. Impressions flowed freely from deep within her. The strong feeling of the correctness of her inner senses prevailed. With her eyes still closed, a smile formed on her face, the first since her babe's death. She could not deny how she felt. She knew the tears would still come and in despair she would sob, but her babe's spirit still existed and he had come for a purpose. Hopefully she would continue to grow stronger from the experience. Smiling again, she wondered how Taja would phrase it. Most likely he would say through the tragedy she would grow in compassion and love.

The Great Sun broke clear of the distant horizon. It illuminated an earth fragrant and teeming with life. A gentle breeze turned the leaves of a nearby tree exposing their silver-green underside. Rarely had Batu seen leaves react to such a delicate breeze. It seemed to be a sign, an omen that stated all was correct in the universe. Stretching her arms, then her legs, she rose from the bench and made her way through the village to the plains. The grasses stretched before her and cavorted under the insistence of the small breeze. At the small grove of trees she sat down next to her favorite one and leaned against it. Her eyes played upon the grass reminding her now, as it did so often, of the running water. It seemed in perpetual motion, ever changing, never constant. Now and then a honey maker flew past her on its way to the cluster of bushes nearby, seeking to collect the opulent nectar from the brilliant flush of colorful flowers. She breathed deeply, capturing fully the sweet fragrance of the flowers being carried her way by the breeze. The scent brought forth memories of the brightly colored blossoms Tomudo had so often presented to her.

A confident smile crossed her face as a small semblance of peace filled her. She was ready to resume living her life with the pain of her loss, in place of living a life in pain because of her loss.

CHAPTER
TWENTY-TWO

Batu resumed her meetings with Taja. The meetings helped her grieve and lessened the pain she felt for her deceased child. The loss made Batu acutely aware of the impermanence of life. That impermanence renewed her desire to seek the Creator. After many prayers, Batu made up her mind to accelerate her spiritual growth. She had approached the Talker Healer about her desire and he agreed to help her.

Seated outside his hut, Taja waited for Batu. She arrived and they embraced. Detaining her at the entrance, he said, "Are you prepared to seek knowledge from your greater self?"

With heart pounding, she answered, "I have prayed to the Creator for help many times, Taja. Yes, I am ready."

A mysterious quality filled his voice. "As you leave the light to venture into the darker presence of the hut, think of it as symbolic of your venture from the outer, smaller self to the inner, greater self. It is there that you will be searching for the truth. You will move inward into your mind and heart, in the same manner as you move inward with your body into the hut. You are well acquainted with the light within you, but not with the darkness therein. You will move into the inner landscape and become acquainted with it as never before."

Stepping aside, he let her enter the hut first. She moved tentatively, expectantly toward the entrance. Entering, she took notice of the hues of light within it and of the different areas cast in shadow. She breathed deeply letting the multitude of aromas stir her senses and easily identified them. As Taja entered, she immediately identified the distinct smell of his body.

He motioned her to be seated and quietly began his instruction. "To reach the inner or greater self, you must still your thoughts and actions."

When he stopped talking, he started humming. The repetitious quality of the humming had a soothing quality that relaxed body and mind.

Softly and slowly, he began his instruction. "Close your eyes. Visualize yourself at the edge of the forest. A brilliant sun is shining on you. You leave the brightness and travel slowly into the thick bush. The bush gives way exposing a faint path. It presents you an easy access to the darker recesses, those residing deep within you. Ahead is a small clearing. Sit down there and construct your prayer to the Creator. Ask for guidance in your quest."

Taja became quiet.

Batu made her petition and waited expectantly.

Taja remained silent.

It concerned Batu that nothing had yet happened. She went over Taja's instruction to quiet her mind. Breathing deeply, she followed the even inward and outward movement of air and steadily relaxed. The mind, so busy in thought a moment ago, slowly emptied itself. A flash of light blazed alerting Batu. The light faded away, revealing a scene of the village. Her father and mother's hut stood straight ahead. Moving to it, she went inside with an effortless, gliding motion. Her mother, father, and Tomudo were talking to several people of the village. She thought it strange to be an observer and not a participant. The people talked animatedly to the trio. Defiance and occasionally anger crept upon the villagers' faces. As they continued speaking, objects spewed forth from their mouths in the shape of tiny dark red arrows and spears. They were piercing the hearts of her mother, father and Tomudo. They winced in pain. Oblivious to their pain, the images kept up the onslaught of words, while the arrows and spears pierced their hearts. Tears appeared in her parents' and Tomudo's eyes accentuating the suffering and helplessness shown on their faces.

Horrified, Batu screamed at the villagers' images to stop talking and firing the instruments of pain. Time and again she tried to hurl herself at the images in an effort to halt the talking. All her attempts failed. Unexpectedly, her screams of horror turned into gasps of pain, as she suddenly experienced the pain that her parents and Tomudo felt. Crying in anguish, she realized the pain they were experiencing came from the callous speech and actions of the villagers because of her own vain words and actions. They were the bearers of their anger and frustration over Batu's actions. Batu realized that she was the cause of the pain her parents and Tomudo were suffering. Fruitlessly, she called to them over and over to forgive her. When she thought she could endure the pain in her heart no longer, the scene faded from view. Drained emotionally, she welcomed the return of the darkness in her mind.

A moment later another flash of light brightened the realm of her mind, displacing the darkness. The village stood before her again. Several women were making their way through the village center toward the running water for their baths. Her image followed them into the water. A small group gathered around her image. Her image spoke confidentially to them. Oliva interrupted to add her viewpoint to the discussion. Unexpectedly, her image's face twisted menacingly as she listened to her friend. With a swift motion Batu's image moved to Oliva, grabbed her hair, tripped her backwards and sent her into the water gasping for air. Oliva struggled to the surface, arms flailing and clawing at her image's arms and hands. The women surrounding them screamed and shouted for her image to release Oliva. Her image took no heed of their distraught pleas. Terror showed in Oliva's eyes as she surfaced gulping air into her lungs. Unmercifully, her image pushed Oliva's face under the water again. Below the water's surface, Oliva struggled desperately to survive. Batu felt Oliva's panic. Desperation raced through her own mind and body as she felt Oliva's frantic efforts to acquire leverage. She felt her own muscles reacting to Oliva's struggle to push herself to the surface. Her friend's strength failed under the superior position of her image. Oliva's air-starved lungs ached, as did Batu's. With her equilibrium gone, all sense of her physical position was destroyed. The sensations roared through Batu, as she felt Oliva's struggles. As Oliva's lungs were about to burst, her mouth shot open in an effort to inhale the air she needed to survive. When it did, Batu felt the water gush into her mouth, stifling the scream only to have it crash into her mind and whirl around in her skull.

Astounded, Batu reeled from the onslaught of emotions and sensations that pummeled her. She felt Oliva's life energies diminishing in her own body. Thankfully, the images and sensations slowly vanished and ceased. In the ensuing darkness, Batu's mind rebelled from the horrid stimulation she had experienced. Seeking to escape from them, she sought the solace of other thoughts, but they were crowded out by the stark vision of Oliva struggling to survive.

A flash of light announced yet another scene slowly unfolding in her mind. This time she saw her image standing in front of her parents' hut. As she watched, her figure reached into a bowl filled with water and splashed some of it upon her body. A man watched her from the village center. She stroked the water slowly, tantalizingly on her breasts. The action reeked of sensuality. Smiling carnally at the man, she burst into a lustful laugh. As Batu's image continued her lewd exhibition, she saw him becoming aroused. Her image bent down and picked up a gleaming long blade. Her image walked to the man waving the blade menacingly. Grasping his erection, her image violently swung the blade and severed the organ from him. The man fell to the ground withering and screaming in pain. Blood gushed from the stump.

Her figure stood over him laughing shrilly. A maniacal look froze on her face.

While her image laughed, Batu was catapulted into experiencing the man's pain. She felt the excruciating pain as the pulsing blood gushed from the organ stump. She screamed in agony as she felt what the man felt. His body contorted and thrashed on the ground. The agonizing pain brutalized her senses. Gratefully, the void of darkness enveloped her in its veil.

The short-lived darkness gave way to the now familiar flash of light. A lush fertile meadow stretched before her. The rich grasses rippled under the caress of a cool, refreshing breeze. Here and there great clusters of flowers stretched their glorious, colored petals toward a sky of iridescent blue. She heard the pleasant gurgle of running water with its moist fragrance easily detectable below the stronger scent of the flowers. Birds sang and darted from tree to tree. In the distance a herd of wapiti grazed contentedly. The pastoral scene, idyllic as it may be, confused her. Based upon the other scenes she had not expected such tranquility. A movement caught her eye. Turning, she saw yet another image in her likeness. Scattered a few paces from her image were blocks of earthen colored material. They were varied in size. Her image began to arrange them one atop the other, placing the largest on the bottom and following it with the next largest until they were all neatly stacked. Placed thus, they formed a tier of nine steps. The uppermost tier stood a little wider than her shoulders.

Batu's image climbed the nine steps and surveyed the meadow. The image's posture conveyed sovereignty over all she saw. The topmost platform on which she stood suddenly turned to feces. Her image sank into it, unmindful of the change. The image continued surveying her domain. The second stepped platform changed, as did the first, and the Batu image sank into it. She stood calf deep in feces. Batu could not believe that her image could not detect the change and feel the fecal matter on her skin, or detect the stifling smell. As she watched, the third and then the fourth platform changed into the foul looking mess. Still her image took no notice of the fact she stood nearly hip deep in it. Recognition came as the figure sank into the seventh stepped platform. It left her mired in it up to her shoulders. At that point, Batu was thrust into the image that bore her resemblance. Her skin quivered attempting to free itself from the clinging feces. All efforts to lunge free from the platform failed. No matter how hard she tried she could not move anything except her head. The eighth stepped platform began to transform into feces. Batu felt herself slowly sink into it. The feces moved up her neck, finally touching her chin. The fecal slime disgusted her. The smell nauseated her. Her stomach churned in revolt. She tilted her head to prevent the feces from covering her mouth. The feces touched her earlobes and worked its way into her hair.

Panic seized her.

She screamed for help.

No one came.

The obnoxious and sickening smells continued unabated. She feared her stomach would expel its contents and add to her revolting situation. Frantic, she felt the last platform turn into feces beneath her feet. She sank steadily into it. Her hopes for salvation also sank. Screaming, she submerged into the last platform of filth. Feeling it crawl up her chin, she closed her mouth to prevent the invasion of the feces into her mouth. Every part of her body reacted in repulsion. Longing to die, but unable to will herself to annihilation, she felt the feces oozing into her ears and nose. With lungs bursting, she opened her mouth to breathe. The overpowering and sickening scene gave way to darkness.

Batu jerked air into her lungs. A shudder ran through her body. Something pounded wildly against her ribs. Startled and fearful, her eyes popped open. The pounding was her heart. Her hands were being squeezed. Taja's hands were upon her own. Finding his eyes she focused on them and breathed deeply to calm her racing heart. A while later she grew calm enough to think clearly. Did he know what had transpired? She looked deeply into his eyes. She stopped wondering upon recognizing the compassion in his eyes. Somehow it softened the shock of her self-examination and her spiritual acceleration. Despite this, she could not hold back the onrushing tears. Weeping, her torso slowly bent until her head rested on the ground.

The tears turned into sobs.

"No! No! No!"

"How could I have done it?"

"Oh Creator, What have I done?"

"Oh no!"

Sobs racked her body leaving her emotionally spent.

"No!" she whispered, "No! No!"

Her tears subsided. She wiped them away roughly. "Oh Taja, what a fool I have been. What a fool. I've hurt so many people with my vanity and pride."

Moving to her side, he wrapped his arms around her. He spoke with the tenderness of a loving father. "Do not berate yourself too much, Batu. A fool is nothing more than a child of Mother Love and Father Wisdom. Like all children, the fool eventually grows to be like its mother and father."

Struggling to contain her emotions, she related all but the last vision. "It was horrible. I felt the pain of those I hurt. I felt it, Taja! I really felt it in my own body. It was as if I inflicted the pain on my own body.

"Why Taja? Why did I feel their pain? Why? How can I ever right those wrongs? How can I ever take back the pain? How can they ever forgive me?"

Taja moved his arms away but held her hands in his. Compassion beamed from his eyes. His voice reflected it. "Know that their greater selves have already forgiven you and participated in the creation of all the events freely. Their cooperation allows you and they to grow in love. Let this venture teach you to perform every thought and action in your life using love as your guide. The reason for existence is to relate to everyone and everything in Mother Nature out of love. If you do this you will not inflict harm."

His head nodded as if to affirm what he had told her. He continued, "You asked me why you had to feel the pain they felt. I will answer you by asking a question of you. How better would you know what others feel then to experience it yourself?

"If you simply talk of someone else's pain it is a cerebral experience. You miss the physical and emotional sensations completely, and thus you miss the major effect it has upon that person. When you make the transition to the Land of No Shadows, you will also be faced with this self-examination. In that self-examination you will again feel the pain you have inflicted upon everyone. The pain you feel stimulates your compassion. All of us go through this form of self-judgment. It is not our loving Creator that judges us."

"Do we ever stop being judgmental of ourselves?" Batu asked.

"When we become enlightened, we are no longer judgmental of others and ourselves."

The words rang true to Batu. She revisited her own words saying, "I never knew that my words would come back upon those I loved and hurt them."

Taja replied, "The things you did to others have a telling effect upon them. When villagers would complain to Tomudo and your parents about you, it hurt them. They suffered through all of that without ever having said anything to you. The accumulation of such tiny injuries can be just as injurious as one large one. The consistency of them is what you must consider. Consistency of even little injuries wares upon people."

With her eyes focused upon her hands, she thought about what he had said. Many moments passed before she turned her eyes to him and spoke.

"Yes, yes I see." She queried him, "Why could I not see my mistakes as they occurred and why could I not see how I caused them pain?"

Taja answered, "Without discrimination, sensitivity and wisdom many of us cannot see our errors. Yours are easy to see. You have dealt with pain that you inflicted upon others. What of those that bear the inflicted pain? Inflicted pain causes tentacles of fear and problems. The worst tentacles arise when pain is inflicted upon the child. For some children, the cause of injury is buried deep within their bodies and consciousness from an event or series of events. These bear tremendous energy that those children may not be conscious of, as they grow older. That inflicted pain can control their thoughts and actions in very strange, negative and unexpected ways.

"It is with the eyes of the truth and the greater self that we are able to see how we inflict pain and how others have inflicted pain upon us. In either case, we must deal with the pain through forgiveness of ourselves and for those that have inflicted pain upon us. Only in forgiveness can we move past our anger. We may never forget the way someone inflicted pain upon us. That is human. That is not the important thing. The important thing is forgiveness. That is divine."

"I never imagined that spiritual acceleration would be so difficult," she acknowledged.

"It is always difficult to recognize and admit the harm you have done. Forgiving yourself for causing harm is also very difficult. Forgiving those who harm you is also hard. Being able to forgive permits us to love unconditionally and deeply. Love encompasses all of spirituality."

"It appears that my greater self spared nothing to humble me," she reflected quietly.

He smiled understandingly. After a moment he asked her, "Are you complete in your understanding of the visions?"

Quietly, she replied, "I think I know the meanings, but I wish to tell you of the worth I see in them. In the vision of Tomudo and my parents, I am certain that my words were sharp and caustic to people I know. I imposed my will on people without regard for their feelings. Those I injured must have gone to Tomudo and my parents and complained. I did not recognize that the words spoken to others would hurt Tomudo and my parents. I now see they chose to be silent because they loved me.

"The scene with the women in the running water made me realize how badly I have treated Oliva. I have always been the center of attention, especially when we bathed. It was I who was beautiful, intelligent and precocious. I lorded it over Oliva and whoever bathed with us. Inwardly, I felt they looked upon me with envy. Their passivity contributed to my feelings of superiority. Oliva represented all of them, and I drowned all who opposed me with my will. I regularly belittled Oliva's and anyone else's accomplishments. I did so because I thought them common and unworthy of discussion.

"As for the poor man in the village center, I acted so wantonly in that vision. I stirred his passion and then hated him for it. When I saw how passionately inflamed he had become I thought him despicable and destroyed his masculinity. I forgot my own actions. For some reason I knew I could not destroy him with words and I picked up the blade and brandished it on him. I stripped him of his manhood, his power and pride. It seemed similar to the dreadful period when I did not bond with Tomudo. I cut him off from the source of his physical means of showing love for me and from creating a babe."

Hanging her head forlornly, she raised her shoulders in a helpless gesture.

Taja became insistent. "In the other scenes you seemed to know everyone, yet in this one you were vague about who he is. Do you find that curious?"

Batu thought about it briefly and answered, "I mentioned, Tomudo... He must stand for all men... And the council!"

Taja let out his breath roughly. "True, but the man is more specific to me."

Batu began to knead her suddenly aching shoulder and neck. Her face turned thoughtful. Kiirt's face popped into her mind. "Oh gods! It is Kiirt. Why did I not see that immediately?"

"Perhaps because you hoped you were over your anger," he offered.

Looking away from him, she nodded in acceptance of his observation. Obviously she had a great deal of work to do about coming to any position of forgiveness of Kiirt.

She sat quietly, uncertain whether or not to continue.

Taja prodded her, "And what of the last vision?"

Scrutinizing him, she wondered if he guessed she had another vision because she had paused, or did he know of it? Brushing the thought aside, she took a deep breath and plunged into describing the vision.

"And how are you interpreting it?" he asked.

"It concerned my vanity and how it suffocated me. I raised myself above everyone. I believed the gods favored me. I believed I could do no wrong. Blinded by what I believed, I built myself up on the steps of pride and vanity, only to realize that each one was created at the expense of others and my inner self. What I created was evil and foul. I created it not knowing I would be suffocated by it. My pride and vanity were the excrement I drowned in. It seems to be at the very root of all of my problems."

In a pleading voice, she asked, "Taja, if I was so intelligent, why did I not see this before? Why did I cause such pain?"

Gently, he answered her, "Intelligence is like a fire, it can cook our food and it can also destroy our village. The traits you possess are the same. The very pride, intelligence and independence that made your back straight against oppression were the same traits that faulted others. What you lacked was love. It is what gives the mind its discerning faculty. You have been able to see your errors only because of your growth in love.

"These visions have permitted you to know how others feel. When you can feel the pain of others you ultimately will have compassion for them."

He became quiet, she ashamed.

She questioned how he felt about her now that she had revealed her vision to him. Without asking him she would always wonder if this moment had changed their relationship.

Without looking at him, she asked, "How do you feel about me now that you know the pain I have caused?"

He did not answer her.

Why did he not speak?

He remained quiet.

Curiosity overcame her apprehension and shame. She raised her head and looked into his eyes. While she gazed into his eyes they changed, taking on a familiar quality. Love shined in his eyes. It enveloped her. In silence she thanked him.

"Even if I had never made a mistake I would not be angry with you, Batu. But I have made mistakes. It is natural to do so, but we must learn from our errors. That is the important lesson."

"Is the Creator angered when we harm others?"

"The Creator is love. Where love is nothing else can exist. The Creator does not judge, become angry or injure. The Creator, through love, simply creates." Knowing the inner journey left her spent he said, "It is late and you have much to think about, much to stir your heart. Go and know that my love is with you always."

He rose. Reluctantly, she followed his movement. They embraced. She clung to him. Fresh tears burst forth from her eyes. Finally, breaking from him she said, "Thank you, Taja, and farewell." As she was about to exit, she turned and said softly, "My love is with you as well."

His eyes closed for an instant. Opening them, he smiled knowingly. She turned and left. He walked to the entrance and watched her walk slowly to her hut in the dim dusk light. Deep in thought, Batu walked away oblivious of his watchful, loving gaze.

CHAPTER
TWENTY-THREE

For many cycles Batu had begun rising before the sky showed the first promise of light. This cycle was no different. She sat savoring the relative quiet. The ominous clouds gathering in the dark sky drew her attention. They had populated the skies in greater number the past few cycles. The rains were imminent. Clearing her mind she began praying. The prayers were yet another recent acquisition in her routine. Concluding the prayers, she breathed slowly and deeply, visualizing her tiny babe. Holding the vision steady, she sent her love to it. Deep in concentration she did not hear the soft thunder in the distance. Upon becoming aware of the rumbling, the images she held so tenuously faded and disappeared. She accepted the intrusion as a word of caution from a well-meaning old friend telling her that the moments she had to enjoy in the company of her family and friends would vanish with the rain. Her mind went back to when she had decided to end her life before the council could banish her. Having become more aware of the meaning of life and its purpose, through her discussions with Taja, she had long ago decided to face the council at the moment of her expulsion. Through those talks with the Talker Healer she had grown enough to seemingly face anything, not with the abandon sense of pride or independence but with courage.

She nodded in recognition of the great strides she had made in her personal philosophy. Yet, in examining herself, she knew that more seasons on Mother Earth were needed to accomplish all that she needed to do. She had made great strides toward lessening her hatred for Romir, Kiirt and the council. But, as hard as she tried, it clung to her tenaciously. No matter how often she had tried, she still felt hurt and betrayed that the council had not changed the law of banishment. The feelings unquestionably, and surprisingly, were more difficult to deal with than the ones that had burned in her gut for Kiirt or even the High Priest. The meetings with Taja had slowly released her from the rage she felt for Kiirt, but anger lingered even though she had worked with Taja to eliminate it. Had Taja not been there for her the feelings would have festered, escalated and consumed her. She felt certain of that.

In the last several cycles, she had resigned herself to death. At least in death, she would be united with Tomudo and her babe in the Land of No Shadows. In the afterlife she would not have to concern herself over the events on Mother Earth and the people of her village. They would be left to an older more confident Coloma and Taja. Hopefully they would form an alliance and convince the others to rescind the law of banishment and confront other intolerable, demeaning and biased laws.

It gave her some comfort in knowing it could happen. Coupled with her search for truth, and having taught Coloma, it did add meaning and purpose to her life. Taja repeatedly impressed upon her that the length of her life was not as important as the quality of love in it. Because of his help she had been able to understand love more fully and to give it more freely. The thought had helped her face the dwindling cycles. If her death would contribute to the growth of the tribe in some significant way, then she would consider herself to have reached a reasonable quality of life, where it concerned the village.

She swayed her torso and closed her eyes. What did Taja say so often, she asked herself? Recalling it she repeated it aloud. "No experience, no matter how small, is lost to the greater self's expression."

Batu unconsciously ran her hand over the facial scar that had robbed her beauty. She found it hard to imagine enduring the personal tragedies she did without Taja's love and guidance. Tomudo's death had sent her to the brink of destruction, and nearly so with the death of her babe.

She prepared her dawn meal and took it outside. Eating leisurely, Batu watched the Great Sun crest the horizon. The beauty and glory of the Great Sun rising had become a spiritual experience for Batu. A love for Mother Earth and the heavens had found a home in her since knowing Taja. Would she see another dawn? The thunder seemed to say if she did she would be fortunate. A strong urging rose within her to see Taja. Walking hurriedly to his hut, she hoped she could catch him before he went to meditate.

The air had changed. It suddenly felt laden with moisture and cool to her skin. Nearing his hut, she heard him singing and stopped outside to listen.

The red-feathered whistler sings
Never knowing or caring
If the Great Sun will shine again
He lives only for the moment
Its nature is to sing
The trill of innocence

Finishing he called, "Come in, Batu."

"The song is lovely, Taja. I have never heard it sung by anyone before. Where did you learn of it?"

Smiling warmly, he replied, "Batu, the song is of you and for you. I sang from my heart so you could learn from my heart how to look upon your life."

"It is beautiful." She crossed the brief space between them and held him. He returned the embrace. They remained enclosed in each other's arms, relishing the feeling of love that washed over them. It was always the same. Every time she opened herself to him, she felt his love. She welcomed the stay in his arms, enthralled with the experience. She rested there reluctant to pull away and end the constant feeling of peace he expressed and security he provided.

A long silence came over both of them. Knowing her moments on earth were dwindling, Batu still sought knowledge. "In spite of all of the things that we have gone through you always remain serene. How have you managed that?"

Smiling in appreciation of her need to acquire knowledge, he seized the opportunity to share his experience with her. "And how have you been able to determine that?"

"Your face never appears to lose its serene look," she answered.

"And what has your stomach told you during those moments?"

Her face turned thoughtful as she searched her memory. "I do not ever remember my belly ever indicating that your face is not what you feel inside of you."

Nodding his head in approval to her answer he went on to ask, "Has that been the case with other people, when you encounter them in situations where you know tension or anger could be present?"

Reflecting for a moment she answered, "No. Prior to meeting with you I was not as aware of it as I am now. It has become more apparent that some people are poor at deceiving others. Some part of their face usually gives them away. Mostly, it is their eyes that give them away, yet some can tell lies and their faces will support what they say. Before my talks with you I could not easily detect their lies. As I speak with people now, I am much more aware of what my body tells me. It seems to be able to sense the truth or falsehood in what they say."

Probing, Taja asked, "Has it also helped you to sense the anger they have within them?"

"Yes."

"We have talked about anger before. I impressed upon you how radically it harms your body and personality. As you gradually rid yourself of this self-destroying emotion, it allows you to move forward in your emotional growth and in your ability to love and understand others. I cannot impress upon you how important it is to overcome your anger."

Batu looked deep into Taja's eyes then asked, "Did you ever have anger in you?"

He chuckled. "Of course. I had to deal with it as a youth. My mother made me very aware of my anger. While it did not debilitate me it did hamper me. Anger in any degree hampers the self. Anger is good only when it comes about because of an injustice that needs correction. If it moves you to take up the cause against an injustice it is of value. It is of no value once you take action to eliminate the injustice. It must be used as the catalyst or stimulus, nothing more."

"How were you able to eliminate anger from your life?" Batu asked.

"My mother pointed out to me those moments when anger ruled me and I reacted to what was said. We talked about why it arose. She showed me it did not serve me to react in anger to what people said. Anger itself often clouded my mind in coming to an understanding of what caused me to get angry. Each time I became angry we talked about the events that caused me to react in anger. As understanding came to me, the length of moments that anger ruled me shrunk and also changed how I reacted emotionally. When I first began this practice my anger lasted two or three cycles. Slowly, it dropped to one cycle, then less than a half cycle, then less than a dozen breaths. Eventually I became aware of what someone's words were doing to me as they spoke it, and I could release it from me with my reply or by my questions. As a youth, it seemed as if it took forever for me to reach that point in my life. It is not an easy task. I still must be very watchful to be aware of how I feel and how I react. I watch what is happening inside of me during my conversations and dealings with people. It is of the utmost importance in dealing with anger that you do not react. You must answer from a position of action not reaction."

"Is that why you speak slowly and sometimes take a moment or two before you reply?" Batu sought to know.

"That is part of it."

"What is the other part?" Batu asked.

"There are moments when I need to seek out the words from a deeper part of myself. I wait for the words to come forth from that area."

"Are you saying that there are parts of ourselves that would reply differently than other parts?"

"I am," Taja offered.

"Can I cultivate this?"

"Most certainly."

She mulled that thought around for a short while before directing the conversation to something he had said previously. "Let us get back to when this all happened. How old were you when your mother helped you, and how long did it take you to come to the point where your reply did not come from anger?"

"We began working on my anger at the age of nine. At eleven I was able to become aware of my feelings as they occurred and not react to what was said. I responded less and less in anger and pressed the person I was speaking to with questions to find out why that person said things he or she did to me. I tried to understand their viewpoint from the question I asked."

"Could the High Priest rid himself of his anger in this manner and that quickly?" Batu inquired.

"I feel the sooner you understand what causes anger in yourself the easier it is to eliminate it, but not many people will choose to work on their anger at the age I did. My mother was singularly unique in what she did with me. Everyone's personality develops along certain lines because of what transpires in their lives. I am sorry I cannot answer that for you emphatically. Many factors contribute to how quickly you overcome anger. Many times anger is tied to what has happened as a youth or even prior to infancy. How deeply you have been injured and at what age it happened are factors. Your present age is yet another. Relationships are another, as is wisdom."

Raising her hand, Batu stopped him asking, "How do relationships affect one's anger?"

"Part of the answer lies in your investment in the relationship. If the relationship is a casual one you do not have to worry about injuring his or her feelings. You can vent your anger on a casual friend for you do not care if you lose that casual friend. Now, if it is a trusted and valued friend you are more cautious of showing anger. You may be afraid of losing that friendship. It is very possible you stuff your anger inside of you, where it creates havoc with your body. Whenever you do not face what disturbs you, you have a reaction. That reaction is what you stuff into your body."

Interrupting him, Batu asked, "Is that 'stuff' you speak of what caused me to be plagued with the silver scales?"

Taja nodded. "Indeed it was, and it can be any type of illness. Even though your face, or voice, may or may not display your anger, depending on how good you are at masking what is going on inside of you, the anger is still stuffed inside your body.

"When angered by your mate, parents, or your children, or any subordinate person, you feel much safer in venting your anger, for they cannot escape your presence. They are living in the same home and have nowhere to go. It can grow to abusive proportions.

"I often liken anger to be rocks that are thrown into the still pond of your serenity. Serenity is what we strive for in life. Anger disturbs the pond's serenity. The longer your anger lingers the longer you are throwing rocks into your pond. Now, I am going to complicate this picture even more by telling you that your pond is connected to my pond and to everyone else's pond. Those ripples caused by the rocks you have thrown in anger are not contained just within your pond. They ripple out to every adjoining pond and affect their serenity as well."

Batu's eyes narrowed. "I see how your anger affects me as we talk, but I cannot see how it affects others at this moment as your metaphor implies."

"Let us take, as an example, your anger at Kiirt and his at you. I know that you have voiced your anger with him to your parents, the council and me and who knows who else knows of it. I have no doubt that he has also voiced his anger with you to others. They have all been affected. Do you agree?"

Without hesitation Batu replied, "Yes."

"Now, on a much deeper level it affects all of humanity for we are all connected just as those ponds are connected. We are literally connected to each other at the greater self level. We are all part of the Creator who created us."

Batu eyes widened. "If we are all connected as you say then that would explain much of what happened during the Age of Corruption. People of one nation reacted to what the other nation did in anger. Even if the leaders of the nations could mask their anger it still resided in them and in their people. If it resided in them, then it spilled onto the other nations. It would be just like your example of the ripples from one pond spilling over to the others, when the rock of anger is thrown into a calm pond. That is truly fascinating."

"Now, I am going to apply what I have shared with you to what is happening in your life. As a village, expelling you will diminish us. Anytime we do not value life it diminishes who we are collectively. I cannot emphasize that enough. Everything we do effects each one of us at a deep conscious level where we are all connected. Every action speaks of our collective values and virtues. On the surface we may choose to ignore, to varying degrees, situations and events, but on that deep conscious level we can never escape it and what it does to us collectively. All events contribute to our collective understanding and growth as a village, nation and humankind. That in turn affects each one of us individually.

"What is to take place soon will be a turning point in the history of the Kahali people. In the past you have been a catalyst with your rebellions toward our traditions, and soon you are going to be one again. People who are catalysts create change. Some of those changes may be good some bad. In every circumstance where you have been a catalyst, it has been for the good of our village even if they do not perceive it as such. It has been an honor to watch you mature and grow in understanding. It was a joy to share with you what little I have, Batu. I am going to miss you, as I have never missed anyone else."

They sat gazing raptly into each other's eyes. Batu broke the silence. "I must speak to you of what is in my heart. When I am with you I realize what deep feelings I have. Perhaps it is because you have broken down my defenses and have given me a way to be in touch with my true self.

"I have wondered many times why it is I find you by my side whenever I am in danger. And now, I am again before you, as my existence is to change drastically. I have come to the brink of expulsion, yet I am at peace. I fear only that I have not done enough with my life. At this moment, I do not fear death. It is because of you, I feel this way."

He nodded slowly.

When she spoke, her voice had a pensive quality to it he had never heard before. "I have smelled the moisture in the air... My moment of banishment is upon me... I am not sure if I will sit across from you again. There are things I want and need to say to you, but I am unsure if I can. If I am unable to tell you all that is in my heart, I can at least tell you how grateful I am for breaking down the barriers which blocked my ability to love. I owe you much dear friend."

Taja's voice filled with emotion as he said, "I will cherish your love forever. Your courage and willingness to search for the love in you will remain bright in my memory."

Looking deeply into his eyes, she whispered, "Before I die I want to know of your experience with the Creator."

Lovingly, he looked at her. "How do you know I have had a union with the Creator?"

"Your eyes speak of it when you talk about the Creator."

He replied slowly, "It is true. I have been graced by the Creator."

A long pause ensued before he began nodding his head and spoke again. "Perhaps when you are alone on the plains you can think of my union with the Creator. It will serve you well to have your thoughts filled with love or of the Creator at the moment of death. What you are thinking of at the time of death is where you will be propelled to in the Land of No Shadows."

He breathed deeply. His eyes moved up and to the left for a moment and then returned to hers. "Oh, Batu, the experience defies description. It has left lasting impressions upon me, ones I cherish beyond any others. I hope I can adequately convey it to you. The union was incredibly intense and beautiful beyond imagination. It occurred in my twelfth season where I always meditate. Of course back then I spent many dreamy moments there and did not meditate much. There I spoke openly to what I called the Presence. Only after the union did I begin to call the presence I felt Creator."

"On an especially serene cycle, I lay in repose on the bank watching the flow of water. I felt enchanted with everything I saw, smelled and heard. I gazed about me totally absorbed in Mother Earth. Lying there, an alteration in my senses occurred, sounds grew distant, my sight much keener. The water shimmered exquisitely. Everything I saw had a rich, vibrant, glowing intensity. Suddenly I began to weep from sheer joy. I lost all knowledge of my body and everything physical. My inner senses heightened.

"A transition occurred catapulting me into what I can only call blissful benediction. In this state, I saw that the Creator created the gods and further that nothing had ever come into existence without the Creator. The sweeping immensity of creation resided in me and I in it. I was not apart from anything created. All of creation filled me, as I filled it. All of creation was in the Creator. The Creator and I were one."

Taja's voice became very soft. He spoke slowly. "A change occurred. A rush of energy engulfed me. It reached an incredible intensity. Suddenly I lost all identity. I was it.... Pure.... Creative.... I had a tremendous sense of creativity.... A moment later I, the energy, became Passive.... Expectant.... In this state I became enriched, vivified and supported by the Creator.... I rested in the loving embrace of the source of all love.... A rapturous indescribable bliss consumed me.... The love I felt was tender and sweet and grew in magnitude and power well beyond my comprehension and imagination."

As his eyes filled with tears, he stopped and looked away from her. He brought his eyes back to hers and continued his narration. "The exaltation of peace, joy and love grew to such proportions I could not contain it all and remain conscious.... I lost awareness.... Later I awoke and found myself lying on the ground. The vividness of the experience sang through me playing upon my heart. On the ground, my body quivered as I savored the sweetness I tasted. The rapture I experienced urged my eyes to pour forth tears of joy long after the rapture waned.

"During the next several cycles, I often found myself weeping whether I thought of the experience or not. Whenever it happened I found myself longing for the wonder, sweetness, tranquility and love I had experienced."

A soft sigh escaped his lips.

They sat in silence.

Batu broke the quiet. "Will I be able to experience a union like the one you have described in some life?" she asked solemnly.

"It is everyone's heritage."

They rose as one and embraced. They clung to each other. Tears flowed freely from them both. With great tenderness he kissed her on one cheek, and on the other, on her forehead, and then on her lips. "The kisses on your cheek are from the friend and the teacher within me, the kiss on your forehead is from the mother and father in me, and the kiss upon your lips is from the lover in me." He embraced her again.

Her voice trembled with emotion as she spoke. "I will carry with me the memory of you, and your love, even as a dweller in the Land of No Shadows."

His face beamed. The smile overtook his face slowly. She sensed his love. Still smiling he finally spoke. "Love well, Batu."

He gathered her in his arms. She clung to him as she said, "I will, gentle one."

She pulled away from him and walked through the entrance. He followed her and stood watching her. She walked away looking at him, unable to stem the flow of tears clouding her vision.

CHAPTER
TWENTY-FOUR

Pensively, Taja watched Batu walk away. Drawing a deep breath, he moved to sit upon the bench outside of his hut. Now and then people passed through the village center. He closed his eyes to concentrate on the immediate problem concerning Batu. A passerby greeted him. Taja returned the greeting. Rising from the bench, he made his way to his refuge at the bank of the running water. There he would not be disturbed. Arriving at the familiar spot, he eased himself down and sat cross-legged as he had done so many times before.

Batu had been correct in her assessment. The rains were imminent. The fate of one he loved would soon be decided. He had to act. He would do it in the only way he knew how. He breathed deeply relaxing himself and opening to the abundant energy whirling around him. He calmed himself, and he felt his consciousness alter. He sensed a familiar presence convey its love. Long ago he identified the presence and came to know her as Malti, a loving teacher dweller in the Land of No Shadows. After expressing his love to Malti, he prepared himself for his internal quest by asking the Creator to cleanse him of undesirable emotions and thoughts. He then asked to be blessed with the light of knowing and love. After the request he quieted his thoughts. In a few moments the colors in his mind gave way to a growing darkness. He prayed that Batu's life would unfold in such a way to provide her with the most beneficial experiences for growth.

Coming to know Batu so intimately brought forth a great love for her. He probed the inner recesses of his feelings for Batu and went over their friendship. A vision of him and Batu embracing emerged to his inner sight. He recalled those rare moments when he became acutely aware of her physical body while embracing. They were fleeting and insignificant interruptions of his concentration, but they had been present. An uncertainty crept into his thoughts. He needed to know the depth of his feelings for her.

He posed the question to his greater self whether he had a shred of desire for Batu. The disquieting answer came in a vision of him and Batu consummating their union by bonding. So it was true! He still held vestiges of physical desires. He knew that being bonded to Batu and carrying on a tempered physical relationship with her would hamper his goal of complete union with the Creator. In his current state of celibacy, it would be far less difficult to attain complete union with the Creator. While an apprentice, he had made the choice to be celibate and never regretted it.

With the images presented in this meditation, it was apparent he had not come as far as he thought. All these many seasons he had set his mind and heart in preparing himself for union with the Creator, and he still possessed the residue of physical desire. Searching his heart, he grudgingly admitted that if he had not renounced being in union, he would have asked Batu to be his woman long ago. She had many attributes that set her apart from other women. Her zest to learn, the ability to share her most intimate thoughts and to pursue the path of love drew him to her more surely than her physical beauty. These things, together with her fierce, independent nature, and her personal ethics, were the very qualities that effectively bound them. The bonding would be secondary to this, but it would be there. He knew full well that his own deep commitment to the Creator would be altered to some degree. Many adjustments would have to take place to insure that he did not lose sight of his purpose. Was he strong enough not let it happen? He rubbed his face fiercely in reaction to his thoughts.

In Batu, he saw someone who would strive to widen the circle of people she loved. He had taken this same task upon himself and found it to be something he wanted to pass on to someone else. Like Batu, he found love more easily given to those who were not disruptive and did not harbor some degree of dislike or hatred for him. During the passing seasons, he had made enormous strides in this area and felt Batu could also achieve it as well. Her personal commitment to remain on the path of love was well rooted, and he sought to help and nurture her in her quest.

Bewildered, but more understanding of his deep personal feeling for Batu, he told himself he would have to examine his feelings toward other people and other situations on a regular basis to avoid fooling himself. Having acknowledged these things he now set them aside to be worked on at a more appropriate moment.

The soft patter of rain on the thatch roof awoke Batu. The short-lived drizzle signaled the end for Batu. Too nervous to eat, she waited for her parents to arrive. In the final moments of her life, Batu wanted to be with them. Upon arriving, she quizzed them about their childhood and her own. Several times she asked for their forgiveness, each time they told her there was nothing to forgive. They laughed and cried while reminiscing. They embraced and kissed often to emphasize the bond of love and blood that tied them together.

The slow trickle of friends and relatives began shortly after their second meal. There were pitifully few. Only two women dared oppose their men to bid their farewells. The others who came pleaded with their men until they relented. The only men that came were relatives.

Those who came gave Batu a small token of their friendship for her journey to the Land of No Shadows. With the presents they sought to assure themselves of her friendship as a dweller. Some asked for her intercession with the dwellers in the Land of No Shadows to assure themselves of a peaceful existence after death.

Batu's most fervent supporter, and her mother's dearest friend, Margit, came with her arm wrapped firmly around her man's arm. Janos was the first non-relative man to make his appearance. Batu saw Margit clutching Janos' arm. It seemed she did it to prevent him from fleeing. In spite of the gravity, she could not help but smile.

Margit clung to Batu in greeting, crying softly and letting her tears wash over Batu's shoulder. Releasing Batu, Margit gathered Szatu into her arms. A soft moan emerged from her.

Janos extended his hand to Batu. "The council has erred in its judgment. I am ashamed of them."

Sensing his earnestness she moved past his arm and hugged him. "Thank you for coming. Not many men have come. It means a great deal to me to have you here."

"I am sorry, Batu, really sorry."

Free now of Szatu's embrace, Margit laid her hand on Batu's arm. "I will never forgive the council. They are insane."

"Taja has no part in what is happening," Batu said defensively.

"I know," Margit replied. "He and Coloma are the only sane ones among them.

"Do you want your mother and I to walk to the plains with you?" Margit asked.

Taking Margit's hands in her own, Batu answered, "Please, Margit, stay here. I am not sure if I could handle that. I have played it out in my mind many times so that when it comes I will somehow be able to do it without breaking down and falling to the earth."

"Are you sure?"

"Yes," Batu said softly, but emphatically.

Swiveling her eyes to Szatu, Margit said, "Oh gods, your child remains courageous to the end. How many times have we seen it? No man-child ever showed such courage. For that matter few of our men have ever shown more."

Managing a weak smile, Margit openly recalled, "It seems just a moment ago I held you in my arms as a newborn and saw the love in your mother's eyes. You have been like my own, Batu, like my own. I could not love you more were you my own." Disregarding her man at her side, Margit confessed, "My life would have been empty without you. You have made me smile, laugh and filled me with pride. A great void will be in my heart. No one will ever fill it. No one."

Batu stepped to Margit and embraced her. "I will carry your words and your love with me."

"I give both willingly."

Margit saw Batu's eyes move reluctantly away to focus on something behind her. Turning she saw Cimini approaching with her babe. A great sigh escaped Margit's lips. "I see others who love you are here." Margit clutched Batu to her bosom and sobbed. "I love you, my child. I will pray for you."

"And I love you."

As Margit released Batu, Janos took her arms and turned to Batu. "Farewell, Batu."

"Farewell, Janos."

Janos escorted Margit to the small group of friends nearby talking in hushed tones.

Cimini's eyes were red. She threw herself into Batu's arms, tears pouring from her eyes. With her free arm she embraced Batu. Tucked in her other arm and squirming lay her woman-child.

With great difficulty she spoke, "Batu, I wish our laws and our men had more heart in them. Casting you out like this is madness. I will truly miss you. Oh, how I will miss you."

"Oh, Cimini, I will miss you as well. You will be in my heart. I will not forget you," Batu said tearfully.

Looking at Cimini's babe she said, "Loviti's face is beginning to fill out. She was so thin before."

Hesitating, Cimini said, "I have been unable to produce enough milk for her. I have had to ask Evana to share her milk with Loviti. She was kind enough to do it. She is still frail, but becoming stronger."

"Forgive me. Mother told me, but I have been so engrossed with what has been happening to me I have not paid much attention to you."

"It is understandable, Batu. No need to apologize."

Gazing at the child, Batu smiled. "She is so lovely and delicate. May I hold her?"

Cimini placed her babe in Batu's arms. Batu began crying with Loviti cradled to her breast. The memory of her own lost creation overwhelmed her. The sudden rush of emotion caught her off guard. A bond formed instantly between her and the babe. It was one she had not fully realized with her own babe. Tears flowed down her cheeks spilling onto the sleeping babe. "Oh, Cimini, how I wanted to hold my babe as I am holding yours. Losing a child is the worst experience in life. Holding your creation brings back all those painful memories."

Batu reached her free arm out to encircle her friend. "Love her well."

Cimini could not hold back the tears. Breaking the embrace Cimini said, "I will. May the gods guide you forever."

"Thank you. I love you," Batu said in return.

Cimini moved to the group that had come to see Batu off. They now numbered nearly two dozen. Margit greeted her to the group with an embrace. Batu watched her friend, wiping at the tears that had wet her cheeks.

Batu spotted Kaathi and her parents coming into the village center headed toward her. The three of them joined the crowd and waited until they could embrace Batu and present their gift to her. Batu expected to see Kaathi near tears like the other young children who were fond of her. She showed no sadness. Something lay in her eyes for Batu to see, but she was unable to fathom its message. She embraced the child and felt from her what she felt from Taja, when they embraced. They parted without speaking, and Kaathi smiled, to Batu's surprise.

Her eyes swept the group closely. Oliva and her mother were among them. Surprisingly, Oliva's eyes portrayed sadness. She had expected Oliva to be among those who were glad that she was being expelled. Oliva's mother's eyes expressed something much different. Smugness and vindication stood out in her eyes. It was obvious that she felt justice was being served. Oliva seemed to be in an inner struggle.

Pulling away from her mother's grasp, Oliva headed toward Batu. With every step, tears filled her eyes. In spite of the many humiliations she suffered at Batu's sharp tongue, she knew she would miss listening to Batu's tales of adventure and misconduct. Living vicariously through Batu had become a large part of her life. That fact pleased her and haunted her. Bittersweet feelings ran through her heart as pieces of the past flashed through her mind in the short walk.

Oliva stood in front of Batu. With tears rolling down her cheeks, she whispered so the crowd could not hear her words. "You have caused me much anguish in the past, but you have also given me a chance to be your friend. I do not have many. I am glad we were friends." Oliva shook her head for emphasis as she said, "You are not deserving of such cruelty."

Batu reached out to Oliva and held onto her hand. "I am sorry for having been cruel to you."

Oliva burst into sobs and threw her arms around Batu saying, "I am sorry this is happening." Withdrawing herself from Batu, she wiped her face with her hands and made her way back to her mother.

As they had held each other, Batu felt Oliva's awkwardness and felt sorry for the way she treated her in the past. If she had more moments left in her life, she would make amends.

Searching the group for Taja and not finding him, she realized he would be coming with the council in a few moments. Szatu and Aahi took hold of Batu's arms and guided her to the bench outside her hut. Seated with her mother and father she felt drops of rain splatter on her leg. Moments later several more landed. Szatu renewed her sobbing.

Batu sat smoothing her mother's hair. The movement at the other end of the village center caught her eye. The council was making their way toward them, with the High Priest and Kiirt in tow. She noticed Taja walking on the outside of the group, his eyes cast to the ground, seemingly deep in thought and not wanting to be a part of them. They made their way slowly towards her. A small group of villagers followed the council a short distance behind. They seemed anxious to see the upstart Batu receive the fulfillment of the law. At the sight of them, Szatu sobbed even louder. Some from the group of friends openly cried.

Batu rose. Her parents followed her move and clung to her arms. They met the council a few paces from the hut. Taja stood looking serene, as always. Batu looked at the faces of the small group of human predators standing on either side of the council within easy earshot. Batu saw Romir glaring at her and looked defiantly back.

The High Priest breathed deeply. Finally, the moment had come for his retribution. Romir gloated openly. The insufferable woman would soon be cast out of the village, and he would be free of her insolence. Aahi was another matter. He made a mental note not to ever speak cordially to Aahi again. Aahi made his insulting position very clear in their last talk. It became obvious why Batu acted the way she did. Her father had encouraged her disrespect. With him as her father Romir understood how she had become so vile.

Kiirt felt Romir's anger as he stood next to him. At certain moments he felt it to be greater than his own. After this cycle they would not have to exert so much energy over this woman that had pained them. His eyes darted to the plains wondering how long it would take for the predators to detect her as prey. His threat of dropping her remains on the plains and letting the predators feast on it was about to come true. The beauty in it was that it was coming to pass without any danger to him. The work of the gods is indeed at play in this event. He nodded his head in acknowledgment and gratitude.

With a somber face, Mihili greeted Batu and her parents. Pausing briefly in his distress he took a deep breath and then spoke, "Batu, no one has come forward and presented us with a reason why you should not be banished from the village. It is my duty as the Elder and spokesman for the council to..."

Taja touched Mihili's arm, stopping him as he himself spoke, "One moment Mihili. I have a question to ask of Batu." His eyes sparkled mischievously.

Everyone's attention riveted on the Talker Healer.

Taja's eyes filled with admiration. "Batu, you have spent many cycles with me in self-inquiry. During those moments together, I have come to know you very well. In those moments I have also come to love you. I know there is much good that you can do if you remain in our village. It would be a privilege to have you by my side as my woman."

The decision had not come easily. Taja had struggled with the decision till dawn. Clearly having Batu as his woman would present many personal obstacles and challenges in his life. The choice also involved contending with the council, Romir and Kiirt. Yet, if she had the courage to defy the High Priest, the council and others in the tribe, then why should he shirk his own challenges, he had asked himself? When more than one path was available to him in the past, he consistently chose the difficult one to embark upon. For Taja, asking Batu to be his woman easily was the hardest path to walk. Voicing his decision at this moment made him breathe easier. He was satisfied that he made the right decision. He continued his proclamation. "Would you consent to be in union with me?" He turned to Aahi and said, "I know full well that it must be agreed upon by you first."

Stunned, the council members stood in silence. Squeals of glee resounded from Batu's friends. The group wanting her to be banished stood in shock, then buzzed excitedly in the background at the strange turn of events. Szatu and Aahi could not believe what they had heard. Their tears of despair turned to joy with Taja's words. Happiness replaced the sorrow upon Aahi and Szatu's faces.

Salvation awaited Batu.

Before she could answer, Mihili regained his composure and raised his voice in bewilderment. "What are you saying? You cannot do this. The moment for proclaiming your intentions has past. You cannot do this! It is breaking our tradition."

A small smile crossed Taja's face. "It is true I am breaking with tradition but not the law. The law does allow such decisions to be made up to the last moment of banishment. The position of being my mate accords Batu the necessary worth for exemption."

Mihili, face flushed, turned to Coloma and asked, "Is this true? Is there such a law saying it can be done now?"

Hesitantly, Coloma recited the law. It stated that a woman about to be banished may be claimed by any man not bonded in the tribe as his mate and thus be saved from banishment at any moment prior to the banishment. The only thing necessary was the consent of the father and of the woman.

Shocked into silence, the High Priest stared at the Talker Healer. A scowl changed his face, as he came to the realization that he had a new enemy to contend with. His stomach burned with anger. Kiirt turned to look at his teacher and saw the dramatic change in Romir's face and felt his ire.

Mihili turned to Aahi and in a faltering voice asked, "It would seem Batu's life is in your hands. Do you accept Taja's offer to be Batu's mate?"

Beaming, Aahi walked up to Taja and placed his hands on his shoulders. "It will be an honor to have you as part of our family. I wholeheartedly agree to have you bonded with Batu."

Looking at Batu, Taja asked, "Batu have you come to a decision?"

Planting her feet firmly on Mother Earth, Batu replied, "I have. Before I give it to you I have need to speak. I speak not only for myself but also for every woman that has had to suffer the feeling of not being worthy. I speak for those women who have had to bear the burden of abuse by men and feel the helplessness of laws that do not protect them. I speak for all women who ever wanted to acquire more knowledge but could not. I speak for all women who ever wanted to voice their opinion in private and in public on any issue. I speak for those children who are punished mentally and physically by fathers who alone in the family are the supreme judge of what to do with an unruly child. That approach lacks the compassion that a mother would give to balance the judgment. I have long been a source of disfavor among you for I have been fortunate enough to be encouraged by my parents to use my intellect to form my own opinions and philosophy. You have come to resent me, and worse to fear me, because I choose to use my mind and heart to determine what is right and just for myself. I speak for every woman who cried for justice and equality. You are afraid of change, and I seem to be the symbol of change.

"You men have come here with the intent of expelling me from the Kahali village." She stared at the High Priest and continued, "Some of you were actually gloating. You felt I had no worth and took comfort that you were following the law by banishing me. But the law will spare me, if I become Taja's woman, and thereby deem that I do have worth. What you all fail to understand is that I have always had worth simply because of my existence. I have not harmed anyone. I have not changed since I awoke before the rising of the Great Sun. I am the same now as then. My acceptance of Taja's offer would change my worth because of the law. I realize that in your eyes, even if I accept Taja's offer, I may still have no worth because of your prejudice. What you do not realize is that your perception of me is clouded by that very prejudice, the law and by the past. You see things too narrowly. Your philosophy does not embrace compassion. This law, which casts out our women may have served, in some unimaginably stupid way, our tribe in the ancient past, but it is useless now. It has done nothing except close your hearts to the women of our tribe, as it did in the past. We women have been subservient to you men for countless generations. That must end!

"You men provide the food, but we women provide you with children. Are not our children far more precious than food? And what of the love we give them? Is it not more significant than food? You have not learned from the past and the mistakes you have made. You have become enslaved to the past and to ingrained prejudices.

"I have prepared myself for death, but in you I sense fear not only of death but of me. As death holds no fear for me, you hold no fear for me. You have no hold on me. No one has. I will remain thus until I draw my last breath of this fragrant air, and my eyes close for the last time."

Breathing deeply again, she pointed at the council. "You have caused me anguish that I need not have endured. No one should suffer such anxiety without having done something drastically wrong. I have done nothing wrong except to point out injustices, which you have been too blind to see, or too prejudiced and fearful to change. Thankfully, I have in Taja, a friend who sees my worth. For the tribe to survive it will need such courage and insight. Unfortunately, I will not see the changes for I have decided to reject Taja's offer."

The crowd gasped. Everyone looked at Batu in disbelief.

Taja eyes never left Batu's as she spoke. He sensed her decision as soon as she began speaking. She knew of his intense desire to be celibate in order to maintain his focus on his spiritual growth. He had chosen to relinquish it to save her life. She had chosen to not allow him to give up something so precious. Sensing her decision, his heart began to race and his hands turned clammy in anticipation. It contrasted to the outer calm he exhibited. As she continued speaking, peace and acceptance came to him. With her decision he clearly saw that in certain areas of her philosophy she had come to match his own philosophy. The will that had served Batu so well had now set her free. Tears collected in his eyes. She was free from the laws and the men who would harm her. The pain in his heart clamped his eyes shut. Tears cascaded down his face. Forcing them open he set them upon Batu. Pride gleamed in his eyes.

Defiantly, she placed her fists on her hips. "You men have caused me to face death twice. If I accept Taja's offer I will have lost what courage I have gained in this life to face death. I know it would not be long before the High Priest and you will conspire to overthrow the law and I would have to go through this agony again. I cannot let you control my life in such a terrible way. I choose to be free of you by leaving my beloved village, my beloved Mother Earth, and my beloved family and friends.

"I am choosing my own destiny. This is as it should be, not just for me, but also for everyone, men and women alike. Perhaps in setting myself free you will see the injustices you have carried out in the name of tradition and law, which should rightly be attributed to fear and ignorance."

Batu looked directly at Taja, eyes blazing. "All of you here, except for Taja, will see my refusal as stupid or insane. He alone understands why I am refusing, and he alone will recognize it as the quality point of my life."

Her eyes changed dramatically as her voice softened. "I hope it is not in vain."

Turning she fell into her mother's arms and grasped her tightly. There in the comfort of her mother's embrace, she silently let the tears flow.

Szatu clung tightly to her creation. Her mind reeled. She could not fathom her child's words. A cry of anguish escaped from her. She whispered desperately in Batu's ear, "Tell Taja you accept. Tell him.... Tell him yes." Sobbing, Szatu begged loudly, "Please, Batu. Tell Taja yes. Please for me.... Please."

Forcing herself, Batu spoke softly. "I cannot, Mother."

"Yes, you can. You can."

"I am sorry, Mother."

Szatu sobbed uncontrollably.

Aahi's short-lived joy was snatched away by Batu's declaration. Dazed, Aahi managed to wrap his arms around his women, suddenly realizing he needed consolation himself. Tears fell from his eyes. He buried his head next to theirs and released his emotions. He could not believe what his child had done. She had a means of escaping from banishment and she refused. Her last act among the Kahali people was one of defiance and bravery. She had not changed her character even in the face of death. He sobbed. The blame rested with him. He had been the one who had never punished her. He had taught and encouraged her to be independent and fearless. He had methodically inculcated the traits she possessed that brought them to this moment. He never imagined this would be the result of his love and desire for her to be better than any man in the village. He moaned in sorrow. The light of his life was being extinguished. He clutched his women tighter.

The High Priest silently thanked the gods for Batu's overwhelming stupidity and for his good fortune. He threw his arm around Kiirt and smiled openly. The thorn in his foot has been removed. Life was again good to live.

Kiirt looked at Batu and wondered if the gods had spoken to her in her desperation. In the darkness he had dreamed he had taken her to his hut and bonded with her and cast her out to be banished with the cycle's first light. His eyes drifted over her body. Lust filled his mind.

On the brink of weeping, Coloma's throat constricted, as he listened to Batu's dramatic speech. When she fell into her mother's arms and released the first sob he could no longer contain himself. He squeezed his eyes shut, but could not stop the flow of tears. He berated himself for having not had the courage to ask her to be his woman. Had he asked her she might have consented and all this would not have happened. The tears came faster.

Mihili listened in disbelief. His stomach soured with each word Batu uttered. This is not what he expected when he accepted the Elder apprenticeship. He did not mean to be a part of such proceedings and never expected her not to be claimed by some man in union. Mihili shook his head in despair. He could not find the strength to say anything. Disturbed and troubled he looked at Taja then Batu. Drained emotionally he remained silent. Bile surged up in his throat.

Neda looked on in shock. How could she refuse to be saved? What manner of woman was this that they were sending to be killed by some savage beast? Hardly comprehending what she said after the refusal, he stood looking at her with his mouth open.

Motum became aware of the change in Batu immediately upon Taja's startling statement. His body picked up on Batu's feelings. Senses poised, he stood next to Mihili oblivious of the Elder's protest.

Release! Motum felt Batu's release.

Laws could no longer bind her.

She had transcended fear.

Freedom! Somehow, unbelievably, Batu set herself free.

He felt it. He soared with her feelings, her freedom.

She was not bound to Mother Earth.

She was free to fly with the feathered ones.

Motum felt small next to her. His courage paled by her standards.

His heart pounded. The blood raced through his body. The experience dizzied him.

Motum glanced at her parents then at Romir, Kiirt, Mihili, Neda, Coloma and Taja. The council members, his senses told him, were at odds with Batu's banishment as he was. Now their hearts were not in it. Their stomachs were rebelling. Romir and Kiirt clearly wanted her dead. Szatu was distraught, as was Aahi, yet Aahi had a sense of Batu's indomitable spirit. Ah, Taja was another story. He knew of Batu's magnificent character and bravery. Taja knew what she felt. It was inconceivable that none of the others could sense her greatness, her courage. Were they so crazed with prejudice that they could not feel it in their gut? Were they so blind not to see what was etched on her face? What has happened to our council and our people? How far had they drifted not to see the immensity of the moment and her heroism?

He breathed deeply drawing upon her courage as he looked at her. He knew what he had to do. If no one else on the council felt it, he did, and he had to show his respect to Batu. He had to be strong. Was that not why he was chosen to represent the warriors of the Kahali. If it meant defying everyone who wanted Batu banished he had to do it. In recognition and admiration of Batu's heroism, Motum boldly stepped forward and called her name. When she looked at him, he bowed deeply in reverence and honor.

The act surprised Batu, along with everyone else present. The unexpected act of honor sent the crowd murmuring in astonishment. Batu recognized the courage it took to do what he did. For the respect he bestowed upon her, she bowed to him in return.

She had accepted his honor with grace. Amazement flooded Motum, one that he had never experienced before. As he gazed into Batu's eyes an understanding flooded him. The woman he honored was perhaps the greatest warrior the Kahali had ever seen, yet none other than he truly knew it except for Taja. Straightening himself, he blocked the delirious voices from registering upon his senses. He concentrated instead on the slightest gesture, emotion or word coming forth from Batu. Even as she turned and fell into her mother's arms Motum felt her strength coursing through his body. Things of this magnitude happened rarely in history. He would not soon forget what he felt this cycle.

Batu stroked her mother's hair with a trembling hand. "Mother, I love you."

"I love you, Batu. I will be praying for you," cooed Szatu.

Turning her attention to her father, she clung to him and rubbed his back softly. "Father, only the bravest man would have gone against tradition and taught me what you did. I have been privileged to be your child. I shall love you even in death."

"You have always made me proud, my child. I love you," whispered Aahi.

Batu tried to free herself from her parents' embrace. They clung to her. Aahi grudgingly released her. Szatu wailed as she let her child slip through her hands.

Batu stepped toward Taja, he toward her. They embraced. Neither of them spoke for a moment, choosing to savor the love they felt. Batu whispered into her teacher's ear. "Thank you for your love."

"It is there forever," he whispered in return.

Their eyes were misty as they parted. Batu moved to the bench outside the hut and slipped the food sack over her head and let it rest on her shoulder. Stuffing the rain slick in with her other clothing, she set the bag on her other shoulder. Sheathing the long knife her father had made, she picked up the new spear he had also made for her defense.

Separating himself further from the other council members, Taja stood next to Aahi.

Batu let her eyes sweep the faces of those who gloated, the small group of friends, the council, Taja, and lastly her parents. Etching them in her mind, she slowly moved backward across the village center toward the rain-dampened avenue leading to the plains. Several times she stopped to clear her eyes of tears. Only when she could see her parents and Taja clearly did she continue with her backward motion.

Aahi, Szatu and Taja moved into the center of the avenue so they could follow Batu's movement out of the village. The others, spellbound into silence, fell behind them in huddled groups.

Batu continued walking backwards until she could no longer distinguish the faces of those she loved. Turning, she faced the plains. Squeezing the spear tightly, she threw her shoulders back and stepped into the unknown.

Taja stood looking at Batu. His heart swelled with pride. He focused his attention on her figure again. There walked a woman who was willing to lay down her life for her principles and for his spiritual commitment. It may well be that he had not fully understood her depth of character. Perhaps she would not have been an obstacle in his spiritual path but a benefit. There was much he needed to reevaluate in his life. A woman of such character was rare and too precious to sacrifice herself. There were many things she had to offer him and the tribe.

Taja raised his voice to be heard by everyone. "Mihili may I ask Coloma to recite a law?"

The crowd stirred. A puzzled look rested on the Elder's face as he replied, "Now?"

"Yes."

"Of course."

With his voice still raised Taja addressed Coloma. "Coloma, please recite the law pertaining to who can be named as an apprentice to a council member."

Without hesitation he answered, "For a member of the Kahali tribe to become a member of the council, the member must have experienced the Rite of Passage. The current council member holding that position must ask the member to become an apprentice, or the member must be appointed to that position by the council, if the position is left vacant by the death of the council member, or if that council member becomes mentally unstable to rule."

Having talked with Tomudo so often, he knew there were no laws restricting women from becoming apprentices. Only the past prejudices kept them from serving. Nothing and no one could keep him from saving her. As his apprentice, she would be able to break down barriers that had been erected numerous generations ago. Alive, she could help point out the inequalities that women were living under. Being the next Talker Healer entitled her to be the first woman to ever sit on the tribal council. He knew Motum had experienced a breakthrough and now felt great admiration for her. In the past, Motum always turned out to be the pivotal vote at the meetings. Now the warrior appeared to be won over to Batu and her position on the council would be secure. Coloma clearly loved her and would become steady in backing Batu.

Taja nodded to Coloma. "Thank you. As you heard Mihili, there is no mention in that law that the apprentice must be a man. The law is clear is it not?"

Mihili's eyes searched Taja's for a long while before he answered. "Yes, that is true."

"Since the law is clear that I can ask a woman to be my apprentice, I am going to ask Batu to be my apprentice. If she accepts, she will be worthy to remain in our village."

The crowd buzzed over the Talker Healer's words.

Romir yelled at Taja. "You cannot do this. Batu is already banished."

"That is true but I can bring her back," Taja replied.

"It is against our tradition," the High Priest roared.

"You are correct, Romir," Taja said firmly, "But the law is clearly on my side, and there is nothing you can do to prevent it from happening."

"The gods will be angered. No good will come of this," screamed the High Priest.

"Right now, Batu concerns me more than what the gods are thinking," Taja countered.

The heated verbal exchange between Taja and Romir caused commotion in the crowd. Mihili groaned. Motum breathed deeply and sighed in relief. Coloma broke into a smile. Neda looked at the crowd. The looks on Szatu and Aahi's faces spoke of their joy. All would be well. As if to emphasize their relief, nearby a songbird filled the air with its voice. The crowd's noise and excitement grew.

Closing his eyes, Taja gave thanks to the Creator. Stepping over to Szatu, he embraced her and whispered in her ear, "I am going to bring back the tribe's next Talker Healer." He released her and headed toward Batu.

Taja's pace was vigorous. His face beamed. The chance to be his apprentice would be far too tantalizing for Batu to resist. Her empowerment would change the destiny of all women in the village and the tribe itself. She would have the opportunity to help lead the Kahali into the future with courage and wisdom.